WORLD ON FIRE

Bad Blood Part II

By Kris Lillyman

For Netty, Scarlett and Dexter.

Prologue

Las Vegas 1977

The two little boys could not disguise their disappointment as Enzo ushered them into the enormous bedroom where their father had insisted they must wait.

They had begged to be allowed to stay, promising to be quiet and not say a word, but their father had said no and they knew not to argue.

So, on his boss' orders, Enzo Pistoli had led them to the bedroom of the fabulous penthouse suite at *The Villa Continental* and left them there to wait until further notice.

The hotel was the most amazing place the ten year-old twins had ever seen and both of them were so excited to be there. What made it all the better was that soon it would belong to their father, Benny Vincenzi.

Today, he had assured them, was going to be his moment of glory; the day when he finally got all he deserved and Jez and Vito, his 'two young bulls' as he referred to them, could not be more thrilled.

It was so good to see their father happy and animated as so often he was stern and morose with mood swings that were difficult to judge. But the boys were delighted to see him so full of joy and each hoped that after today, his ebullient mood would continue.

The twins did not see much of their father as he was often too busy to give them his time, so for him to bring them here, on this momentous occasion, to be part of his success, was an extremely big deal for both of them.

Jez and Vito had been brought up in privileged style, mostly by their mother. Although they had been doted on by their grandfather, Carmine, and great uncle, Tito, who they also called 'grandfather' at his specific request - not really understanding what a huge honour this actually was.

Indeed, these two seemingly kind old men were, in fact, the two most powerful capos on America's Eastern Seaboard and Benny's marriage to Carmine's daughter, Lucia, had been purposely designed to unite the two families.

Yet Benny's personal success had been limited and he remained a disappointment to both his uncle, Tito Vincenzi, and father-in-law, Carmine Carboni who considered him something of a liability.

But today that was going to change.

Today he was going to secure them *The Villa Continental*, thus giving them that all important foothold in Las Vegas.

Aside from the huge financial rewards associated with this, it would also give the Carboni/Vincenzi organisation a firm foundation in the city from which numerous other streams of revenue could undoubtedly be generated.

What is more, Benny would be stealing it away from his two most hated enemies, Joe Cassidy and Sean Noakes, who currently part-owned the very lucrative property.

Vincenzi had been fighting a blood feud with them since his days as a black marketeer back in the East End of London - when Cassidy and Noakes were just kids doing grunt work for one of the big South London firms.

They had done well since then and *The Villa* stood as an impressive testament to their achievements. But soon Vincenzi would be relieving them of it - and they would not know a damn thing about it until afterwards, when he would have the delicious pleasure of telling them.

Benny had somehow convinced himself that Cassidy and Noakes - who went by the name of 'Reilly' back in the day - were the ones responsible for all his misfortunes. But, in truth, he was a deranged psychopath who had brought much of it upon himself.

Over the years this psychotic obsession had caused Joe and Sean a great deal of heartache - both had lost loved ones and had their lives ripped apart by Benny's relentless campaign against them.

His bloody vendetta began thirty years earlier when his own murderous actions and those of his associates, gave Joe and Sean no alternative but to react, which proved to be the catalyst that sparked Benny's insatiable rage.

Since then Vincenzi had been setting himself against them at every turn but somehow they consistently managed to evade him - although Benny had always left tragedy and devastation in his wake. He had even played a contributory part in the death of Joe's first wife, right there at *The Villa Continental*, but still it was not enough for Benny.

Now, however, with the aid of Carl Napier, who was the manager of *The Villa*, and the movie star Virgil Nash, who owned the governing shares of the property, Benny was finally going to destroy Cassidy and Noakes for good - and he could not wait.

In anticipation of this, Benny had flown his sons out to Las Vegas to witness his greatest triumph, going against their mother's express wishes. Yet to placate her, he had agreed to confine the twins to the bedroom until everything had been finalised.

This was much to Jez's chagrin, who was the oldest of Benny's boys by fifteen minutes.

Jez Vincenzi - short for Giuseppe - was much like his father in many ways; arrogant, volatile and impatient. Vito, by contrast, was softer, kinder and more like his mother in nature. Yet, in appearance they were identical and it was difficult to discern one from the other especially as they were all but inseparable. However, as soon as they opened their mouths there could be no mistake.

Jez was undoubtedly the dominant twin and was not shy about letting people know it.

Nevertheless, whether Jez liked it or not, Enzo left the two boys in the bedroom as instructed then returned to the main living area of the penthouse suite to join Benny and the others.

Along with Enzo Pistoli, Benny had brought two other trusted soldiers named Sammy and Guido. In addition, there was also Carl Napier, the current manager of *The Villa* who purported to be a friend of Joe Cassidy's but was, in fact, in league with Vincenzi.

Unbeknownst to Joe and Sean, Carl and Benny had been secretly buying up large chunks of shares in the hotel and currently owned a total of forty-eight percent.

Cassidy, Noakes and his former employer, Louretta Wild, owned another fifty percent between them whilst the remaining three percent belonged to Noakes' friend, Virgil Nash.

However, Napier had recently discovered evidence of Nash's involvement in a porno flick early in his career and had set about blackmailing the star out of his shares.

With Nash's three percent added to Vincenzi and Napier's forty-eight, it would give them the magical majority of fifty-one percent, effectively giving them overall control.

At any moment, Nash was expected to arrive at the penthouse where, in exchange for the damning footage of his ill-advised porno, he would sign over his shares.

Jez had some grasp of all this from overhearing snatches of his father's conversations, purposely positioning himself where such discussions were likely to take place.

However, neither he or his brother knew that their father had been born Benny *Mottola*, not *Vincenzi*. Nor that he had once

4

escaped from prison in England, only to re-emerge in America with a new face, a new name and the opportunity to prove himself in his uncle's organisation.

They would have been horrified to learn, too, that he was, in fact, a rapist and a murderer who had killed and maimed many people.

All they knew was that he was their father; an elusive, often absent figure who showed them precious little in the way of love. So the opportunity to spend some time with him in Las Vegas was a chance, perhaps, to earn his affection.

Regardless of their ignorance to Benny's past, the twins did understand that they belonged to a very powerful family and that their grandfathers were men most others were afraid of.

Indeed, since the boys were very small, Carmine and Tito had drummed it into their heads that money was power and power was everything and, after today, they were convinced their father would have both.

***

Jez was pacing the floor like a caged animal in a zoo. He wanted to be out there, in the thick of the action, to see Virgil Nash sweat and to see his father relieve Cassidy and Noakes of their prized hotel.

Jez was young, but his mind was sharp. Even though he had never been specifically told, he knew exactly what business the Carboni and Vincenzi families were in and it did not trouble him in the least.

What is more, his father had let him watch the movies *The Godfather* and *Scarface*, ignoring the fact that they were highly unsuitable for a boy of his age and Jez had loved every single minute of them.

Indeed, they had made quite an impression and he had watched the videos repeatedly. He dreamt of being just like *Michael Corleone* or *Tony Montana* when he grew up - only even more ruthless and despotic.

Hell, Jez Vincenzi was going to set the world on fire.

For now though, he was content to learn all he could from his father; the man he rather misguidedly admired almost as much as those tyrannical characters on his VCR.

Jez had often eavesdropped on his father's meetings and telephone conversations, particularly those involving Carl Napier, so he was under no illusions about what was going on that afternoon at *The Villa Continental*.

He just wished he was able to play a bigger part in it.

Vito, however, was not so concerned.

Yes, he would liked to have been in the main room and was anxious to know what was going on but that was pretty much it.

Unlike Jez, Vito had no interest in the family business or whatever it was that his father and grandfathers did. His brother had tried to explain but it all seemed too grown up to matter much.

All Vito wanted was to spend a bit more time with his father and being with him there, in Las Vegas, meant he could do just that.

However, the boys both knew just how hated Cassidy and Noakes were by their father. Indeed, they had heard the names spat with venom or spoken of in a disparaging manner for as long as they could remember.

Their father was seemingly obsessed by these two apparently loathsome individuals - so the twins were well aware of the importance of today and were excited on Benny's behalf.

If destroying Cassidy and Noakes meant their father was finally going to be happy, then nothing on earth could be better.

Both of them had their ears pressed against the door, trying desperately to hear what was going on in the outer room, listening intently as the elevator door to the penthouse 'pinged' open, signalling the start of the proceedings.

The sound was muffled but they could just about make out

what was going on.

"Is that Virgil Nash arriving?" Vito whispered.

"Ssh, yeah. I'm trying to listen," hissed his brother vehemently.

"Ah! If it isn't Judas Iscariot - and right on time too," Jez heard his father say to Nash in the outer room

"Sammy, Guido - search 'im!" Benny ordered. Jez smiled at Vito. Their father sounded just like *Michael Corleone.* It was so exciting.

"He's clean, Boss," Guido said a moment later.

"Good. Get 'im over 'ere." Replied Benny.

"This shouldn't take too long." The boys then heard Carl Napier say.

"Great, cos the air don't smell too good in here!" Virgil Nash said. There was then a muffled thud, as he received a punch for his insolence. The sound of the obvious blow travelled to the boys listening in the bedroom which gave them cause to snigger with delight.

"Now, now, Nash," their father said in his half cockney, half American twang, "This ain't Hollywood, you don't have to play the hero - not here. Besides, it's a bit too late for that don't you think? Heroes don't sell out their friends now, do they? At least, not in the movies I've seen."

Jez was loving the machismo of this exchange and continued to listen with glee to the back and forth between his father, Napier and Nash. The movie star, it seemed wanted to see the incriminating cine-film before signing over his shares.

This cued much rustling and the sound of a briefcase being opened. Jez guessed this was Benny showing Nash the evidence which he had witnessed his father putting in the case earlier.

"Satisfied?" Benny finally asked.

"Satisfied," replied Nash.

"Good, then let's get down to business."

Jez and Vito could hardly contain themselves. Indeed, Jez was almost certain he could hear his father scribbling his signature on the share transfer document.

"Okay, Nash," he then heard his father say, "Time to make good your part of the deal."

Jez thought he was going to burst with excitement.

"C'mon, Nash," Napier sneered, clearly irritated. "We ain't got all day."

Suddenly Jez had a feeling of unease, a premonition that something might be wrong.

"What's the matter Nash?" He heard his father say. "Gettin' cold feet? You startin' to feel like the cowardly snake that you are? Well get used to it, cos you're gonna feel it every single day of your life. But it's too late now, there's no turnin' back - the buck stops here with you signin' those papers."

"I can't," Nash said so softly that Jez could barely hear him. *What did he say?*

"What's that?" Benny asked. "Did I hear you right? Did you say you can't?" Their father's voice was calm but both boys recognised the menace in it.

"Just sign the goddamn papers Nash - and let's get this over with!" Napier was clearly becoming agitated, too.

"I can't - I really can't." Nash's voice was stronger now, seemingly more confident and Jez's feeling of unease intensified. *Something was definitely wrong and their father did not know it.*

"Don't push it, son," Benny replied, "I'm not a guy you wanna upset."

"Listen, Nash," Napier snapped, "Do you really think that copy of the film you're holding is the only one? Do you really think we'd be that stupid?"

Jez smiled. Of course, their father still held all the cards. Nash had no way out of it, no wriggle room. *Surely he understood that, didn't he?*

"Now for chrissakes," continued Carl Napier, "pick up that fuckin' pen and sign your goddamn shares over to us!"

Yes, that's it. Make him do it.

Yet, much to Jez's incredulity, Nash sounded unbelievably calm as he revealed the devastating reason why he could not sign the papers.

"No. That's what you don't understand," he said. "They're not my shares, not any more. You see, I've already sold 'em."

Jez was stunned. Surely it was some mistake. Maybe he had misheard. *He's already sold them? What did that mean?*

"You've done *what*?" The boys heard their father roar loudly, the sound of him lunging towards Nash unmistakeable.

However, at that moment, something else happened, something equally unexpected, as the boys heard a rush of footsteps and what sounded to be several people storming into the penthouse uninvited.

"What the fuck?" Their father growled.

"Oh, my God!" Napier shouted, clearly alarmed.

Vito looked at Jez, "What's going on? What's happening. Is this supposed to hap—"

"No. Shut up!" Jez snapped. "Let me listen."

Vito did as instructed, placing his head next to his brother's as they stood side by side at the bedroom door, trying to understand exactly what was happening in the room beyond.

***

It sounded as if all hell had broken loose. Interlopers had obviously stormed into the apartment intent on ruining their father's best laid plans.

They could hear the sound of scuffling, of punches being thrown. As fighting seemingly broke out in various places in the room beyond it became clear that Cassidy and Noakes were the ones who had gatecrashed the party, tipped off by Nash who had

9

apparently betrayed Benny by selling his shares to them.

It all sounded so desperate as Jez and Vito listened transfixed; rooted to the spot with dreadful fascination.

Suddenly there was a gunshot and everything stopped for a moment but then another shot rang out, crashing through the silence before everything went still once more.

The boys looked at each other, fear etched on their faces. Vito began to cry whilst Jez just looked utterly dumbstruck.

But then they heard their father speak and the relief was immense.

Benny had won and the intruders had been vanquished.

There was more talking. Their father breathless from all the exertion but clearly enjoying his victory.

Jez could not hear with absolute clarity but he managed to surmise that his father was about to kill Cassidy and Noakes and his heart began to beat faster with excitement. It was just like the movies - just like *Tony Montana* and *Michael Corleone*.

Fabulous.

But then there was a loud crash - the sound of the fire escape door being flung open - and someone else burst into the apartment.

Again there was scuffling and two more shots were fired.

Then two more and in that moment Jez Vincenzi's life changed forever.

***

Jez and Vito had been standing next to each other, trying to hear what was happening in the main room; one minute filled with hope, the next with despair as the battle raged and the power shifted from one party to the other.

But then there was a deafening sound as something blasted violently through the door. Suddenly needle sharp splinters of wood were showering Jez's face and arms, stinging his skin as he was thrown to the floor.

He lay there on the plush carpet for several seconds, slightly dazed and drenched in what he assumed to be water; his face wet and his clothes soaked through.

He could feel Vito beside him. Both were lying in a pool of liquid yet Jez could not understand why. *Had there been an explosion? Had a water pipe burst?*

He sat up slowly. "What the hell was that?" He asked his brother, noticing the giant ragged hole that had appeared in the door.

"Vito?" He said. But there was no response and he looked down to see his brother beside him, laying on his side. He appeared to be sleeping yet Jez was more concerned to see that he was not actually covered in water but in blood. Indeed, he and Vito were in the middle of a giant puddle of it.

Jez was horrified. *What had happened? Where had all the blood come from? He was not injured, nothing seemed to hurt. So if not him, then—*

"Oh, no! Vito," he exclaimed, immediately placing a bloody hand on his brother's shoulder and nudging him frantically. "No, no - wake up! Please wake up!"

But Vito did not.

Becoming more distressed with each second, Jez pulled his brother over so that he lolled from his side onto his back.

The moment Vito's face flopped over to face him, Jez recoiled in fright. "Jesus!" He cried with terror.

One side of Vito's face was perfect, a mirror image of Jez's own. Yet the other side had been completely blown away to leave a bloody, cavernous hole.

Jez immediately had an overwhelming desire to throw up and did so, right there, on the carpet; his vomit mingling with the blood, brain matter and skull fragments that covered the carpet surrounding them.

As he wiped his mouth with the back of his hand, he stared

for a moment longer at his brother, his horror tinged with a morbid, somewhat detached curiosity. *So this was what death looked like.*

However, this was soon replaced by the realisation that his twin was gone and he felt the pain of it deep down in the pit of his soul - as if part of his own flesh had been brutally ripped away.

Very gently, Jez picked Vito's body up in his arms and carried him out of the bedroom into the main room where, one by one, everyone turned to face him, their struggles instantly forgotten.

Benny, himself, was staring horrified, unable to quite comprehend what he was seeing. Then his face seemed to crumble and he began to emit a low, mournful wail; a sound so full of utter despair that it was gut-wrenching for all to hear.

For a moment it looked as if he might collapse but somehow he managed to stagger over to Jez where he carefully took Vito from him.

Benny Vincenzi then sank slowly to his knees, tenderly cradling his son in his big powerful arms and sobbing loudly as he studied what remained of the boy's ruined face.

***

Jez stood by his father's shoulder and stared into a bloody scene of complete devastation.

Carl Napier lay dead, a gaping hole in his chest. Virgil Nash, who Jez immediately recognised from the movies, was also down, shot in the thigh but still alive.

Three other men were in the room, too. All now staring back at Jez.

One; blonde and muscular, similar in appearance to Nash. This, Jez would later learn, was Sean Noakes.

The second was younger, maybe late twenties, long hair, very cool, no doubt popular with the girls, too. Before today, Jez might have envied him. But not any more. Indeed, he would discover that this was Matt Mason, Joe Cassidy's eldest son, who had entered the apartment via the fire escape.

Finally the third one; dark, brooding and quietly assured. This, Jez would find out, was Joe Cassidy - and he was holding the gun that had killed Vito.

But things were not as they appeared to be and Joe was, in fact, innocent of the atrocious crime Jez suspected him of.

What the boy did not know was that moments before, Joe had wrestled the gun out of Benny's hands. Nor did he know that it was actually his own father who had killed Vito, *not* Joe Cassidy.

Furthermore, Benny had also killed Carl Napier.

Neither killing had been intentional but that did little to alter the dreadful reality of the situation.

Vincenzi had fired two wild shots in blind fury that destroyed everything he had and everything he dreamed of.

But whilst Benny wept, Jez's hate burned.

***

Joe and Sean knew they no longer belonged there. Vito's death had ended it and Benny needed to be left alone with his grief and the dreadful knowledge of what he had done.

Virgil suddenly groaned with pain and without thinking about the consequences Sean quickly rushed over to him. But the moment he moved, Sammy, Guido and Enzo lifted their guns.

"Leave 'im!" Benny ordered. "Leave 'im alone. Don't ya think there's been enough killin' today?" His voice was heavy and full of despair, but the authority in it was unmistakable and the three goons stood down.

"You up to moving?" Sean asked Virgil in a hushed voice.

"Hey, if it means I get outta here in one piece, I reckon I could goddamn fly!" He replied.

"Let's not get too ambitious eh?" Sean said, then gestured for Joe and Matt to help.

Very slowly, Sean and Matt lifted Virgil up, his arms draped over their shoulders as they helped him hobble to the elevator. Joe stood guard, still holding the gun he had wrestled from Benny, just in case.

The room was totally quiet now, everyone watching the four men leaving the penthouse - except for Benny. He was still staring at the bloody mess that used to be his boy. He knew what was going on though, and just before they got into the elevator, he said in a soft, almost gentle voice, "It's not over Cassidy. You know that don't you?"

Then Benny paused for a second, the deep regret he felt for bringing his sons to *The Villa* eating away at his evil soul. "You too Reilly." He added, using Sean's real surname. "Keep looking over your shoulder 'cos I'll be coming for you."

Joe looked directly at Benny. "Yeah," he replied simply.

Sean just nodded. Would it ever be over?

***

Before the elevator doors slid shut, Matt Mason caught the expression on Jez's face.

It was dark and murderous and Matt wondered, just briefly, if this was perhaps a premonition of things to come.

Maybe. Maybe not. But either way, Jez Vincenzi was someone he hoped never to see again.

***

As for Jez, himself, he was raging.

Benny's enemies were now *his* enemies and he would never be convinced that anyone other than Joe Cassidy had killed Vito.

But he did not hold Joe solely responsible.

All those who had stormed the penthouse uninvited had played their part. Indeed, had they chosen *not* to oppose his father then Vito would undoubtedly still be alive.

As they retreated to the elevator, Jez studied the intruders carefully.

Joe Cassidy. Sean Noakes. Matt Mason. Virgil Nash.

Making certain that he remembered the face of each and every one of them.

Because in that moment he resolved to kill them all.

PART ONE

Chapter One

TEN YEARS LATER
London 1987

The pub was a haze of cigarette smoke. It smelled of it too, along with beer and sweat and furniture polish. The brass fittings and heavy mahogany furniture had changed little since the place was built back in the 1900s. In fact, *The Golden Gloves* was what the tourist board might call a typical London pub. Owned by old-time villain Alfie Noakes and run by his daughter, Violet, the clientele were mainly gangsters of the old school; big-hitters of the fifties and sixties who had now been put out to pasture by their younger replacements. Most were over seventy but they still tottered in every day - the slicked hair and dark suits of their heyday now replaced by bald heads and warm cardies to keep the chill off their aged bones. It was like a retirement home for crooks, with Alfie holding court at his favourite table every evening.

Members of rival firms talked like old friends, ignoring the fact that at one time they would have cheerfully sliced each other's throat. Those things were forgotten now, only the memories of 'the life' remained and it was spoken of constantly. Even Big Jack Anderson, a particularly nasty piece of work, had taken to frequenting *The Golden Gloves* and had, for the past few months, been buddying up to Alfie.

Alfie was the keeper of a closely guarded secret and at his

age it was only a matter of time before something slipped. When it inevitably did, he wasn't even aware of the huge error he had made. Age and an addled mind were not a good combination for someone with the kind of information Alfie was in possession of.

"Sorry, what did you say?" Big Jack said, unable to believe what the old man had just told him. "Did you say Joe Cassidy was still alive?"

Alfie was pushing eighty-six now, a doddery and frail shadow of his former self who was losing his faculties, just a little. That's why he was talking to Big Jack who, even though no spring chicken himself, was every bit as scheming and ambitious as he ever was. If Alfie had been on top of his game there was no way he would have allowed himself to be so easily coerced into speaking of the thing he'd kept secret for the last ten years. But he was into his fourth whiskey and Jack was being friendly enough as they reminisced about old times. About old friends and old enemies.

"Course, Joe's still alive. You knew that already, didn't you?" Alfie was a little confused.

"Yeah, course I knew", Jack bluffed, "What happened again, I forget?"

"Well, they faked their deaths, didn't they", Alfie seemed placated and continued, "Both Joe and Sean. Fooled 'em all. The whole bloody lot of 'em. Never suspected a bleedin' thing. Good on 'em I say. They was good lads them two. Didn't deserve all that crap that happened."

"No. Good on 'em," Jack said through gritted teeth and a fixed expression of sympathy.

"They was always clever them boys," Alfie continued, "I knew they was. Saw it right from the word go".

"Oh, yeah, they was clever alright", Jack couldn't believe his good fortune, couldn't believe what he was hearing. "Where are they now then - I mean if they're still alive? I ain't never seen 'em about."

20

"Ah, no. Well you wouldn't would you. They're gone, mate. Long gone and I don't reckon they'll be comin' back neither. Bloody sure I wouldn't".

"Gone where though?" Jack pushed. He had to be careful, Alfie had lost it but he had never been stupid.

Jack was aware, too, that Violet was looking over, watching out for her dad, knowing he was easily addled and worrying about what he might say, but she was busy serving and unable to come to his aid and Jack smiled inwardly as he let the old man talk.

"I can't remember exactly," Alfie said. "Somewhere hot - one of them bloody banana islands, weren't it?"

"What, you mean the Caribbean?"

"Yeah. That's right. Somewhere like that. Not sure exactly where, my boy Richie knows though. He still keeps in touch".

"You sure that's where they went?"

"Yeah, I'm sure. 'Ere, why you so interested any how?" The question was proof enough of Alfie's mental state. Had he been firing on all cylinders he'd have known that Jack would have gladly sold his soul to find the whereabouts of Joe Cassidy and Sean Reilly. And the people Jack worked for would reward him handsomely for the information.

"No reason. Shouldn't mind sendin' the boys a note that's all. Be good to hear from 'em' after all this time".

"Yeah, course. S'pose you're right. I miss 'em you know. They were like me own kids at one time".

"I know Alfie, mate. You was good to 'em that's for sure. You sure you don't know what island?"

"Course I'm sure - I ain't bloody senile, you know. But Richie does, I told you".

***

Big Jack returned to the *The Golden Gloves* two nights later with Bass Stone; a violent, ruthlessly ambitious brute of a man whom

Anderson had taken under his wing some years earlier.

It was way passed midnight when Bass jemmied open the back door and snuck into the lounge bar where Violet was vacuuming the carpet, oblivious to the sound of the door being forced or the intruders now inside who were committed to dangerous intent.

Alfie was in bed upstairs, the only other person in the pub.

By the time Violet saw the shadow of the man standing behind her it was too late and as she turned, Stone grabbed her and held a knife to her throat.

A minute later she was tied to a chair, looking directly at the powerfully built, half-caste man before her.

Bass was the illegitimate son of a Jamaican porter and a dockside whore. He had tightly cropped hair and a hard face with a jagged white scar above his right eye which shone white in contrast to his caramel skin.

At thirty-two, he was mean and murderous in nature with a growing impatience to find the one big score that would propel him into the big time. He had saddled his pony to Big Jack's in his early twenties, hoping that someone with Anderson's connections would lead him to the riches he so desperately sought. But they had been a long time coming.

Or at least they had, until now.

Anderson had left Bass to guard Violet, whilst he went through to the back room where Joe Cassidy's office had once been many years earlier, to see what he could dig up.

Alone with Stone, Violet glared at him with a burning fury in her striking green eyes; her dark hair tumbling around her shoulders as she struggled to be free. But the ropes were tied securely around her wrists and ankles and a balled up rag had been shoved into her mouth to keep her silent.

Stone was wearing a light grey suit and a pale blue shirt. Both were covered in dried blood, as were his hands. He noticed her looking and smiled, the polished gold of his capped incisor gleaming in the lamplight.

"You're looking at the blood?" He said. "Don't worry, it's not mine, darlin'. It's your brother's."

Violet was suddenly aghast, utterly appalled. She started to pull against her restraints with renewed vigour but it was useless, the tears springing from her eyes as she thought about Richie. *What the hell had Anderson and this monster done to him?*

Bass Stone let his words hang for a moment as he watched Violet struggle. She was a stunner, no doubt about it, and always had been. At thirty years old it was a small wonder she had never married, yet she had devoted her life to running the pub and taking care of her father.

She had never been short of male attention, however, which was unsurprising as she was strikingly beautiful with a spectacular figure; full, firm breasts, a slender waist and long, shapely legs that any red-blooded male would kill to have wrapped around him.

Stone felt his loins stir as he admired her.

He had dragged his way up from nothing; his alcoholic father heading straight back to Jamaica the moment he was born and his pox ridden slut of a mother murdered by his own hand before he was twelve years old. He had killed her for the few coins in her purse and the meagre scraps of food she had sold herself for in an effort to feed them both, yet he did not regret it for an instant.

She was weak, he was strong and one person was easier to feed than two, it was simple mathematics.

After his mother's death, Bass had fought for survival, using his guile and his fists and whatever else came to hand. And he had endured it all, from orphanage to school and from borstal to prison, Bass had earned the nickname 'Bad To The Bone' Stone and emerged with a reputation few would dare test.

Violet, on the other hand, was South London royalty; an

entitled, spoilt princess, in Stone's opinion, who knew nothing of the hardships he had lived through.

She was the youngest daughter of Alfie Noakes, one of the most respected and revered men in the whole of the London underworld. A villain of the old school, back when gangsters had a certain panache, in the days of Vinnie Reece and Joe Cassidy.

But Bass cared little for style or panache. To his mind, Noakes was a dinosaur, a fossil whose time had long since expired.

All Stone cared about was results and money and would stop at nothing to get both.

Bass had always lusted after Violet but felt that she considered herself too good for him, regarding him as if he was little more than shit on her shoes.

But not any more. Stone could now do exactly what he wanted with her and she would be powerless to resist him.

A delicious thought.

When he was certain that Violet had absorbed the news of her brother's murder fully he spoke again. "Yeah, old Richie put up one hell of a fight. To his credit he wouldn't say a bleedin' word, no matter what I did to him - nor his bum chum - that Irish monkey who was always by his side. What was it with them two anyway?"

But it was a rhetorical question. "It don't matter," he went on, "cos me and Jack reckon old Alfie must 'ave something 'ere that'll tell us what we wanna know. Bound to 'ave. He probably don't even know it."

Violet continued to fight against her ties, tears streaming down her face as she thought about poor Richie and his best friend.

"Question is," Stone continued, "What is it you and me can do while we wait?"

Violet froze, immediately aware of Stone's intent as he suddenly loomed over her. She tried to cry out, to scream, but her cries were muffled by the rag in her mouth.

She was wearing a loose floral dress with buttons down the front and a hem just above her knees. A heavy silver pendant hung on a chain between her heaving breasts.

Violet was unable to stop Stone as he grabbed the flimsy neckline of her dress and dramatically tore it open, ripping the material apart, the buttons pinging off in all directions, to expose her ample cleavage.

As the buttons scattered about the floor like hail stones, Bass pushed a calloused hand into her lacy white bra and roughly grabbed a handful of one of her plump breasts, squeezing it hard.

"Is that nice? Is that what you like, Princess?" He snarled, his voice thick with lust.

Violet wriggled wildly, fighting as best she could to fend him off, but it was futile, there was nothing she could do as he pawed her lasciviously, hurting her tender flesh as he pulled out the breast and pinched the nipple.

Violet wailed mutedly at the pain of it.

"Ah, that's it, is it? That's what you like," Stone said as he pinched harder, causing her to cry out again.

Then he reached down with his other hand and pushed it between her knees, forcing her dress to ride up around her thighs as his thick, probing fingers found the lacy edge of her silk knickers.

A second later one of his blood engrained fingernails was clawing urgently at the thin gusset of her underwear as Violet desperately clamped his forearm with her knees, trying frantically to prevent him from penetrating her womanhood.

She was screaming madly, fighting with everything she'd got, using every ounce of her strength to keep him at bay.

Then somebody else spoke.

"Get off her - now!" A gruff voice said behind him.

Bass turned to see Alfie Noakes standing there in his pyjamas, clutching a sawn-off shotgun in his frail, liver-spotted hands.

"You heard me, scum. Get your fuckin' hands off my daughter!"

Immediately, Stone removed his hands from Violet, the stain of her brother's blood still on them.

"Alright, Grandad - it's okay, no harm done - just a little fun, that's all," Bass said, his voice calm and even. "Let's not get too excited, eh?"

"Get away from her!"

Bass did as instructed, slowly edging away from Violet with his hands half up in a submissive show. "Okay, Gramps, no problem - there you go, see? I'm away from her."

"Whattaya doin' in my pub?"

"Ah, well, you'd best ask him that," Stone nodded, gesturing to the man who had just entered the room behind Alfie.

"Don't move, Alfie!" Big Jack ordered. "I'll shoot ya, you know I will."

Anderson was holding a revolver in one hand and a scrap of paper in the other.

"Who's that?" Alfie asked, his back to Jack, as his eyes darted from Violet and then back to Stone.

"You mean you don't recognise my voice? Well Alfie, I'm hurt. Really I am."

"Jack? Is that you?"

"Hey, hooray! Give the man a cigar," Anderson said. "You're obviously not so bleedin' senile after all."

Big Jack Anderson was not so 'big' anymore. His body had shrunk with age and he was a shadow of his former self, but he was still a treacherous snake, just as he always had been. Some things never change.

"What do you want?" Alfie demanded, "Why are you here?"

"And there you go again," said Jack, "I'm surprised you even have to ask. I came for this Alf, this little bit of paper."

"What?"

26

"I know, hardly seems worth it does it? But believe me, this little bit of paper is worth an absolute fortune. It's gonna bring me everything I deserve - money, power - all the things that should have been rightfully mine years ago but were denied me thanks to Joe fuckin' Cassidy. Well not anymore. This bit of paper is gonna make me a king."

Alfie was confused. *What was he talking about and what did a piece of paper have to do with Joe?*

But presently that did not matter. All that mattered was that Anderson had invaded his pub and Bass Stone had tried to rape his daughter.

At nearly eighty-six years old, Alfie had been lucky. His life had been good. But his kids had all grown up and moved away and his wife had died long ago. All he had left was Violet, his youngest and most precious. Her and his pub, they were the only things worth living for now and without them he was nothing.

Without Violet his life would be unimaginable.

As his aged brain ticked over, a cine film played in his mind. He saw Joe Cassidy and Sean Reilly, Vinnie and Ray Reece, his wife, his kids, amongst them Richie and Violet.

A good life. And as good a day as any to die.

His time on this earth was done.

Then, with all the speed and strength he could summon into his tired old body, Alfie span round and fired both barrels of the sawn-off in rapid succession.

Big Jack, surprised by the agility of the old man, managed to fire off one wild shot before the blast from the shotgun blew him backwards, ripping through his stomach, decimating his torso and taking off his whole left arm.

Anderson was dead before his body hit the back wall.

His corpse then fell to the ground in a mass of blood and butchered flesh, leaving a huge red stain on the wall where it had hit.

However, Alfie did not wait to look and turned back to face Stone. But in the seconds it took for Alfie to kill Jack and turn back around, Bass had pulled a semi-automatic from his belt and fired off four rounds into the centre of Alfie's chest.

Alfie staggered only slightly at the impact, before looking down at the four fresh new holes in his pyjamas which were now oozing blood. Yet he was somehow immune to the pain and merely observed his wounds with a detached curiosity, not quite able to comprehend their significance.

Slowly he lifted his head and saw Violet slumped in the chair.

The stray bullet from Big Jack's gun had caught her below her left shoulder, an inch or so above where Alfie imagined her good, kind heart to be.

Her eyes were open, filled with pain, tears trickling down her cheeks.

Alfie had failed to save her. His final act in this world had ended with the death of his daughter and his only comfort was the knowledge that he would be joining her very shortly in the afterlife.

Bass Stone stood between him and Violet; evil of a kind Alfie had not witnessed in many a long year.

Magically, Alfie's confusion abated, as if in dying a cloud had lifted. His mind suddenly as clear and as sharp as it had been thirty years before. Furthermore, he now understood the reason for Anderson and Stone's visit that night, the reason why Violet and very shortly he, himself, had been murdered. He realised with absolute certainty what was on the scrap of paper that Jack had discovered and cold fear flooded his belly.

But in that moment of terrible realisation, Stone shot him between the eyes, sending him, at last, to death.

***

The night had certainly not gone as planned but all things considered it had not turned out too badly at all for Stone.

28

He studied the carnage around him. Big Jack, Alfie, the girl. There was also the six they'd left dead at *The Galaxy Club*, too.

A busy and bloody night. But Stone had survived. He smiled at his good fortune and wandered casually over to where the piece of paper lay face down on the floor. Jack had let go of it as the shotgun blast tore through him.

Bass paused only briefly to glance over to where Big Jack's body had fallen; his mentor and the closest thing to a father he had ever known, but he felt nothing except maybe a slight buzz of exhilaration. With Jack out of the picture no one could stand in Stone's way.

Bass bent and picked up the scrap of paper but before he had the chance to look at it he heard a slight murmur. He turned to the sound and saw that it was coming from the girl.

Miraculously Violet was still alive.

She lifted her head wearily, blood pumping from the bullet wound high in her chest. She coughed and spat the balled up rag from her mouth as her eyes met Stone's.

"I'll kill you, you bastard," she whispered weakly. "I swear it, if it's the last thing I do. I'll kill you."

Stone smiled. *What was it with these Noakes'?* They were certainly a tough breed. Her brother took a tremendous amount of punishment before Bass finally shot him out of pure frustration. Alfie, too. Eighty odd years old and he still stood after taking four bullets to the chest. Incredible.

And now Violet, seemingly back from the dead. Bass was growing weary of killing this family. He'd thought two was enough for one night but apparently not.

"You're gonna kill me - is that right?" He said to Violet, his voice incredulous. "Well maybe you could have if you'd just played dead and kept your pretty gob shut for a while longer. Hell, you'd have had a pretty good chance, too, cos I'd have never known Jack hadn't killed you. But now, Princess, I do. And what is it they say?

Forewarned is forearmed - ain't that right?"

Stone raised the semi-automatic and aimed it directly between Violet's breasts. "Silly, silly girl," he said.

And then he fired.

Violet's body flipped backwards in the chair, her hands and feet still bound to it as both she and it slammed down onto the floor, the chair smashing as it collided heavily with the ground.

"Yep. Silly girl," Bass said again as he turned and headed for the door.

As he reached it, he turned the scrap of paper over and read the name and address that was written on it.

The address was of a place somewhere he had never heard of, and the name was not the one he had expected. But clearly Jack had thought it of significant importance, so it was a good enough place to start.

The name written on the paper read, *Michael.*

***

Manno O'Keefe slid across the floor of the night club leaving a gruesome snail trail of blood in his wake. His death was imminent; he'd seen enough killing, and caused enough of it, to be certain.

He had lasted more than an hour but now he was weak from blood loss and fighting unconsciousness. If he closed his eyes he knew that he would never re-open them, and the person whom he had taken the torture for, the man whom he had given his very life to protect, would go unwarned.

Five more feet was all that was left to go, but both Manno's knee caps had been blown away and three fingers on each hand had been sliced off making it incredibly difficult for him to manoeuvre across to the telephone by the corner booth in which he usually sat.

The five feet may as well have been five miles, but Manno was determined to make it.

On this, the last journey of his life, he had slid his squat, stocky body passed those of four of his men and finally, most tragically, passed that of his lifelong friend and business partner, Richie Noakes. Their men had all been shot and had died almost instantly, but not Richie. He, like Manno, had been tortured, but in frustration, after Richie had held out for an incredible three hours, Bass Stone had put a bullet through his head at point blank range, spilling his shattered brains over the polished, bloodied dance floor of *The Galaxy Club*.

Richie and Manno had dominated London's underworld for a decade but their reign had now come to a gruesome end at the hands of Stone and Big Jack Anderson, the man whose life they had spared ten years earlier.

It was one of their very few mistakes but ultimately it had done for them as Joe always said it would.

Manno's eyes kept blurring and objects were moving in and out of focus at a confusing rate. Minutes passed as he dragged himself those last desperate feet, his hands ghostly white as they clawed their way to the phone by the booth from where he and Richie had, until this night, governed their empire. Just one more push, slithering and slipping his tired form through the moving puddle of lifeblood that was draining, nearly to completion, from his wasted body.

Six more inches. He reached out and, with his thumb, managed to hook the phone cable that hung down from the private booth. Both handset and receiver came tumbling down, only narrowly missing his head.

Slowly, painfully, Manno pulled the receiver towards him and wedged it under his sagging chin as he took his last gasps of breath.

Making an effort to ignore the grotesque stumps that used to be his fingers, Manno shakily tapped in a number with his thumb that he had memorised long ago. After an almost insufferable wait as the long distance exchange rattled through the digits, Manno at last heard the phone ringing.

It was several more vital breaths later that someone eventually picked up.

"Hello?"

Manno tried to speak but his voice would not respond.

"Hello, who is this?"

Manno tried again and this time forced a hoarse whisper. "Joe?"

"Hello?" The voice on the other end of the line said again. "Manno? Is that you?"

"They know, Joe," Manno managed to make his voice a little more audible. "They know and they're comin—"

"What?" Joe asked, hearing the pain and distress in his friend's voice and becoming instantly concerned. "I'm sorry, I can't hear you properly. Did you say *they know?*"

But it was too late. Manno had achieved his objective, he had warned his mentor and performed his last service to the man he respected above all others. But now his time had, at last, run out.

His head had slumped to the floor and his bloodied, ruined face was, at last, clear of pain.

Manno was dead.

Which is where, after a ten year respite, it all began again.

Chapter Two

The Cayman Islands

Joe Cassidy awoke early. He liked this time of the morning, when the house was peaceful and everyone else was still asleep in their beds, with just the sound of the ocean and the chattering of the birds for company. It gave him an enormous sense of well-being, a sense that everything was right in the world.

Rose was laying with her back to him, breathing heavily, still dozing happily. Joe bent and kissed her lightly on the shoulder then slipped out of bed without disturbing her.

They had been married for nearly fifteen years and were still as much in love now as they were on the day she became his wife, although much had happened in the intervening years which would have tested most relationships. But not theirs; they remained strong and firmly united. For better or worse.

However, in recent years things had been pretty good and mostly uneventful. Indeed, since making their home in The Caymans things had been fairly idyllic.

They lived on a sprawling estate, which he and Sean had dubbed 'Far Point' as it was situated at he furthest point of the island.

Sitting high on a cliff top, it had fabulous views of the ocean on one side and lush, green lawns to the other.

The house was large and colonial in style with bleached

clapper board panelling that was more reminiscent of a mansion in The Hamptons than a home in The Caymans, giving it an air of established prosperity.

Either way, it remained a fabulously impressive property, as did its identical twin which sat on the other side of the bluff; the two houses separated by just over a quarter mile and joined by a private road.

Each house had its own driveway lined with white stones which stretched down to a gated perimeter fence. This fence marked out the boundary of the entire estate which hugged the coastline of the beautifully picturesque peninsula it sat upon. With the sea at its back - a sheer drop from the cliff top dwellings - and its own secluded stretch of white, sandy beach, it was a fortress retreat which had served to keep Joe and his family successfully hidden from the outside world for many years.

To ensure this continued, the estate was also defended by two security teams, comprising four highly trained men in each, who patrolled the perimeter and guarded the high gates of both properties 24/7.

Eight guards for two dwellings was an awful lot of protection but Joe considered it an excellent investment and afforded him the peace of mind which enabled him to sleep at night - at least for the most part. However he could never let his guard down fully as there was always that little niggle in the back of his mind; the little niggle that was constantly asking *'What if?'*

But he was managing it better as time went on.

Joe pulled on some sweat pants then grabbed a T-shirt and sneakers from the giant walk-in closet before heading downstairs. At fifty-four he was still in fabulous shape with a physique that most men half his age would seriously envy but then he had always been obsessive about fitness and still worked out on a daily basis.

He had aged well; his black hair was now streaked with grey

but this just seemed to lend him an air of distinction whilst the crow's feet at the corners of his eyes somehow had the effect of making him look even more handsome, which many had not thought possible.

Joe pulled on his T-shirt as he jogged downstairs en-route to the large, luxuriously appointed kitchen. This was Rose's domain where she reigned supreme. She had designed it herself; personally choosing all the high spec appliances and overseeing the making of the bespoke maple cabinets and sleek marble worktops.

The only item which Joe laid claim to was the chrome plated Italian style coffee machine - his pride and joy - and he clicked it on as soon as he entered.

Whilst he waited for his first, glorious cappuccino of the day, he snatched a bottle of juice from the huge larder fridge and took a few refreshing gulps, then he pressed the cap back on and stuffed the bottle into his pocket.

A few minutes later he was sitting out on the deck by the pool, his cappuccino steaming nicely on the table in front of him and the warm sun on his face.

The air was completely still, the Caribbean sea tranquil and calm; an eager bee buzzed around the flowers somewhere in the background and the birds were still singing the last bars of the dawn chorus as the huge yellow ball of the sun gradually rose up from the deep green of the ocean to the clear blue of the sky to mark the start of another perfect morning in The Caymans.

Joe was not a religious man, but at this time of day he could well be convinced of some higher power such was the glory of what he surveyed.

It was a very far cry from the war-torn streets of his South London birth.

Joe took a revitalising sip of strong coffee; the sparkling ripples of the infinity pool looking wonderfully inviting as they floated off into nothingness - seemingly running over the edge of the cliff. In reality this was just a cleverly constructed illusion which allowed for an uninterrupted view of the distant horizon. Nonetheless, illusion or not, it was a sight that Joe would never tire of.

He would take a dip in the pool later, after his workout, as he did every morning, before reading the newspapers - even though the English ones were always several days old, which was the price he paid for living in such a remote location.

However they enabled him to keep a semi watchful eye on his share prices and to catch up with what was happening in the wider world.

First, however, he needed some exercise.

He drained his cup then made his way barefoot to the gym, which was situated in its own purpose-built block at the far edge of the pool deck to the side of the main house.

Before entering, Joe took a few more moments to enjoy the feel of the morning sun on his body as it warmed his tanned skin. It truly was a wonderful setting. He was a lucky man.

He pulled the juice bottle from his pocket, popped the cap and took a long swig for a welcome blast of freshness and to cleanse his palette from the harsh taste of the coffee. Then he dropped his sneakers on the ground and scotched his feet into them.

A minute later he stepped into the light airy interior of the gym. It was spacious and fully air conditioned with state-of-the-art equipment that would put most pro gyms to shame.

The far wall was made completely of glass; a wide, floor to ceiling expanse which, like the pool deck, offered spectacular views of the calm Caribbean Sea.

Joe flipped a switch beside the door and the glass wall slid silently aside to allow the morning in.

It was like something out of a Bond movie.

He smiled, it certainly beat the cold, scruffy gym back at *The Golden Gloves* which he used to frequent in his youth. *'I wonder what*

Alfie would make of this?' He wondered, thinking fondly of the man who had played such a pivotal role in his life.

Joe wished that he could see him again in person but knew that to do so would be unwise and it made him sad.

To rescue himself from the melancholia he suddenly felt, Joe powered up the treadmill and got down to business, after a few miles he would feel better.

Sure enough, five miles later, the blood pumping through his veins, his heart racing, Joe felt invigorated.

After the treadmill he did thirty minutes on the rowing machine and another thirty on the bike. He then took another long, refreshing slug of juice before setting to work on the bag.

This was his favourite form of relaxation; it worked out all the knots, unleashed all the aggression and kept him sharp.

As he hammered away at the bag, he again thought of *The Golden Gloves* and the old ring there in which he and Sean used to spar, taking on all comers and winning.

Back then they were still just kids but it seemed like they had the whole world at their feet.

It was Alfie Noakes who had seen their potential, given them their break and set them on the road to becoming the men they had eventually turned out to be.

Yet the road had been long and fraught with danger, many had suffered and too many had died, but through it all Joe and Sean had remained tight; their bond rock solid no matter what.

And Alfie had been loyal to them both.

In the intervening years, Violet Noakes, Alfie's daughter, had proved just as loyal, just as trustworthy and Joe would be forever grateful to her for that.

Joe resolved to write to Violet later, after he had finished in the gym. Alfie was old and ailing now and if there was anything he could do to make the old man's life a little bit more comfortable then he would do all in his power to make it happen.

Joe Cassidy always remembered his friends and Alfie and Violet Noakes were among the very best.

For now though, Joe had another thirty minutes of aggression to work out on the bag and as he landed yet another blistering punch on the worn leather, he tried not to dwell on events of the past that no distance and no amount of time could ever erase.

***

By 7am Sean and Sarah were cantering along the cliff top; he on his favourite chestnut mare and she on the white maned Palomino that had been his gift to her on her fiftieth birthday.

The couple had loved each other since they were both very young but tragedy and circumstance had kept them apart for many years. However, for the past ten they had been almost inseparable, trying to make up for all that lost time. They spent every day together, indeed almost every waking moment but neither could ever get bored of the other.

Nowadays their lives centred around their combined love of horses. Sean had been involved with horses since his early twenties and had a deep understanding of them. He still spent a great deal of time in the corral breaking and training them for which he had a particular skill.

Sarah, however, was relatively new to horses. In fact she was well over thirty by the time she even saw one up close and into her forties by the time she first got to ride one. But, like Sean, she had fallen in love with them immediately.

Now the pair of them reared horses together. Their stable was not extensive but the quality was unmistakeable and had earned them a very discerning and exclusive clientele. Yet Sean and Sarah stayed firmly in the background and all trading was conducted through a trusted intermediary - namely Sean's ex-mother-in-law, Louretta Wild, a horse dealer herself and a tough old broad to boot.

Together, Sean and Sarah had even coaxed her twin brother, Joe, into the saddle and occasionally he would join them on their morning ride; his house being just a short distance away on the other side of the bluff.

But not this morning. They both knew that at this time of day Joe would still be in the gym and very little could keep him from his morning exercise. So they were on their own, which was absolutely fine.

Indeed, their house, which was normally a hive of activity was fairly quiet at present. Michael, their son, was usually there and handled all their business affairs, but he was away at a retreat for a couple of weeks and Sean's son, Josh, from his first marriage, was visiting his mother in California.

Only Josh's sister, Olivia - or *Liv* as she now preferred, Sean's twenty-one year old daughter, was at home with them but 7am was far too early for her. Besides, whilst Liv loved the horses and was a gifted horsewoman in her own right, she was much more into cars and motorbikes and generally getting her hands dirty. Currently she spent nearly all of her time under the hood of the classic 1970 Chevy Monte Carlo which she was busy restoring to its former glory - but never until around mid morning as her bed was far too cosy.

So Sean and Sarah left her to sleep as they headed out on their morning ride.

They rode hard along the cliff top, Sarah's long black hair flowing out behind her. Like her brother, she, too, had worn extremely well and could easily pass for a woman in her mid-thirties. She was slim and fit and still incredibly beautiful with those dark beguiling eyes that had entranced Sean all those years before.

Sean was in good shape, too. His work had kept him so, with his body hard and muscular - honed from the long hours spent in the corral. However, his strawberry blonde hair had thinned in latter years so he now preferred to keep it tightly cropped which made him look sleek and chiselled.

Indeed, it was hard to believe that he and his wife were both in their fifties.

The couple followed the cliff path for a while before heading down the narrow, roughly hewn track to the pretty little cove that lay hidden below the rock face and the white sandy beach beyond.

The beauty of the location always reminded Sean of the paradise island he imagined Robinson Crusoe to have been shipwrecked upon, with the aquamarine sea lapping the shoreline and gently swaying palms lining the meandering expanse of deserted beach.

To his mind, with Sarah by his side, there was no better place on earth and he counted his blessings every time they rode out of the cove, through the mouth of the natural rock archway that had been formed through centuries of gradual erosion, and out onto the powdery white sand.

Within the depths of the cove, which had been used by pirates and smugglers over the years, there were a couple of modern innovations which Joe and Sean had deemed prudent to install, although each hoped they would never have to be used, but it was wise to be prepared.

However, Sean gave the innovations only the scantest regard as he and Sarah passed through.

Within seconds of hitting the beach, both horses were wading through the waves, up to their withers in the warm sea water, Sean and Sarah still in their saddles.

The pair of them were bare legged with their naked feet slipped free of the stirrups to allow the salt water to wash gently between their toes.

Sean, in a T-shirt and cargo shorts, and Sarah in a bikini top and cut-offs, giggled and joked as the horses frolicked in the water; the early morning sun, already warm and soothing, shining down upon them, making everything perfect, just as it did every day.

40

After a while, they led the horses back onto the sand. The animals walked for a short distance along the shoreline, away from the cove, before Sean and Sarah nudged them into a trot and then into a full gallop, really letting them go, allowing them to run carefree as fast as they could along the beach.

They raced towards the track at the far end of the bay that would lead them up the cliff face on the opposing side of the bluff which would bring them out a short gallop from Joe and Rose's house.

With luck, if they had timed it correctly, Joe would have finished his workout and Rose would have made a start on breakfast.

***

At twenty-three, Brett Cassidy looked just like his father at the same age; tall, broad shouldered and impossibly handsome. Indeed, his dark good looks had been the cause of many a young girl's broken heart but Brett was just not ready to be tied down.

Like one of Sean's prize stallions, Brett was wild and untamed with a restless spirit and a fire in his heart.

When he was just fourteen, he had been forced to kill a man - an evil man intent on murdering his father - but a man nonetheless and the experience had changed him somewhat. He had always been cool and resourceful with a strength of character not common in others of his age, but after the incident Brett had ceased to be a child.

That had been ten years ago but he had never once doubted it had been the right thing to do. However, it had shaped him, made him realise just how precious life was. To that end he was determined to make the most of his own life - to grab it with both hands and give it a damn good shake.

But on a small island in the Caribbean it was not so easy, particularly when his family were supposed to be in hiding.

However, Brett made the best of things and was well aware of the risks should their whereabouts become known to the outside world. He also had far too much respect for his father and uncle to flout their trust in allowing him to lead a relatively normal life - regardless of the obvious danger it could potentially put them all in.

So, during the high season, with Joe and Sean's blessing, Brett crewed on a luxury motor yacht, taking rich tourists deep sea fishing. His job was to cater to their every need and ensure that they were satisfied enough to leave him a big, fat tip.

In the low season, Brett worked at a *Calico Jack's Bar and Grill* in the town, serving beer and burgers to the locals. Almost every penny he earned was spent on fixing up his own boat, *The Rachel*, which was a much smaller, far less glamorous affair than the one he currently crewed on.

But he had grand plans and *The Rachel* was merely the start. One day he hoped to own his own small fleet of cruisers, running trips around the Caribbean - taking rich tourists hunting for sharks, fishing for marlin and diving the reefs.

It was not exactly life in the fast lane, but it would be one lived on his own terms with plenty of opportunities for adventure - and what could be better than that?

The fact was, however, that Brett did not need to work at all; his father was a multi-millionaire and would have gladly helped him turn his dream into a reality - but Brett was determined to make it on his own. He loved his father, admired him above all others, but he adamantly refused to ride on Joe's coat tails.

He wanted to earn it for himself and Joe respected him for that.

The only concession to this was the Harley Sportster that Brett rode around on. Joe had bought his son the bike when he turned seventeen to enable him to get around the island - flatly refusing to let Brett pay him back for it, even though he had tried.

The bike was now six years old but it still started first time as Brett sat astride it that morning and pushed it off its stand by the jetty where it had been parked for the last two days.

He had just finished what was supposed to be a four day

excursion with a wealthy industrialist from Pennsylvania. But the client had been called back on urgent business so they had put ashore early, after just two days at sea.

This meant Brett found himself back on dry land much sooner than expected, although the business man had left him with a healthy tip so it had certainly been worthwhile.

Better still, if he hurried, he could get home in time for one of Rosie's fantastic English breakfasts - sausages, bacon, fried bread, the works - just like the ones she made when they lived in South London.

So, with the thought of freshly cooked bacon on his mind, he set off along the quayside, purposely riding past *The Rachel* which was moored up nearby, making a mental note of the areas on which his bumper tip might best be spent.

Briefly, he considered pulling over and putting in a few hours work on her as there was always something that needed doing. But the delicious thought of breakfast was too tempting especially after a couple of nights away.

The boat would still be there later. He would come back then when he'd had his fill of bacon. *Mmm, he could almost taste it now.*

Wearing only a T-shirt, faded Levis and pair of battered deck shoes, Brett revved the Sportster and sped away from the quay, his muscular arms and tanned face enjoying the kiss of the early morning sun as he roared out along the coast road towards home.

Ten minutes later he was being waved through the gates by Freddie, the head of the security team that guarded the *Far Point Estate* - where both Brett's father, Joe, and his Uncle Sean lived in the only two houses on the whole property.

As he rode up the long curved driveway and headed towards his dad's enormous house, Brett could have sworn he smelt the delicious aroma of fried bacon on the air and his stomach rumbled with hunger at the mere thought of it.

Sean and Sarah's two horses were tied up outside, chomping at a trough of oats, leading Brett to believe that they, too, had been enticed by the prospect of Rosie's cooking.

Instinctively, as he slowed to a halt, he glanced across the bluff to where his uncle's house sat high in the distance, unconsciously searching for any sign of Liv. However, he then caught himself and quickly looked away.

Liv Noakes was strictly off limits he reminded himself.

Yet it did not stop him wishing she was not. Why was it out of all the girls on the island he had only ever really been interested in the one beyond his grasp?

Liv was his cousin, or at least technically. She was Sean's daughter by his first wife. But now Sean was married to Sarah, Joe's sister - Brett's aunt.

Liv and he were not related by blood but had known each other for much of their lives. To begin with she had been like an annoying little sister but in latter years, as they both grew older, something between them had changed. Something that both of them were very aware of but never spoke about.

Yet the chemistry between them was undeniable. Indeed, Brett's feelings for Liv had been a contributory factor to his spending so much time away from the estate - keeping his mind occupied so that he did not have to think about the beautiful girl who lived next door.

However, Liv had taken this as an affront to her personally, feeling that he was purposely trying to avoid her and not understanding why. Consequently their relationship had become somewhat fractious as a result of it.

Nonetheless, Brett was convinced it was for the best.

But, try as he might, he could not stop thinking about her as he lent his bike on the stand and headed out to the veranda following the smell of bacon.

Liv stirred at around nine. She needed to pee, yet her bed was just too warm and cosy. Nevertheless, she could not put it off any longer so, very reluctantly, she crawled out from under her duvet and staggered across the bare wooden floor to the bathroom.

She sat on the lavatory; her elbows on her knees, her head resting in her hands as she closed her eyes and dozed whilst passing a long, tinkling stream that seemed to go on forever.

When she was finally done, she sat there in silence for a few moments still half asleep and too tired to move; the house completely silent except for the distant sound of the ocean.

And then she heard something else. The unmistakeable sound of a motorbike. A Harley Sportster, she would have known the rumble of its engine anywhere.

Brett was back.

A little tingle of excitement fluttered in her stomach. Her dad had told her Brett would be away for four days and she had felt that familiar rush of disappointment at the news. The same disappointment she always felt whenever he rode away from *Far Point*. Yet now he was back.

Liv wiped herself quickly then sprang off the toilet and ran to the window. Sure enough, there he was, his black mop of hair blowing in the wind as he sped up the driveway to Joe's house.

Even at this long distance he was a sight to see.

Then, suddenly, she admonished herself and a prickle of anger crept in as she thought about how he had dropped her - just like that.

They had got on so well, spent long hours together, working on bikes and cars and riding around the estate on horseback; swimming in the sea and exploring the coves, strolling along the beach completely at ease in each other's company. She had even helped him with his restoration of *The Rachel*. It was wonderful.

But then it all ended. For no apparent reason Brett seemed to tire of her. He no longer wanted to be around her, could barely even speak to her and was rarely on the estate long enough nowadays for her to find out why.

The truth of it was that she missed him dreadfully. Deep down in the pit of her soul it truly hurt her - although she purposely avoided asking herself the reason why it hurt so very much for fear of what the answer might actually be. Indeed, the regard she had for him went far beyond mere friendship but she was loathed to admit it to anyone - especially herself.

Yet it did not stop her from being mad at him. In fact, she was madder than hell.

There was no way she could go back to sleep now as her mind was too full of questions, too wrapped up with issues that had been unresolved for much too long.

So, there and then she decided to go and confront him; to find out just what in the hell she had done so terribly wrong.

She stomped back into the bedroom and stood stark naked in front of her dressing table; a twenty-one year old goddess with the figure of a supermodel and a mane of shiny golden curls, but Liv, although not blind to her natural charms, certainly did not concern herself with such superficial things - although she was not beyond using them to her advantage when it suited her.

However, this morning, her appearance was the last thing on her mind.

The slight morning breeze gently flapped the white muslin drapes through the open window as she hastily rummaged through the top drawer and dug out some mismatched underwear.

She gave herself a cursory glance in the mirror as she pulled the knickers on, up her long, tanned legs and over her perfectly pert posterior, despairing at the tangle of unbrushed blonde hair that hung messily around her shoulders. But she had no time to make herself presentable as she had to get over to her Uncle Joe's before

Brett headed off again.

Liv pushed her generous breasts into the silky bra and clipped it together at the back before shrugging on her trusty green overalls, which were covered in the oil and grease of the Chevy Monte Carlo, as well as that of her dad's old Indian motorcycle and numerous other automotive projects she had worked on over the years - usually alongside Brett, or at least until recently.

The grubby overalls did a spectacular job of completely obscuring Liv's wonderful figure but she seemed quite oblivious to this as she scrunched her hair into a shaggy ponytail and pulled on a dirty red baseball cap to keep the remaining wayward curls off her strikingly pretty face.

Finally, she sat on the bed and tugged on a pair of tatty Converse sneakers before rushing downstairs and out to the garage.

A moment later, she was roaring down the short stretch of road that linked the two houses in her prized Monte Carlo, its chrome rims gleaming in the sunlight.

The car was still wearing its base red undercoat, however once Liv had finished tinkering about under its hood, it would receive a lustrous new paint job.

But not today. Today was going to be all about confronting Brett Cassidy.

***

Ray Reece sat in his wheelchair at the table on the veranda, next to his wife, Ruby. Both had white hair now and had spent the last ten years growing old together.

Ray still looked like a pirate, with his wild hair, pointed goatee and shiny black eye-patch - and he had never lost that impish sense of mischief that had influenced his roguish reputation. Yet Ray had never fully recovered from his fall - or all that other business back in London, prior to their departure from the city that had been his home for the greater part of his life.

47

However, The Caribbean suited him, and as long as Ruby was by his side he could have been happy anywhere on earth.

That feeling extended to his adopted family, too, and as he looked around the breakfast table he felt like an extremely fortunate man.

There was Ruby, of course, making a fuss of him as usual, sorting out his plate and loading it up with piles of sausages, bacon and eggs. Alongside her, setting down a steaming pot of coffee and a crystal decanter full of juice, was Rose; a stunning, remarkably kind woman who had become something like a daughter to him; who cared for both him and Ruby as if they were her own parents. Sitting opposite, were Sean and Sarah who, over the years, he had come to like and respect as much as Joe did. Next to Sarah, was Joe himself; a man who Ray could not have had a higher regard for, whom he was proud to call his greatest friend and even more proud to be the person Joe considered to be his father. Alongside Joe was Brett; a chip off the old block, almost identical to his father in every way. If not for Brett taking decisive action ten years earlier, Ray would undoubtedly have been dead. He owed the boy his life. Yet in saving Ray, Brett's childhood had been stolen away and he had become an adult at just fourteen. But if anyone could carry the weight of it, it was Brett. He was strong, just like Joe and Ray loved them both as if they were his own.

Rose was busy making sure everyone had enough; filling glasses with orange juice and topping up mugs with piping hot coffee. She was bright and vivacious, always quick with a smile and a kind word, which made her the ideal hostess.

Slim and tanned, with long auburn hair, Rose was blissfully happy in the bosom of her family. Her only slight sadness was that Matt, her and Joe's eldest son, was not there but he was a wanderer and a free-spirit who preferred to go his own way. However, they spoke regularly and all got together several times a year, which made his absence a little more bearable.

Nonetheless, with Matt not there, it was Brett who was the object of her affections. Even though he was not her own son, she treated him as if he was and, in return, he regarded her as his mother - although preferred to call her 'Rosie' rather than 'Mum'.

Rose could not disguise her happiness that Brett had returned sooner than expected and planted a big smacker on his cheek as she placed an extra sausage on his plate. "There you go," she said, ruffling his hair, "I know how much you love a full English."

"Hey! What about me?" Joe complained playfully, "Don't I get one?"

"No, you don't - you'll get fat. Brett's a growing boy and needs to keep his strength up - don't you sweetie?"

"Yeah, Rosie, that's right," said Brett busily carving up his sausage. "Sides, I'd hate you to get fat, Pop," he grinned mischievously, knowing how unlikely that was given his father's supreme fitness.

"Hmm," Joe sighed, raising an eyebrow and giving Brett a sideways glance. "You would, would you?"

"Uh-huh," nodded Brett, smiling widely as he tucked into his breakfast.

"Boy's gotta point," chimed in Ray. "You wouldn't want to get all flabby now would you?"

Joe chuckled. "Don't you start you old pirate - I notice Ruby snuck a couple of extra sausages on your plate *and* a triple helping of bacon."

"Hey, I'm old and feeble. I need the sustenance."

"Old and feeble my arse! I've known weaker ox's," replied Joe.

"Yeah, I don't remember you being too feeble last night, lover boy!" Said Ruby, causing the whole table to fall about laughing.

"Thanks, Ruby," said Sean, "I reckon that's an image I could live without over my breakfast!"

"You and me both!" Agreed Joe.

"Oh, I don't know. I think it's romantic said Sarah."

"Me, too," added Rose as the rumble of Liv's finely tuned Monte Carlo made its presence known outside causing Brett to shift uncomfortably in his chair.

"Dunno what's so romantic about an old man having—" began Joe but he was interrupted by the sound of the telephone.

"Don't worry, I'll get it. You have your breakfast," Rose said. But Joe was already out of his chair and crossing the veranda.

"No, don't be silly," he said to her, "You've been busy cooking all this - now sit down and enjoy it. I'll get it." Then he winked at her and said, "Besides, a bit more exercise might stop me from getting flabby."

She smiled adoringly at her husband. "Don't worry, I'd still love you regardless."

Joe blew her a kiss.

"Hey!" Rose called as Joe vanished into the kitchen, "It might be Matt - come get me if it is."

"Will do" his disembodied voice yelled from inside the house.

A moment later Liv marched onto the veranda, her face like thunder.

"Oh, hello sweetie," said Rose, "you're just in time for breakfast. Sit yourself down and I'll go get you a plate."

"No, thanks, Aunt Rose, I'm not staying. I just need to have a quick word with Brett if that's okay?"

"Yes, of course you can, sweetie, no problem. He's just got back from work." Rose then turned back to the table and called her step-son. "Brett, honey, Liv's here, she just wants a quick chat!"

Again Brett shifted uneasily.

"Uh-oh, looks like you could be in trouble, boy," Ray whispered under his breath.

"Yeah," agreed Sean, conspiratorially, "I've been on the receiving end of that look before and believe me, it don't mean anything good."

"Thanks guys," muttered Brett sarcastically before saying to Liv, "Can't it wait 'til after breakfast? I've just got back and I'm starv—"

"No!" Liv snapped. "It can't wait. Please, I need to speak with you now."

"Told you," Sean whispered as Brett shrugged his shoulders and very reluctantly stood up.

"Good luck, kid," said Ray. "Say, can I have that extra sausage if you don't make it back alive?"

Ruby nudged him in the ribs. "You be quiet you silly old sod, can't you see that the girl's upset?"

"Just trying to lighten things with a bit of levity, that's all."

"Well it's not working," Ruby hissed.

Like a man heading towards the gallows, Brett slowly walked over to where Liv and Rose were waiting, dreading what she might be about to say, knowing that he fully deserved whatever it was and feeling like the scum of the earth because of it.

She was surely going to ask him why he had been avoiding her but he could not tell her the truth. He just couldn't. It would ruin everything.

But then, Joe walked out of the kitchen, his face deathly pale, the shock clear to see on his face.

Brett was instantly concerned, all thoughts of Liv suddenly washed from his mind.

"What is it, Pop? What's the matter?"

Instantly Sean was on his feet and rushing over. "Joe? What's happened? Who was that on the phone?"

Immediately Rose thought of her son. "Not Matt? Please tell me nothing's happened to Matt?"

"No," Joe said. "It wasn't Matt."

"Who then?" Demanded Rose.

"It was Manno," said Joe, finally. "At least I think it was him, I couldn't really hear very well—"

"Manno?" Said Sean. "Why what's happened?"

"I dunno, Sean," Joe's voice was grave, "But I think he might have just died."

"What?" Sean was aghast. Sarah was on her feet, too, now.

"Why Joseph?" She said, hurrying to her twin brother, "What did he say?"

Joe looked at her, then at Sean. Then at everyone. "He said *'They know'*."

"*They know?*" Said Sean.

"Yeah, at least that's what I think he said. I can't be sure, I could barely hear him. But I think he said *'they know'* and then I think he died." Joe then looked at Ray, his old partner from the South London underworld, the only other person there who knew Manno as well as he did. "I think he died, Ray."

"Jesus," said the old man in the wheelchair, "the poor bastard."

"Uncle Joe?" Liv's voice suddenly snapped Joe out of his thoughts. "What does that mean?"

Joe looked at Sean who, in turn, turned to his daughter. "It means we've got trouble, sweetheart - or at least we might have."

"Is that right, Joe?" Asked Rose, incredulously. "Have we got trouble? Could we be in danger?"

Joe's face was set as he turned to his wife and said, "Maybe. Wouldn't hurt to let everyone know, just in case."

Rose put her hand up to her mouth in shock. Their perfect life had just been shattered but she had no time to think about that now. "Tell me what you want me to do," she said.

"That's my girl." Said Joe proudly, then added, addressing everyone in general, "Right, we'll try and get hold of Matt. I'll also call Louretta and put her on alert. Sean, you try and get a message to Michael - wouldn't hurt to let Vicky and Virgil know, too, just to be safe. In the meantime, I'll try and figure out some way of getting hold of Violet in London, see if she knows anymore. Hopefully it's nothing to worry about - hopefully I misheard and Manno's fine but if not, then we'd better get ready."

"Ready?" Asked Liv. "Ready for what?"

Sean looked into his daughter's scared blue eyes and said, "Whatever's sure to be coming our way, honey."

Then he turned and gazed out to sea, his mind seemingly drifting back to some other place in time as he said once more, in a voice thick with resigned foreboding, "Whatever's sure to be coming our way."

***

Forty-eight hours later, Joe was feeling extremely frustrated. He had not been able to contact Violet Noakes or, indeed, get any answer at all at *The Golden Gloves* despite the risks associated with telephoning there directly. The same applied to *The Galaxy Club* which, again, proved fruitless. Joe knew it was madness to call and it went against all his better instincts but he *had* to know.

Was Manno dead and, if so, were they all now in harm's way?

Caymans news channels focussed mainly on local issues and world news extended only as far as America. Any information about the rest of the world was patchy at best so Joe was completely in the dark about what might be happening in London. Even more frustrating was the fact that the UK newspapers would not be flown in for at least a couple more days and by that time anything could have happened.

Furthermore, no one had been able to get hold of Matt. His lifestyle meant he was never in one place for too long and even when he was, he was rarely contactable by telephone.

However most of the others had been alerted and advised to take care. Although in Michael's case, Sean had only spoken to his doctor, who thought it best not to inform Michael himself as it might cause him unnecessary distress and perhaps even harm his recovery. Yet Sean was assured that security would be stepped up at the gated facility and that no one would be permitted to enter the grounds without a thorough check.

Yet this still did not put either Sean's or Joe's mind at rest. Both knew from the bitter experiences of their past what could happen if the wrong person discovered that they were not dead after all, as was long believed but, in fact, living happy lives in The Caymans.

They were both well aware that the repercussions of such a discovery could put them and their families in a great deal of danger and, after ten years of peaceful anonymity, that was something neither were willing to contemplate.

Nonetheless, something told them - perhaps it was instinct, perhaps it was just the fear that one day this would happen - but whatever it was, Sean and Joe were convinced.

Trouble was coming.

Chapter Three

Miami

Carmine Carboni, capo di tuti and Godfather supreme of crime syndicates on both the East and West Coasts of America, including New York, Miami, Las Vegas and Atlantic City, had always disliked his son-in-law, Benny Vincenzi, and had shed no tears when he was killed.

Yet Benny's marriage to Carmine's daughter had been extremely beneficial to both the Carboni and Vincenzi families, the union resulting in the twin grandsons, Jez and Vito, whom both Carmine and Tito utterly adored.

Yet Vito had been snatched from them all too soon and the pain of losing him at such an early age had never dulled. It had been ten years since his death, but Carmine had never stopped grieving.

Then there was Jez, Benny's remaining boy. Carmine's beloved grandson, who was still a child when his twin brother was killed. He was not much older when he lost his mother to cancer and prior to that came the news of Benny's death. Although this was actually something of a relief to Carmine as, in his latter years, Benny's behaviour had become increasingly erratic. His obsession with Cassidy and Reilly had driven him to the brink of insanity and he had become a serious liability.

He would not be missed.

Nevertheless, in spite of Benny's death, it did not change the fact that Carmine had still lost a grandson and Jez his only brother.

All because of Joe Cassidy and Sean Reilly.

But they had reportedly died, too, so could not be held accountable.

However, neither corpse could be formerly identified, which seemed strange considering that they had each died within days of each other on opposite sides of the Atlantic.

Supposedly Reilly had died in a car wreck on the outskirts of Vegas, his body burned beyond recognition and Cassidy's face had been blown off in a gangland shoot-out in London's docklands.

Their deaths and the lack of positive identification had always seemed a little too convenient for Carmine and if there was one thing that he did not trust it was 'convenience'.

Yet his and Tito's combined efforts had tried and failed to find evidence to the contrary.

But still Carmine's gut told him that something was amiss and his gut was rarely wrong.

What is more, Jez had always been convinced that Cassidy and Reilly were still alive - indeed, as he got older, the idea had all but consumed him.

It had changed him, too.

Jez had always been the dominant twin and lacked the kinder, sweeter and more compassionate nature of his brother. Indeed, Jez was altogether tougher, much more aggressive and far less easy to placate.

After Vito's death, all these traits were amplified. He became quicker to anger, difficult to control and very demanding.

But his mother had indulged him and so did his two powerful grandfathers. The very fact that he survived made him even more precious to them, even more cherished and even though he was a difficult child, neither could see any wrong in him.

He was their young prince, the heir to both their crowns. Indeed, in the event of his grandfathers deaths, with him as the sole beneficiary, Jez alone would inherit everything, thus completing the merger of the two families that had begun with the marriage of his mother and father.

It would also make him a very wealthy and extremely powerful individual.

Unsurprising then, that few amongst his peers would dare take issue with him. So rather than being guided by the well meaning advice of trusted friends he was instead surrounded by fawning sycophants who eagerly complied with his every wish and demand.

Even Carmine and Tito were not immune and would happily have given him anything he desired. Yet the very thing he wanted above all else they were unable to provide.

And what Jez so desperately desired was vengeance.

Yet for all Carmine and Tito's combined wealth, for all their power and influence, the truth or, indeed, conclusive proof, as to whether Reilly and Cassidy were alive or dead still eluded them.

But Jez firmly believed that somehow they had escaped the fates that had apparently befallen them and would not be satisfied until his vengeance had been properly served.

He had just turned twenty-one; his birthday party a hugely lavish, wildly expensive affair in the grounds of Tito Vincenzi's Miami mansion. Carmine was there, too, of course, as was every member of both families.

Old men in expensive suits and heavy set women in twin sets and pearls talked, ate and sat in lawn chairs whilst the younger generation; tanned, toned and up for fun, partied long and hard into the hot afternoon.

The party was Tito's present to Jez, along with the yellow Lamborghini that was sitting outside on the driveway and the solid gold Rolex that now adorned his wrist.

Carmine, however, had not yet presented his grandson with anything. "My gift will be here soon," was all he would say, somewhat mysteriously.

Jez did not seem too impressed by this but was placated by his grandfather's assurance that 'it would be well worth the wait.'

Jez was handsome in a cruel way; his face chiselled with sharp cheek bones and a square chin, yet his lips were thick and rubbery like his father's and his dark eyes were cold and void of emotion. His shoulder-length hair was black with a long fringe that was swept back off his forehead.

Jez's body was tight and muscular and presently clothed in a canary yellow silk suit that had been purposely made to match his gleaming new sports car.

The suit was cut in the loose style and worn over a tight-fitting black T-shirt. A pair of soft, black, handmade, Italian loafers were on his feet, minus socks, as was the fashion and being stylish was important to Jez's overblown sense of vanity.

Jez was lounging in a luxurious seating area, in a nest of comfortable sofas under the shade of a large pergola that had been erected just beyond the vast pool. The pool itself sat directly in the centre of the beautifully manicured lawns that stretched all the way down to the tranquil waters of Biscayne Bay. The sound of the gentle waves lapping at the edge of the private island completely drowned out by the loud disco beat of the party.

The lawn, pool and wide paved pathway that led up to the expansive veranda of the huge waterfront property were all bustling with young party people in bikinis and board shorts. The older generation staking their claim on the veranda itself, keeping as far away as possible from the boom boom beat of the disco where they could talk to each other in peace without having to shout over the din.

But Jez was not concerned with their comfort, they had only

been invited as a courtesy, because they were family, but whether they were enjoying themselves or not made little difference to him.

Jez, himself, was swigging mai tais and enjoying the attentions of three bikini clad girls who were all but throwing themselves at him; flaunting their ample wares and flirting outrageously as they, too, swilled down mai tais by the glass full; kissing and cavorting and putting on a brazen show for the birthday boy, giving him a little taste of what he could expect later in the privacy of his bedroom.

The four of them had all just done a few lines of coke - away from the disapproving eyes of Jez's ever watchful grandparents who had warned him never to go near the merchandise.

But what did they know? They were old men, echoes from the past. Jez was new, switched on, ambitious - the future - and he could do whatever the hell he pleased.

Besides, the coke had spiced things up nicely and had significantly enlivened what was proving to be a pretty dull party.

Jez was eager for his present. Carmine had intrigued him, *what was it that the old man had bought him?*

Another car? A boat maybe? Whatever it was it better be good after making him wait for so long.

Jez had downed several more mai tais by the time an aide of Carmine's came to fetch him. His gift had finally arrived and Jez was to follow the aide to the boat house where he was to be presented with it.

He had been instructed to come alone and not bring any of his friends.

This did not sit well with Jez.

The boathouse, really? How obvious could his grandfather make it?

Clearly he was being given a new boat. Great. So what was the big deal? Why the wait? And why couldn't any of his friends come along to see him receive it?

Nevertheless, Jez gritted his teeth and decided to indulge his grandfather. Let the old man have his moment of glory, it surely would not be for much longer.

Jez duly arrived at the boathouse several minutes later, removing his black wrap around sunglasses as he stepped in through the door.

The boathouse was a large Art Deco style structure that sat directly behind the private dock. Big enough to house two luxury motor yachts along with a couple of speed boats and several jet skis; all the essential millionaire toys.

"Hello?" Jez shouted into the seemingly empty space.

"Back here, J-Boy!" Replied Carmine from the far side of the boathouse, the sight of him obscured by the smooth lines of the two enormous, ocean-going cruisers.

Reluctantly, Jez made his way around the dock to where he at last saw both of his grandfathers standing in a group with three of their bodyguards. Alongside them was a tall half-caste man and another smaller, skinnier person who was bound at the wrists and had a hood over his head.

Immediately intrigued, Jez hastened over to them, a curious expression on his face. This was not what he had been expecting.

Carmine Carboni was smiling widely, as was Tito Vincenzi; the two most powerful heads of organised crime in America waiting anxiously to please their beloved grandson like a couple of devoted Labradors.

"What's all this?" Asked Jez, noting the hooded man's bedraggled, scruffy appearance, clearly the victim of some serious 'roughing up'. The ropes tied around the man's wrists had obviously been in place for sometime as they had worn away the skin leaving angry, bloody burns.

"This, J-Boy," Carmine said grandly, "is my birthday present to you."

"What? I don't under—" Jez began to say before Carmine whipped off the bound man's hood.

Carboni grinned wickedly as he said, "Jez Vincenzi, meet Michael Walsh - or perhaps I should say Michael *Reilly* - the son of Sean Reilly, nephew of Joe Cassidy - and your answer to where both of those bastards actually are!"

***

In the thirty-seven years since his birth, Michael Walsh had endured an awful lot; facial disfigurement, kidnapping, enforced drug abuse and the brutal attentions of a sadistic killer, amongst other things, and it had all left him extremely scarred and particularly vulnerable.

Over the last ten years he had been coming to terms with what had happened and with the comfort and love of his parents and the tight bond he had formed with other family members - his uncle, aunt, step-brothers and sister amongst them, he had at last managed to find some sort of peace.

However, years of therapy had also been a significant factor in his recovery. He visited a therapist at least once a week and twice a year spent two weeks at an exclusive sanatorium situated on its own private corner of Nantucket.

It was a place ideally suited to the type of convalescence and treatment Michael needed. Regular therapy sessions went hand in hand with one-to-one mentoring and peaceful periods of relaxation. All of it geared towards the improvement of mental health and physiological well-being.

Afterwards, Michael always felt refreshed and invigorated, the demons of his past assuaged just that little bit more than they had been before.

During his down time at the sanatorium, Michael would enjoy walking alone along the white sandy beach of the island which traced the outer edge of the sprawling complex. He relished the peace and tranquillity with just the melodic sound of the softly breaking surf lapping at his feet as he meandered along the shoreline.

However, it was on one such day, when Michael was strolling barefoot along the sand, wearing only a T-shirt and cargo shorts, that he noticed a small motor launch speeding towards the shore.

He looked on curiously as the boat drew nearer until it eventually slowed and came to a halt in the shallow water close to where he stood.

Michael raised a hand and shaded his eyes, watching as a tall, powerfully built, half-caste man jumped into the sea and waded ashore.

The man, who was smiling broadly - a gleaming gold incisor twinkling in the sunlight - was dressed in a similar style to Michael although he towered above him as he approached.

"You Michael?" Said the man in a pleasant, friendly manner.

"Yes?" Replied Michael, assuming the man to be a member of the sanatorium staff although not entirely sure what he was doing approaching him from the ocean or, indeed, why he was out there in the first place.

"Good," said the man, "thought so." Then, quick as a flash, he punched Michael hard in the face, knocking him to the ground.

Michael lay on his back looking up, his head spinning, his vision starry, the strange man looming over him, silhouetted against the brightness of the sun.

Then the darkness came and he blacked out.

***

When Michael awoke he was bound at the wrists and ankles. He was sitting on the floor at the stern of the small motor cruiser, his back thumping against the rail in time with the dramatic rise and fall motion of the vessel as it sped out to sea; the waves crashing under the hull, the sound of them beating out a steady rhythm as fear filled Michael's belly whilst the echoes of his harrowing past resounded his brain.

A wiry old man in scruffy fisherman's attire was sitting under the canopy of the wheelhouse several feet away, navigating the speeding vessel over the swells. Whilst sitting on a padded bench seat, just opposite Michael, with one hand on the rail and the other holding a pistol, was Bass Stone - but Michael was not aware of who he was.

Stone had never even heard of the island of Nantucket prior to seeing the address of the sanatorium written on the scrap of paper found at *The Golden Gloves* along with Michael's name but upon investigation, he discovered the facility was run by a former South London doctor with connections to Joe Cassidy.

As such, he guessed that the sanatorium had become a convenient postal address where information could be easily passed back and forth without detection by certain interested parties.

And it had worked well until now but Stone had put the pieces of the puzzle together easily enough.

He was aware of Michael's importance to the overall scheme of things as Big Jack had told him most of the details of what had happened in the past or, at least, his version of them.

What is more, Bass knew that finding Michael was the key to his ascension from mere foot soldier to fully fledged General.

Also, just one look at the skinny, strange looking man he had spotted walking along the beach - right where his sanatorium informant had said he would be - told Stone that this one would be a much easier nut to crack than Richie Noakes or Manno O'Keefe.

Now, as the boat headed out to the deep water, en-route to their final destination, Bass was confident that Michael would tell him all he needed to know. After all, it would take a long time to get to Miami from Massachusetts and in that time Stone was confident he could persuade almost anyone to tell him anything.

Stone relished the prospect and smiled when he saw that

Michael had finally roused. This was going to be fun.

"Ah, hi there, Mike," he said, in a pleasant, friendly tone. "Glad to see you're back with us after your little nap."

"What do you want with me?" Michael demanded. "Why are you doing this?"

"Oh, okay. Straight to the point, then, no chit-chat?" Replied Bass conversationally, "Fair enough, I get it. Well then, what I want from you, Mike, is information. Why I'm doing this is because there is someone who will pay me a great deal of money to deliver you to them."

Michael felt his stomach churn with dread and he began to struggle wildly with panic, tugging at the ropes around his wrists, kicking his feet desperately to try to free himself from the tight restraints around his ankles.

He could not face the prospect of any more pain as he'd already been through enough for a lifetime. He would rather throw himself overboard and take his chances with the sharks or drown in the depths of the ocean than endure anymore suffering. But he could not escape, his bonds were too tight, there was no way he could even stand up let alone leap over the rail.

"I won't tell you anything!" Michael yelled defiantly. "I won't - *I won't*. Please - just let me go!"

"Oh Mike," Bass said in a sympathetic tone. "I'm afraid I can't let you go - and yes, you will tell me everything".

Then he leant in, staring at Michael hard in the face, his cold eyes full of evil intent as he added, "And I do mean *everything*.

Michael felt his bowels shift, the terrifying memories of the torture and beatings he had endured in the past suddenly flaring brightly in his brain once more. *Not again*, he begged silently to God. *Please not again*.

He fell back against the rail in utter despair and began to weep.

Bass Stone smiled. This was going to be so much easier than

he had expected.

***

As it transpired, it was actually harder than he anticipated. Michael held out for much longer than Bass had thought someone like him possibly could. He showed balls, Stone would give him that. But eventually, after much suffering, he had ultimately cracked.

Michael lay slumped on his ropes, still tied to the rail. His face was a bloodied pulp; four of his teeth had been knocked out and his nose was broken. His skinny body was purple with bruising and several of his ribs were cracked. Stone had gone to town on him, relishing every blow, every punch.

Michael had lost consciousness many times during his ordeal and was vaguely aware of the passage of the sun each time he awoke. Yet, as the sun finally sank below the horizon on their second day at sea, he at last gave up the information Stone so badly wanted to hear.

Now, however, Michael felt like a traitor. He had betrayed the trust of his father and uncle, told this brutal madman of their location and he was desperately ashamed.

Late in the evening, as the small motor launch moored up on the dark and lonely jetty of a scruffy, run-down harbour somewhere in the Florida Keys, Michael wished he was dead.

He spent the night shivering and aching on the cold, damp floor of a warehouse near the dockside, tied up like a dog with no water to drink nor food to eat. But as the long hours of the night passed, Michael vowed to make things right, to make amends for being so weak.

Bass Stone came to fetch him several hours after sun up. Stone was dressed much more smartly now; a light beige suit, a cream silk shirt and polished brown shoes.

The wiry fisherman-style helmsman was no longer around as Stone bundled Michael back into the boat and took the wheel himself, safely guiding the launch back out to the open sea.

65

Judging by the position of the sun in the clear blue sky, it was sometime around mid-afternoon when Stone pushed a cloth sack over Michael's head, obscuring his view and preventing him from seeing their final destination.

A short time later, the small vessel docked again and he was led by Stone and two other men to a cooler place; a building of some kind Michael guessed, although still quite close to the water as he could hear the waves lapping at the edge of what felt to be a wooden deck under his bare feet.

Michael was being held securely by the arms, although there was little chance of him escaping as Bass Stone pressed his mouth next to his ear and whispered, "Journey's end, Mike. Time to make me look good."

Michael felt too weary to struggle and guessed he would very soon be dead, but if an opportunity presented itself for him to atone for being so weak then he was determined not to squander it.

He would do right by his father and uncle if it was the last thing he ever did.

***

Jez Vincenzi looked into Michael's eyes and smiled coldly.

"You like your present, J-Boy?" Asked Carmine Carboni victoriously. "Mr. Stone here assures me that Joe Cassidy and Sean Reilly are alive and well - and that this piece of shit can tell you exactly where to find them."

Michael blinked a couple of times, accustoming himself to the light, the sack having been removed from his head.

He looked about him, ignoring the glare of the snappily dressed young man in front of him. To Michael's left stood Bass Stone, emotionless and silent, immediately next to him stood the man who had just spoken, Carmine Carboni. Grey haired, heavy set with thick framed spectacles and a white bowling shirt over grey seersucker slacks. Michael guessed it was what passed for Mafia chic.

To the left of Carmine was a chubby, bald-headed man chomping on a fat Cuban cigar. He, too, wore glasses, although his were tinted aviators. This was Vito Vincenzi; smiling and slug like, with a loud silk shirt hanging loosely on his sizeable bulk and a lightweight pair of beige trousers covering his chunky legs.

Holding one of Michael's arms was a man of about thirty with curly hair and a muscular physique. He was in a dark grey suit with a black shirt.

On Michael's other arm was a smaller, stockier man with a crew cut, also in a dark grey suit and black shirt.

Both of these guards were carrying Uzi sub-machine guns.

Strangely, the sight of the guns gave Michael just the slightest glimmer of a chance.

"Hey, ugly!" Snapped Jez, grabbing Michael firmly by the jaw and twisting his head to face him. "Is that true?" He snarled. "Can you tell me where they are?"

Michael was tired. He had been through a lot. Endured much. "Yeah," he replied softly. "I *can* tell you where they are."

Jez Vincenzi turned and grinned at his grandfathers excitedly. This was the news he had been waiting to hear for over ten years. All his suspicions had been confirmed, his instincts validated.

Cassidy and Reilly were alive.

Finally vengeance would be his. The best birthday present ever.

However, his 'gift' had not yet finished speaking and as Jez turned back to him, Michael smiled and added, "But I'm not going to tell you."

Then, with all the strength he could muster, Michael shoulder-barged the stockier guard as hard as he could, taking him and the other guard completely by surprise.

Crew Cut staggered sideways into Bass Stone, knocking him off balance, as Michael made a desperate grab for the machine gun.

Suddenly, amazingly, Michael found that he actually had the

Uzi in his hands and immediately he started firing it wildly. The machine gun juddering uncontrollably as he pressed his finger hard down on the trigger, but he did not stop.

Michael watched aghast as bullets ripped across Carmine Carboni's chest, blowing huge holes through his pristine white bowling shirt as thick fountains of blood erupted from them.

Yet Michael clung onto the weapon, still spraying bullets in a mad, indiscriminate frenzy. He witnessed Vito Vincenzi's head detonate as several shots slammed into it at near point blank range, the sight of it utterly horrifying but still Michael held his finger on the trigger, knowing it was his only hope of saving Joe and his father.

Jez dived to the floor, bullets ripping through the tails of his bright yellow jacket as Michael swung the Uzi around, blasting Curly Hair through the neck, separating his head from his shoulders in a burst of deadly machine gun fire.

With his whole body shaking to the ghastly vibration of the weapon, Michael attempted to spin back around, knowing that Bass Stone and Crew Cut were behind him.

He had to get Stone.

At his lowest ebb, after being beaten half to death, Michael had told Stone everything and, as such, made him the only other person to know of Joe and Sean's whereabouts.

But as Michael wrestled the Uzi around he felt something slam into his shoulder, which immediately released his finger from the trigger. Indeed, he could no longer feel the trigger or the gun at all and the Uzi dropped from his grip and clattered to the ground as another violent jolt hit him hard in the belly.

Michael sank to his knees, knowing he had been shot, the pain of it suddenly intense and all-consuming. He looked up to see Bass Stone, whose smoking semi-automatic was aimed directly at his head.

Michael knew that he had failed his father and his uncle but hoped, at least, he might have given them some sort of chance by taking out Carmine and Vito. Maybe without them Jez would prove to be nothing, meaning what Michael had divulged to Stone would end up being nullified, but either way, Michael could do no more.

As he contemplated this, he smiled because as Bass Stone pulled the trigger, Michael knew that his time of suffering had, at last, come to an end.

***

Jez Vincenzi lay cowering in fear, his hands clasped tightly over his head. Only when he was certain that the gunfire had ceased did he dare lift his face from the decking to see Michael's body slip silently into the water where it floated face down and lifeless.

Jez looked at the absolute carnage about him. Blood and guts everywhere and both his grandfather's obviously dead, cut down brutally by the spray of machine gun fire.

Crew Cut rather guiltily picked up his Uzi from the deck then stepped over to Jez and offered his hand to help him up.

"Get the fuck away from me you useless piece of shit!" Jez barked, slapping Crew Cut's hand away as he hauled himself to his feet.

As Jez stood, he studied the holes in his yellow jacket in amazement, unable to believe that he had survived without injury. The bullets must have passed within mere inches of him.

"See that?" He snapped at Crew Cut. "See these fucking holes? I coulda been killed you fucking moron. My grandfathers *were* killed. You had one goddamn job to do and you couldn't even do that!"

"But Boss, I—" began Crew Cut.

"Shuddup! Don't you fucking speak to me. In fact gimme that fucking gun - gimme it now!" Jez demanded.

Crew Cut was suddenly very scared, suspecting what might happen if he gave Jez the gun. Bass Stone saw the hesitation and took it upon himself to intervene.

He pointed his *Glock 17* semi-automatic at Crew Cut and said, "You heard the man. Give him the gun."

Jez glanced very briefly at Stone then turned his attention back to the underling and held out his hand.

Crew Cut was now clearly terrified and after another moment's hesitation reluctantly handed over the weapon.

Jez snatched it out of Crew Cut's hands and pointed it back at him. "You won't let my family down again you useless bastard," he snarled.

"Please, Boss, please'" begged Crew Cut, "I won't I swear. Please just don't—" but his pleas for mercy were silenced by yet another deafening burst of machine gun fire. Jez's face a picture of cruel delight as the bullets ripped through his underling's belly, very nearly slicing him in half.

Crew Cut fell back into the water with a loud splash as Jez turned the smoking weapon on Bass. "As for you, I don't know you from the fucking next guy. But since you turned up both my grandfathers are dead and so's the only guy who could tell me what I want to know."

"Woah! Wait a minute!" Stone yelled. "I just saved your life!"

"So?"

"So Walsh would have killed you if I hadn't shot him."

"Maybe, I guess. Don't mean I shouldn't kill you."

"Yeah, but I can help you—" Bass said calmly. "—I know where they are."

"What do you mean, *you know where they are?*" Asked Jez, preparing to fire.

"I know where Cassidy and Reilly are - and all the others. Walsh told me. I can lead you right to them all."

Jez mulled this snippet of information over for a moment. Stone certainly did seem like a useful guy to have around and he *had* just saved his life. Jez also rather liked the idea of *'all'*. Not just

Cassidy and Reilly but *all* their associates too. *All* those responsible for killing his brother Vito.

He studied Stone. Tall, powerful, seemingly fearless. Obviously resourceful, too, and well capable of taking care of himself.

With his grandfathers dead Jez would need someone reliable like Stone around - a bodyguard, a protector, someone he could trust with his life.

Suddenly it struck Jez that with his grandfathers out of the picture it was now he who ruled their empire. In the space of maybe less than five minutes he had just become the most powerful man in organised crime in America.

But it was a position others would undoubtedly want for themselves and who amongst his grandfathers' men would stay true to Jez when the chips were down?

He needed someone detached from the family, someone with no prior knowledge of all the internal politics and power struggles who could remain objective. An outsider who would be loyal to him and no one else.

Could Bass Stone be that man?

On first impressions alone, he seemed to fit the bill perfectly.

"You're right. Maybe you can help me," Jez said, lowering the gun. "Maybe you can help me a whole lot and perhaps I can make it very worthwhile that you do."

Bass' interest was immediately piqued. "Please, tell me what I can do for you," he said, sensing that opportunity was about to knock.

"Sure. But first, let's get out of here. It's all become a bit of a downer and it is my birthday after all."

"Oh, then happy birthday," Bass said.

"Thanks," said Jez, placing his hand on Stone's shoulder as he led him out of the boathouse.

Jez only glanced briefly at the bodies of his dead grandparents as he passed.

They had given him everything but now they were gone. The kings were dead. Long live The King.

Chapter Four

Arizona

"Lookin' for a good time, baby?" The girl with fake breasts and bottle blonde hair asked. She wore a mesh top with no bra, an ultra short mini with stiletto boots and white fishnets on her long tanned legs. She was very attractive in a trashy way, but it was a look that definitely worked for her. As for the sales pitch, the guy at the bar had heard better, but not recently. He took a long slug of *Bud* and eyed her up and down. "Sure," he said, "pull up a chair and we'll have us some laughs".

"How 'bout we have us some laughs back at my place? I got plenty of beer and a real cosy apartment".

The guy smiled, a million dollar Hollywood smile on a movie star face. The photo the girl had received in the envelope did not do him justice. In it, she could see he was good looking, but close-up he was a knockout with a body to match; broad shoulders, muscular frame and, from where she was standing, what looked like a real tight butt. This was going to be a dream assignment made all the sweeter by the five thousand bucks that had accompanied the photo.

But Matt Mason wasn't a movie star, he was a driver. A damn good one with a good run of first places under his belt. Of course Mason wasn't the name he raced under, that would have been stupid and easily traceable. Barton was the name he had used for the last ten years and, so far, it had kept him safe.

Matt had never settled down or got married or had kids. Once he'd wanted to, but those dreams had died along with the girl he'd planned to share them with. Now he was thirty-eight years old, lived in motels and trailers and called nowhere in particular home. He travelled all across the States visiting race meetings and kept up with old friends whenever he was nearby but, for the most part, he spent his time alone. If he'd wanted to he could have had the choice of pretty much any woman he wanted, but that would mean commitment and Matt, since his early twenties, was no longer good at that. He preferred to pick up women in bars, just like this one. Women with no strings attached and no more desire than he for anything other than a one night stand. It was easy, it was emotionless and nobody got hurt, which was just the way he liked it.

"Well, baby, waddaya say?" Asked the girl.

Matt glanced around the bar, a typical redneck place somewhere east of Phoenix, a place full of truckers and bikers and few good looking women. He knew the girl was a hooker, but that didn't matter. She was pretty and she had a sexy smile and that sure beat the hell out of a game of pool and a night in the back of his truck.

"Well you sure get straight to the point, don't ya?" He said, still smiling, his California accent revealing no trace of his English birth.

"No sense screwin' around, baby. I like what I see an' I could sure use some company. I'd like it to be you but I guess it could just as well be any one of these other guys. So what's it to be?"

"Well, seems like you've talked me into it then. Your place it is."

"Good choice, honey - you won't be sorry I promise - I'm real good company."

"Hey, that's good to hear. No sense goin' somewhere that ain't gonna be fun. What'll I call ya?'

The girl leaned in, her breasts resting heavily on his arm as she took his hand and kissed him lightly on the cheek. 'Mmm, you smell as good as you look. I'm Marcie. What's your name honey?'

"I'm Matt", he said, throwing a couple of dollars on the bar and picking up his hat.

"Matt, honey, I just know we're gonna have us the best time", she said as they headed for the exit.

***

Matt was awoken by a noise outside the bedroom. Just the slightest click of a latch and the merest creak of a floorboard, but years on the run had made him jumpy. Being a light sleeper, even after a heavy night, had kept him alive. The space next to him was warm but empty. Marcie was gone. The two of them had partied pretty hard, just like she'd promised but, tired from the previous day, he had passed out sometime after two. When she was sure he was asleep, Marcie had gone to the window and signalled to a green sedan parked on the street two floors below, thereby completing the deal she'd made several hours before. She had not asked questions as she had not required answers. Just the five grand, an amount for which she would have just as easily sold her mother.

For just a second, Matt sat motionless to make sure his ears were not deceiving him. But then he heard it, whispering, right outside the bedroom door. It was Marcie, he was sure of it, her and a guy, perhaps even two guys, but the voices were muffled. Something felt badly wrong, could this be a set-up he wondered. His instincts told him that it undoubtedly was.

Silently Matt slipped out of bed and quickly pulled on his jeans and T-shirt. He searched for a weapon but could see nothing. Thinking quickly, he stuffed three pillows length-ways down the bed and covered them with the blankets, hoping that, at first glance, they looked man-shaped and would fool someone long enough to give him a chance.

As the bedroom door knob turned, Matt dived behind the

door, the room illuminated only by the neon of the signs outside Marcie's apartment window. Slowly, as Matt's pulse quickened, the door inched open allowing another slither of light to enter the room. A hand appeared through the gap, gloved and holding a silenced semi-automatic, a finger resting nervously on the trigger. *Phut, phut.* Two muffled shots spat from the gun blasting two holes into the pillows on the bed with two equally muffled thuds. A shower of feathers burst from the bedclothes betraying the truth of what lay beneath.

"What the— " the would-be assassin began to say, just as Matt slammed the door against his outstretched wrist, causing him to cry out in pain. The semi-automatic dropped to the floor as the man's arm vanished back through the gap in the door, which Matt slammed shut. 'Sonofabitch!' The intruder yelled, "He's behind the goddamn door - the bastard's been expectin' us!"

"Double-crossing, bitch!" Another man exclaimed, "What, five grand not enough for a cheap whore like you?"

"No! I didn't tell him, I swear—"

Then another shot rang out, but not silenced this time and Matt heard a brief yelp before something heavy hit the floor. He guessed Marcie had just received her pay-off.

Matt grabbed for the semi-automatic as a shot blasted through the door, missing his head by inches, the splinters from the thin wood hitting his cheek. Another shot burst through lower down, again missing him by inches as he sprang backwards, flattening himself against the wall behind the door. However, the noise of his back hitting the wall alerted his attackers to his whereabouts and third shot exploded, this time through the wall, slicing away the flesh from Matt's bicep as it flew past. Stung from the wound, he leapt from his hiding place, turning as he ran, and fired off several shots at the door and wall, not knowing whether any hit their unseen target.

Making it to the window, he urgently tugged it open just

moments before the door burst open. Two men flung themselves into the room, although only one was firing, the other, thanks to Matt, was unarmed. Matt returned fire as he desperately tried to scramble out of the window and this time he was sure he winged the one with the gun. He fired again, but the clip was now empty, rendering the automatic useless, and the trigger just clicked harmlessly. Matt threw it aside in frustration as he at last made it onto the fire escape and frantically threw himself down the first flight of stairs. A bullet ricocheted off the metal beside him and another hit the stair below as he dropped onto the second flight, half running, half falling. A third bullet buzzed past his ear and struck a trash cart on the street just feet away.

Matt made one last desperate leap and hit the street running, barefoot and bleeding but still breathing. The men after him were not far behind, already one was on the second flight of steps the other shouting instructions from the half-landing under Marcie's window.

Matt dived down an alley, the adrenaline pumping through his veins, his instincts for survival in overdrive. The man with the gun arrived at the entrance to the alley maybe ten seconds later, his partner twenty seconds after that, but Matt had vanished.

Several cars were parked on either side of the alley, including Matt's Chevy pick-up. The unarmed man, who had now retrieved his gun and replaced the clip, nodded to his friend and smiled, then gestured to the pick-up. *Like shooting fish in a barrel.*

Both men, with guns held high, confidently closed in on the dusty Chevy, taking aim at the driver's door as they inched towards it.

Suddenly, an engine sprang to life on the other side of the alley just a short distance away. Then a screech of tyres filled the air as a dark blue Dodge roared out from its parking space and rocketed towards them.

The two men turned to see Matt behind the wheel, with the

heavy truck bearing down on them, both managing to fire off a couple of wild rounds as it sped forwards.

The windshield of the Dodge shattered and Matt felt something slam into his shoulder, then again into his side, just below his armpit, but he did not waiver as he gripped the steering wheel and kept on course.

The first man held his ground and took aim again, the other was less brave and attempted to dive aside but neither stood a chance as the Dodge ploughed into them, thrusting them backwards into the side of the Chevy, pinning them between the two heavy vehicles and trapping them metal to bone.

Once he was certain the danger had passed, Matt put the Dodge into reverse then turned off the engine. All was quiet as he stepped out the car, the two fresh bullet wounds hurting like hell but he ignored the pain.

The two assassins lay on the ground. One, obviously dead, his legs separated from the rest of his body by some distance having been dragged away by the fender of the Dodge as it reversed. There was blood everywhere, a total mess. The other guy was alive but in bad shape.

It had been a long time, but Matt recognised him. The guy's name was Enzo - used to work for a man named Benny 'The Bull' Vincenzi who had been dead for the past ten years.

There had been bad blood between him and Matt's father for years but it had been hoped that Benny's death would finally put an end to it.

However, Matt always suspected that Vincenzi's son, Jez, might pick up from where his father left off.

That now appeared to be the case and somehow, some way, Matt's past had caught up with him.

"So, he's finally found one of us, has he?" Matt asked as he stood over the dying man.

Enzo smiled agonisingly, blood spilling from his lips, staining his teeth red as he replied, "Not just one of you, asshole. *All of you.*"

Matt went cold as the guy on the floor laughed victoriously. A police siren sounded in the background, then another and another. Matt had to move. Quickly.

He grabbed the goon by the scruff of the neck and dragged him aside but as he made to walk away, Enzo caught him by the ankle and stared directly into his eyes. He was no longer smiling, but coughing weakly, blood erupting from his lips, as he took one final look at Matt and said again, "Not one, but *all.*" Then he died.

Matt had no time left for further reflection. He jumped into his dented Chevy pick-up with his shoulder throbbing badly, and sped away, the trailer slewing wildly behind.

Twenty minutes later he was on the highway, heading towards Vegas and a doctor he knew there. He had only one thought in his mind, to warn all those who were now, most definitely, in harm's way.

***

California

It was a beautiful night, with the warm Pacific breeze whipping through their hair as they sped down the coastline towards Malibu and the fabulous beach house that they called home.

They had been to the première of his latest movie, a detective thriller set in San Francisco, which was set to break all box office records.

At fifty-five, Virgil Nash was still a big star, probably one of the five most bankable in Hollywood. His wife, Victoria Wild, was also an actress, although her movie career had waned latterly and she now spent much of her time on Broadway where she enjoyed immense success. Together they were a golden couple, happy and devoted to each other and completely unspoiled by the trappings of fame.

They had no children together, although Victoria had two by

her previous marriage to Sean Reilly, Virgil's best friend. They were now grown up and spent their time equally between Malibu and the Cayman Islands, where their father now lived.

It had been awkward at first, but they had got through it and all had come out the other side happier and wiser. They made it work.

Victoria had insisted they take the convertible from Frisco as she hated limousines having once had an especially bad experience in one. Nor did she like dancing to the studio's tune, who had arranged for a suite for them at the Golden Gate Plaza. But she wanted to get away, to be with her husband, to get home and snuggle up to him in their big bed that overlooked the ocean. Virgil had not argued.

Furthermore, her son Josh, now nineteen, and her mother, Louretta, had also been at the première and they were driving back to Malibu that night, too, so Victoria could spend some family time at home with them the next day.

Amongst her several other residences, Louretta owned her own beach fronted property just a short distance down the coast from Victoria and Virgil in Santa Monica but the plan was for her to stay at her daughter's place overnight. The two of them had a whole schedule planned for the following day; both wanting to make the most of Josh being home from college - even though he was only at *CalTech*, less than an hour away.

As a special treat, Josh had been given the honour of driving his grandma home in her 1967 Shelby Mustang GT500 - a car much too cool for a woman in her seventies but Louretta had never been one for convention.

Josh was a car nut just like his sister and knew Liv would be green with envy when he told her about it - which only added to his enjoyment.

Nonetheless, Josh being allowed to drive the extremely powerful automobile went against Victoria's better judgement but Louretta was inclined to indulge her grand kids and once she had set

80

her mind on something there was little chance of changing it.

As it was, even though Louretta and her grandson had set off for home first, they would actually be following along behind as Josh had made an unscheduled stop which would inevitably delay them. Claiming that he was starving after the long, arduous première, he had headed for a Drive-Thru *McDonald's* to satiate his youthful appetite. However, Virgil, Victoria and Louretta all suspected it was more to show off in the classic car to the crowd of girls that were gathered there.

So it was some miles down the road that Virgil noticed the headlights in his rear-view mirror and thought it was Josh and Louretta catching them up - although he was surprised that they had managed to do it so soon.

However, as the lights drew nearer, Virgil could tell they did not belong to the Mustang.

Just another car then, he thought absently, maybe another couple heading home in the early hours of the morning.

But then, after a few more miles, the headlights seemed really close and the guy was driving right up Virgil's ass. "Just pass, goddamnit," he said angrily to the mirror.

"It's alright, honey," Victoria said, who was curled up on the passenger seat, "He's just eager to get home I guess - maybe he's onto a sure thing too." She smiled wickedly, as did Virgil but his feeling of unease did not go away. Something was definitely wrong.

Sean's phone call a few days earlier had unnerved him. Joe had apparently received a message from London - a warning of some kind - but the details were sketchy and they were still looking into it. But Sean's message had been clear; 'be vigilant, because trouble might be coming.'

Suddenly Virgil was regretting letting Josh and Louretta drive back alone, indeed, the decision for any of them to drive back at all tonight now seemed foolhardy.

As if to confirm this, the convertible was suddenly shunted by the car behind. Victoria squealed, "Hey, what's up with that guy!"

Next thing the car, a Jeep Cherokee, was up beside them, travelling just inches away on the deserted highway. The drop to the ocean on the other side separated from them by a steel barrier.

"Holy shit!" Virgil exclaimed. "This guy means business, honey. Put your seat belt on - put it on now!"

But Victoria wasn't listening. She spun around in her seat and yelled "Hey, buddy - back off will ya!"

But at that moment the Cherokee slammed into the side of the Mercedes convertible causing Virgil to swerve wildly. Victoria was thrown into him as their car scraped down the side of the steel barrier, sparks bursting from the metal like fireworks in the moonlight.

"Jesus!" Virgil exclaimed again, "What the fuck—!" But his words were cut short as the Cherokee slammed into them again. The Merc was all over the place as Virgil fought for control, but there was no let up as again the Jeep connected hard with the side of the car.

With the passenger door being steadily crushed in, Victoria was almost on Virgil's lap as she tried to avoid being struck by the Jeep - which made her husband's efforts to control the convertible even harder.

Suddenly, with a burst of speed and a roar of power, the Cherokee hit again, the impact far greater than all the previous attempts. Virgil could not hold it and the Mercedes span and ploughed into the barrier. It then cartwheeled twice, as easily and as gracefully as a piece of paper being flipped in the breeze, before landing with a violent crash on the barrier where it slid along on its mangled axle, for several yards.

When the car finally came to a smoking, metal-creaking halt, it balanced precariously, see-saw like, between the closeness of the road and the distant drop to the ocean.

The Cherokee slowed to a halt, as the two men inside inspected their handiwork.

Virgil Nash was slumped over the steering wheel; his face was a bloodied mess and his eyes were closed.

Next to him, the destroyed passenger seat was empty. Victoria Wild, it seemed, had met her end in the warm blue waves below, her body no doubt dashed against the rocks by the unyielding force of the sea.

The wrecked Mercedes teetered on the edge of the abyss and was clearly going to slide over at any moment.

"Hey, movie star!" One of the men shouted. "Jez Vincenzi sends his regards!"

"Don't waste your breath, Rocco," said the other man, "The guy's dead and the broad's gone over the edge."

"Yep. Looks like you're right, Bobby. Guess there ain't gonna be no Virgil Nash or Victoria Wild movies any more."

"Nope. Guess not. And thank God for that - gimme a goddamn Stallone picture any day over one of their faggoty flicks."

"Amen to that, brother. A-fuckin'-men!"

There was a roar of laughter from both men and then a screech of tyres as the Cherokee sped off.

Both were satisfied that their evil work was done.

***

The Mustang handled like a dream; the throaty roar of its powerful engine music to Josh's young ears as he guided it smoothly down the winding coastal road towards Malibu.

Louretta had enjoyed watching the girls admiring her handsome grandson at the Drive-Thru, even though it was the car which had originally caught their eye.

But to a teenage girl a hunk of high-powered metal could only do so much and Louretta knew it was the boy sitting behind the wheel, and not the classic car, that had held their attention.

It was no surprise as Josh was an impressive young man. He

seemed to have inherited the best parts of both his parents; his mother's tanned good looks and platinum blonde hair along with his father's muscular physique and easy-going temperament and Louretta felt extremely proud of him.

Indeed, she was proud of Liv, too - although she had inherited her mother's wild streak which made her much more of a handful.

Yet, somehow, Louretta enjoyed that side of her - even though she had not particularly appreciated it in her own daughter when she was growing up.

Louretta considered Sean's warning from a few days earlier, knowing the hell he and Joe had been through years before. But that all seemed so long ago now and surely times had changed. Benny Vincenzi was dead after all. For all intents and purposes Sean and Joe were dead, too, so she was certain that they were perhaps just being overly cautious and that there must be a simple explanation.

Indeed, if Louretta thought for a moment that any of them were in danger - particularly her grand kids - then there was no way she would have allowed Josh to accompany her alone.

No, she was convinced that they were all perfectly safe and that there was no need to worry.

Her mind at ease, and tired from the hustle and bustle of the première, Louretta settled down in the passenger seat and happily let her grandson drive her home - and he was certainly in his element behind the wheel.

The Mustang cornered as if it was on rails; the windy coastal road perfect for the ultimate driving experience. In fact, Josh's attention was so focussed on the road directly in front of him that he failed to notice the smoking wreck of the Mercedes until he was almost on top of it.

But when he did at last see it, he felt as if he had been kicked in the gut and was immediately struck by a sickening sense of dread.

"Oh, Christ, Grandma, it's Mom and Virge!" He yelled,

screeching the Mustang to a dramatic halt and leaving two long lines of burnt rubber on the tarmac behind it as he leapt hurriedly from the vehicle.

The sudden stop jolted Louretta forward in her seat, snapping her awake. Briefly she was confused, still groggy from sleep, but then, through the windshield, she saw Josh rushing towards the wreckage of what she instantly knew to be her daughter and son-in-law's automobile and suddenly the bottom fell out of her world.

The Mercedes was gradually slipping over the edge; the harsh, grating sound of metal scraping metal as the axle slid across the barrier, tilting the passenger side of the vehicle down toward the ocean below.

Josh reached the driver's door and forced it open, causing it to creak loudly in dented protest.

"Virge!" He shouted desperately, seeing his step-father slumped over the wheel and noticing with horror that the passenger seat was empty. "Wake up! Where's Mom?"

But Virgil was lifeless as Josh pulled him back from the steering wheel and fought to free him from his seat belt. Blood was steadily seeping from a gash on Virgil's forehead as the car slid ever nearer the drop with every second that passed.

The car creaked and groaned as Josh tugged frantically at the belt catch, the mechanism seemingly jammed and unwilling to release Virgil from its clutches, all the time the vehicle balancing precariously on the precipice, set at any moment to slip into the sparkling blue two hundred feet below.

Then, just as Josh snapped the seatbelt free, the Mercedes gave out one final, deafening metallic rasp before slipping off the rail and over the edge.

As it fell away, Josh hastily grabbed Virgil by the lapels and pulled with all his might, steadfastly refusing to let his step-father get sucked over the ledge by the drag of the car.

A moment later Josh found himself flat on his back with the weight of Virgil on top of him, hearing the distant crash as the mangled Mercedes hit the rocks at the foot of the cliff before splashing into the ocean.

Miraculously Virgil was safe although he remained motionless and unconscious. What is more, Josh still did not know what had happened to his mother and he was becoming increasingly more concerned by the second. *Where was she?*

In an instant, Louretta was beside them. She rolled Virgil carefully off her grandson to allow Josh to clamber to his feet then immediately set about performing CPR on her lifeless son-in-law.

"Josh, quick, check around for your mom!" Louretta ordered, at once in control of the situation yet desperately concerned for the safety of her daughter. "She might not have—" but she was unable to finish her sentence as the possibility of what might be was utterly unthinkable.

Josh did not need telling twice and set about scouring the surrounding area for his mother, hoping that she had been thrown free - with luck she might have landed safely in the soft scrub on the far side of the road. But he was working in darkness, visibility was poor and the headlights of the Mustang were behind him.

Then he heard an encouraging shout.

"He's alive!" Louretta called urgently. "Virgil's alive. Thank God!" Josh heard his step-father cough as he regained consciousness. Then his grandmother added, "Any sign of your mom? Can you see her Josh?" Her voice cracking with despair.

"No, I—" he began, before hearing a rustle from beyond the barrier on the cliff side of the road.

"Help!" A weak voice yelled. "Help me, please!"

Like lightning, Josh bolted across the road to where the voice was calling from. As he reached the barrier a slim, feminine arm reached up and clawed frantically at the air. "Help, please, I'm slipping - I can't hold on—"

Josh latched on to the arm with both hands and held on for dear life as he hauled his mother up from the tiny ledge upon which she had been clinging, the earth beneath her feet crumbling away to nothing at the very moment Josh grabbed her.

He pulled her into his arms and held her tightly. "Thank God, oh thank God! I thought you were dead - we really thought—"

"I'm fine, honey - thanks to you," Victoria gasped with relief. "Just a few cuts and bruises. But what about Virge? Where is he? Is he okay?"

"He's alright Mom, he's safe. He's alive. Grandma's looking after him.

Victoria kissed her son lightly on the cheek to thank him, then untangled herself from his embrace. Her face was grazed and bloody and she had a sprained ankle but fortunately nothing more serious as she hobbled over to where Louretta was kneeling beside Virgil.

"Christ, baby, you're a sight for sore eyes," breathed Louretta, her joy at seeing her daughter alive clearly apparent. "You okay?"

Vicky nodded. "Yeah, I'm fine, honest. What about Virge?"

Louretta looked down at her son-in-law who was slowly rousing. "Not sure yet but okay, I think," she said. "Could be his arm's broken. Got a nasty cut on his head, too, but that looks to be it. He was out for a while and wasn't breathing - I'll admit he had me scared but I reckon he'll be alright now."

"Goddamn!" Virgil groaned, as if to prove Louretta right. "My head hurts like a son of a bitch!"

"Careful," Louretta warned. "You got a pretty bad cut, so no fast movements, okay?"

"You got it. What about Vicky?" He asked instantly. "Is she—"

"I'm here Virge. I'm safe, it's okay. We're all okay."

"Jesus, what a relief," he said, seeing his wife's face as she leant over him, "Nothing broken? You look pretty beat up."

"Gee, thanks" Vicky laughed. "No, I'm fine, honey. Just some bruises and a sprained ankle. I'm more concerned about you."

"Hey, I'll live. Don't worry about me."

"What happened anyway?" Josh asked. "How come you crashed?"

"Yeah," said Louretta, "You get a flat or something?"

"No." Replied Virgil gravely. "We were run off the road—"

"What?" Cried Josh and Louretta together.

"Yeah, two guys in a Jeep - they kept comin' at us. Lucky we didn't end up over the edge," said Victoria.

"Hey, you nearly did," said Louretta. "If it wasn't for Josh you'd have gone over with the Merc. He saved your life, Virge - there was no way he was letting you go."

Virgil looked over at Josh, wincing in agony as a jolt of pain shot down his broken arm. "Thanks, son, appreciate it."

"Hey, don't sweat it. No problem - but why were those guys trying to run you off the road? What did you do to them?"

"It's a long story, kid." Said Virgil. "A very long story."

"What do you mean?" Asked Louretta.

Virgil turned his head and looked directly into her worried eyes. "Joe was right. Trouble *is* coming and those guys were the welcome wagon."

"What? How can you be sure?" Louretta queried.

"Yeah, we don't know for sure - do we Virge? I mean, how do we know?" Said Victoria.

"Cos I heard 'em." Said Virgil, his words heavy. "When I was slumped over the wheel, before I blacked out. I heard 'em speaking - heard 'em laughing. One of 'em said 'Jez Vincenzi sends his regards.'"

"Jez Vincenzi?" Asked Josh. "Who's he?"

"Somebody I hoped I'd never see or hear from again," replied Virgil.

"You absolutely sure?" Asked Vicky.

"Positive."

"Christ!" Said Louretta. "How could I have been so goddamn stupid? Why the hell didn't I listen?"

"Hey, it's okay, Mom. None of us took the warning seriously. We all thought it must be some mistake."

"Why?" Said Josh, sounding more than a little alarmed. "What warning - what does it mean?"

Victoria turned to her son, her face deadly serious. "It means that your dad and Uncle Joe were right, Josh."

"Right? Right about what?"

"Trouble, honey. Big trouble and it's only just begun."

***

The highway was deserted as they all clambered into the Mustang. Victoria and Louretta were squeezed together on the tiny back seat, Virgil was in the front passenger seat with a handkerchief pressed to his bleeding head and Josh was once again behind the wheel.

As he started the engine Louretta said, "We'd better not head back to Malibu now. It might not be safe."

"Just what I was thinking," agreed Virgil. "They may think Vicky and me are dead but somebody might be waiting there for you and Josh and it's best not to take any chances."

"You think?" Asked Vicky, already suspecting that her husband might be right.

"Maybe. But I'd rather not find out. Sides, I think for the time being it's best that you and me stay dead for a while."

"Good idea," said Louretta, "It worked well enough for Joe and Sean for ten years - or it did until now."

"If not home then where?" Said Vicky.

"Somewhere I can get this arm set without anybody taking snapshots or asking for autographs - if I'm gonna be dead then I can't go to a hospital - nor can you, Vicky. Our faces are too well known."

89

"There's only one place I can think of," said Louretta. "The doc there won't ask questions and it'd be a good place to lay low for a while."

"You mean—?" said Victoria.

"Uh-huh," seems to make sense."

"It's got my vote," agreed Virgil, instinctively knowing the place to which his wife and mother-in-law were referring.

"Is someone gonna let me know where it is you're all talking about? I mean, if we're not going to Malibu then where the hell are we going?"

Louretta smiled. "Vegas, kid. Where else is there to go when you're in trouble?"

Chapter Five

London

When she first opened her eyes Violet briefly thought she was in heaven - although was quite surprised to find it smelled so strongly of disinfectant.

But then she heard the beeps of the monitors and the chatter of the nurses.

And then she felt the terrible pain.

Immediately after that she remembered being shot - once by Jack Anderson and once by Bass Stone. Worse still, she remembered Stone shooting her father - murdering him right in front of her.

He had killed her too. Or so she thought.

But now, here she was in what was clearly a very noisy hospital ward, lying in a bed, rigged up to some kind of monitor.

Alive.

She tried to sit up but the pain in her chest immediately intensified and her movements were seriously restricted by some heavy strapping around her ribs. She looked down at herself and saw a big wadded pad taped over her breast bone and another taped directly below her shoulder.

Both pads were held in place by swathes of bandages that were wrapped generously around her chest and back.

Violet also noticed that she was attached to a drip.

With some effort she tried to sit up again but with all the strapping it was difficult and the pain was immense.

A nurse saw her struggling and rushed over.

"Hey, be careful you'll pull the stitches - also you're sternum's very bruised and it's going to hurt like hell," said the pretty young nurse.

"Yeah," replied Violet wincing, "I just worked that out for myself."

The nurse smiled. "You know, you're very lucky to be alive - if it wasn't for your chain then you'd have undoubtedly been—"

"Chain?" Queried Violet.

"Uh-huh. The chain with the silver pendant you were wearing when you were shot. The police have taken it away now but it saved you. The bullet struck the pendant dead centre - which is why you've got the bruise. But better a bruise than a hole through the chest, right?"

"I suppose," Violet agreed. "But I was shot twice wasn't I?"

"Yeah, but the other bullet passed clean through - missed your heart by a couple of inches - but it's fine, don't worry. The other one though - if that had hit home then well - like I said, you're very lucky."

Presently Violet did not feel very lucky as all she could think about was her beloved father, Alfie, and how Bass Stone had shot him dead.

Stone had all but admitted to killing Richie, too, and the loss of her big brother was almost too much to bear.

Suddenly, thinking of them - her dad in particular and her last memory of him, Violet was overcome with grief. She could not hold back the tears and they started to stream down her cheeks; her shoulders heaving uncontrollably even though it made her chest ache.

The nurse seemed a little uncertain of what to do at this outpouring of emotion and simply placed a steadying hand on

Violet's shoulder. "Oh you poor dear," she said, "You've really been through the mill haven't you? But please, try to be careful of your chest as you'll only make things worse."

Violet wanted to snap at her and ask how it could possibly be worse, but instead she sniffed up her tears and took control of herself; crying would not solve anything.

After taking a few calming breaths, she eventually asked, "How long have I been out?"

"Over three days," said the nurse. "You took a pretty nasty whack on the head - banged it on the floor, I think, anyway we were beginning to wonder if you'd ever wake up."

Violet could not believe it. *Three days*. It felt like just minutes ago that it had all happened.

"You said that the police were involved?" She asked.

"Yes. I'm afraid they've asked to be informed the moment you wake up. They're very keen to find out exactly what happened."

"Yeah. I bet. Have they had any luck finding the man who killed my father and brother?"

"Sorry, I don't know. They didn't really tell me much - just that they wanted to speak to you when you woke up. But I get the impression they're pretty much in the dark. Nobody seems to know what happened. I'm so sorry about your family by the way. It must have been awful - I can't imagine."

"Thanks. Yeah, it was."

The nurse smiled sympathetically. "Can I get you anything - some water maybe? Something to eat?"

"How about my clothes? The sooner I get out of here the better."

The nurse smiled again, her face apologetic. "Sorry. You can't leave until the doctor says so - and not until the police have spoken to you either. They made me promise."

"Fine." Violet said with resignation. "You'd better just make it a water then, please."

With her head aching and chest throbbing, Violet lay on the bed mulling things over.

Bass Stone had made the mistake of not killing her, even though he obviously thought that he had, and that was his fatal error because somehow, some way, Violet intended to make him pay for what he had done to her dad and Richie.

But how? What could she do? A woman alone. She would definitely need help that was for sure; an ally with as much of a reason for wanting Stone dead as she did.

Immediately two people sprang to mind yet she had no idea of their whereabouts. Indeed, Violet was almost certain that it was the search for their whereabouts that had led to her father and brother being killed.

Anderson and Bass Stone had been hunting for Joe and Sean and now she must, too, but for an entirely different reason.

Violet had corresponded with both of them over the years but always through an intermediary - namely Richie - but never directly. Her father, of course, knew where they were, or he had once when his mind was still in tact, but she, herself, did not.

She also assumed that Stone had taken the only clue to their location from *The Golden Gloves*.

What she did have, however, was a point of contact. Joe had said to her in one of his letters that if she should ever need him, if there was no other way of reaching him, then she should try this place. He told her to leave her name at the desk and sooner or later he would be in touch.

Now that place was her only hope.

***

The police came to see Violet a short time later and she answered all of their questions as best she could - leaving out any details of Joe and Sean of course - but otherwise telling them the truth of what had happened.

As for the motives for the attacks at both *The Galaxy Club* and *The Golden Gloves,* she said they were a mystery to her but claimed, quite rightly, that Jack Anderson had always been jealous of Alfie, Richie and Manno's status and believed that to be good enough reason for him to have them killed. Bass Stone, on the other hand, was just an animal who killed for pleasure.

In turn, the detectives had nothing new to impart, except to confirm Richie and Manno's deaths, much to Violet's dismay. Bass Stone's involvement, however, came as news to them but they said the information would go some way to helping them with their enquiries.

Yet Violet knew that Stone would be long gone, undoubtedly heading for whatever location was written on the scrap of paper Big Jack had found in the back room of the *The Golden Gloves.*

Nonetheless, seemingly satisfied with what she had told them, the police left Violet alone after about an hour, passing the doctor on his way to her as they ambled unhurriedly off the ward.

The doctor gave Violet a thorough examination, reiterating just how lucky she was to be alive and telling her she would be kept in hospital for observation for the next few days.

Violet quietly nodded her acquiescence but once he had gone on his way she asked the pretty young nurse to help her out of bed and fetch her clothes.

Much against her better judgement, the nurse reluctantly agreed and less than forty minutes later Violet was pulling up outside *The Golden Gloves* in the back of a black cab where she instructed the driver to wait.

Moving very stiffly and extremely carefully, Violet found the spare key to her flat above the pub under the flower pot by the back stairs door.

Once inside, working as quickly as her injuries would allow, she packed a suitcase then went to the wardrobe and removed a hat box from the bottom shelf. She placed the box on her bed and lifted the lid to reveal several thick wads of ten pound notes. She took out a couple of bundles and threw them into her suitcase. Then she put the box back where she had found it.

Finally, after retrieving her passport from her dressing table, she locked her flat and gingerly made her way downstairs to the waiting cab, her chest throbbing badly.

"Where to luv?" The cabbie asked.

"Heathrow please. Quick as you can," she replied breathlessly.

***

Violet bought spare bandages, a bottle of *Detol,* a tube of anti-septic and a roll of sticking plaster from the *Boots* in the Heathrow departure lounge then sat patiently and waited for her flight.

She had paid for first class; an extravagance she would normally forego but with her injuries she thought it might be prudent to have the extra space and comfort. Also, she hoped to sleep through most of the long flight which might help with her recuperation in some small way.

Anything to hasten the healing process was worth a try because as soon as she reached her destination she was damn sure she was going to be ready for whatever might come next.

***

California

Bass Stone sat on the terrace looking out over the sparkling blackness of the ocean. It was a clear night and he could easily make out the distant horizon. The air was warm with just the slightest sea breeze which was cooling and most welcome to Bass who was unaccustomed to the hotter climate. Back in the UK he would still be wearing a jacket at this time of year.

Indeed, until a short time ago he had barely set foot out of London his entire life but now here he was, his third paradise location

96

in as many days and a whole world away from South London. But it was a lifestyle he was determined to get used to and no less than he believed he deserved.

The chair he was sitting in was made from a dark coloured wicker of some kind with thick, comfortable padding - the most comfortable chair Bass had ever sat in - and probably worth more than his whole flat back home. *A goddamn patio chair!* Bass smiled at the thought. If the boys from borstal could see him now.

He had helped himself to a beer from the well stocked fridge which was stuffed full with all kinds of fancy shit - stuff that Bass had never even heard of let alone eaten. Fortunately though, alongside that, alongside the bottles of expensive Champagne and chilled wines there was a case of *Bud*. At least someone in the house had taste.

The house itself was unbelievable; the likes of which Bass could not previously have imagined in his wildest dreams; spacious and plush, amazingly luxurious with an open fireplace and a stone built chimney stack around which a vast open plan living area had been beautifully conceived. Every wall was made of glass allowing panoramic views of the sea and surrounding area to make it nothing short of breathtaking.

It was special now, in the dark, at night, but in the daylight, with the sun streaming in, Bass was willing to bet it would be magnificent.

Christ, how the other half lived.

He had previously thought the Vincenzi mansion in Key Biscayne to be the most opulent and lavish place he had ever seen; with all its old school style and classic, grandiose architecture but this place beat it hands down. This place was much more to Bass' taste. Modern and chic - what he now understood to be minimalist in design - very contemporary, very cool and, so it would seem, very Californian - at least to those who could afford it.

One day soon Bass, too, planned to own a place like this; classy, luxurious, no expense spared - and in the last few days he had made significant progress in achieving that goal.

He had successfully ingratiated himself to Jez Vincenzi and tentatively earned his trust. By presenting him with Michael Walsh he had also managed to position himself next to Vincenzi - and with the boy's powerful grandfathers conveniently out of the picture, it was potentially a position of great influence.

But that would take time and for now Jez was still listening to the advice of others - although for the most part ignoring it in favour of his own misguided ideas.

Ideas which Bass knew to be flawed but had nonetheless led him there, to Malibu, where he found himself sitting in the dark waiting for Louretta Wild and her grandson to arrive. Someone on the Vincenzi payroll had informed Jez that the old woman and the boy would be staying the night there, at Virgil Nash and Victoria Wild's house - not in San Francisco, where the première was being held.

Bass had been instructed to take care of them whilst two other Vincenzi men, Rocco and Bobby, had been given the more important task of killing Nash and his wife.

Yet, so far, the old woman and the boy were 'no shows'.

Bass had been patient. He had sat there on the terrace for over two hours, sipping Virgil Nash's beer and admiring the view.

Before that he had searched through the house, looked through the cupboards and the drawers, poured over all their private things.

He had even rummaged through Victoria Wild's underwear and jerked off into a pile of her silk panties whilst pressing a soiled pair, which he'd found in the laundry hamper, to his nose.

Afterwards he had stuffed them into his pocket as a little memento of his time with her. The knickers of a movie star, *now they were something worth keeping*.

He had then taken a dump in the en-suite bathroom and

'forgotten' to flush. *Fuck these rich pricks - they probably had someone to wipe their goddamn arses for them anyway.*

As he absently explored the house, picking up trinkets, flicking through the record collection and perusing their substantial video library, he had also pocketed a pair of Nash's cuff links and was now wearing one of several gold watches he had found in the vast walk-in closet off the master bedroom.

Whilst there, he had also tried on some of the clothes but even though Nash was tall and well-built he was considerably smaller than Stone who could find nothing to fit him. Even the star's elegant, hand-made shoes were too small.

No matter, Stone would soon be able to afford his own.

Finally, he sat on the terrace bored; his trusty semi-automatic resting on his lap - the same gun which had killed Michael Walsh, Alfie Noakes and Noakes' daughter, Violet - or so he assumed.

He thought of Violet now. *What a waste.* He would liked to have sampled her delights just once before she died; a woman of such ample charms that Bass' mouth watered at the very thought of them - those eyes, those legs - *those tits.* Now there was a woman who should have been a movie star not some jumped up bar maid in a grotty South London pub.

But she had to die.

Oh well, it was no big deal. When he was rich there would be many other beautiful women for him to choose from, of that Bass was certain - and they would be a lot less picky than Violet bloody Noakes.

Stone looked at the new gold timepiece on his wrist, the one he had liberated from Virgil Nash's closet. It was late now - or early - depending on which way he thought about it.

Louretta Wild and her grandson - Sean Reilly's kid - should be back there by now and Bass should have killed them already.

Indeed, he should have been on his way back to the air field in

Bakersfield by this time, not still waiting for them to return.

Something had gone wrong, he was sure of it.

Which was where Vincenzi's strategy fell down.

Jez was adamant that he wanted Matt Mason, Louretta Wild and her grandson along with Virgil Nash and his wife all dead before mounting an assault on the *Far Point Estate* in The Caymans.

All so that Vincenzi could have the pleasure of looking into Joe Cassidy's and Sean Reilly's eyes and telling them that their family was dead before he killed them too.

Bass fully understood the pleasure derived from this but to his mind it also left too many margins for error.

If just one part of the scheme failed then Cassidy and Reilly might possibly be forewarned and therefore prepared for whatever Vincenzi had planned for them.

But there was no changing Jez's mind. He was dead set on this course of action and Bass had absolutely no hope of dissuading him.

So, regardless of Stone's opinion, Jez had dispatched a team to Arizona to kill Matt Mason - who was apparently some sort of stock car driver. Yet the men Vincenzi had chosen seemed overly confident and extremely cocky which, Bass guessed, might translate as 'sloppy.'

Bass did not like who Jez had sent with him to California either. One of them, Rocco, was the brother of one of those sent to Arizona. The other, Bobby, was his none-too-bright partner.

Bobby was just the average goon on a payroll - an obedient soldier who was blessed with more muscle than brain. Stone knew the sort and had met his like many times before. The other one, however, Rocco, was clearly a psychopath who got a particular kick out of killing. He was in it for the blood and the thrill of causing pain - traits that Stone recognised in himself - although for him the money always came first, killing was just an added bonus.

Rocco was also close to Jez which made him doubly dangerous and Bass knew that he would have to tread carefully as he could potentially hamper his own designs on getting closer to Vincenzi.

Nonetheless, he suspected that both Rocco and Bobby were waiting for him back at Bakersfield, their part of the plan fulfilled.

It was almost dawn and it was now clear to Stone that no one was coming back to the house. The old woman and her grandson must have opted to stay the night in San Francisco after all. Either that or something had gone wrong on Rocco and Bobby's end - perhaps there had been unforeseen complications, who knew?

Either way, Stone's time had run out. He had to get going or risk missing the flight back to Miami - they were on a clock and the pilot would not wait.

Bass hated leaving the job unfinished especially as he was eager to impress Vincenzi but, if Rocco and Bobby had done their part, then it was only a matter of time before the cops came sniffing around the house and Stone had no intention of being there when they did.

Louretta Wild and Josh Noakes could wait. There would be many more opportunities to kill them - he would just have to convince Jez Vincenzi of that.

For now though, it was time to go.

***

As Bass pulled into the parking lot of the airfield in Bakersfield almost three hours later, the first reports were coming in on the radio about an accident which was thought to have involved the movie stars Virgil Nash and Victoria Wild. Information was sketchy but it appeared that their car had apparently left the road and plunged over the cliff on Route One. Early indications left little hope of the glamorous couple's survival.

Grief stricken fans had begun to gather at the crash site, all praying for news that their idols were alive and unharmed.

Bass smiled at the eulogies which were already coming in from Hollywood's great and good - never too shy to miss an opportunity for a sound bite or the chance of some free publicity.

Nonetheless, Stone was curious to note that so far Louretta Wild had not been available for comment and no statement had been issued on her behalf. Indeed, it appeared that Victoria Wild's mother had suddenly disappeared and had not been seen since the première of her son-in-law's movie in San Francisco the night before.

According to the radio, concerns were growing for Miss Wild's safety and the police were keen to hear from her as soon as possible.

Bass, too, would have liked to have known where she was and he felt a prickle of frustration by his failure to complete the first assignment for his new employer.

But the fact that his intended victims had not turned up was beyond his control. Maybe Rocco and Bobby knew more.

As Stone approached the tiny Piper Cheyenne aircraft that was prepped and ready to take him and the others back to Miami, he saw Rocco and Bobby waiting for him on the tarmac.

Rocco had that smug, over-confident smirk on his tanned face, whilst Bobby just looked nervous and eager to get going.

Bobby Assante was short, stocky and prematurely bald with a flat expressionless face. Rocco Pistoli, on the other hand, was tall and slim with sharp, pointed features. A long hairline scar ran diagonally from the top right of his forehead to the bottom of his left earlobe, the result of a knife fight in his youth, which somewhat marred his otherwise handsome face. His demeanour was very much relaxed, almost lazy, belying his supreme fitness and ruthless nature.

He was not someone to take lightly but then again, neither was Stone who had a scar of his own to rival Pistoli's. Whilst the Italian's was long and thin, Bass' was wide and jagged; a daily reminder of the first man he had killed and the broken bottle that had sliced him as they fought.

"Hey, you're late." Said Rocco. "You get any problems? The old lady give you a hard time?" Again there was the smirk which Bass would love to have punched off. But now was not the time.

"She never showed. I waited all night - thought you might know something about it?"

"Us, why?"

"Cos you had eyes on 'em at the première didn't you? Thought you might've killed two birds with one stone if you know what I mean?"

"Uh-uh. We watched 'em drive away from the theatre - her and the kid in that fancy Shelby - but we didn't take 'em out."

"Hmm," pondered Stone. *Where the hell were they then?* "And you didn't see 'em en-route?"

"Nope." Said Rocco. "Nash and Wild followed along a little later and we swung in behind. No sign of Granny though. You sure you didn't just blow it?"

Now Bass *really* wanted to punch him. He looked at Rocco hard in the eyes, his displeasure at the blatant slight unmistakeable. "No. I did not blow it," he said firmly through gritted teeth. "The old lady was a no show, same with the kid. You got a problem with that?"

Rocco smiled broadly and held up his hands in mock defeat. "Hey, man - no I ain't got a problem. If the broad didn't show then she didn't show - you can't kill what ain't there, right? Just ain't too sure if Jez will see it like that - that's all."

"Yeah? Well you let me worry about Vincenzi. He's my problem, not yours, okay."

"Sure man. Sure thing," replied Pistoli, with a shrug, enjoying how easy it was to rile Stone. He did not particularly like this big, English half-caste that Jez had brought in and knew how much it must grate on Stone that he had failed to complete the first task he had been given.

Yet Rocco sensed that the Brit could also be very dangerous and decided it would be smart to play it cool for the time being.

Although there was no harm in having a little fun at Stone's expense in the meantime. Indeed, he intended to exploit the other man's failure regularly throughout the long flight back to Miami.

As they all climbed into the Piper Cheyenne, Rocco smiled in anticipation of directing a few well-aimed barbs in Stone's direction.

After all, he had to pass the time somehow.

***

As it turned out, Stone was much harder to get a rise out of than Pistoli anticipated - in fact Bass had slept through most of the flight. Then, when they finally touched down on the tarmac in Miami, Rocco was greeted with news that made him forget all about the trivial power-play between himself and Stone.

Because he had just learned that Matt Mason had killed his brother.

Chapter Six

Las Vegas

Dr. Ethan Ridgeway had not practiced medicine for over five years. He had retired back in '82 and had since seen his three kids get married and his wife of forty years die of cancer.

Now he rattled around in their big old house up on Canyon Hill Drive all alone and he had just about had enough of it.

Recently his kids had persuaded him to move into an old folks home - although it was called something a little fancier but that was basically what it was - and for want of a bit of company Ethan had agreed.

The realtor had hammered the sign into the lawn just that morning which now made it all a reality.

It was sad but life had to go on and his beloved Ellen would not have wanted him to mope. So it was the beginning of a new chapter which, Ethan hoped, might lead to the chance of a bit of excitement - although he could not imagine *The Cedar Pines Community for the Elderly* being a lot more exciting than what he had now, but at least he would not be alone.

Maybe there would be some like-minded folks there, people who might well be old but not quite ready to up and die - who still wanted to live, not just exist.

It was what Ellen would have wanted and - now he had at last accepted she was gone - what he wanted too.

Once, when he was a much younger man, he had been quite the catch. Indeed, before Ellen he had once dated a movie star - who was the first great love of his life. But their lives were headed in different directions - his into medicine and hers into global stardom - so they had eventually parted. But they still kept in touch at least semi-regularly. In fact, it was only ten years earlier that she had called at his door late one night and begged him for a favour.

Ellen had been in hospital that night, recovering from her first debilitating bout of chemo so she knew nothing of the clandestine visit and Ethan had never mentioned it. He did not want to trouble her as she had more than enough to contend with and where was the sense in mentioning a visit from an old flame. After all, nothing happened between them, it was all perfectly innocent - at least in the romantic sense.

Yet he could not deny there was still a spark.

Ethan had often wondered since that night how different things might have been if he and his first love had stayed together, even though the life he had chosen for himself had been far from dull. Three kids and a busy life as surgeon - then later as doctor with his own private practice - meant there was little time left for very much else.

As it was, Ellen had made him a wonderful wife and he had loved her deeply but still he could not help but wonder if he had maybe missed out on some excitement along the way.

Now, though, it all seemed a little too late to want for something more but he lived in hope.

As Ellen used to say, *'you never know what's just around the corner.'*

Ethan smiled as he thought fondly of his wife, much like he did most days at around that time when the pair of them used to sit on the porch, high on the hill in their house that stood alone on Canyon

Hill Drive.

Now his kids would tell him it was not safe to be so secluded, to live so far away from any other houses and he guessed they were right but he did enjoy the peace and quiet, especially with a cup of mint tea - sometimes even a whisky if he was giving himself a treat.

He would certainly miss the old place but it did make sense to move. It was too big and too much work for a man in his seventies even though he was still extremely fit for his age.

Indeed, the ladies of the neighbourhood still considered Doc Ridgeway to be something of a catch - with his silver fox looks and suave Cary Grant air but after Ellen there was no other woman for him - except maybe one and that ship had most probably sailed long ago.

Nonetheless he sat there on the porch with a cup of mint tea in his hand, surveying his beautifully maintained lawn and gazing at the ugly new 'Sale' board that had been freshly stuck into it, wishing he was forty years younger and that his whole life was still ahead of him. Maybe then he would do things differently.

However, he was snapped out of this reverie by the sound of an engine which cut abrasively through the silence of the tranquil afternoon. Ethan turned to see a beat up Chevy with a trailer on tow heading up the street towards the house.

The pick-up was swerving all over the road, the engine lurching as if the driver was drunk and applying only intermittent pressure on the gas pedal, causing it to kangaroo up the street like a kid on his first day at driving school.

Ethan jumped to his feet; spilling the contents of his china cup all over the porch as he watched the Chevy veer wildly to and fro. Finally he watched aghast as it mounted the sidewalk on his side of the street, careering straight towards his property.

He could do nothing as it then ploughed through his hedge, ripping through the lovingly tended flower beds and across the

107

immaculate lawn before smacking headlong into the sale sign, breaking it in two. The heavy vehicle finally came to a juddering halt several yards later, the realtor's masthead of the brand new sale board crushed under its wheels.

Ethan was unable to believe what he had just witnessed and was temporarily rooted to the spot with amazement as the driver's door slowly creaked open and a man fell out onto the churned up grass.

Without thinking, Ethan threw his cup aside and rushed to help. The man was lying on his back, his long brown hair partially obscuring his face. The man's shirt was completely covered in blood, his jeans too. He had been shot, Ethan could tell immediately - twice for sure, maybe more - and he had lost a lot of blood.

"Hold on, son!" Said Ethan, "I'm a doctor, I can help you - but I must fetch my bag first - I'll be back in a second, I promise. Please hold on."

He made to move but the man grabbed him firmly by the arm, his grip surprisingly strong considering his weakened state. "They're coming, Doc," gasped the man, clearly in a great deal of pain. "Tell 'em they're coming—"

Ethan was uncertain of what the man meant but knew that he must act quickly if he was to have any chance of saving him. But then, looking into the man's eyes, he suddenly recognised him.

It had been a long time but it was definitely the same man. The same man who had been with Louretta Wild that night long ago when she had come to ask for a favour.

"My God!" Ethan said out loud as it all came flooding back.

But then, before he had a chance to say anymore, Matt Mason released his grip on Ethan's arm and slumped into unconsciousness.

***

Ten years earlier, at the urgent request of his first love, Louretta Wild, Ethan had helped the movie star Virgil Nash out of a pretty serious jam.

Nash had been shot, which seemed somewhat odd, but Ethan patched him up and promised Louretta, an ex-movie star herself, that he would never speak of it to anyone. He had kept his word but had always been curious of the circumstances that led Louretta to his door that night.

He knew the incident had occurred at *The Villa Continental*, a large hotel on The Strip which Louretta part owned, he also had her word that Nash was merely a pawn in a much bigger game which sought to relieve her and her partners of their prime piece of Las Vegas real estate. Virgil, she promised, was an honourable man and deserved Ethan's help. Nash's movie career, however, would not stand the scandal of him being shot, hence the need for discretion.

There was obviously much more to the story but Louretta did not want to tell Ethan the rest for fear of involving him further in matters that had already proved hazardous to so many. 'Maybe one day,' she had promised. But that day had so far never come.

Accompanying Louretta and Nash that night were three other men. All seemed decent enough, yet one of them, the youngest of the bunch, had now returned and was currently occupying the bed in Ethan's surgery at the rear of the house.

Even though he no longer practiced medicine, his surgery was still well stocked and perfectly maintained - and he had lost none of his skill as a surgeon. Indeed, he had saved the young man's life who would undoubtedly have died had he arrived any later.

As it was, two days after crashing so dramatically onto Ethan's property, the man was now out of danger and in a stable condition, although still unconscious. But he was young and strong and Ethan expected him to make a full recovery in time.

In his efforts to save him, Ethan had pulled a bullet out of the man's shoulder and one out of his side, just below the armpit. He had also sewn up an extremely nasty gash in his bicep.

The man was fortunate indeed.

Particularly as Ethan had refrained from calling the police, suspecting it might possibly not be the best course of action given the circumstances of their last encounter.

With that in mind, Ethan had parked the Chevy out of sight in the garage and thrown a tarpaulin over the trailer which he had stationed out back in the yard where there was no chance of it being seen by the casual observer.

However, he had watched the news that morning and was gravely concerned by what was being reported from Route One out in California. They were saying that Victoria Wild and Virgil Nash were thought to be dead whilst Louretta herself was missing.

Ethan was deeply worried for Louretta's safety yet he was certain that there must be some connection between the incident in California and the young man in his surgery as it was just too much of a coincidence.

It was also clear to him that events might still be unfolding.

If he knew anything, it was that Louretta Wild was a resilient, resourceful woman and it would take one hell of a lot to defeat her. If she was dead then they were going to have to show him the body because until he saw it for himself he was damn sure not going to believe it.

**

Ethan had slept little over the past two days as he had been keeping a vigil by Matt's bed, monitoring his patient for any change in condition - either good or bad.

However, since hearing the news about Louretta that morning, he had been frantically flicking through the channels desperate to find out more.

Nonetheless, no matter how concerned he was, by mid-day his last reserves of energy finally depleted and after forty-eight hours of very little rest he fell into a deep sleep in the armchair beside Matt's bed.

He was rudely awoken from his slumber half way through the afternoon by the constant ringing of his doorbell.

Ethan rubbed his eyes and stumbled out of the surgery as he made his way through the large house to the front door, worried that it might be the police and trying desperately to conjure up a plausible story which would explain why he was harbouring a possible criminal.

Yet when he looked through the glass window in the centre of the door, it was not a policeman he saw but Louretta Wild and his heart leapt with joy.

Quickly he pulled open the door and threw his arms around Louretta. "Oh, thank God!" He exclaimed. "I knew you couldn't be dead."

"Hi, Ethan," breathed Louretta through the tightness of his embrace. "It's good to see you, too, honey," she said, giving him a kiss on the cheek. "Really it is."

"You've been all over the news, Rett, everyone's so worried—"

"Hell, I'm fine. But you might not be when I tell you why I'm here."

"Why, what's the matter?"

"Plenty. And I'm afraid I need your help yet again."

"Of course, of course," said Ethan, releasing her, "Please, come in."

"Yeah, well, it's not just me - that's the thing. There's a bunch of us and well, we're in a whole heap of trouble."

"A bunch?"

Louretta nodded then signalled to the Mustang that was parked on the driveway.

Ethan watched as three people climbed out, two of whom he instantly recognised - not just because they were world famous movie stars but also because he had pulled a bullet out of one of them ten years earlier.

He held the door whilst they filed in, all looking rather sheepish. "Hi, Doc," said Victoria.

"Hello." He replied politely.

"Me again, Doc. Sorry," said Virgil, who looked pretty beat up, as did his wife.

"Hi," Josh said shyly, bringing up the rear.

Ethan nodded his welcome and closed the door behind him, then turned and said to Vicky and Virgil, "The TV says that you two are both dead - says you're missing, too, Rett."

"Yeah, well I ain't," replied Louretta firmly. "I'm here and I'm safe - we all are - and with your help I'm hoping we can stay that way."

"Sure, of course, anything - are you hurt, too?"

"No, just Virge, his arm's busted pretty bad, I think. Vicky's just got cuts and bruises but she'll need you to look at 'em."

"Yes. Of course. Follow me," Ethan said as he led them through to the rear of the house. He was acting on auto-pilot, his medical instincts kicking in before anything else but his mind was buzzing with questions about what had happened.

Louretta guessed what he was thinking. "Thanks Ethan," she said. "I know I owe you an explanation and I'll do my best to tell you everything, I promise - it's just that there's so much it's hard to know where to begin."

"It's okay, tell me later, when you've had a chance to rest. Let me help Virgil and Victoria first - then you and me can have a nice chat over a cup of mint tea."

Louretta smiled. Ethan and his mint tea, it was one of the things she remembered about him, one of the many things. "I think maybe I'd rather have a whisky today if it's all the same to you," she said.

Ethan grinned in response. "Yes, I think you might well have a point."

However, as they reached the surgery door, he suddenly remembered Matt was in there and said, "Oh my goodness, I quite forgot. I'm sorry, Rett, I should have told you. A couple of days ago someone else turned up at my door in need of help. Someone I think you might know."

Louretta looked at him curiously. "What do you mean?" She asked as he ushered her into the surgery, Virgil, Vicky and Josh all shuffling in after her, equally curious as to what he meant.

But there was no need for Ethan to reply as the answer was self evident.

They could all see Matt for themselves, lying there on the bed, hooked up to the monitor, his eyes closed and his body swathed in bandages.

All of them stared at the bed with utter astonishment until Josh rushed forward. "Christ, Matt!" He yelled.

"Well I'll be goddamned," stated Virgil. "Not him, too."

"Is he okay, Doc? Is he alive?" Pleaded Josh.

"He's alive, son, and he'll be fine - don't worry," assured Ethan. "He just needs to rest up a while, he's been through it the last couple of days but he's over the worst now."

"My God, what happened?" Asked Vicky, clearly shocked at seeing Matt there.

"I don't know exactly but I took a couple of bullets out of him. God only knows how he made it to me but he was nearly dead when he arrived."

"Did he say anything?" Said Louretta.

"Not really, he's been pretty much out since he got here - he did say one thing though. He said 'Tell 'em they're coming.' Does that make any sense to you?"

By the look on Louretta's face Ethan guessed that it did.

"Christ," she said. "I've been such a goddamn fool— Ethan, please, I need to use your phone, straight away. It's important."

113

"Yeah, of course, Rett. Anything. It's through here. I'll show you."

Louretta followed him back along the hall to a small table at the bottom of the stairs upon which the telephone sat. "Please, help yourself. Make all the calls you need."

"Thanks, honey," she said. "But I only need to make one. I just hope I'm not too late."

However, as Louretta reached for the receiver, the phone began to ring and her hand shot away from it as if she had been stung.

She looked at Ethan who, in turn, looked back at her, a little baffled. It was undoubtedly just some innocuous call from a friend or maybe one of his kids phoning to check on him, but Matt's arrival and the subsequent appearance of Louretta had him second guessing himself.

Louretta saw the doubt in his eyes. "It's okay, honey. Nobody knows I'm here. I'm certain of it. Pick it up, it'll be fine," she said, although not feeling quite as confident as she sounded. After the last few hours she could not be certain of much at all.

"Yes, of course," replied Ethan, "I'm just over reacting. Silly of me." He then reached past Louretta and snatched up the receiver. "Hello," he croaked nervously.

There was silence for a moment as he listened to the caller. "Yes, this is Doctor Ridgeway, how may I help you?"

There was silence again, yet as Louretta watched she saw Ethan's face drain of colour.

"Erm, I'm sorry, er, please, would you hold on a moment?" Ethan sounded really quite scared as he cupped his hand over the mouthpiece and whispered in a panicked voice to Louretta, "Christ, Rett. It's somebody called Bernie - wants to know if you're *here?*"

She stared back at Ethan, shock written all over her face. Then, after a long moment, she held out her hand and said, "Let me talk to him."

By the time she had collected her suitcase from the luggage carousel Violet felt utterly spent.

Over thirteen hours of rest, a good amount of which was spent sleeping, yet still she felt exhausted and in a great deal of pain.

She had changed the dressings on her injuries a couple of times during the flight and was concerned to see a few of the stitches had torn out of the wound in her shoulder; a result of her ill-advised exertions she assumed. Yet ironically it seemed to be her chest that was hurting more than anything else. The bruise was a livid rainbow of colour - purple, blue, yellow and green - spreading out like a stain across her breasts and ribs. It would heal, she had been assured, but presently it hurt like hell and she would be glad to get to the hotel.

She staggered out to the line of waiting taxis and all but fell into the back of a cab, hoarsely telling the driver where she wished to be taken before collapsing in agony onto the back seat.

Fifteen minutes later, the cab pulled up under the impressive canopy of the largest, grandest and undoubtedly most spectacular hotel she had ever seen.

So this was Las Vegas.

Now she understood the hype, although at present she was not in the best condition to appreciate it.

Violet forced herself out of the cab and somehow managed to tip the driver after he had retrieved her suitcase from the trunk of the car.

Immediately a bell hop in a smart blue uniform and pristine white gloves snatched up the case and placed it on a trolley.

"Good afternoon, Ma'am," he said, "Welcome to *The Villa Continental*, we hope you'll enjoy your stay. If you'd just follow me I'll direct you to the front desk."

"Thank you," Violet managed breathlessly, her head swimming and her chest throbbing badly as the bell hop wheeled her case in through one of a whole line of ornate gold entrance doors. She followed along behind as best she could.

The inside of the hotel was quite remarkable; wide marble floors and tall ornamental columns, fine sculptures and beautifully carved embellishments - the centrepiece was a huge marble fountain which would not have looked out of place in Ancient Rome. Violet was staggered and had she not known she was in Las Vegas she could have quite easily believed herself to be somewhere in the Mediterranean.

"They're you go, Ma'am, I'll leave it right here," said the bell hop, removing Violet's case from the trolley and placing it down on the ground in the waiting area by the front desk, where she joined a queue of other weary travellers all eager to check-in.

A whole phalanx of staff, also dressed in smart blue uniforms, were busy helping the new arrivals from behind the long expanse of sweeping desk that stretched from one side of the vast lobby to the other.

"Thank you," Violet said again, feeling extremely light-headed as she handed the bell hop a couple of dollars."

"Appreciate it, Ma'am," he said, tipping an imaginary hat before studying her a little more closely. "Say, you okay? You look a little—"

"No, no - I'm fine, thanks. Just a little tired, that's all." She felt as weak as a kitten but Violet did not want any fuss.

"Okay, Ma'am. Well then you get a good rest - you've sure picked the right place. Enjoy your stay with us."

Violet nodded her gratitude and the bell hop went on his way, leaving her to wait in line for the next available desk clerk.

She was completely unaware of the sharply dressed man who was observing her from a short distance away.

Indeed, the only thing Violet was aware of was her growing sense of dizziness and the overwhelming feeling that she was about to pass out.

She stood there swaying for a moment as everything around her started to spin then, finally, her legs buckled and she fell. However, before she could hit her head on the highly polished marble floor, the sharply dressed man rushed forward and caught her in his arms.

Violet was fighting the blackness but her vision was starry as she looked up at the man who was now holding her in his arms.

She desperately tried to focus on his face but she could not, it was merely a blur. "Please," she said, her voice but a whisper. "I need to speak to Joe Cassidy. I *must* speak to him, it's urgent, his life's in danger - *please*—"

But then, her eyes rolled up into her head and Violet said no more.

***

Bernie Dufresne had been the general manager of *The Villa Continental* for ten years.

Prior to that he was concierge of the five-star *Paris Matador,* one of the most exclusive hotels in the whole world. However, earlier in his life he had spent some time as an actors agent in Hollywood and before that he had worked as a personal assistant to the star he would eventually represent.

Indeed, Bernie Dufresne had been with Louretta Wild through most of the important moments of her life, seeing her safely through three marriages and three subsequent divorces as well as an enormously successful movie career. However, when Louretta decided to retire from the movies to breed horses full-time, Bernie's life suddenly became a lot less interesting and he moved onto pastures new.

Through the years, the two remained close and talked regularly on the phone even though they saw each other less than they would have liked.

During that time, Bernie became something of a confidante who Louretta could trust with her most closely guarded secrets, yet they had never become lovers as Bernie's tastes lay in an entirely different direction.

However, he did know intimate details about her love life that she would not dared to have told anyone else and even though Louretta had a famously tough exterior he knew her to have an extremely soft centre which she revealed to very few.

It was Bernie who comforted her years earlier when she and her first love broke up; he remembered well her crying on his shoulder the night that she and Ethan decided to go their separate ways.

He knew, too, that it was to Ethan she went to after all the horror of what happened at *The Villa* when Benny Vincenzi and Carl Napier tried to steal it out from under her nose.

Ironically, it was that incident that led Bernie to become general manager of *The Villa* himself.

Louretta was in desperate need of a new manager after Napier's betrayal and the subsequent fallout from it. She needed someone she could rely on to revive *The Villa's* damaged reputation and restore it to its former glory.

Bernie had the necessary hotel experience, he also knew a lot of influential people including many Hollywood movie stars who could easily be persuaded to add their names to *The Villa's* exclusive clientele which, in turn, would attract the masses.

In addition, he had all the relevant business acumen and the deft people skills that the position required.

But above all he was someone whom Louretta could trust so it was an easy decision which Joe and Sean, her equal partners in the venture, happily got behind.

As a result, Louretta had invited Bernie back to The States where she told him everything, knowing that it would never go any further. She told him about Benny Vincenzi, about Joe and Sean, about Virgil Nash and how Ethan Ridgeway had given them his unconditional help.

Louretta told Bernie all of this because as her friend it was important that he knew exactly what he was getting in to before accepting the job.

The rest, of course, was history and they were now ten years down the road into what had become an extremely successful union.

Bernie was one of the very few people who knew that Joe and Sean still lived, indeed they were still silent partners in *The Villa* and technically his bosses, although their involvement was very carefully hidden and Bernie had never breathed a word of it to anyone.

Furthermore, like many other people around the world, Bernie had watched the news that morning with grave concern, although he was far better acquainted with those that were being reported dead or missing than almost anyone else.

He was so worried about Louretta. To him, it seemed more than merely a coincidence that she was missing when her daughter, Victoria, was being reported dead. The Louretta he knew would have been out there, in front, demanding answers whether she was grieving or not.

It simply did not make sense that she was nowhere to be seen.

Bernie drew two conclusions from this. The first was almost unthinkable; that something equally bad had befallen Louretta, too. The second, was that she purposely did not want to be found and that there was a damn good reason for her absence.

It occurred to him that maybe her disappearance was linked to the events of the past but he dismissed it almost immediately as there was nothing that he had seen on the news to corroborate the theory.

However, it did nothing to alleviate his concern.

For most of the day he had not been able to get his worries for Louretta's safety out of his mind. Indeed, his thoughts had largely been about her welfare and not the business of running a hotel and casino.

He had returned to his suite many times during the day to

catch the news on the TV but in each case there was nothing new being reported.

It was on one of these occasions, when returning from his suite, that he stepped out of his private elevator into the lobby with the weight of the world on his shoulders.

However, almost immediately, his eyes were drawn to an extremely attractive woman who had just joined the line at the front desk and he watched her absently for a few moments, briefly forgetting his worries over Louretta.

But then the woman began to sway dramatically and instinct told him that she was about to pass out.

Bernie raced over just as her legs buckled and caught her a split-second before her head hit the floor.

She looked into his face but he could see she was struggling to stay conscious.

And then she spoke, leaving Bernie utterly stunned by what she had said.

**

When Violet awoke she was lying on a bed in a vast bedroom with tall windows that offered a magnificent view of the Las Vegas Strip and the wider city beyond.

The room was luxurious in the extreme and expensively decorated in a tasteful, Mediterranean style, leading Violet to believe she was still at *The Villa Continental*. As for anything else, she had not got a clue. She knew not whose room she was in nor how she got there or, more importantly, how long she had been out.

Yet she did feel much better. Her head was no longer spinning and her wounds were less painful.

She looked down at herself, shocked to discover that she was naked. Someone had obviously undressed her and put her to bed. They had also re-dressed her injuries with fresh, clean bandages.

Suddenly she was scared. *Had the person who stripped her done anything else to her?* Instinct told her they had not but there was no way she could be sure.

Then she remembered briefly seeing a man and saying something to him before blacking out. *Was it him who had undressed her?*

Violet noticed that her clothes were neatly folded on a chair beside the bed. Her suitcase had been placed on the floor next to it, the lock still intact.

Slowly, very carefully, she slipped out of bed and got dressed, easing on her T-shirt and jeans gently so as not to cause too much pain.

Yet she knew there was no time to waste. As much as she would have liked to stay in the comfortable bed and give her wounds an opportunity to heal, she still had to get in touch with Joe and Sean before it was too late.

Furthermore, it was not her bed and not her room, which meant it was time for her to go.

However, before she could leave there was a gentle knock on the door. Violet froze as she watched the door handle turn, her eyes darting about the room for anything she could use as a weapon.

As the door inched open, she snatched up a vase in desperation. "You come near me, I'll hurt you!" She yelled. "I don't want to but I will!"

"Please, there's no need to be afraid. I've no intention of hurting you," said Bernie as he tentatively stepped in. "You're safe, I promise and you won't be harmed."

"Yeah? You say that now but how do I know that you mean it?"

"I'm sorry but you don't. But I can assure you I won't. My name is Bernie Dufresne and I'm the general manager here. This is my apartment. I'm the man who caught you when you fainted—"

"You the one who took my clothes off too?"

"No, no. Good God, no. That was a female nurse - I promise.

121

She is a trained professional - works here on staff. She's the one who undressed you - the one who took care of your wounds and put you to bed. I swear it."

Violet studied him for a moment. He certainly did not look like a rapist or a murderer, not in his impeccably cut suit or with that perfectly groomed appearance. He also had an honest face with kind eyes and a friendly, warm smile.

"You swear it?" She said.

"I do. You have my word, you'll be perfectly safe here."

Violet thought for a moment then lowered the vase. She was really in no fit state for a fight anyway.

"Well okay, then," she said.

"Thank you," replied Bernie. "Now, please, Miss Noakes, sit down, rest a while longer and tell me how I might help you."

"You know my name?"

"I'm afraid so, yes. I took a look at the luggage label on your case. "You're from London, yes?"

"Yeah, that's right, but look, it's okay - I've really got to get—"

"Forgive me," Bernie interrupted, "You said something, before you passed out. Do you remember what it was?"

The fact that Violet had mentioned Joe had given Bernie cause for concern. For all intents and purposes Joe was dead, so why would anyone show up at *The Villa* asking for him ten years after he supposedly died? Especially somebody with the surname *Noakes*.

That together with Violet's wounds and the disappearance of Louretta, as well as the apparent deaths of Virgil and Victoria had given him much to ponder in the few hours that she had been out.

Violet's arrival and Louretta's disappearance were linked somehow, he was sure of it.

"Listen, I really don't want to trouble you. I'm so sorry I've put you out but I really must be going," she said.

"Please," said Bernie. "It's important. More important to me than you could possibly know. Trust me, I beg you."

It was a risk, he knew, but he was desperate. He had never seen or heard of this woman before, but there was something about her that told him her intentions were good and she meant Joe Cassidy no harm.

In return, Violet studied him. He certainly did seem trustworthy and she had come here specifically to get a message to Joe or Sean. Who better to ask than the manager? After all, she *had* to trust somebody.

Violet took a deep breath and threw caution to the wind. "When I arrived here, I said that I needed to speak to Joe Cassidy, as I'm sure you remember."

Bernie nodded as she continued. "I know he's alive and that he's a part owner of this hotel along with Louretta Wild and Sean Noakes. My father is - or rather, was, Alfie Noakes, a good friend of theirs - he even gave Sean his last name who was like a son to him." She paused for a moment whilst her heart broke all over again thinking about her father.

"Please, take your time," said Bernie, seeing her distress, "It's okay."

"They trusted each other," she continued at last, "Dad, Sean and Joe. The boys trusted Louretta, too, I think - after all, they opened this hotel together, didn't they?"

Bernie nodded and smiled. "They did, yes."

"Anyway, the truth is, I don't know much more, except that something bad happened and they had to fake their own deaths to escape whoever it was who was after them. But they're good guys, I know that. Honourable men." Then, as an after thought, she added, "I'm hoping you are, too."

Bernie smiled once more, his heart going out to her. "Yes, I am, I promise," he said. "So why are you trying to find Joe?"

"Because a few days ago a man named Bass Stone killed my

father and brother and tried to kill me too—"

"My God, I'm so sorry—"

"That's not all," continued Violet. "Stone found some information that my dad had hidden - I don't know exactly what but I think it might lead him to Joe and Sean - and they're who he's after. Their lives are in danger, Mr. Dufresne - you must help."

"Me?" Said Bernie, "But how?"

"Joe told me in a letter once," replied Violet. "He said that if I ever needed to contact him, then I should leave my name here at the front desk and eventually he would get in touch."

For a second Bernie was puzzled. "I don't understand it. I'm the only person here who could possibly know they're alive. But I don't know where they are or how to get hold of—" suddenly he broke off as a thought struck him.

"What, Mr. Dufresne? What is it?"

"Louretta," he said. "She knows. She's the person who Joe meant would be in touch."

"Great - that's great - then please, give her a call, we need to get word to Joe and Sean as soon as poss—"

"No. I'm sorry. You don't understand, it's not that easy."

"Why, what's wrong? She owns this place, right?"

"Yes, Miss Noakes, she does. But you see, Louretta has gone missing and I think whoever this Bass Stone is, he might well have tried to kill her, too."

***

It explained everything; the strange circumstances surrounding Virgil and Victoria's apparent deaths as well as Louretta's disappearance.

Bernie was now sitting next to Violet on the couch in the spacious living room of his luxurious penthouse suite where, for the last ten minutes he had been telling her all that he knew.

Currently they were watching the latest news report on the TV

124

and Violet was shocked by what she was seeing. Now suspecting, too, that everything was all linked.

Bernie was quiet, clearly very worried for Louretta's safety. Yet something told him that she was not dead, indeed he was convinced of it.

So where the hell was she?

He was wracking his brains, trying to think of the most logical place she would go - somewhere her enemies would not know about.

Few knew her as well a Bernie did but still he could not think. But then, in a flash of brilliance, it suddenly struck him and a name popped into his head.

Dr. Ethan Ridgeway.

Louretta's first love. The man she had never forgotten and the one who she had turned to for help ten years earlier after all that had happened with Benny Vincenzi.

Even though Bernie had never met him, he knew that Ethan was Louretta's safe port in a storm and if she was in trouble or hurt then it was to him she would undoubtedly go.

It was a light bulb moment and Violet immediately recognised the change in Bernie's demeanour.

"What is it?" She said. "What are you thinking?"

Bernie smiled widely as he turned to her and said, "I know where she is - she's alive, I know it and she's right here in Vegas."

"What? Where?" Asked Violet, stunned.

But Bernie was already off the couch and heading for the phone.

Chapter Seven

Miami

"No one kills those two mutherfuckers before me - understand?" Said Jez Vincenzi, to the small, fifteen man army sitting before him as he addressed them from the front of the plane. "If you find 'em, then bring 'em to me - but you don't kill 'em - cos they're mine."

Jez knew now that Bass Stone had been right and that his plan had been flawed from the outset.

Now, due to this lapse in judgement, Matt Mason had escaped and Louretta Wild possibly had too.

Furthermore, thanks to their botched efforts in Arizona, two of his best men were now dead. This had not gone unnoticed by those gathered before him and he sensed he was quickly losing what little respect they had for him.

Jez's plan was unravelling. Cassidy and Noakes would no doubt have been alerted to the danger, forewarned of his knowledge of their whereabouts, so it was imperative that he now acted swiftly and decisively, to show strength in front of his men.

As the new boss of the Carboni/Vincenzi crime family it was time to prove himself worthy of the crown.

Jez was aware that those that were faithful and unflinchingly loyal to his grandfathers were yet to be convinced of his ability to lead them and his cause had not been helped by the events in Arizona.

But, after tonight, he was determined that their opinion of him would change.

Only the new guy, Bass Stone, seemed unquestioningly loyal even though he had failed his mission in California - however, his explanation had been plausible enough as the old bitch had not turned up. Jez was willing to overlook this, just this once, mainly because he badly needed Stone as an ally in the face of dwindling support.

But he would not be so forgiving if it happened again - no matter what the circumstances.

Jez Vincenzi did not handle failure well.

Rocco Pistoli, was also an ally; a good friend, too, or at least he had been until he heard of Enzo's death. Now he was just hungry for blood and would be willing to follow anyone anywhere for the chance of revenge. Yet he was not entirely trustworthy and should Vincenzi falter, then Rocco's loyalties would be available to the highest bidder.

However, Jez had assured him that the attack on the *Far Point Estate* would lead Rocco one step closer to the revenge he now desperately craved and had promised to back him all the way. After all, Jez knew all too well what it was like to lose a brother and, in his distorted view of things, it was those they were visiting tonight who should be held accountable.

Whilst Stone, Pistoli and Bobby Assante were flying back from California, Vincenzi had assembled the troops - a team of his grandfathers' top men - killers and enforcers who would get the job done.

As soon as the little Piper Cheyenne touched down on the tarmac he had taken Rocco aside and told him the news of his brother. Then, as Pistoli absorbed the information, Vincenzi's team of killers, which now counted Stone and Assante amongst them, boarded a larger aircraft which was destined for The Caymans.

Time was of the essence.

So as not to give Cassidy and Noakes the opportunity to escape, Jez and his men would have to reach them as quickly as possible.

And that meant giving Stone, Assante and Rocco Pistoli no chance for rest.

However, judging by the look on Pistoli's face when Jez turned back to face him, rest was the last thing on his mind.

Now, as the pilot began his descent onto the small, private airfield in The Caribbean, Jez finished his speech to the troops.

"You kill everyone and every thing. You hear me?" He said. "No man, woman, child - not even any cat, dog or fucking chicken escapes alive - is that clear? Everyone dies. But remember, Cassidy and Noakes are mine. You find 'em, you bring 'em to me. The rest are yours - do what you want with 'em, but when you're done, kill 'em, understand?"

Finally, Jez grinned and said, "When we leave that fucking island later, we're gonna be covered in the blood of our enemies - and it's gonna be fucking beautiful."

***

The Cayman Islands

Joe and Sean were down in the cove at the foot of the cliff making their preparations. Normally when together they would chat cheerfully about this and that, maybe enjoy some harmless banter, but today they were stern, focussed and determined. They were both also extremely concerned for their families.

Joe had spoken at length with Louretta on the phone and knew now, thankfully, that she, Matt and the others were safe at Ethan Ridgeway's place in Las Vegas.

The Doc had also given him a full report on Matt's condition and it appeared that he was now out of danger although, as yet, still unconscious.

Louretta's old friend had been of invaluable assistance to them and they were in his debt once more.

Incredibly, Violet had made her way to Doc Ridgeway's too, with the aid of Bernie Dufresne, and the story she related to Joe chilled him to the bone.

He was shocked and deeply saddened to hear that Alfie, Richie and Manno were all dead. Angry, too, that their murderer, Bass Stone, had also tried to kill Violet.

Moreover, Joe was concerned that Stone was now in possession of information that could threaten their existence at *Far Point*.

What Virgil had told him supported this theory as it was apparently Vincenzi's men who had tried to run them off the road in California.

Since Benny's death, neither Virgil or Victoria had hidden themselves away as their careers had always kept them in the public eye. Indeed, if Tito Vincenzi or Carmine Carboni wanted them dead then they could have taken them out at any time. But they had not and Joe guessed this was because Virgil and Victoria were too high profile; that their deaths would cause too much of a media furore and spark an intense investigation.

But if that was the case, then Joe had to ask himself, *Why now?*

One possible answer was that Jez had recently come of age and it was in fact him, not his grandfathers, who had orchestrated these acts of violence. *So was Jez now calling the shots?*

Another explanation could be that Jez now held information which would enable him to take out all his enemies in one fell swoop. This implied that Bass Stone had taken whatever he found at *The Golden Gloves* directly to Vincenzi.

A troublesome thought.

Nonetheless, Joe was thankful to hear from both Violet and Virgil and glad that they had made it to the safety of Doc Ridgeway's. However, he knew that they were just the entrée on Bass Stone and Jez Vincenzi's menu whereas he and Sean and all those at *Far Point* were the main course.

Presently, however, what concerned Joe and Sean most of all was Michael and the fact they had not heard from him in many days.

Sarah was frantic with worry. She and her son had only properly known each other for the last ten years. Prior to that she had spent her life in a near-comatose state brought on by traumatic events in her late teens whilst still pregnant with Michael.

She had remained silent and unresponsive throughout his birth and had played no part in his subsequent upbringing which continued to be a constant source of bitter regret even though circumstances had been beyond her control.

Worse still, due to the events which brought about Sarah's condition, Sean had also been absent from Michael's early life, although not before leaving him in the capable hands of Ruby and Ray who had raised him as their own.

They had done the best job that they possibly could but Michael had been a difficult child. His problems, however, had been greatly exacerbated by Benny Vincenzi and those who acted for him. At their hands Michael had suffered a great deal - kidnap, abuse, facial disfigurement and horrific mental scars that time would never erase.

All of this had left him with a skewed view of the world and a misplaced sense of loyalty which had put Joe, Sean and both their families in terrible danger.

However, they weathered the storm and ten years ago, after Benny Vincenzi's death, Michael finally saw the truth of things. Since then he had been rebuilding his relationships with both his parents and family as a whole.

Over time they had all reached a place where everything was finally good.

Michael was loved, cared for and, for the first time in his life, properly happy. The demons of his past had at last been laid to rest and his regular visits to the sanatorium in Nantucket made sure things stayed that way.

But now he had gone missing and Sarah and Sean could not help but fear the worst.

Sean had been on the phone to the sanatorium day and night, desperate for any word, but there was still no clue as to his whereabouts.

After hearing what Violet said about Bass Stone, Sean had no choice but to assume something terrible had befallen Michael - that maybe Stone had found him, perhaps even Vincenzi.

It occurred to Sean and Joe that Michael was possibly being held hostage somewhere in a bid to draw the two of them out of hiding.

However Michael was clever and if there was any way out he would find it. Yet he would have to remain focussed as after what he had been through in the past, any new trauma might have an adverse effect on his delicate state of mind.

The only hope was that he had somehow escaped and was currently trying to make his way back to the comparative safety of *Far Point*.

Sarah was at her wit's end and her first instinct was to get on the next plane to Massachusetts to try and find her son herself. But Sean and Joe managed to dissuade her.

They were confident that if he was able, Michael would send word. With luck he might even be on his way back to them.

Far Point had been a sanctuary for them all for the last ten years, a safe haven where the outside world could not harm them and Michael had appreciated this more than most.

Joe and Sean knew this safety was now compromised and that forces might well be on the way which would threaten their idyllic existence. But they could not risk leaving with Michael still unaccounted for.

Besides, *Far Point* was an eminently defendable stronghold

with a formidable security force in place. It would be as safe there as anywhere.

Furthermore, the estate was their home and they were damn sure not going to give it up without a fight.

To this end, the security team had been put on high alert and the estate had been locked down - no one in, no one out, not without either Joe or Sean's express permission.

Years earlier, when they first came to *Far Point*, Joe and Sean had the foresight to install a munitions locker in the cove, together with a couple of rubber dinghies. Each dinghy was equipped with an outboard motor, a case of flares and an emergency supplies chest with which to make good their escape if so required.

Joe had also taken the precaution of putting a plane on standby for them in Jamaica - strictly off the books. If things went bad at *Far Point* and the dinghies proved necessary, then it was just a short sea voyage to Montego Bay. From there they could be in Vegas within a few hours and meeting up with the others at the comparative safety of Doc Ridgeway's.

Presently, however, Joe and Sean were busy cleaning and checking everything, making sure the dinghies were sea worthy and that all the equipment was free from dirt and in good working order.

At the top of the cliff, at the entrance to the narrow path that led down to the cove, sat Ray Reece in his wheelchair, a double-barrelled shotgun resting across his knees and a smoking pipe clenched between his teeth.

Even though he claimed to like the peaceful life, it was all just a façade as this was really what Ray Reece lived for. He loved to be in the thick of the action and it was what he excelled at. However, in latter years, his disability and his reliance on the wheelchair had hampered his activities somewhat.

But with a shotgun there was still no one better.

Although at the moment his services were not necessarily

required - not in broad daylight and with an armed security force patrolling the estate - but he was desperate to be involved and simply refused to be treated like an invalid.

Besides, in Ray's view, there was no sense in being too careful.

Nonetheless, the wheelchair did prevent him from using the pathway as it was simply too cumbersome and awkward to navigate the steep, uneven track.

In the event of the cove having to be used as a means of escape, Ray would have no choice but to abandon his wheelchair and be carried down the narrow track, which did not sit well with him but there was simply no other way.

Yet Ray's pride would not allow him to admit it. "I reckon I'd rather keep my dignity if it's all the same," was all he had to say on the matter.

Joe and Sean just smiled. The old pirate could blather and bluster all he liked but if the need arose, they *would* get him down to the cove.

***

Brett hated being cooped up and caged in like some wild animal in a zoo - no matter how luxurious his prison was or how necessary he knew his confinement to be.

He yearned to be free, to be out there on the ocean, or working on his boat - hell, at present, he would even be happy to work a double shift at *Calico Jack's*, because at least then he would be doing something other than just waiting.

To keep himself occupied, he had ridden the perimeter of the estate on his Sportster numerous times to check for possible breaches in the fence.

And each time he found none.

It was getting to the point where he was wishing there was such a breach, because then he could fill his time repairing it.

But instead, he was out on the driveway, tinkering around with his bike, trying to keep his mind from wandering to places he dare not let it go, but he was failing miserably. Indeed, far from thinking about his bike or, more importantly, concerning himself with the threat currently hanging over *Far Point*, his mind was filled with thoughts of Liv Noakes; of her lustrous blonde hair, her big blue eyes and her long, long legs that seemed to go on forever.

He cursed himself for this - cursed this whole damn situation - yet still he could not help but keep peeking over to Liv's house where he could see her out in front of the garage happily working on her beloved Monte Carlo, seemingly oblivious to his furtive glances.

Brett was almost hoping that Vincenzi *would* attack. It would certainly end this insufferable waiting and keep his mind off the girl he was trying so desperately hard not to be bewitched by.

He kept telling himself that Liv was off limits, forbidden fruit and a complete no go. They had grown up together and she was almost like his little sister.

Except she was not his sister, not even a blood relative and there was no reason why they should not be together.

Liv was a beautiful, fiery, passionate, young woman yet she was also his friend - or was until recently - so how could he now declare his true feelings for her without ruining all that they had once been.

Christ how Brett wished something would happen that would stop all of this from buzzing about in his head. He was not familiar with uncertainty or indecisiveness yet Liv Noakes had him second guessing his every move and he did not like it one little bit.

***

That morning, Liv had taken delivery of the package she had been waiting on for the last three weeks.

She had ordered it from a specialist dealer in California and when she opened the box the shiny new *Quadrajet* carburettor was every bit as beautiful as she knew it would be.

It was late in the afternoon by the time Liv emerged from

under the hood of her Monte Carlo, a wide smear of oil on her cheek and a big, wide grin on her delighted face, the *Qjet* finally in place and the powerful engine purring like a contented tiger.

However, with the new part installed, she was dying to take the Monte Carlo out for a spin, to hear the full throaty roar of the beast and not just the tantalising purr.

But she had been given strict orders by her father. On no account was she to leave the bounds of the estate, Sean had told her, as it was just too dangerous.

However, the new carburettor and the seductive rumble of the engine had all but persuaded her to defy his orders.

Surely a quick test drive wouldn't hurt. Besides she would be back before anyone even knew that she was gone.

Her father and her Uncle Joe were still down in the cove with Ray standing guard above. Whilst Sarah, Ruby and her Aunt Rose were busy stowing their valuables and securing any breakables - just in case.

Brett was on the driveway in front of Joe and Rose's house, working on his bike, clearly immune to the anger Liv felt towards him.

She knew he was there because she had checked almost every ten minutes; seething that he appeared not to have noticed her at all.

With all that had happened recently she had still not had an opportunity to confront him about why he was suddenly being so cool towards her. Indeed, even though he, too, had been confined to the boundaries of the estate, he had managed to make himself scarce whenever Liv so much as came within a hundred yards of him.

It was all extremely infuriating and clearly evident that he would not care one jot if she took the Monte Carlo for a spin or not.

The only question was, how could she get passed the guard on the gate.

Freddie, *Far Point's* head of security, would never go against either her father's or Joe's orders, nor would any of his eight man team - except maybe one.

Clinton Fine was a local lad, born on the island and only slightly older than Liv, herself. The pair of them enjoyed a good rapport and whenever she saw him there was always a twinkle in his eye.

Liv suspected that if she asked him, there was very little Clinton would not do for her and, as such, saw him as the key to her escape from the estate.

As there were two separate driveways on the estate, so too were there two guard houses; one on the West Gate, which secured the Cassidy property and one on the East Gate, which protected the Noakes'.

Clinton would take over from the guard on the East Gate in just a few minutes when the shift changed at 6pm, which would give Liv her opportunity.

She closed the hood on the Monte Carlo and surreptitiously glanced over again at Brett. He was now sitting astride the Sportster, the sleeves on his T-shirt rolled up even further so that he might catch the last of the afternoon sun on his muscular arms.

Why the hell did he have to be so damned good looking?

A moment later she heard the Sportster's engine spark into life as Brett headed off again on yet another tour of the perimeter fence.

But he would be back soon and if she was to go then it had to be now.

Liv slipped into the driver's seat and switched off the engine as she looked down the hill to the gate. Scott, the previous guard, was already driving away in one of the little golf buggies the security force used, making his way back to the guardhouse at the Southern edge of the estate for a well earned rest.

Clinton had relieved Scott of his duties and was now sitting in the little booth beside the gate, looking smart in his dark blue uniform and peaked *'Far Point Security'* baseball cap.

Seizing the moment, Liv released the hand break and slowly, silently, the Monte Carlo began to roll down the hill, steadily picking up speed as it free-wheeled down the long stretch of driveway to the gatehouse.

"Hey, pretty lady," Clinton Fine said, greeting her with his customary grin as the Monte Carlo rolled up to the edge of his hut, "Where you headed all quiet and stealthy like?"

"Hi, Clint," replied Liv, batting her eyelashes coquettishly and looking deeply into his dark brown eyes, using all her feminine wiles. "Ruby's taking a nap so I didn't wanna wake her - you know how noisy this baby's engine can be."

"Yep. Sure do," he smiled, staring dreamily into her grease-smeared face, yet barely noticing the dirty blemish.

Whilst Liv did not care about her looks she was certainly not oblivious to how others saw her - particularly the local boys who all seemed to fall over themselves to gain her attention. However, the only boy whom she had ever wanted to fawn over her seemed immune to her charms.

But Clinton Fine was not so immune and she sensed that he was already falling under her spell.

"I just wanna take the Chevy out for a run - try out the new carburettor."

"New carb, huh?"

"Yeah, a Qjet - should make it run real smooth."

"Cool, yeah. I'll bet," replied Clint, pretending he knew what the hell Liv was talking about.

"Yeah, so if you'd just be a sweetie and open the gates—"

"Sorry, Liv. No can do. You're pop gave us all strict orders. Something's going on and the whole estate's on lock down."

"Oh, yeah, I know but I've cleared it with Dad and he says it's fine," she lied, "I'm only gonna be gone for a little while."

Clinton looked confused. "He said it was okay?"

"Yeah, just a few minutes ago - you could ask him but he's still down in the cove."

"Strange. Freddie didn't say anything. Maybe I'd better just clear it with him first—"

"No need to bother him. Freddie's obviously got lots of stuff to deal with around here at the moment and I don't wanna be any trouble." Again she batted her lashes. "Sides, you don't need his say so. This is your gate right now - surely you can say who goes in or out?"

Clinton looked a little flustered. "Er, yeah, well I guess—"

"Sure you can. Say, have you been working out? That uniform looks real good on you - fits great on those broad shoulders of yours." It was an utterly shameless tactic and she did feel a little guilty at being such a flirt but she was still angry at Brett and it felt good to get some male attention.

Clinton looked pleased with the compliment and puffed his chest out proudly. "Yeah, I workout a little. I hit the gym maybe two, three times a week."

"Well it's working. You're looking *fine* Mister Fine." God, this was cringe-worthy and she knew it was beneath her to toy with Clint so blatantly but it was the only way she was going to get off the estate to test the Monte Carlo.

"Thanks. You ain't looking so bad yourself."

"What, in these greasy overalls, I'm sure that's not true."

"Hey, you'd look good in a potato sack," replied Clint, the flirtatious glint in his eye now a positive sparkle."

"Ssh, you're making me blush - I think you'd better let me go before I start to swoon."

Clint beamed back at her, a bright white grin on his burnt mahogany face.

"You sure your pop said it was okay?" He asked.

"Course, yeah. It's no problem." She was crossing her fingers as

138

she said this, hating the lie but it had now gone too far and it was too late to back out.

"Well, alright - but be careful - I'd hate to get in trouble with your pop."

"You won't, honest," replied Liv guiltily, hoping that her father would forgive Clinton's part in things should her actions be discovered. However, as the naive young guard opened the gates, she was confident she could talk Sean around should the need arise.

With the gates finally open, Liv turned the key in the ignition and the Monte Carlo roared into life.

"Thanks Clint!" She yelled, "Promise I won't be long!"

Then she pressed her foot firmly on the gas and with a screech of tyres and a cloud of blue smoke the Chevy tore off down the road, soon leaving *Far Point* way behind it in the distance.

***

Liv drove down the long stretch of tree lined road, which led from the estate to the main highway. The Monte Carlo growled noisily as she sped along the unpaved road, the loose gravel spitting out from under the wide tyres of the souped-up American muscle car as it rushed by.

Once she hit the highway, Liv turned right, flicking her headlights on in the dimming light of dusk as she headed for town.

After a couple of miles she passed two black panel vans which were parked up on the side of the road, but she barely noticed them as she roared onwards, putting the Monte Carlo through its paces.

She would drive once around the town then head back to the estate, she promised herself, which would bring her back just after nightfall but, with luck, no one would know she was ever gone.

It was a chancy strategy and if her father found out he would be livid but with the window open, her hair billowing wildly in the warm evening breeze and the rhythmic beat of the engine playing a glorious melody in her ears, it was a thrill ride well worth the risk.

Chapter Eight

B ass Stone took a long drag of his cigarette as he lent nonchalantly against the back doors of one of the two black panel vans.

He and the other members of the fifteen man force were waiting for nightfall before launching their attack on the *Far Point Estate*, all of them dressed in dark fatigues and armed with automatic weapons.

Some of Vincenzi's men were dozing in the vans, others were milling around beside them, concealed from view by the vehicles themselves. A few were lying in the long grass that lined the verge, killing time before the time came to kill men.

Jez Vincenzi, himself, was pacing up and down, anxious for what was to come, hungry for the kill and impatient for night to fall.

Pistoli was up front in one of the cabs, his feet up on the dash, his head resting on the door frame and his eyes closed. Rocco knew to save his energy for what was to follow, no point in wasting it now.

As for Bass, he was just enjoying his smoke, making the most of the calm before the storm. His hands were steady and his heart rate even.

This was what he lived for, what he thrived on.

And he was good at it.

The same, however, could not be said of Jez Vincenzi who was, as yet, untested in such matters - although for eagerness Stone's new boss could not be faulted, even though his preparation was somewhat questionable.

Indeed, Bass watched as Jez quite openly removed a little glass vile from his inside jacket pocket and proceeded to pour a small amount of cocaine onto the back of his hand. Quickly, he snorted it up his right nostril, then immediately repeated the process with his left.

As he felt the euphoric effects wash over him, Jez could not help but notice Stone's calm demeanour and be impressed by it.

He was glad now that he had brought him along as he was a calming, steadying influence; his experience instilling confidence in Jez that the other men might not otherwise have felt.

Jez offered Bass the vile but he declined to partake. "No thanks, I'll pass," he said.

Bass preferred to do his killing with a clear head and narcotics somehow diluted the buzz.

As he regarded Stone, Jez heard the sound of a vehicle approaching and looked out from behind the van in time to see on old Chevy Monte Carlo flash past. The car was stripped of paint and was wearing just a base undercoat but it still looked good as the harsh roar of its powerful engine cut abrasively through the silence of the evening.

A girl with long blonde hair was driving, Jez only saw her for an instant but he could tell that she was an absolute stunner - as was the car, or at least it would be when it was finished.

Maybe he would get himself one just like it when he got home, he thought absently - after all, he could have whatever the goddamn hell he wanted now that he was in charge. A classic American muscle car such as that would look good parked in his garage next to his yellow Lamborghini, his bright red Ferrari and his silver Porsche.

Perhaps he would get himself the girl, too, he mused, when all this was over. Once he had finished with his business at *Far Point* he could go into the local town and find her. If he flashed some money around, she should not be too difficult to track down and she would surely be impressed by a wealthy young stud such as he.

She could be his little reward for killing Cassidy and Noakes.

However, the thought soon passed as Bass Stone stubbed out his cigarette and said, "It's gonna be dark soon, Boss. Time to get ready."

Jez turned to face the man whose efforts had brought him to this point and smiled widely.

"I've been ready for ten fucking years."

***

After doing all they could in the cove, Joe and Sean emerged onto the narrow track that led up the side of the cliff just as the sun finally sank below the horizon.

By the time they reached the top it was totally dark.

Ray was waiting for them, his pipe glowing bright orange as he puffed away contentedly in the darkness. "You all done?" He asked them.

"Yeah. Everything's in good shape and should do the job if it comes to it," replied Joe.

"Let's just hope it doesn't," said Sean.

"Amen to that," agreed Joe, "but at least we're as ready now as we can be."

As he spoke, the single light of a motorcycle could be seen bobbing up and down as Brett navigated his way along the cliff top towards them having completed his tour of the boundary.

"Here comes the boy," said Ray, squinting into the darkness with his one good eye through a cloud of pipe smoke, the loud hum of the Sportster now filling the air.

As he watched his son approach, Joe could not have been more proud.

Brett had grown into a fine young man, the death of his mother and the events of the past could easily have traumatised him or had

142

some other negative effect but, fortunately, they had not.

Of course Rose's steadying hand had helped to keep Brett on track. She had welcomed him as her own and loved him just as much as she did Matt. As it turned out, the two boys had been good for each other and even though Brett was considerably younger than his step-brother the two of them got on remarkably well.

Matt had been great with him; taught him karate, taught him about cars and mechanics - as he had with Liv and Josh, too. Indeed, Matt had been the kind of older brother that anyone could have wished for.

Brett missed Matt when he was away, whose job took him all over The States, but whenever he came home the two of them just picked up from where they left off.

However, Brett had made a good life for himself on the islands even though Joe knew it was not necessarily the life he would have chosen had things turned out differently. But he never moaned or whined, he just got on with things, which was one of the traits Joe most admired about him.

"Everything alright?" Brett asked as he pulled the bike over beside them.

"Yeah, all done," said Joe. Then added, "Say, you seen Liv, Brett?"

"Er, no, not really," he replied somewhat guiltily, "I mean, she was out on the driveway about half hour ago, I think. I didn't really notice, sorry."

"You didn't notice, eh?" Said Ray mischievously, mercilessly teasing the lad he fondly regarded as his grandson.

"No," replied Brett firmly, staring daggers at the old man. "I didn't."

Ray raised his arms in surrender, "Okay, fair enough," but there was a knowing smile on his face as he spoke. He may have been old but he was definitely no fool.

"So what now?" Said Brett, changing the subject.

"Well I'm going back to get a shower, I'm covered in dust from the cove," said Joe.

"I'll come with you" said Ray. "You can give me a push - be good exercise for you."

"Thanks," said Joe with a smile.

"I could do with a shower, too, but I'm gonna check on the horses first." Said Sean.

"Do you want a hand, Unc?" Brett asked, desperate to keep busy. "I could give you a lift down to the stables?"

"Sure, that'd be great."

"Okay, good. See you two later then," said Brett to Joe and Ray as Sean climbed onto the back of the Sportster.

"See ya, son!" Said Joe.

"Yeah, be lucky," added Ray, not suspecting for a moment that all of them would be in much need of that advice long before the night was through.

***

The women of *Far Point* were attempting to maintain some semblance of normality even though each of them were acutely aware that their very existence was under threat.

They did not enjoy living under lock down or confining themselves, wherever possible, to the general proximity of their respective homes but it was a small price to pay for their safety and considerably more preferable than the alternative.

In keeping with this forced normality, Rose had just baked a cake which was cooling on the kitchen table and she was now upstairs with Sarah who was helping her to put fresh sheets on the beds. Life had to go on regardless of the circumstances.

Ruby, meanwhile, was downstairs in the living room, having a much needed nap. In her younger days very little could rattle her as in her time she had pretty much seen it all but recently age had caught up with her and now the most innocuous of things seemed to trouble her greatly. So with all the uncertainty surrounding Michael's disappearance she was beside herself with worry.

Even though Sarah was Michael's biological mother, it was Ruby who had raised him and she was desperately concerned for his safety, as was Ray but he disguised it much better.

It was not like Michael to go wandering off, especially not from the sanatorium, a place where he was always so contented. Furthermore, had he gone off on some random jaunt, it was even less likely that he would not have told someone at the sanatorium first.

Both Ruby, Ray and Sarah had come to the same dreadful conclusion as Joe and Sean; that something dreadful had befallen Michael and the thought of this was tearing them apart.

Ray was deeply concerned for his wife and feared that if the news came that they were all dreading the grief of it might possibly kill her.

As it was, Ruby had only slept sporadically since hearing of Michael's disappearance and now she was utterly exhausted. She had fallen into a deep sleep on the sofa, her knitting on her lap, and Rose and Sarah had decided to leave her alone to rest. It would do her good.

***

They had left the vans in a stand of trees a short distance from the gates and hiked the rest of the way through the densely wooded area that lined the approach road so as not to be seen.

Once they had reached the perimeter fence, the fifteen man squad - sixteen including Jez - had split into two teams of eight.

Their first objective was to take out the two gatehouses - silently, so as not to raise the alarm. Then the guardhouse itself, eliminating the entire security force before they had a chance to react to the incursion.

After that, they would swiftly move on up to the houses killing any and all that happened to get in their way - except, of course, for Joe Cassidy and Sean Noakes as they were to be left for Jez Vincenzi alone.

***

Freddie, *Far Point's* head of security, was absently flicking through the log book on the small desk inside the white painted hut that sat adjacent to the West Gate. It was just one of a series of random checks he had devised in order to keep his men on their toes during this heightened state of security.

The duty guard, an older man named Barclay stood beside him. Normally at around this time he would be half way through the sports section of his newspaper and two thirds of the way down his cup of strong, black coffee, but Freddie's presence had forced him to be more attentive.

Occasionally, Freddie would ask him a question about a certain entry in the book and Barclay would make a show of thoughtfully considering it for a moment before answering. Yet in truth, he and the other men thought Freddie's new regime to be all a bit pointless.

Eight security men guarding eight people. How hard could it be?

Surely all these spot checks and new-fangled security measures were over the top. After all, *who were these people they were guarding - the Royal family?*

Nevertheless, Barclay went through the motions of paying attention and Freddie made much of each meaningless entry in the book.

By the time both of them heard the slightest of noises behind them it was too late.

The serrated blade of the hunting knife slid between two of Freddie's ribs and then up into his heart, slicing his life away in an instant.

Before Barclay could understand what was happening, the

garrotte was around his throat, severing his carotid artery. He fought for the briefest time but was dead long before his killer laid his body down on the hut floor beside Freddie's.

The West Gate had been successfully secured.

***

Clinton Fine was manning the East Gate, listening to the ball game on the radio and thinking about Liv Noakes, wondering if there was any way that she might ever go out with him.

Sure, he worked for the estate and her dad was his boss but there might still be a chance. *Maybe?*

Suddenly he heard a faint rustling sound from outside the gatehouse and he sat up in his chair and looked out of the window into the dark. For a moment he thought it might be a snake as he had seen one before, slithering across the road into the woods.

A shiver ran down his spine, he did not like snakes.

Then he heard the noise again and this time it sounded like something much bigger. *A fox, possibly? Maybe even a deer?*

However, a flicker in the corner of his eye made him swivel round in his chair, which was when he saw the man standing at the door of the hut smiling at him. He was a half-caste, with tightly cropped hair and a jagged white scar above his right eye.

With horror, the young security guard saw the silenced gun in the man's hand and opened his mouth to scream but the only sound that could be heard was the almost inaudible *phut, phut* from the barrel of Bass Stone's automatic as he fired two bullets into Clinton's chest and the muffled thud as he fell off the chair and onto the wooden floor of the gatehouse.

The East Gate had also been secured.

***

One man in a *Far Point* baseball cap and dark blue uniform patrolled the Western perimeter another, identically attired, patrolled the Eastern boundary, both armed with flashlights and sidearms.

However, neither stood a chance when attacked by the concealed figures who had snipped their way through the wire and lain in wait for them in the shadows of the darkened estate.

The two guards had both been garrotted and despatched just as easily as Barclay had - without a sound uttered from their lips which may have alerted those they had been employed to protect.

Which left just the three off-duty men in the guardhouse.

They were playing cards when Rocco Pistoli entered and all of them died within two seconds of seeing him walk through the door. Each of them shot in the dead centre of their foreheads, killed with barely a sound from his silenced automatic. Three sitting targets, three perfect shots.

This was just too easy.

***

Jez Vincenzi stood at the bottom of the hill, looking up at the two big, white, clapper board houses, watching his plan unfold.

The elegant homes stood proudly on the twin bluffs of the undulating cliff top, the calm, Caribbean sea painted black as oil in the background.

A secure, unbreachable stronghold - or so their owners had so arrogantly assumed yet, as Jez's small force fanned out across the hillside, infiltrating the estate like a virus, he took pleasure in knowing that this arrogance would be Cassidy and Noakes' downfall.

Arrogant and stupid, he thought, as he again reached into his jacket and removed the small vile of white powder.

Just another small hit to keep the engine revving nicely.

As he snorted the powder off the back of his hand, he watched three of his men entering the stables; their job to torch it - raze it to the ground; wood, brick, animals and all.

He smiled.

Then he looked over at the house to the right of his gaze, and saw his dark menacing minions swarming around it.

More of them were entering the house on the left, shortly to be joined by the others from the stables.

Everything was going perfectly to plan. Noakes and Cassidy did not stand a chance.

But then suddenly a gunshot rang out and everything went to hell.

***

The engine died in a huge cloud of steam a mile or so from the estate, midway down the heavily wooded approach road.

Cursing her rotten luck, Liv lifted the hood but even with the light of the headlamps it was impossible to see what the hell had gone wrong as it was just too dark.

She needed a flashlight and her tools and she had neither.

She kicked the front tyre with frustration and swore again, "Sonofabitch!" She yelled. This was not at all what was supposed to happen.

The only thing for it was to walk the remaining distance to *Far Point*, grab her tools and beg someone to bring her back so that she could fix the goddamn car. This would not sit well with her father.

Boy, he was gonna be mad!

It was a warm night so Liv shrugged off her overalls and threw them onto the back seat, leaving her in just a vest top and Levi cut-offs for the walk back, which would be much cooler.

And if there was one thing she needed to do at present it was cool off.

So, leaving the stranded Monte Carlo where it was, Liv stomped off angrily down the dark, deserted road that would eventually lead her to *Far Point*.

However, before too long, she soon began to enjoy the walk; the peace and quiet, the smell of the trees carrying on the warm night breeze, it was exhilarating.

She was completely unafraid of the menacing dark shadows of

the forest or what might lurk beyond in its hidden depths.

Indeed, her first indication that something was amiss came much later when she noticed two black vans parked in a stand of trees a little way from the roadside.

Her eyes were now accustomed to the dark so her vision was completely unimpaired by the cover of night and it seemed to her that someone had purposely attempted to conceal the vehicles from view.

Alarm bells started to ring in her head and immediately she broke into a run, her Converse trainers crunching on the loose gravel road as she rushed home, desperate to warn the others of the possible danger.

However, her heart sank when she was within a few yards of reaching the East Gate and she skidded to a halt.

The gate was wide open and the gatehouse was seemingly empty.

Her first thought was for Clinton and she raced to the tiny hut and burst in through the open door but immediately pulled up sharp, slapping her hand quickly over her mouth to prevent the scream from escaping.

Clinton Fine, the handsome, fun-loving young man with the irresistible smile whom she had been flirting with barely an hour earlier was now lying dead on the floor surrounded by a huge pool of blood. He was on his stomach with his face turned to the side; his skin grey and his glassy eyes open.

Liv was shocked and for a second she could not move.

But then she thought of the others - of her father and Sarah, of her Uncle Joe and Aunt Rose, of Ray and Ruby.

And then of Brett.

Quickly, she darted out of the gatehouse and looked beyond the gate, up to the estate and the houses on the cliff top. She could see the dark figures of many men swarming across the lawns.

One man in particular was only a short distance away, his back towards her. To Liv, he appeared to be the one in command, orchestrating things from a strategic vantage point whilst his men set about their dreadful work.

Was that Jez Vincenzi? Liv wondered briefly.

But it was merely a passing thought as her main concern was to alert the others - to warn them of the impending danger and hope to God that she was in time.

Thinking clearly now, she nipped back into the gatehouse and rolled Clinton over onto his back, apologising to him under her breath for being so rough.

His gun was in its holster and his flashlight was tucked into his belt. Hurriedly, Liv took them both. She pushed the flashlight into the back of her shorts and then took hold of the pistol with both hands.

She crept out of the gatehouse once more and planted herself just inside the gate, her feet apart, her shoulders relaxed, then she took aim at the intruder she assumed to be Jez Vincenzi.

And fired.

Chapter Nine

A floorboard creaked beside the sofa upon which Ruby Walsh was napping. It made only the slightest of sounds, but it was enough to rouse her from her slumber.

Bobby Assante froze in his tracks just a few feet away from her, cursing the heavy boots he was wearing for their lack of stealth. Then he shot a guilty glance at Bass Stone who was standing directly in front of the old woman and shrugged his shoulders apologetically.

Yet Stone merely smiled. What was about to happen was inevitable, it made no odds to him whether the old crone was awake or not - although out of preference, awake was definitely better.

Ruby stirred and opened her weary eyes - eyes that had seen much in a life filled with colour, vivacity and an ample portion of wickedness. Yet she had also known heartbreak and tragedy too and now, with the disappearance of Michael, they had become known to her again.

Since marrying Ray Reece her life had transformed and the last ten years, spent with him and Michael, on this paradise island had been the best of her almost eight decades. Yet now she was old and tired and Ray was an invalid - although he would be loathed to admit it - and the worry for their adopted son had taken its toll on both of them.

Ruby could not imagine her life without Michael in it. Aside from Ray, he was her everything; a gift that she never thought she would ever deserve.

But Sean and Sarah had given her that gift and even though he was their son by birth and they loved him desperately. No one could love him like Ruby did.

No one had forgiven his faults and failings or his youthful petulance like she had. Indeed, from the moment he was entrusted to her care, Ruby had loved him unconditionally - warts and all, through thick and thin.

And without him life would be utterly unthinkable.

So when she roused, startled to see Bass Stone standing in front of her, she knew without question that Michael was dead and that very shortly she would be joining him.

She regarded Stone for a moment, remembering him as a little boy even though he had no memory of her.

He was a nasty, spiteful child with an evil temper she recalled; a bully who always craved what the other children had - whether he had use for it or not.

This attitude earned him the nickname 'Bad To The Bone Stone' and in Ruby's opinion it was fully deserved.

Stone's mother used to be one of Ruby's girls; a sad, troubled young woman who made a lot of wrong decisions. She had fallen in with a bad lot - namely an alcoholic Jamaican dock worker - who left her pregnant and destitute with her half-caste son, Bass.

Ruby tried to help her, offering support and a roof over her head, but she would not accept and instead left the safety of her employ to go it alone.

Occasionally, as the years passed, Ruby would see her on the streets of South London touting for business. Each time she looked slightly more dishevelled, slightly more downtrodden. Sometimes the boy would be with her, sometimes he would not - Bass always went his own way even as a child.

Then, one day, Ruby saw her no more.

Word had it that Bass had killed her himself - stealing the money she had earned in an effort to feed them. It was never proven but Ruby never doubted it for a moment.

As he got older, Stone was forever in trouble and Ruby suspected that either prison or a gruesome death in some back alley awaited him but then she left London and never thought of Bass Stone again.

Not until very recently.

And now here he was, in *her* paradise, in *her* living room. A knife in his hand.

Ruby looked directly into his eyes, recognising the jagged scar and remembering well the night he got it; his head sliced with a broken bottle in a fight outside *The Golden Gloves* when he was no more than thirteen against three older lads. Yet Stone had emerged victorious.

Now he was here, staring back at her.

"He's dead, isn't he?" Ruby asked quietly, already knowing the answer but needing to be absolutely certain.

Bass tilted his head quizzically, "Who?" He asked. After all there had been so many.

"My boy. Michael," responded Ruby, her voice barely a whisper. "You killed him didn't you?"

Bass smiled. "Oh, him. Then yes, of course he's dead. Very, very dead indeed."

Ruby felt as if she had been kicked in the stomach and emitted a low gasp of utter despair. Even though she had been prepared, there had always been a sliver of hope, a small glimmer of light that burned in expectation of Michael coming back to her. Yet now it had been brutally extinguished.

"I shot him myself," continued Stone gleefully, "watched as his blood spilled all over the floor. I'll say this for him though, for a skinny fucker he sure had a lot of blood."

Ruby whimpered involuntarily. "Joe and Sean are gonna kill you," she hissed, "and I'm gonna be laughing in my grave when they do!"

"I've got news for you, darlin' - your precious boys ain't gonna be living after tonight either, so you're all gonna be in your graves together. You and your whole fuckin' family."

Suddenly Ruby was seized by the desire to protect those that she loved. She snatched up a knitting needle from her lap and desperately jabbed it in Stone's direction but he was well out of reach and she was far too slow for a man such as he.

He laughed at her derisively as Bobby Assante grabbed her shoulders from behind and pinned her back on the sofa.

But Ruby was not done, she would not die without a fight and she shot her arm backwards and stabbed Assante straight through the throat. He squealed loudly and fell away behind the sofa in agony, a gruesome fountain of blood jettisoning from the mortal wound.

However, as Ruby grinned with the sure knowledge that she had disabled one of her attackers, Bass Stone pushed his hunting knife deeply into the soft flesh of her stomach.

She glared at him with angry defiance as the cold steel slid into her, the pain of it no greater than that which already filled her heart.

Then she blinked as Bass twisted the blade and pulled it out slowly. Ruby could hear the suck of her innards clawing against the shiny metal of the knife as it withdrew from her.

She coughed and felt warm blood spill onto her lips, although there was a smile on her face from the sure knowledge that she would soon find Michael waiting for her in the next life.

She had no desire to fight now, merely to just succumb, to welcome death as it rushed towards her. However, as she allowed the darkness to wash over her, she watched in horror as Bass Stone turned to see her husband, Ray, emerging through the doorway in his wheelchair.

But by then it was too late to cry out, too late to warn him of the imminent danger, because at that moment everything went black.

***

There was nothing that Ray Reece loved more than a slice of Rose's homemade chocolate cake so when he saw it there, freshly baked and sitting on the kitchen table where she had left it to cool off, temptation got the better of him and he helped himself to a large slice.

After watching Brett and Sean ride off on the Sportster to the stables, Joe had wheeled Ray back to the house along the cliff path, leaving the old man in the kitchen whilst he ran upstairs to take a quick shower and wash off all the dust from the cove.

The house was quiet and Ray suspected the women were somewhere about, busying themselves as was their want. He knew that they, like all of them, were trying to keep themselves occupied, trying to keep their minds off Jez Vincenzi and Bass Stone and what they may have done to Michael.

However, try as he might, Ray could not help but think about Michael.

In days gone by, he would have been out there looking for him, trying to save him - indeed, that had been both Sean and Sarah's first impulse, too - but common sense prevailed. None of them knew where Michael was and their best hope was that he would find his way home to them eventually.

Yet none of them truly believed he would. Not now.

Ray had always been an amiable soul; a big-hearted, larger-than-life character. Famously fun loving and mischievous, he often played the fool. Indeed, the impression most had of him was as a wild-haired, one-eyed, scallywag.

But Ray was much more than that.

He was something of a legendary figure in South London and certainly one of the toughest to ever emerge from there - back in the days when tough men were two-a-penny. He was feared and respected in equal measure and although his amiable manner ensured that he had many friends, his fearsome reputation suggested that it was far better to have him as an ally than an enemy.

And as an ally, no one could want for better, particularly not Joe, as Ray Reece had stood beside him through thick and thin. Joe knew, without question, that Ray would always have his back and would fight with him to the bitter end, no matter the cost.

Indeed, if toughness alone meant anything, then it should have been Ray, not his brother, Vinnie, who became head of the South London underworld. It should have been him, too, that took over when Vinnie died, not Joe - even though Joe had been a reluctant heir.

But Ray was simply not interested.

He wanted a life of fun, of no complications or responsibilities and it was a lifestyle he excelled at for many years; a brawling, boozing, bawdy bachelor is how he could best be described in his wild days.

But then he fell in love with Ruby and his whole outlook changed.

She and Michael became his world. Joe, too, whom he looked upon as a son - and latterly Joe's whole extended family became Ray's family too.

They were all that was important to him now and without them he was nothing.

However, Ruby stood at the pinnacle. Since marrying her he had found a happiness that he never previously knew existed and even though South London would always be the place he called home, his life with her on this island paradise had been nothing short of idyllic.

But now that was over and Ray knew that one way or another, life would never be the same again.

Moreover, he suspected that Ruby would not be the same either and this troubled him greatly.

He had been attempting to lighten things, to keep jovial and maintain a sense of calm, assuring his wife that Michael was most probably just lost somewhere, that he would undoubtedly turn up sooner or later.

Yet it was all a charade. He knew it and so did Ruby.

But sitting there all alone in the kitchen, as he prepared to bite into an enormous chunk of Rose's delicious chocolate cake, he finally allowed himself to drop the carefree facade.

His shoulders drooped and his head slumped; the cake which just moments ago looked so inviting now sat untouched and unwanted on the plate, Ray's appetite mysteriously evaporating.

He was tired all of a sudden and his limbs ached. He rubbed his legs and winced slightly; old wounds and old pain, his rakish past at last catching up with him.

Again he thought of Michael as he so often had since hearing of his disappearance. Then he thought of Ruby and the torture he knew she was going through with all this damned uncertainty and this insufferable waiting.

It occurred to Ray that he had perhaps been selfish in helping Joe and Sean with their preparations in the cove - which had been his way of keeping his mind off things.

But thinking about it now, it would possibly have been more considerate to stay home and comfort Ruby. Indeed, she needed his support more now than ever before.

Immediately he decided to go and find his wife to make amends. So, putting the cake down, he wheeled himself out of the kitchen with his trusty shotgun still resting on his lap and headed for the living room.

However, halfway across the wide, wood panelled hallway, he heard hushed voices coming from the direction he was headed. He assumed it to be Ruby, although he could not distinguish what was being said as his hearing was not as good as it once was.

Unperturbed, he wheeled himself in through the open door of the living room to see a large man with his back towards him.

Alarmed by the sight of this intruder, Ray pulled up sharply, causing the rubber tyres of his wheelchair to squeak noisily on the polished wooden floor.

Hearing the sound, the strange man quickly turned to face Ray who immediately recognised him as Bass Stone. Momentarily he was shocked but what concerned Ray far more was that in the very same instant, he also saw Ruby and the dreadful, heartbreaking image of her made his blood run cold.

To his absolute horror, he realised Bass Stone had killed her and as this devastating fact registered in his brain he decided that he no longer wanted to live either.

But the instinct for survival was burned deeply into his DNA and desperately he grabbed up the shotgun from his lap. As he did so, Ray heard the sound of distant gunfire but he had no time to consider it further as Bass Stone was already pulling on the hilt of his holstered automatic and in less than two seconds he would be firing it directly at Ray's head.

***

Joe bounded up the stairs and strode across the landing to his and Rose's bedroom to find his wife and sister already in there plumping pillows and tucking in sheets.

"Hi, Darlin'," he said to Rose, giving her a quick peck on the lips. "Everything okay?"

"Yep, it's all quiet. Where's Brett and Ray?"

"Brett's gone with Sean to the stables and Ray's downstairs in the kitchen."

Sarah smiled at Rose. "There goes the chocolate cake then!"

Rose rolled her eyes, knowing that her sister-in-law was right. Ray's love of cake was famous.

"Did you see Liv?" Sarah asked Joe.

"No, but I think she's working on that car of hers - least she was a while ago. Probably back home now. He says he hasn't but I think Brett's been secretly checking on her."

Rose smiled wickedly. "I bet he has."

"Stop it!" Sarah admonished. "Mind you, I suspect Liv might've been checking him out, too."

"Makes me laugh how they don't think we've noticed," said Joe.

"Well I think it's sweet," Rose said.

"Me too," agreed Sarah.

"Hmm, well let's just see, shall we," added Joe, heading for the en-suite. "Could cause problems down the line. Say, have I got a towel Rosie? I wanna take a quick shower."

"Oh don't be such a grump," said his wife. "I think they'd make a lovely couple - and your towel's on the airer where it usually is."

"Thanks."

"Yeah, go take a shower, grumpy!" Sarah teased, "Maybe you'll find your sense of romance while you're in there!"

"What do you mean?" Said Joe, with a wink, "I'm nothing if not romantic - ain't that right, Rosie."

Yet before his wife had an opportunity to deny it, he shut himself in the en-suite.

A moment later they heard the shower running.

***

Suitably clean, Joe stepped out of the shower feeling instantly refreshed and quickly towelled off.

Once dry, he ran a comb through his dark hair and slipped on some fresh underwear but then, just as he was pulling on his jeans, he heard the sound of a distant gunshot.

He paused for an instant, just to be certain, yet in that moment a shotgun blasted downstairs.

He knew then, without question, that *Far Point* was under attack and that Ray was in trouble.

Without wasting another second, Joe burst into the bedroom to find Rose and Sarah anxiously huddled together. However, before he could say a word he heard more gunshots and yet another explosion of shotgun fire, indeed, it sounded as though all hell had broken loose.

Whilst he was worried about Ray, he knew the old pirate was well capable of taking care of himself, so his immediate concern was for the safety of Rose and Sarah.

"You need to leave, *now!*" He told them. "Use the back stairs and get to the cove as soon as you can. Take one of the golf buggies - it'll be quicker."

The women nodded as Joe grabbed a T-shirt out of his drawer and flung it on. From the same drawer, he pulled out a small snub-nosed revolver and checked it was loaded before handing it to Rose. "Here, take this," he said. "Use it if you have to - don't hesitate." He looked at her with fierce intent. "Understand?"

"I understand," she said.

"And Rosie, Sarah—?"

They looked at him.

"—Please be careful."

They nodded. "You, too," whispered Rose. "You make sure you come back to me Joe Cassidy, you hear me?"

"Don't worry," he said. "I'll be fine."

Then he crossed to the bed and reached underneath, pulling out a *Browning 9mm* semi-automatic that he had stashed there. He released the magazine to check it was full before snapping it back in, then pulled the slide to be certain that a round was in the chamber.

Satisfied, he then sidled stealthily over to the bedroom door and checked their exit. It was clear, no signs of life. He signalled to the women to move and they did, quickly.

"Go. Hurry," Joe whispered as they slid past him and scurried along the landing to the back stairs whilst he covered their exit.

Once he saw them disappear through the door that led through to the back stairs, he left his vantage point and stalked silently down the main staircase, his bare feet making no sound on the wooden treads as he guarded his descent with the *Browning*.

Once down, he made a very quick sweep of the hallway before heading into the living room where he knew the sound of the shotgun had come from, no doubt in his mind that it was Ray who had fired it.

However, the sight that greeted him as he crept into the room, was nothing short of horrific.

***

Even though Ray was old and crippled, he was just a split-second faster than Bass. He had no time to aim properly but managed to fire the first barrel in Stone's general direction. However, it was not as accurate as it might have been as he was trying desperately not to catch Ruby in the scatter of shot.

Stone dived urgently aside, narrowly avoiding the full impact of the blast which would have ripped him in two had he not been so quick to react.

However, a few pellets buried themselves in his upper arm and ruined his aim so that the bullet he fired in return only hit Ray in the shoulder, not the head.

Bass fired again as he frantically scampered away. In his desperate bid to escape the deadly power of the twelve-bore, he charged headlong into the closed french windows - smashing both doors to smithereens as his hefty bulk ploughed through them with sheer brute force.

As he made his escape, another blast from Ray's shotgun

crashed into the wall beside Stone's head, causing the door frame to explode in a hail of brick and wood. Bass' face caught the brunt of the detonation and in the shower of splinters that rained down on him, a needle sharp slither of oak pierced the cornea of his right eye and buried itself deeply in his pupil, blinding him instantly.

Bass yelled with pain and slapped a hand over the agonising wound, but still he kept on going, blundering determinedly through the shattered framework and out onto the veranda. Howeve, as he thundered off into the darkness, he knew the injury would prevent him from playing any further part in the gruesome work that was still yet to be done there that night.

***

The first thing Joe saw was Ray's blood spattered wheelchair, turned on its side and empty.

Beyond that, lying on the floor beside the sofa, was the body of a man he did not recognise, a knitting needle sticking grotesquely out of his throat.

Then Joe saw Ray himself, a bullet wound in his shoulder and another high in his chest, the result of Stone's second shot. Both looked bad but much to Joe's relief the old man was still alive.

The most shocking sight, however, was of Ruby. She looked deathly pale; her once bright red hair now silvery white, giving her an almost ghostly air.

Somehow Ray had managed to drag himself up beside his wife and was now holding her in his arms, tears streaming down his face.

They were both soaked in blood from their injuries, making it a grisly, yet truly heartbreaking scene.

For a second Joe was convinced Ruby was dead but then he saw her eyes flicker slightly and he rushed to be by her side.

Mortified by what had happened, Joe gently took her hand. She, along with Sean's mum, had been the closest he had ever come to knowing what it was like to have a mother.

He looked at Ray in desperation but the old man's eyes said it all. She was beyond hope and fading fast.

Joe closed his eyes, the pain of it almost too much to bear. But then he looked at Ray again. "You okay?" He whispered.

"No son," he said, his voice weak and gruff. "I ain't." Yet the words only partially related to his injuries.

Joe nodded his understanding. There was nothing he could possibly say which would give his friend any comfort.

Then, in a voice so faint that it was barely audible, Ruby said, "Joe?"

"I'm here, Ruby," he replied attentively.

She was wheezing, her breathing laboured and slow, speaking was clearly an effort but she was determined to get the words out. "It was Bass Stone," she gasped. "He's killed me and he—"

Momentarily she was unable to continue, the pain from her wound and the pain in her heart making it hard to go on.

"Save your strength Ruby, please don't—"

"No." She said firmly, her eyes suddenly wide as she stared fiercely at Joe. "He killed Michael. He told me. My boy is dead."

"My God, Ruby. I'm so sorry. Truly I am. I never thought for a moment it would ever come to—"

"You stop that Joe Cassidy!" She admonished, squeezing his hand with her last reserves of strength. "It's not your fault - nor Sean's - you hear me?"

Tears filled Joe's eyes as he listened to her speak.

"You've been good boys, the pair of you. Good *sons* and I'm proud of you. I've had a good innings. Me and Ray both have and these last years I wouldn't have swapped for the world."

"Ruby, I don't know what to say, I just wish—"

"Wish nothing," she interrupted, her voice now less than a whisper. "Just promise me you'll settle the score for Michael."

"I will Ruby. I promise."

The old woman nodded almost imperceptibly, "Good boy," she said, "I know I can always count on you."

Then she turned her attention to her husband. "Save your tears, darlin," she said. "We'll be seeing each other soon enough and both me and Michael will be there to welcome you."

Ray was almost too grief stricken to speak, "See you soon, darlin'. I love you," was all he could manage before being overcome with emotion.

"I love you too my beautiful, glorious, scoundrel of a man," she said.

And then, without another word, Ruby Reece quietly passed away.

Chapter Ten

Sarah and Rose made it down the back stairs and out through the kitchen without being seen.

Two golf buggies were parked at the rear of the property which were often used to ferry items between the houses. Ruby had also used one to save her the effort of walking to Sean's place which, even though only a short distance away, had become more of a struggle in latter years.

Tonight, however, they were to provide a means of escape.

Quickly, Sarah jumped in behind the wheel of the nearest one whilst Rose climbed into the passenger seat. A moment later the little buggy whirred into motion as Sarah pressed her foot down hard on the accelerator.

The buggy was not especially fast but it was certainly quicker than running and, more importantly, it made very little sound as it sped away from the house and up onto the cliff path.

However, once they had emerged from the shadow of the building, Sarah was alarmed to see the glow of flames on the other side of the bluff. Then, to her horror, she realised that her house was on fire and as she stared wide-eyed in disbelief, she saw that the stables were alight, too.

"My God, Rose!" She exclaimed, "The house and stables are on fire - the horses, they'll be burned alive!" Then she remembered what

Joe had told them and terror filled her heart. "Christ, Rosie! Sean and Brett are in the stables, aren't they? They're going to be killed!"

Rose stared aghast. "Oh, Jesus, no!" She cried, slapping her hand to her mouth in dread. Yet before she could say more, she caught a flicker of orange out the corner of her eye and turned to see that her house was on fire, too.

"Bloody hell, Sarah, look," she said, nudging her sister-in-law in the ribs. "The bastards have torched our place, too!"

"What—?"

"Joe, Ray and Ruby are in there," Rose yelled, "we must go back!"

"No, Rosie. We can't," replied Sarah, sounding anguished yet determined. "You promised Joe, remember? You've got to trust him. He'll get them to safety, I know he will. We'll just get in his way!"

Rose knew that Sarah was right, although running away did not feel right to either of them.

"But what about Sean and Brett?" Said Rose, "Shouldn't we try to help them?"

The buggy slowed momentarily as Sarah pondered this terrible dilemma. Years ago, she had not been equipped to deal with such dramas, the harrowing events of her youth making her understandably fragile - indeed, she had locked herself away in a self-imposed coma for over twenty years to escape them.

But she was strong now. Determined. Sean and Joe had proved to her that she was capable of anything - that she could survive the worst life could throw at her as they, themselves had.

"No," she said at last, her voice firm and decisive. "Sean and Brett will be fine. I *know* they will and they will not appreciate us getting in their way. We must go to the cove like Joe told us to."

Rose stared at her sister-in-law for a moment then nodded. "Yes. Okay, that's what we'll—"

Before she could finish speaking, a black-clad figure rushed out of the darkness on her side of the vehicle. The man, dressed in fatigues and army boots was brandishing a large hunting knife and growling wildly as he sprinted towards them.

"Quick, Sarah!" Rose yelled, "Move it - now!"

Sarah turned in time to see the man bearing down on the buggy, roaring like an angry bear, the knife held high in readiness to stab down into Rose's heart.

"Shoot him!" Sarah cried as she pressed her foot down hard on the gas, "shoot the sonofabitch!"

Suddenly Rose remembered the little snub-nosed pistol in her hand that Joe had given her and immediately she raised it.

The man was less than five feet away now. Two more seconds and she would have been dead.

But instead, Rose fired. Once, twice, three times.

She saw the shock register on the man's face, then watched the knife drop and his legs buckle as his hurtling body collided heavily with the side of the buggy, rocking it sidewards. The wheels bumped roughly over his head as he fell to the ground and Sarah powered onwards.

However, in that brief moment of relief, when they thought the immediate danger had passed, two more black-clad figures came racing out of the darkness.

One was so close that Sarah had to swerve the buggy in an effort to miss him, yet she still managed to catch him a glancing blow.

She heard him cry out in pain and then watched as he fell away out of sight.

By now, though, the other man had his hands on the rail at the back of the buggy and was busily trying to clamber on.

Rose was swivelling in her seat, attempting to get a clear shot, but the track was uneven and with Sarah swerving the buggy all over the place it was difficult to keep the gun still.

Then suddenly, the man was inside the buggy, his bulk

seemingly massive in the tight space.

Before Rose had a chance to react, the brute grabbed a handful of her long auburn hair, pinning her backwards so that she could barely move. In the same instant, he locked a muscular forearm around Sarah's throat who was still trying desperately to steer the vehicle and prevent it from plummeting over the edge of the cliff.

In her peripheral vision, as she struggled to be free, Sarah could see her house to the side of her, the fire now raging and out of control, flames clawing at the upstairs windows and licking the scorched eaves.

The smell of burnt wood stung her nose as the buggy ploughed into a dense, black cloud of noxious smoke, the toxic fumes searing her throat and charring her lungs, yet still she fought.

Sarah could feel something banging against her chest. "Take the gun!" Rose yelled, her head still pinned back as she blindly tried to hand Sarah the pistol, "Kill the bastard."

With the man's arm tight around her throat, slowly choking her to death as she sightlessly tried to navigate the haphazard track, knowing that the buggy was just feet from the edge, Sarah felt for the weapon.

A second later Rose slapped it against her hand and she snatched it up.

As they finally burst through the cloud of acrid smoke into the clear night air, Sarah saw with horror that they were heading directly for the edge.

With less than ten feet to go, she raised the gun over head until she felt it butt up against something hard behind her.

Hoping that this object was the man's head, she shut her eyes and squeezed the trigger.

The shot was deafening, yet suddenly she was free, the man's arm falling immediately from her throat as a hideous shower of blood and bone rained down on her.

Clearly she had found her target but with no time to celebrate, she shouted, "Jump Rose! Jump now!" Then, without a second to spare, she leaped from the speeding golf buggy.

As she smacked down in the soft grass just inches from the lip, Sarah watched the buggy plummet headlong over the edge. It fell gracefully for a long, silent moment, then crashed down hard on the rocks below, smashing noisily to pieces.

"You okay?" She heard Rose ask.

"Oh, thank God!" Sarah replied, scrambling to her feet and rushing towards her. "I didn't know if you got out or not!"

The two women embraced. "Yeah, I did - thanks to you."

"You mean thanks to your quick thinking," Sarah replied.

"Well, maybe. But we're not out of it yet."

They broke off the hug and looked about them, seeing both houses and the stables completely engulfed in flames.

"So what now?" Sarah said.

"Well, we do what you said," answered Rose. "We follow Joe's orders and head to the cove."

"And then?"

"And then we pray."

***

Gus Golino rubbed his thigh in the spot where the golf buggy had hit him. Fortunately it had only been a glancing blow and nothing was broken but he was going to have one hell of a bruise in the morning.

However, as ex-Italian Special Forces, Golino prided himself on being tough and a little bruising meant nothing to him, especially when two women still needed killing.

He jumped up and hobbled away, shaking off the injury, managing to maintain a reasonable running pace as he followed the direction in which the golf buggy was headed, knowing that he could not be far behind.

A few minutes later, he emerged through a thick cloud of black smoke that was pothering out across the cliff top from the burning house up on the bluff, to see the two women in the distance.

Keeping his eyes on them, he smiled, then again broke into a steady trot, still limping, but the exercise easing the stiffness.

As he watched, he saw the women suddenly vanish as if they had perhaps taken some hidden pathway down to the beach. Yet he was so close now that he could almost smell them and soon enough, they would be in his grasp.

Golino's loins stirred at the thought of this; his injured leg would not prevent him from having some fun with the two ladies before they died.

***

Sean and Brett each took a large bale of hay from the barn that adjoined the stables, then set about feeding the horses.

The spacious stable block had two rows of ten neat stalls separated by a central concrete avenue - Sean took the right side and Brett the left.

The building itself was immaculately maintained; each stall and trough pristinely kept and the central walkway swept to perfection.

Indeed, Sean and Sarah went to painstaking lengths to ensure that each animal was not only beautifully groomed but also happy and well cared for in facilities that were quite simply outstanding. This love and commitment to their highly valued stock had earned them the patronage of a most discerning and loyal clientele.

As for Brett, he had helped out in the stables many times in the past so needed no instruction on how things were done.

This evening, however, he was merely required to feed and water the animals on his side of the aisle and was grateful for the opportunity to be kept busy.

He and Sean set about their work; filling each trough and whispering soft words to each horse in turn, making sure that each had a fair share of fuss.

Yet, tonight, the horses seemed unsettled and far from content which was most unusual. In fact, they seemed positively skittish and Sean wondered at first if they might be picking up on the heightened anxiety that presently surrounded *Far Point*.

In his experience, horses were highly intuitive animals so it was entirely likely that they knew something was wrong.

However, as he fed and watered Chica, his prized, chestnut mare, the normally mild-mannered horse seemed almost scared and was dancing around nervously in her stall.

"It's okay, girl," Sean cooed, as he rubbed her nose and tried to calm her. "Everything's gonna be—"

But then suddenly Chica reared up on her hind legs and whinnied loudly, clearly scared out of her wits.

What is more, all the other horses started to neigh and whinny and kick in their stalls.

"What's the matter with them?" Brett asked as Sarah's Palomino kicked over her trough and began to buck and rear in fright.

"I dunno, I—" began Sean, but as he looked down the avenue towards the bottom end of the stables, he thought for a moment he saw a shadow of something. A person, he thought. *Was it Liv or Sarah?*

"Hello?" He called. "Liv - is that you?"

By this time the horses were going wild and the noise they were making was almost deafening.

And then Sean saw why and a second later, so did Brett.

An orange flicker of flame began to creep around the last stall at the far end of the stables. "Fire!" Both Sean and Brett shouted simultaneously; each staring in horror as the initial flame was quickly accompanied by another, then another and within seconds the whole stall was ablaze.

With the wooden building as dry as tinder and an abundance

of hay to act as kindling, Sean knew the fire would spread with terrifying speed. Therefore, his first thought was for his valuable livestock, although their monetary worth played no part in his reasoning.

"Quick, we need to get the horses out - now!" He yelled, "Open the gates, let 'em run free!" As he spoke, he released the latch on Chica's gate and swung it open so that she could escape. The mare needed no encouragement as she bolted from the stall and out through the open side of the stable block at the top end of the building.

The Palomino gave chase behind her as Brett followed Sean's lead, rushing from stall to stall, setting the horses free.

Sean was hurriedly doing the same on the other side of the block, steadily working his way down the stalls, each horse desperately scared, terrified of the fire which had now fully taken hold, engulfing at least two of the stalls on Sean's side and one on Brett's.

Thankfully, these stalls were unoccupied as due to a recent sale the stables were only half full. This meant there were ten horses only, five on either side of the walkway. Thanks to Sean's quick reaction, seven of these had already been released and were now running free across the *Far Point Estate*, out of harms way.

However, as Brett fought to release the latch on the eighth stall, he was certain he heard a gun shot through the melee of whinnies, hoof beats and roaring flames.

"You hear that?" He shouted to Sean.

"Yeah, sounded like gunfire!" He yelled back, his face fraught with worry. "You go check - but be careful. I'll take care of the horses!"

Brett nodded his agreement and sprinted out of the stables.

As Sean released the final horse on his side, he heard yet more gunfire. He thought about Sarah and Liv and everyone else at *Far Point* and hoped to God that they were okay. In just a few moments he would go and help but first he had to save the horses.

He ran across the aisle to free the last two animals and at that moment Brett ran back into the stables and called out to him.

"Sean - we're being attacked. Intruders are all over the estate."

"Jesus!" Sean exclaimed.

But there was worse news yet to come.

"Liv's in trouble!" Brett shouted over the din of the horses. "I can see her, she's down by the East Gate - I've gotta help her!"

Sean's immediate instinct was to save Liv - to forget about the stables and go help his daughter - but he could not just let the horses burn as that would be just too diabolical.

He felt dreadfully torn between duty and humanity, but in the end humanity won out.

"Yes - save her, Brett!" Sean begged, knowing that he had no choice but to stay with the horses. Yet he was still desperately scared for his daughter, "Please - I know you can do it. Save my little girl for me!"

"Don't worry - I will, I swear it." Replied Brett firmly, understanding the dilemma Sean faced and respecting his impossibly difficult decision. "But if we can't make it back to the cove, I'll get her out on *The Rachel!*"

Sean nodded. He would trust Brett with his life. What is more, he would trust him with Liv's life. If anyone could save her then Brett Cassidy certainly could. "Go, boy. Go now!" Sean yelled. "Go save Liv!"

And with that Brett was gone.

***

The fire was raging as Sean pulled back the final latch, burning his hand on the scolding metal.

The horse was frantically bucking and kicking, rearing up and whinnying in terror as it skittered anxiously around the stall. Yet before Sean had a chance to swing the gate open, the scared animal leapt forward and crashed into him, throwing him backwards onto his butt.

174

The horse continued to buck and kick, unaware that the unlatched gate was sitting ajar.

Sean looked up, desperate to help the terrified horse but instead saw a large man in black fatigues staring down at him.

This was the fire bug. The one who had set light to the stables and destroyed all that Sean and Sarah had worked for; whose shadow Sean had seen just a minute or two earlier.

The man smiled, knowing that his new boss would surely be pleased with the prize he had found.

However, at that moment, the frightened horse saw its opportunity and made a sudden bolt for freedom. Rearing up, it forcefully kicked the gate wide open, taking the intruder completely by surprise.

The man turned with alarm as the horse loomed over him, too late to react as it crashed back down catching him hard on the forehead with one of its lethal hooves and opening up a wide, bloody gash.

The dazed man staggered backwards as the panicked horse charged past him, kicking out with its hind legs as it went. Another hoof thumped the man in the stomach which sent him sprawling backwards into the blazing inferno that had consumed the opposite stall. The fire enveloped him instantly; his terrible screams soon quashed by the deafening blaze as his body burned.

But for Sean the danger had still not passed.

As he climbed to his feet, he heard the crackle and splinter of wood breaking above his head. He looked up to see the fire ravaged central beam, which was now charred and blistering under the volcanic heat of the blaze.

In that instant, he heard another almighty creak as the whole ceiling shifted.

With the horses all free, he dashed out of the flaming stable block into the dark uncertainty of the night, not knowing if his wife and daughter were alive or dead.

Chapter Eleven

The bullet missed killing Jez by the slightest fraction and instead sliced his cheek as it whizzed past.

"Jesus fucking Christ!" He exclaimed as he dived to the ground for cover.

Rocco Pistoli, just back from killing the three off-duty men in the guardhouse, saw his boss go down and rushed over to him.

"Boss - you okay?" He asked, kneeling by his side just as Liv fired again. This time the shot struck the ground an inch in front of Pistoli's knee and immediately he ducked, although his eyes were on the girl who was firing.

"Some asshole is shooting at me - *do I fucking look okay?*" Jez yelled, his hand pressed to his bleeding cheek.

But Rocco's attention was now on Liv.

She realised quickly that he had seen her and as he sprang up and bolted towards her she fired off another couple of rounds. But the shots were hurried and wild and before she could fire again Pistoli ploughed into her, grabbing her around the waist and bowling her to the ground like a linebacker taking out a quarterback.

"Fucking bitch!" He growled, slapping her hard around the face before grabbing hold of her gun hand and shaking the pistol free so that it slid out of reach across the grass.

Liv fought wildly but Pistoli was too strong. He sat across her stomach and pinned her arms beneath his knees whilst holding her delicate wrists in his rough, calloused hands.

She spat in his face but as her saliva dribbled off his lip back onto her own cheek he just smiled.

He had her and she knew it.

They stared at one another for a long moment before a voice said, "Okay, Rocco, bring the bitch over here."

Pistoli smiled again as he stared into Liv's eyes. "Sure thing, Boss," he replied.

He dragged Liv up and even though she fought again he held her tight. There was no escape.

She could now see the man she had shot. He was holding a bloodied handkerchief to his cheek and wincing with pain.

He was young, around her age, maybe a little less. Tanned and Italian in appearance with long hair and cold eyes.

"You nearly shot my fuckin' head off, you know that?" He barked.

"Yeah, well that's what I was aiming for, so think yourself lucky," she snapped back.

Jez raised his hand to strike her but she just stuck out her chin defiantly. "Go on," she said, "see if I care!"

His arm hung in the air for a moment as he studied her. Then he smiled and lowered it again, impressed by the girl's spirit even though she had almost killed him.

"You know who I am?" He eventually said, dabbing his bleeding cheek with the handkerchief.

"Sure I do," she replied with a sneer. "You're a murdering bastard."

Jez regarded her for a second then smiled again. "You're funny. Good, I like that."

However, his interest had been piqued by the girl whose long blonde hair was flowing in the breeze as she stood staring at him.

It was the hair that made him remember her and he knew now where he had seen her before.

She was the same girl who was driving the muscle car earlier - the one he had intended to track down after finishing at *Far Point*. But now she was here, in front of him, her blue eyes blazing with anger, her firm breasts heaving in the skimpy vest as Pistoli restrained her.

Christ she was something.

"My name is Guiseppe Vincenzi," Jez said. "You know that name?"

"Yeah. I know it," replied Liv.

"Then you must be—"

"It's none of your goddamn business who I am!"

Jez laughed mirthlessly. "But please, let me guess."

Liv shrugged. "Knock yourself out." *There was no way he could know who she was.*

Yet he did. "You must be Olivia," he said.

Unintentionally she showed a flicker of surprise. "Ah, yes," Jez grinned, "Obviously I've guessed correctly - the beautiful, sexy, Olivia Noakes in person. The daughter of Sean Reilly - AKA Sean Noakes - step sister of the very ugly, very dead Michael Walsh."

Liv felt it like a knife to the heart. Michael was dead and she could not help but gasp with shock.

"Oh jeez," continued Jez with mock sympathy, "I just kinda blurted that out didn't I? Guess it surprised you, huh?. But yeah, honey, your brother's dead - squealed like a little girl, too, if memory serves." He grinned, then walked forward and stood admiring her for a moment, taking in the full splendour of her abundant charms. Then, unable to resist, he placed both of his hands on her breasts and fondled them roughly.

"Get your filthy hands off me you murdering creep!" Liv hissed, as she fought helplessly in Pistoli's grip, her tears for Michael spilling onto her burning cheeks. "My father will kill you for what you've done, you sonofabitch - and I'm gonna be there when he does!"

Jez chuckled. "Oh, dear. You just don't get it, do you, baby?"

As he spoke, Jez was looking at her chest and groping her repeatedly, as if appraising ripened fruit, "You see," he said matter-of-factly, "very soon your father will be dead - as will your uncle and the rest of your fucking family. Then you and me are gonna have a little fun together." He then looked from her breasts to her face and stared coldly into her eyes. "And believe me, baby," he added, "I can go all night."

It was at that moment they heard the motorbike and Jez Vincenzi turned to see Brett Cassidy bearing down on them, his face as black as thunder.

In Liv's eyes, Brett had never looked quite so wonderful and with Pistoli momentarily distracted she stomped hard on his foot and wriggled free of his grip.

As Rocco cried out in pain, she gave Jez an almighty kick in the balls before diving for the bike, lunging desperately to reach Brett's outstretched arm.

As Brett grabbed her up, Liv glared victoriously back at Vincenzi. He was doubled over in agony, clutching his injured testicles as she snarled, "In your goddamn dreams, asshole!"

***

Brett plucked Liv up and swung her round onto the saddle behind him, the bike almost slipping from underneath him as he fought to keep it upright and he had to use his feet to prevent it from tipping over.

However, once Liv's arms were tightly wrapped around him, Brett twisted the throttle and the Sportster's front wheel lifted off the ground as they sped off at a tremendous lick.

Immediately Pistoli gave chase. Forgetting the pain of his stomped on foot, he sprinted after them like an athlete out of the blocks, his gun held out in front.

He was losing ground to them fast but still he fired off three shots in quick succession. The first struck one of the Sportster's mirrors and it exploded into tiny pieces; a fragment of jagged glass scratching Brett's cheek as it brushed by.

The second bullet glanced the petrol tank and ricocheted off out of harm's way whilst the third struck the engine then pinged across the back of Liv's bare calf, grazing it a little. She squealed and ducked down as far as she could, trying to make herself as small as possible, fearing that at any moment she would surely be killed.

Yet by now Pistoli had stopped running. Instead he was standing stock still, several yards beyond the East Gate, in the centre of the gravel approach road, where he was taking aim.

The bike was moving fast and it was dark but he was an excellent marksman. However, at the point of pulling the trigger, Jez distracted him. "Kill the fuckers!" He shouted right behind Rocco, "Don't let the bastards escape!"

It was enough to spoil Pistoli's aim and the bullet which should have hit Liv in the centre of her back, missed her by the slightest of margins.

Instead, however, it struck Brett.

He felt it like a bee sting in his right side and jarred forward sharply with the impact of it, although Liv thought he was merely ducking the fire as she was. But Brett kept on riding and within seconds they were out of Pistoli's range who was now merely a fading shadow in the distance.

Yet Jez Vincenzi was already shouting into his walkie-talkie, ordering two of his men to steal a vehicle and give chase immediately, demanding that they pick up Pistoli en-route.

Meanwhile Brett rode flat out, all the way up to the junction where the approach road met the highway. As he guided the Sportster towards town, he reached down and gently touched the place where the bullet had struck him.

It hurt like hell and when he pulled his hand away his fingers were slick and wet and dripping with blood which, even in the darkness, looked extremely bad indeed.

But he did not tell Liv.

Brett's first priority was to get her to safety, just as he promised Sean he would and even if it killed him, that was exactly what he was going to do.

Unfortunately, what he did not know was that Pistoli and two of Vincenzi's best men were less than a minute behind him, speeding up the approach road in a pick-up they had stolen from the *Far Point Estate*.

What is more, the bullet which struck the Sportster's engine had caused considerable damage and less than a mile down the highway, as Brett and Liv sped towards town, the bike suddenly began to sputter and lose power.

***

Joe watched solemnly as Ray kissed Ruby gently on the forehead, saying his last goodbye to the woman he had loved for the best part of his life.

However, as Joe looked on, he could hear the crackle of flames chasing through the walls and scampering over the eaves. Indeed, he knew even before he saw the fire that his house was burning.

But he could not do a damn thing about it as there was simply no time.

His home would soon be gone and he had to accept it.

Yet it was only bricks and mortar and there were far more important things to be concerned about at present.

He let Ray say his final, heartbreaking farewell to Ruby then, whilst the old man was still weeping for his dead wife, Joe hoisted him up off the sofa and bundled him over his shoulder.

Ray did not want to go. "Leave me, boy!" He yelled, his voice heavy with grief and despair. "Let me stay with her!"

But Joe was heedless. To leave Ray there to burn was unthinkable. "I can't, Ray," he said. "I just can't. I'm so sorry."

The old man briefly tried to fight but he knew that Joe would never allow him to stay - and deep down he loved him for it - but it did not make the thought of leaving Ruby there alone any easier to bear.

However, whilst Joe was deeply sympathetic to Ray's plight, his more pressing concern was how they could both escape the burning house before it crashed down around them.

With the *9mm* tucked in his belt and Ray slumped over his shoulder, Joe stooped and with some effort picked up the shotgun.

"I hope you've got some cartridges left, old man," he said, "Cos I reckon we'll need 'em if we're gonna make it off this peninsula."

"Course I've got some cartridges," Ray barked in return. "I might be nearly dead but I ain't fuckin' stupid!"

Joe smiled. That was the Ray Reece he knew. Ever reliable, even when his whole world had turned to shit, and in that moment Joe could not have respected him more.

"Glad to hear it - you had me worried for a minute," he said, handing his friend the shotgun as he made a dash for the door, "Now let's get the bloody hell outta here!"

***

They made it out of the house without incident, although the fire was now raging and the billowing smoke stung their eyes and charred their lungs.

Unfortunately, however, the remaining golf buggy had succumbed to the flames, ignited by sparks showering down from the wood panelled building. It was now ablaze at the rear of the house, ruling out any hope of them using it for their escape.

"Shit!" Joe exclaimed, knowing now that they would have to make a bolt for the cove on foot - with him carrying Ray all the way. "You up to a bit of exertion old man?"

183

"Don't worry about me, boy," replied Ray, his head hanging over Joe's shoulder as he loaded two fresh cartridges into the twin chambers of his twelve bore. "You just set the pace and I'll cover your arse - same as always!"

Joe smiled again. "Yep. Sounds about right," he said, setting off at a fast trot, anxious not to jolt Ray around too much and aggravate his wound any more than absolutely necessary.

As he ran he could hear gun shots; some far away, some nearby and he drew the *Browning* from his belt as a precaution, hoping to God that his family were safe.

Yet, no sooner had he drawn the weapon than he saw an armed figure, dressed all in black, unexpectedly illuminated from where he was lurking in the shadows by the glow of the two burning houses.

The figure, suddenly aware that he had become visible, raised his gun in response but Joe already had him covered.

Reacting quickly, he twisted from the waist, whilst still on the run, and fired off two shots in rapid succession.

The invader dropped to his knees, discharging his weapon harmlessly into the dirt before falling on his face.

Joe kept on running but there was to be no respite. As they approached Sean and Sarah's house Ray saw another man burst out of the darkness brandishing an Uzi. "Watch it, Joe!" He shouted urgently.

But before Joe could heed the warning, Ray noisily emptied one of his shotgun barrels into the man's chest, blowing it open and propelling him back into the darkness before he had a chance to cut them down with the deadly machine gun.

Joe nearly fell over from the violent recoil of the twelve bore, his balance misplaced by the awkward weight of Ray on his shoulder. But he managed to remain upright and staggered onwards.

"Jesus! That was clo—" he began, but his voice was snatched away as a bullet hit him in the upper arm.

This time there was no stopping the momentum and, whipped sideways by the force of the strike, Joe lost his footing, spilling Ray from his shoulder as the pair of them crashed to the ground.

The sound of more shots rang out. Joe was struck again in the thigh and he cried out in pain. "Sonofabitch!" He yelled as another bullet whizzed past his ear so closely that he could feel the breeze from it.

"Fuck!" Ray shouted as he, too, was struck. "Aaah!" He growled again as yet another bullet hit him.

"You okay old man?" Joe cried, keeping his head down to prevent it from being blown off as more shots struck the ground around him.

"Yeah, I'm fine," Ray replied through gritted teeth and excruciating pain, whilst also keeping his head low. "And less of the old man, eh!"

But in truth he was not fine. Neither of them were. They were pinned down by an unknown assailant - a sniper somewhere out in the darkness who, at any moment, was likely to kill them both.

***

Sean saw his friends fall as he ran up towards the cliff path from the burning stable block; their silhouetted forms black against the glow of fire in the night sky.

He saw the shooter, too - just up ahead, lying flat on his stomach, his camouflage fatigues making him almost invisible on the dark ground as he took aim at Joe and Ray.

Sean proceeded stealthily across the narrow roadway that led from his house to Joe's, pausing only to pick up one of the large, white stones that lined its verge.

Then, very carefully, he crept up behind the shooter who was too busy taking pot shots at those in front to notice Sean approaching from behind.

Seconds later, Sean was looming over him. Yet as he heaved

the stone over his head in preparation to smash it down onto the man's skull, a twig snapped under his foot, alerting the shooter to his presence.

Sensing the imminent danger, the man rolled quickly onto his back, raising his gun instinctively, but he was just a moment too late to prevent the attack.

The heavy stone crashed with devastating force against the shooter's forehead, shattering his frontal bone and killing him instantly. Yet his reflexes did not die so suddenly and as stone connected with skull, before the man's corpse finally stilled, he squeezed off one final round.

Sean was thrown backwards as the bullet struck him, landing hard on his backside with a burning, all-consuming ache high in his chest, just below the shoulder. He knew he was shot but had no time to dwell on it and instead scrambled to his feet and grabbed the semi-automatic from the dead man's hand.

Then, with an awkward gait as he nursed the painful wound, he sprinted off to help Joe and Ray, praying that he might find them alive.

***

Sean skidded to a halt beside them. "You okay?" He asked quickly, then immediately saw that they were not.

"We've been better, I reckon," said Ray, his voice harsh and raspy as he lay there bleeding on the ground.

He was badly shot up; a bullet in his chest, another in his leg and one more in his stomach which looked particularly worrisome. Joe, too, was wounded; shot in the arm and leg.

"Christ almighty!" Sean exclaimed, stunned by the bloody sight of the pair of them.

Indeed, such was his concern that he briefly forgot about his own injury until Joe looked up at him and said, "Jesus! Forget about us - what about you? That looks pretty bad."

Only then did Sean glance down at himself and see the blood pumping from the hole below his shoulder. Suddenly feeling weak, his legs buckled and he fell to the ground beside Joe.

"Hey, man, you okay?" Exclaimed Joe, instantly alarmed.

"No, I don't think I am," replied Sean, aware now that he actually felt dreadful. But that was not his immediate concern.

"What about Sarah and Rose?" He asked. "Are they safe?"

"I hope so," replied Joe, "I sent them to the cove and I've not seen them on the path so with luck they made it safely."

"What about Ruby? Did she go with them?"

Joe was unable to find the words to tell him but Sean read it in his eyes and was horrified. "What? No, surely not." He looked at Ray, hoping desperately to be told that it was not true. Yet Ray just nodded, his eyes squeezed tightly shut as he tried to block out the pain of it.

"Oh my God!" Said Sean, stunned. "I'm so sorry Ray - truly I am."

"It's okay, son," Ray whispered. "I'll be with her soon enough."

Sean was uncertain of how to respond to this and was still trying to process it all when Joe asked, "What about Brett and Liv - they okay?"

Sean shook his head. "Brett was with me - we were trying to put out the fire in the stables when we heard gunfire. Liv was in trouble down by the East Gate and Brett went to save her but I haven't seen either of 'em since."

"Shit," said Joe, his face grave with concern.

"There are intruders everywhere," continued Sean. "Up here, in the stables, down by the gates - they're all over the fuckin' place. Must be a dozen of 'em at least."

"We need to get to the cove," Joe said. Rose and Sarah might be in trouble."

"And Brett and Liv?" Asked Sean.

Joe thought for a moment then said with certainty, "Brett will save her, I'm sure of it."

"He promised me he would," said Sean, "Told me if he couldn't get back to the cove then he'd get Liv out on *The Rachel*."

"Then you can be sure that he will," said Joe with confidence.

"I know," agreed Sean.

"For what it's worth," added Ray, "I don't doubt it either. What I do wanna know, though, is how the hell we're gonna make it to that cove? Two of us can't walk and one of us is too fuckin' shot up to even stand."

"Not to mention we don't know how many more men are out there trying to kill us," said Joe.

"Yeah, that too," said Ray with a wry smile. "I was tryin' to keep it upbeat."

"I can stand," said Sean defiantly. "I just needed a breather, that's all, but I'm fine now."

"You look it," said Joe sarcastically.

"Hey, you don't look too great yourself."

"Nope. Can't argue with that."

"If I help you up do you reckon me and you could support Ray between us - if you don't put too much weight on that injured leg of yours, I mean?" Asked Sean.

"Sure. No problem." Joe replied with a confidence he did not feel.

"You two go on," said Ray. "I'm fuckin' dead anyway, I'll just hold you up."

"Bullshit, old man," snapped Joe. "You're coming and that's the end of it."

Ray knew better than to argue.

Without another word, Sean clambered slowly to his feet, agony etched all over his face. He then helped Joe to painfully stand, after which, with a great deal of effort, they pulled up Ray. All of them were in a bad way but the old pirate was definitely in the worst shape.

In his free hand Sean gripped the semi-automatic he had taken off the sniper, whilst Joe held the *Browning*. Ray, who was being supported by the pair of them, was still clutching his trusty shotgun.

Slowly, very slowly, they made their way along the cliff path towards the cove, trying hard to keep in the shadows, ever aware that more attackers could be coming at them through the darkness.

***

They were less than fifteen feet from the narrow track that led down the cliff face to the cove below when a gruff voice called out to them from behind. "Stop right there or I'll fuckin' shoot!"

Joe and Sean, supporting Ray between them, stopped in their tracks. "Bollocks!" Joe spat with frustration. *Nearly made it.*

"That's right you English asshole," said the man with the Uzi behind him, "I got you cold."

Joe glanced at Sean who nodded a reply. They still had the implicit understanding which made them so formidable back in the old days when they were working for Alfie Noakes, almost as if they could read each other's thoughts.

It was the same with Ray, too, and Joe whispered to him under his breath, "You up to this old man?"

Ray, by this time, was almost unconscious. He had lost so much blood that he was ghostly white whilst his breathing was no more than a deathly rattle. Yet still he held onto the shotgun.

"You just do what you gotta do," he gasped, "I'll be ready."

"Turn around!" Demanded the intruder, "Hands where I can see 'em!"

"Okay, okay - just don't shoot, alright?" Said Joe.

"That's a good boy," sneered the man, waving the Uzi in their direction. "Slowly - I don't want no surprises."

As the three of them turned, the man shouted loudly over his shoulder, carelessly taking his eyes off his quarry for an instant, "Hey, Jez! I got 'em - they-re here! Cassidy and Noakes, they're both—"

With their captor temporarily distracted, Joe and Sean seized the moment. In unison, they whipped up their guns and shot him several times in the chest. The man juddered violently; his body dancing a grotesque jig as the bullets struck him. Yet in the violent throes of death, he involuntarily squeezed down on the Uzi's trigger and fired it in a mad, frenzied arc.

With bullets buzzing wildly around their heads, Joe and Sean dived for cover - Joe keeping a tight hold on Ray as they all hit the ground.

Sean flattened his injured body into the dirt and did not look up again until the Uzi had fallen silent.

Slowly he lifted his head and saw the intruder in a crumpled heap several feet away. Joe was to his right, sitting upright, supporting Ray with an arm around his shoulders.

"All good?" Asked Sean hopefully.

However, Joe shook his head almost imperceptibly and gave him a grave look. *No, all was not good.*

"Reckon I'm getting too old for this shit," said Ray, who had a hand pressed against his stomach. "Just as well I'm gonna be giving it up."

As Sean watched in horror he saw blood trickling through Ray's fingers from a fresh wound in his gut.

"You ain't gonna be givin' up nothing," said Joe, "so don't even think about it."

"No point sugar coating it, boy, "Ray wheezed, "I'm done for."

"No, Ray—" began Joe, not wanting to hear it.

"It's okay, son," said the old man. "I'm fine with it - Ruby and Michael are waiting for me."

By now, Sean had shuffled over to them. "Christ almighty!" He exclaimed, recognising the severity of his friend's injury.

However, as Ray lay there dying, his face was calm. "I've got cartridges in my pocket," he gulped, "Reach 'em for me would ya Sean?"

Trying desperately to keep his emotions in check, Sean quickly did as instructed.

"Now I'll keep the bastards at bay," said Ray, taking the cartridges off him, "whilst you boys make your escape."

"No! I ain't leavin' you" said Joe, a single tear running down his cheek. "I got a plane waiting in Montego Bay to take us all to Vegas - we'll get you there, get you to Doc Ridgeway's, you'll be—"

"No boy. Give it up!" Ray snapped, his voice suddenly strong; assertive. "For once in your goddamned hard-headed life, give it up. I'm dying and there ain't a bleedin' thing you or me can do about it."

Joe was silent and knew the old pirate was right. It was useless.

"Now hand me that shotgun," continued Ray, "and let me get you out of the shit one last time."

After a brief pause, as he mentally processed the inevitable, Joe finally grabbed up the shotgun and placed it in Ray's bloody hands. "You give 'em hell - you understand?"

"Don't worry, boy," Ray grinned wickedly, "I intend to go out in a blaze of bloody glory!"

Joe's tears were undisguised now; tears for a mentor; tears for a friend. *Tears for a father.*

Sean was choked too; Ray Reece meant the world to him and he owed him so much, yet he knew that these last few moments should be for Joe and Ray alone. He reached out and squeezed the old man's arm. "Ray," he said, "It's been an absolute pleasure. Sleep well old friend."

Ray nodded weakly. "The pleasure was all mine, son," he said.

Then, reluctantly, Sean slipped away, knowing he would never see him again.

Joe waited for a moment then looked at Ray. "Just you and me now, old man," he said.

"Yep. And I wouldn't have it any other way."

"I owe you everything," Joe said earnestly, "You know that don't you?"

Ray smiled. "I reckon we're about even on that score."

"Yeah, well maybe," Joe agreed, "but I think this act of blatant bloody stupidity might just tip the balance in your favour."

Ray tried to laugh but instead coughed painfully.

As traces of blood spilt from Ray's lips, Joe heard voices in the distance - voices he did not recognise. "They're coming," he said quietly.

Ray winked. "Then they're gonna get a bit of a surprise, ain't they?" Then suddenly grimaced in agony as a huge surge of pain shot through him. "Go on boy - get outta here," he coughed, "I got this."

Joe did not move and Ray could sense his reluctance. "Go, son," he said. "It's fine. It's my time."

Knowing it to be true, Joe solemnly placed a hand on top of Ray's then stared directly into his pain-stricken face. "Vic Cassidy may have dragged me into this world," he said, his voice catching in his throat as he slowly stood, "but he wasn't ever my father."

Ray looked up at the tall, strong man above him, his one good eye wet. "No?" He asked quizzically.

"No." Said Joe, bending and kissing his wild-haired friend lovingly on the forehead. *"You were."*

Ray could not have been more proud, yet before he could summon any words in response, Joe disappeared silently into the night.

But then, as Ray sat there alone, his lifeblood seeping away, Joe called out to him from the darkness. "Blaze of glory, you old pirate - nothing less. Show the bastards how *real* hard men die!"

Ray smiled, his eyes glistening with tears as Joe then shouted his last words to him.

"I'll be seeing you in the next life, old man - you can count on that!"

As Ray's throat tightened with emotion, he adjusted his grip on the shotgun, and with a tear running down his cheek, he grinned widely. *Yes, he certainly would.*

Chapter Twelve

The Sportster's engine sputtered and choked. "What's wrong?" Liv asked, as the bike began to slow dramatically. "What's the matter?"

"Dunno - it's just losing speed," replied Brett. "A bullet must've severed the fuel pipe or something but there's no power, nothing left, and I can't do anything about it."

"Shit!" Cried Liv as she looked down at the engine, immediately seeing petrol spurting from the hose situated directly under her leg. "Yeah, you're right. Its the fuel line. Hold on, I might be able to—" she wriggled back in the saddle behind Brett, bending low so that her head was almost under his arm as she reached down and blindly felt for the small length of tubing.

The Sportster was moving ever slower and by now was just puttering along but Liv found the hose quickly, her knowledge of mechanics serving her well, as she pinched her fingers around it, effectively preventing any more fuel from escaping.

"Try that!" She yelled to Brett above the slowing drone of the engine.

Brett twisted the throttle and immediately the bike responded. Although the Sportster was instantly faster it was still travelling at nothing like the speed it should have been but hopefully it would be enough to get them into town and down to where *The Rachel* was docked.

But they had lost a great deal of time and the pick-up that had been trailing them since escaping from *Far Point* had made up an awful lot of ground. Indeed, as Brett glanced in his last remaining mirror, he saw its headlights in the distance. He had no clue that the vehicle he could see behind him carried Rocco Pistoli and two of Jez Vincenzi's most deadly killers but his instincts told him to be wary.

Turning his attention back to the road in front, Brett was relieved to see the lights of town glowing up ahead. Another couple of miles, another few minutes, that was all they would need. If the fuel would just last until they could get to *The Rachel* in safety then, shortly afterwards, they would be out on the open sea where no one could harm them.

Next stop Montego Bay and after that it would be onto Las Vegas, just as his father had planned.

First though, they had to make it to town.

They rode on in silence for several more minutes, each of them praying that their fuel reserves would last until they got to the boat. But then, as they passed the town sign, the Sportster suddenly began to kangaroo violently. Then, after a series of dramatic judders, its engine finally died.

Brett quickly glanced behind him and saw the trailing headlights much closer now. Indeed, he could even recognise the shape of the vehicle they belonged to and instantly knew it to be a pick-up. *Could it even be one that he, himself, had driven?*

"Goddamnit!" Liv cursed, at last letting go of the fuel pipe, knowing the futility of holding it any longer. They were out of gas, simple as that and there was nothing she could do now that would keep the bike going.

Brett let the Sportster coast for as long as possible, steering it towards the first few buildings of the town, which were little more than wooden shacks belonging to the poorest of the small population.

He free-wheeled the bike off the main drag and bumped it over the dirt track that skirted the mishmash of huts, finally bringing it to a halt next to one of them.

As he and Liv climbed off, Brett noticed the pick-up again, the light emanating from the shanty town helping him to clearly make out the *Far Point Estate* logo painted on its door. Sadly his instincts had been correct.

"Don't look now," said Brett, leaning the bike on its stand, "but I reckon we might have company."

"What?" Asked Liv, with alarm.

Brett nodded to the vehicle that had been troubling him which was looming ever nearer.

"Shit!" She said, certain that she could see Rocco Pistoli sitting up front in the passenger seat. "That's the guy who was shooting at us."

"Yep," Brett replied. "You up for a jog?"

"You betcha."

"Good. C'mon, let's go - we can take the back streets to the harbour."

Without another word they set off at a run, Brett wincing with every step from the pain burning in his side, blood now soaking his T-shirt and jeans. However, he was careful to keep Liv on the opposite side of him so that she could not see. *If they could only make it to* The Rachel, *then everything would surely be fine.*

Or, at least, that is what he was hoping. Yet, his hopes were dashed almost instantly because at that moment a gruff voice called out, "There they are - over there!"

Then there was a screech of tyres as the pick-up swerved off the main road and chased after them.

***

In the darkness, the uneven pathway, which hugged the sheer face of the cliff, was dark and treacherous. All the familiar foot falls which guaranteed safe passage were all but invisible yet Sarah and Rose navigated it as best they could.

As they made their way down, they could hear the sound of gunfire coming from above and feared for their loved ones who were still caught up in the desperate battle raging all over the estate. Many times they thought of turning back, to see if they could help, but Joe had been insistent and both women knew that he and Sean would only be hampered by their presence. Yet that knowledge did little to ease their concerns.

The best they could do was get to the cove as quickly as possible and ready the dinghies for a quick escape.

When at last they made it to the weather-worn crevice that formed the entrance to the cove, Rose reached under a little rocky outcrop to find the couple of flashlights Joe had stashed there.

"Wow!" Exclaimed Rose, clicking on a flashlight and shining it into the cavernous interior. "I haven't been down here in a while. I'd forgotten just how big this place is."

"Wow's right," agreed Sarah, standing beside her and directing the beam of her own torch into the vast space. "It looks so different in this light, - like a prehistoric cathedral carved out of rock."

Sarah passed through the cove every morning with Sean as they took the horses down to the beach. In fact, even though she usually entered lower down, through the much larger, naturally formed archway, she saw it so often that she barely even noticed it anymore. But, seeing it now, by torch light, the enormity of the cove was truly awesome.

Yet neither of the women had the luxury to stand and wonder as time was of the essence.

Joe and Sean had situated the dinghies close to the entrance so that in the event of an emergency they could be easily dragged across the beach to the sea. However, with their outboard motors secured to the back and the boxes of supplies stored within, they were surprisingly heavy. It would take all of Rose and Sarah's combined strength to drag each one the fifty feet to the sea.

"C'mon," said Sarah, "Let's get started, the others might be in a hell of a hurry when they get down here and we might need to make a quick getaway."

"Yeah, I know," agreed Rose, "I reckon those boats are gonna take a bit of shifting, though."

"Hmm, think you might be right."

Using the flashlights, the two of them scrambled down to the lower level and ran across to the dinghies where they immediately set to work.

***

Gus Golino was struggling to find his way in the darkness, petrified that at any moment he might fall to his death. He had been trailing the women down the path; slipping and scrambling and clinging onto anything he could find, worried that his next step might be his last.

But the thought of the women kept him moving downwards, certain that his reward when he caught them would make it all worthwhile.

At last he saw the flicker of torchlight; two moving beams on the beach some twenty feet below, he could even smell a hint of perfume on the evening breeze. *Delicious.*

Stealthily, he proceeded downwards until he came across the crease in the rock wall that led into the cove. He slipped silently in and crouched down behind a huge boulder where he could spy on the proceedings below unseen.

A single lantern was burning on a natural shelf above a grey dinghy which illuminated the immediate vicinity around the women, allowing Gus an unobstructed view of them.

They appeared to be worn out; their plump breasts heaving enticingly with exertion. A wide drag mark in the sand suggested that something heavy had recently been where they were standing. *Another dinghy perhaps?*

Whatever it was, it was clear to Gus that they were preparing an escape.

Both women looked to be around the same age; not young but definitely not old either and each very sexy. One was dark, the other auburn and Gus licked his lips. *Which one to pick first?*

They were dressed almost identically; T-shirts and tight jeans and Golino ogled them as they took hold of the rope at the front of the dinghy; his loins stirring, his bruised leg, from where he had been hit by the golf buggy, completely forgotten. He was a predator now and all he could think about was the thrill of the hunt.

Very gently he placed his Uzi down on the ground then slipped his trusty Baretta from the shoulder holster strapped over his combat fatigues. Then, from the sheath on his belt, he pulled out a long, razor sharp hunting knife with a jagged blade - his weapon of choice for close work.

As both women took hold of the rope at the front of the boat, their torches tucked under their armpits, Golino stepped out from his hiding place and pointed the Baretta directly at them.

"Stop right there, ladies," he said, his voice echoing loudly around the cavernous interior, "Put down the rope and rest those flashlights on the side of the dinghy."

Rose and Sarah looked up, startled by the sound of his gruff voice, to see Golino's darkly clad figure standing on the ledge above them.

"That's it, c'mon, quickly now - I ain't got all night."

They glanced briefly at each other in defeat, knowing they had little choice.

Golino grinned with wicked delight as they did as instructed. "Put those torches down so the beam faces you," he commanded. "I wanna see exactly what you got for me."

Again, they did as they were told, the expressions on their faces set with fear.

"Great," said Gus with glee, "now I've got you in the spotlight, we're gonna have us a little show."

"Please," Rose begged, "You don't have to do this—"

"Shuddup!" Snapped Gus, as he jumped down to their level. "No talking."

Again, Sarah and Rose looked at one another apprehensively, both clearly terrified.

"Don't look at each other!" Barked Golino. *"Look at me!"*

The women quickly turned their attention back to him, squinting into the glare of the torchlight, neither now able to see the person directing them.

"Good, that's very good ladies," said Gus. "Now, let me see you strip - and make it good otherwise I might just have to kill you!"

***

Sean and Joe knew the pathway to the cove well as each had travelled it many times before. Indeed they had used it less than an hour earlier so the rocky undulations of its uneven terrain were particularly familiar to them. However, in the darkness and with them both so injured it was proving difficult to navigate.

Joe was limping badly from the bullet hole in his thigh, whilst the wound in his upper arm was throbbing painfully with the arm itself all but useless.

Sean was losing a lot of blood. He was weak and light-headed but was managing as best he could.

The pair of them were supporting each other as they limped down the steep incline; the thought of Ray up on the cliff top giving his life to save theirs playing heavily on their minds.

Halfway down they heard the blast of a shotgun followed by a short burst of machine gun fire. Joe and Sean stopped in their tracks, bitterly aware that Ray Reece, their good friend, was making his last stand.

However, in order to make his sacrifice worthwhile, they had to press on, to make the most of the time he was buying them. So they hobbled on in the dark whilst the battle raged up above.

The twelve bore blasted again as Ray discharged the second barrel and Joe and Sean assumed him to be finished; the shotgun now empty.

For a moment everything was quiet but then there was the crackle of an Uzi and yet another blast of shotgun fire. Somehow, even though he was weak and close to death, Ray had managed to reload and Joe's heart swelled with pride.

Blaze of Glory.

Nevertheless, after both barrels emptied for the second time and yet another clatter of machine gun fire, there was silence again.

Then came the solitary report from a pistol.

Joe and Sean knew this to mean that Ray's fight was over and at last he had gone to join Ruby and Michael.

He would never be forgotten.

Yet first they had to survive this night themselves.

***

Joe and Sean staggered on in silence until they saw the soft glow of lamplight being emitted from the gap in the rock face. They were tired, weak and close to collapse.

But then they heard the echo of Gus Golino's voice as he shouted at Rose and Sarah in the cove and knew their work for the night was not yet done.

To save the women they loved, they must rally themselves once more.

Chapter Thirteen

B rett held tightly onto Liv's hand as they raced desperately through the narrow streets; the red *Far Point* pick-up chasing them every step of the way.

However, the bulky vehicle was hampered by its chunky dimensions and could not reach optimum speed in the tight, higgledy-piggledy of the shanty village so, for the moment, the pair were managing to evade their pursuers, but it would not last for long.

Rocco Pistoli was in the passenger seat of the pick-up, his hands gripping the dashboard and a determined expression on his scarred face. Falco, one of Vincenzi's heavies, was driving and another, Nicolino, was standing up in the flat-bed at the rear, clinging onto the roll bar.

Running flat out, Brett and Liv soon burst free of the outlying shanty huts and with the pick-up still in pursuit, hurried into the more affluent suburbs of the town where the road became wider, unfortunately allowing the chasing vehicle to significantly increase its speed.

Also, in stark contrast to the poorer outskirts, there were street lights in this part of town and Brett and Liv clung to the shadows as they sprinted along the sidewalk.

Brett was flagging badly by now and Liv was all but pulling him along completely unaware of the painful wound in his side which was restricting his movements; agony shooting through his whole body with every footfall.

"What's the matter?" Liv yelled, "Why are you slowing down?"

"It's nothing - I'm fine," Brett called after her, "Just a bit of stitch, that's all!"

This struck Liv as odd as she knew Brett to be supremely fit but there was simply no time to question it as the pick-up was hot on their heels. Indeed, they could hear the roar of the engine and the crunch of its gears right behind them.

Another few seconds and it would be right on top of them but Brett knew a shortcut to the harbour which the pick-up would find impossible to pass through.

Just up ahead, there was a tiny alleyway that led passed the storage yard of *Calico Jack's*, the bar where Brett worked during the off season. Beyond that it was just a short dash to the quayside and on to where *The Rachel* was moored.

The downside was that it would telegraph to their pursuers exactly where they were headed - although the pick-up would have to take the much longer route to the quayside by road. Brett hoped this would buy him and Liv the precious time needed to get the boat untied and out to sea - but it would be tight.

"Quick!" Brett shouted, "down here!"

"What? Down where—?" Liv cried as he yanked her sideways and into the dark little alleyway.

"Short cut," he replied. "Trust me!"

She did as instructed as the pair of them ran down the uneven track towards *Calico Jack's*.

A couple of seconds later the pick-up screeched to a halt at the entrance. "Shit!" Pistoli cursed, slapping his fist down angrily on the dashboard, furious that his prey had evaded him. Then, through the windshield, he noticed a tiny hand-painted sign with an arrow that pointed down the narrow pathway which read *Harbour* and he smiled.

Brett hoped his local knowledge of the town might pay off but it was not the case as he heard Pistoli shout, "Nico, quick - get after 'em - we'll head 'em off at the harbour!"

Brett looked behind him to see a man leap from the flat-bed of the pick-up and hit the ground running. He was broad with a buzz-cut and a mean expression. He was muscular, too, with a machete gripped in one of his paw-like hands as he set off after them.

Desperately, they carried on running, Brett continuing as best he could but he knew he could not keep up the pace; knew that long before they made it to *The Rachel* Vincenzi's soldier would cut them down.

As they sprinted past the rear gate to *Calico Jack's* storage yard, Brett gasped, "You keep going - get to the boat and start her up - I'll be right behind you."

"What?" Replied Liv, horrified. "Why - what are you gonna do?"

"I gotta stop this guy behind us," he panted, "I've got to Liv. Please, don't argue - just do as I say otherwise we're both dead."

"No - you can't, Brett - please—"

"Too late," Brett said, suddenly stopping in his tracks. "Now go!" He called after her, "Quick as you can!"

Still on the run, Liv turned to see Vincenzi's goon less than twenty-five feet from Brett. Her heart pounding in her chest, terrified for what was about to happen. "Brett!" She yelled, tears immediately springing from her eyes.

"Go! Don't stop!" Brett shouted as Nico charged towards him. "I'll be right behind you, I promise!"

***

Brett had no time to think. It was about instinct now as Nico's huge bulk filled his vision.

Although wounded, Brett had agility on his side. He was smart too and as Nico barrelled towards him, Brett rolled at his feet, using the big man's own inertia to bring him down.

Unable to stop, Nico clattered over Brett's tightly balled body and went sprawling to the ground in the close confines of the alley.

Pain exploded through Brett like a jolt of electricity yet he sprung up onto his feet preparing for the attack which was sure to follow.

However, as he turned he saw Nico still on the ground, his body motionless and the long blade of the machete sticking out of his back, its lethal edge dripping with blood. Clearly he had stuck himself with it when he fell.

It was a grotesque sight but Brett had no time to dwell on it as he had to get after Liv, guessing that by now she would be approaching the quayside.

The pain in his side was now excruciating, the way in which he had brought Nico down had pulled open his wound and weakened him considerably but he had to press onwards, acutely aware that Liv was still in danger.

Favouring his injured side, he was about to limp away when he noticed a gun, a *Colt .45*, shoved in Nico's belt. Quickly, he tugged it out then set off with a slow, painful gait, desperately hoping that he was not too late.

***

Liv emerged out onto the quayside and with relief saw *The Rachel* moored just ahead of her. However, as she rushed towards it she noticed the headlights of the red *Far Point* pick-up round the corner at the opposite end of the harbour. Clearly the men pursuing her had wasted no time by taking the long way round.

Liv guessed that she only had about a minute to reach the boat, untie it and get it away from the quayside before the truck drew level.

Without a moment to waste, she sprinted over to *The Rachel* and leapt onboard, darting straight to the wheelhouse to retrieve the keys from the box under the seat where Brett kept the spare set.

Quickly she started the engine and thanked her lucky stars that it fired first time; the sound of the small cruiser sputtering gently in the water was one of the most gratifying noises she had ever heard.

Then she ran to the front of the boat and with some effort threw off the bowline tethering it to the dock.

In the periphery of her vision she could see headlights drawing close and her stomach filled with dread. But she did not panic and instead scurried along the edge of the deck, passed the wheelhouse to throw off the rope on the stern. Unfortunately, such was her rush along the narrow ledge that she slipped and very nearly fell into the water. She caught herself just in time, clinging onto the chrome grab rail but landing hard on her bare knees.

Nonetheless, the fall had cost her valuable seconds and by the time she had regained her feet and shimmied along the edge of the boat to the stern it was too late.

The pick-up skidded to a halt by the dockside and Rocco Pistoli jumped out waving an automatic in her direction. "Give it up, Blondie," he said victoriously, "It's all over."

"You sonofabitch!" Liv said contemptuously.

"Uh-huh," Rocco replied with a smile, as if she had just paid him a compliment. "C'mon, let's go - best not to keep Jez waiting, not if you know what's good for you."

"I couldn't give a damn about Jez Vincenzi. He can wait until Hell freezes over for all I care!" Liv sneered defiantly.

"Yeah well, that's as maybe but it ain't gonna change nothing. C'mon, get in the truck - or I can just as soon take you back dead, makes no odds to me."

Liv had run out of options. Slowly she stepped off the boat and onto the quayside. Falco was holding open the rear passenger door for her and reluctantly she slid in and onto the seat.

Then something strange happened.

As Rocco climbed into the front passenger seat, Falco closed the rear door, shutting Liv in. However, as she glanced out of the open window at him, she saw him suddenly freeze; a look of surprise on his tanned face.

"Make a move and I'll blow your goddamn head off!" Brett snarled from behind Falco, pressing the barrel of the Nico's *Colt .45* hard into the back of the Italian's neck. "You too!" He snapped at Rocco. "Try anything and you're dead - and believe me, I'm looking for the slightest excuse!"

***

Liv's heart leapt at the sound of Brett's voice. *He had made it! He had actually made it!* However, she had no time to celebrate as Brett was still giving orders, "Liv, take his gun," he said, referring to the semi-automatic Rocco was holding, "then get out and on to the boat, quickly."

She did not need telling twice. "Give it up, big boy," she said to Rocco, leaning over the back of his seat and speaking softly into his ear, "You wouldn't want to make him mad cos I've seen that and it really ain't pretty!"

Without any choice, Rocco handed over the gun. "Laugh it up while you can, Blondie, cos when Jez catches up with you, *that* ain't gonna be pretty either - I can promise you."

"Yeah? Well both him and you can kiss my pert little ass!" She said.

With that, she took the gun and slipped out of the pick-up on the opposite side to Brett, then hopped back onto *The Rachel*.

"Get her untied," Brett called. Then he turned his attention back to Rocco and Falco. "Okay, you two, it's time you went for a little swim."

For a moment they both looked a little stunned. "C'mon, quickly, let's not be shy!" Said Brett.

After a couple of beats, Rocco got out of the pick-up and walked over to the edge of the quayside. Falco followed with Brett behind him, pointing the .45 in the general direction of both of them.

"Right, jump into the water, now," he demanded.

"You gotta be kidding—" protested Rocco.

"Do I look like I'm goddamn kidding?" Yelled Brett, who was standing awkwardly, clearly badly injured and favouring his wounded side. "Now get in the fuckin' water before I push you in!"

Meanwhile, Liv had untied the stern line and was now in the wheelhouse.

"Okay, Brett!" She called. "We're all set!"

"Great!" He called back, trying to keep the pain out of his voice. "Okay boys," he said, now speaking to Rocco and Falco, "Time to make a big splash."

As the two Italians looked uncertainly at each other, Brett straightened his aim on them. *"Now!"* He demanded.

Rocco shrugged, "We'll meet again, boy, I can promise you that," he said, "and when we do, circumstances are going to be different."

"Yeah, well, you might be right," Brett said with resignation, too weak to argue the toss, "but for now just get in the goddamn sea."

Rocco gave him one last meaningful stare then he turned and jumped off the quay, landing in the water with a loud splosh.

Falco, too, gave one final, uncertain look at the dark, uninviting water below, then leapt into it feet first.

A few seconds later, both men were bobbing up and down, treading water as best they could in their combat fatigues and heavy boots.

However, by this time Brett was on board *The Rachel*. "Okay, Liv," he called, "take her out!"

Slowly, the little cruiser pulled away from the quayside, Brett covering Rocco and Falco as *The Rachel* headed out to the safety of deep water.

Ten minutes later, the quayside was just a dark blur on the land, the tiny lights of the town twinkling like stars in the night sky.

Liv turned down the motor and let the boat drift for a while as she left the wheelhouse and went back to join Brett who was leaning against the upright of the sun canopy at the stern, looking back at the land.

"Okay," she said, "Where to now?"

He did not reply so she went to him and touched him on the shoulder. As he turned, she could see now that he looked deathly pale; a light sweat on his forehead.

"Brett?" She said, immediately concerned.

"It's okay, Liv," he croaked, "You're safe now," then his eyes rolled upwards, his legs gave way and he collapsed in a heap at her feet.

Chapter Fourteen

Sarah and Rose froze for a moment, neither willing to comply with Golino's command to strip.

Years earlier Rose had been the victim of an attempted rape yet fortunately, her son, Matt, had saved her.

Sarah, however, had endured prolonged suffering in her past; sickening abuse which had taken her years to finally put behind her.

She was stronger now than she had been in her youth but the thought of Golino's sweaty hands pawing at her flesh was revolting and the idea that he might actually violate her was utterly unbearable.

She began to shake with fear, terrified that the violence of her harrowing past was about to repeat itself but she desperately tried to keep it together and when Rose reassuringly reached out and took her hand, sensing her dread, it steeled her somewhat.

She would not be a victim again. *Ever.*

Nevertheless, Gus Golino had other ideas.

"C'mon ladies, I ain't got all night!" He snapped.

"Okay, okay!" Rose responded, immediately stepping protectively in front of Sarah, her chin jutting out with defiance. Even though she loathed the thought of what Golino might do, she could not in good consciousness allow Sarah to re-live the horrors of her past for fear of it causing the catastrophic damage to her mental state as it had so devastatingly before.

This time Sarah might not ever recover so if there was a way in which Rose could possibly prevent it then she certainly would do - no matter the cost to her personally.

"I'll go first, alright?" She said, with as much grit as she could muster.

"No, Rose, you don't have to—" Sarah began but Rose cut her off.

"It's okay sweetie," she said with forced determination, "I've got this, I can handle this creep."

Oddly, this seemed to amuse Golino. "Oh, you got this do you, honey?" He said dismissively. "Well I'll tell you what then, let's make this a little more interesting shall we?"

Without warning, he suddenly flung the jagged edged hunting knife at her; the murderous weapon spinning quickly through the air and sticking into the sand directly between her feet.

Rose flinched with alarm as the knife spiked into the ground beneath her.

"What say we spice things up a little then, huh?" Sneered Golino, "and instead of you just taking them pretty clothes off, you *cut* them off, okay?"

"What? No, you can't be serious!" Rose replied aghast, her eyes widening as she cast them over the partially buried blade.

"Oh, I'm serious, honey," continued Gus gleefully. "Serious as a fuckin' heart attack - so get cutting - *now* - or so help me I'll slice your goddamn throat!"

Rose took a beat. She had no choice, it was do or die.

Slowly she bent and took hold of the hilt of the knife and tugged; sliding it out of the soft sand to expose its full, deadly length.

"That's it, honey. That's good!" Encouraged Golino eagerly, "Now slice off that tight little shirt of yours and let me see those firm, round titties."

Very reluctantly, Rose pulled the hem of her T-shirt away from the tanned skin of her midriff and offered up the jagged edge of the knife, being careful not to prick herself with the razor sharp blade.

The moment the keen edge touched the thin cotton cloth, the material tore, startling Rose by how deadly sharp it truly was.

She heard a slight gasp of shock from Sarah as the shirt began to tear.

Nonetheless, she continued.

Very gingerly, with her hand trembling, she cut a straight line up the centre of her T-shirt until the bright pink of her lacy bra showed and the two pale pink domes of her breasts could clearly be seen encased within.

"Yeah, baby. That's it!" Said Golino, his voice thick with lust and his trousers bulging with excitement. "Cut it right off - then the bra - show me those big, juicy jugs!"

Rose sliced the T-shirt all the way up to the neck so that it hung like a ragged bolero from her shoulders.

"C'mon, now the bra - quickly. *Do it!*" Gus was clearly having the time of his life.

Rose stared daggers at Golino, her face set, defying his loathsome gaze.

Even so, she could barley keep her hand still enough as she tentatively pulled the elastic of her bra away from between her breasts and slipped the tip of the terrifying blade underneath.

Almost instantly there was a loud twang of elastic and her generous breasts bounced free.

Golino's tongue was hanging out like a dog on heat and he was about to speak when suddenly a deafening shot rang out and the dinghy beside him dramatically deflated.

"Don't make a fuckin' move, asshole, or the next one's gonna kill ya!" Joe growled.

***

Joe and Sean, the walking wounded, had hobbled into the cove

212

as silently as they could and had heard most of what had been said.

However, Sean could barely stand upright; his vision blurring in and out, and Joe's shooting arm was all but useless.

But they were a team and together they could mount an attack, although in their present state how effective that might be was highly questionable. But there was no alternative, their women needed them and they had to be up to the fight.

Without the need for words, Sean stood in front of Joe, trying his best to stay still.

Joe, still in possession of the *9mm* but now holding it in his left hand, which was now his one good one, even though it was not his natural choice, lifted it up and rested it on Sean's shoulder.

Joe was an excellent marksman with his right hand but had not so much as fired a single round with his left so needed all the assistance he could get.

Very carefully, he took aim, using Sean's shoulder to steady his hand but due to his injured leg, he was having to place all of his weight on one leg so his balance was slightly off.

Yet still, as he watched the infuriating sight of his humiliated and terrified wife cutting her own clothes off at gunpoint, he had to slow his heartbeat and compose himself.

Finally, he took a deep, calming breath and fired.

Simultaneously with the sound of the gunshot, the rubber dinghy 'popped' like a toy balloon and instantly deflated.

"Great shot!" Encouraged Sean in a whisper.

"I was aiming for the guy's head," replied Joe under his breath.

Even though the situation was far from amusing, Sean could not help but crack a smile.

However, this brief moment of levity was extinguished immediately by Joe's next words, barked angrily at the man below.

"Don't make a fuckin' move, asshole," he yelled, "or the next one's gonna kill ya!"

Golino span round, searching for the source of the gunshot and immediately saw the two men standing on the raised ledge opposite him. Gus also saw the *9mm* in Joe's hand. However, even in the flickering lamplight, he noticed the gun waving around unsteadily and could see that both men were seriously injured. Indeed, the one with the gun was having to use the other's shoulder for support.

Yet still they had the advantage.

Golino lowered his weapon in defeat, realising his fun was over, at least for the moment.

"Rose!" Joe ordered, "Take his gun and don't take your eyes off him."

Rose could not disguise her relief to see Joe, although quickly she dropped the knife and pulled the tattered remains of her T-shirt together to cover her nakedness, feeling slightly ashamed that she had allowed Golino to ogle her.

What concerned her more, though, was the pain in Joe's voice; she could hear a rasp in it which told her he was suffering. Worse still, she knew Golino heard it too.

Quickly she shot a glance up to where her husband was standing on the ledge. He looked pale and injured but Sean, who was standing in front of Joe, looked to be in terrible shape, his shirt was drenched in blood and his face was as white as a ghost.

"Oh my God!" Cried Sarah in horror, as she, too, saw Sean. "Sweetheart, are you okay? What's the matter - have you been shot?"

"It's okay, darlin', I'm alright," Sean replied croakily, sounding none too convincing. "It's just a flesh wound, that's all. I'll be fine."

However, as the words left his mouth, his eyes rolled upwards and he began to sway dramatically.

As Joe tried to catch him, Golino seized the moment. Yet as he raised his gun Rose made a desperate dive for it, managing to grab it with both hands just as he fired off a shot, spoiling his aim.

The bullet ricocheted loudly off the stone ledge under which Joe was struggling with Sean, sparks flying off the rock as it struck with a deafening clap.

As Joe and Sean hit the dirt, neither able to remain standing without the aid of the other, Rose wrestled fiercely with Golino.

But the Italian was stronger than Rose and he was easily overpowering her; forcing her down onto her knees with the physical strength of his thick forearms, the pistol just inches from her face.

Golino was grinning like a madman as they fought, his eyes playing over Rose's breasts which were exposed once more.

Rose could not hold on to the gun any longer, try as she might Golino was just too strong. As he at last wrestled the weapon free from her grip, she fell backwards onto the soft sand; her T-shirt and bra cut in two, her bare breasts laying heavily on her chest. She looked bedraggled and vulnerable, her hair all mussed up after the fight.

"That's it, baby," Golino grinned, thick yellow spittle spraying from his excited, wet lips as he spoke, the gun pointed casually at the rock ceiling. He had the upper hand now and was flaunting his dominance over her. "I got you just where I want you now, and it's time I had some fun."

"Oh yeah?" Snarled Sarah, "Not if I can help it, asshole!"

Having been forgotten about in the tussle, Sarah had snatched up the knife and was now standing behind him with it held tightly in her grip.

Seeing Golino standing there, lording it over Rose sickened her.

She despised depraved monsters like him - like her father - indeed, the scene before her evoked appalling memories of her dreadful experiences long ago and she could not just stand there and let it happen again, not while she still had breath in lungs.

A rush of volcanic anger surged threw her body and with all the force she could muster, she plunged the knife forward into Golino.

Suddenly Gus felt an excruciating pain in his back as Sarah stabbed the knife deeply into him. He fired off the pistol three times in quick succession, each shot slamming into the rock ceiling overhead with a deafening crack, as agony shot through his body.

In desperation he dropped the gun on the floor and reached over his shoulders with both hands, trying madly to pull the knife free, but it just made the pain worse.

Rose quickly scrambled away as Golino blundered helplessly about, the hilt of the deadly hunting knife sticking out from between his shoulder blades.

Then there was an almighty crack as the ceiling of the cove gave way above Golino, the gunshots loosening the centuries old rock.

Gus looked up, surprise registering briefly on in his anguished face before a mass of rubble collapsed on top of him, killing him instantly and burying him under a pile of rock and stone.

Rose, dragged herself backwards as fast as she could, trying to avoid the hail of debris, managing to escape the main rush of it with just a few small stones glancing off her legs. She would sustain several bruises but fortunately nothing more.

As she retreated to safety the dust began to settle and she could see her sister-in-law standing in the background, her face blackened with dust.

Sarah's eyes were set with determination. She would not be a victim again. *Ever.* And nor would any of her friends.

***

Quickly, Sarah snatched up one of the bright yellow waterproof jackets that had previously been stashed in the now deflated dinghy and threw it to Rose who had swiftly clambered to her feet. Then the pair of them raced up to where their husbands had fallen.

Sean was laying on his back, his eyes closed. Joe was beside him, leaning up on his good elbow.

"I'm okay," he said immediately as they rushed up to him. "But Sean's lost quite a bit of blood."

"Quick, honey, out of the way. Let me take a look," said Rose to Joe. "I'll examine you in a second."

Rose had left London in her late teens, heading for the pub in Northamptonshire run by her aunt and uncle. She pulled pints in the evenings but during the day she studied to be a nurse at the local college. As it turned out, she never qualified and eventually became landlady of the pub but she did glean enough medical experience to get by in an emergency and the knowledge had never left her.

Without a second thought, she tore off the ragged remains of her T-shirt and folded it into a tight, square pad. "Sarah, press this down on the wound," she said. "Press it hard, keep the pressure firm - it's the only way to stop the bleeding."

"Will he be okay?" Sarah asked.

"If we can get him to a doctor soon then maybe," Rose answered, shrugging on the yellow waterproof to cover herself, "but I honestly don't know for sure, sweetie. Sorry. But you keep pressure on that wound and he's got a fighting chance."

"How long?" Croaked Joe.

"Again, I can't be sure," said Rose, "But I'd say twenty-four hours, max. Certainly no more."

"That's okay," said Joe firmly. "We can do that. We can be at Doc Ridgeway's by tomorrow morning - but we gotta go now."

"Hey, not so fast, tiger. What about you? You're hurt - and what about the others? Brett and Liv, Ray and Ruby?"

"I'll be fine," Joe replied, "You can take a look at me once we get off the island."

"And the others?"

Joe frowned. Now was not the time. They had to get Sean to a doctor urgently. "It's a long story, I'll tell you on the way."

217

"It's a long story?" Rose queried. "What do you mean? Where are—"

"They're not comin', Rosie." Joe interrupted firmly. "I'll tell you later, I promise - but now we've gotta get going."

Rose regarded him briefly, looking deeply into her husband's eyes and seeing the emotion. "Okay, honey," she said quietly. "Let's go."

"Sure, but please tell me the other dinghy's alright?"

"It is, don't worry. It's down by the water. Not too far."

Joe smiled. "That's my girl."

Sarah was tending to Sean, whose eyes were sporadically flickering open and closed. "Hello, darlin'" he said to her hoarsely.

"Hello," she replied. Her voice cracking. "You think you're up to moving?"

"Just you try and stop me," he breathed.

"No chance of that," she beamed, even though her heart was breaking. She had heard Joe speaking of the others and suspected the worst but for now she had to focus on Sean.

"Sis?" Said Joe, reluctantly disturbing her.

"Yeah?"

"You think you and Rosie could help get Sean to the other dinghy?"

"Sure. What about you?"

"One of you will have to come back and give me a hand but I'll manage okay."

"Fine. C'mon then," said Sarah determined to do anything necessary to save her husband. "Let's get moving."

***

It took a full fifteen minutes for all of them to get safely across the beach and into the remaining dinghy. A further ten for Rose and Sarah to push it successfully off the beach and out over the breakers, Joe in no fit state to lend a hand. Yet, half an hour after their struggles in the cove they were out on the open sea; the twin outboard motors of the streamlined dinghy humming quietly as it sped rhythmically over the waves.

Sarah was sitting at the bow, cradling Sean's head in her lap, pressing the padded T-shirt firmly down on the wound below his shoulder. He was flitting in and out of consciousness but breathing steadily. Sarah knew he was strong and fit and she was praying on everything she held dear that would be enough to see him through that night and into the next day.

Joe was sitting in the stern with Rose. She had dressed both of his wounds as best she could but he, too, would need a doctor as soon as possible. His injuries, although not as serious as Sean's, could soon become fatal if they did not receive proper attention soon.

Rose, meanwhile, had control of the tiller and was steering the small craft over the ocean.

Joe had a chart and a compass on his lap which he was reading with the aid of a flashlight, ensuring that they stayed on the quickest course to Montego Bay where their plane was waiting to fly them to Vegas.

In the background the night sky was aglow with the distant fires of their homes burning.

Yet no one said a word.

**

The raid had been a complete disaster for Jez Vincenzi; a mismanaged, ill-conceived fuck-up from start to finish.

He had taken fifteen of his best men to the island and now, somehow, inconceivably, they had been all but wiped out.

Fifteen hardcore soldiers who formed the upper echelons of the Vincenzi/Carboni organisation - indeed, the very backbone upon which it had been built.

The men, hand-picked by Jez for the operation, were the established hierarchy of trusted enforcers who had been with

Carmine and Vito, Jez's all-powerful grandfathers, for years - men who were instrumental in their rise to the top.

But now, thanks to him, they were all dead.

In his first act as leader, he had single-handedly managed to decimate the organisation his grandfathers had built up.

Any respect, or indeed, any good-will that Jez may have inherited from his grandfathers would surely evaporate; his tenuous control over the huge and sprawling organisation gone.

Furthermore, without the aid of those men he had taken to *Far Point*, the very same men who he knew would be so vital in keeping his underlings and ambitious rivals in check, the whole Vincenzi/Carboni operation would soon crumble into disarray.

And for what? Cassidy and Noakes were still alive.

For all Jez's efforts the men he came to kill had somehow evaded him.

They, together with a pair of old farts, two middle-aged women and a couple of kids not much older than Jez, himself, had wiped out his entire army of skilled, experienced soldiers.

It was just unbelievable.

Jez walked almost shell-shocked up the small rise of the bluff, the sky lit orange as the nearby buildings burned; Cassidy and Noakes' paradise destroyed, their world on fire.

But it was scant reward for his efforts and he took little comfort from it.

The left side of his face and left arm were speckled with tiny pellet wounds where he had been struck by the spread from a shotgun blast. Two feet in the wrong direction and he would have undoubtedly lost an arm, possibly even been killed - as it was, the two men who had remained by his side had been; both blown apart by the devastating force of a twelve-bore.

But he had been lucky.

Less could be said of the man laying at his feet who had inflicted those wounds, who Jez now studied.

Vincenzi had killed him, himself, with a single round to the head as the man lowered the discharged shotgun, but the victory seemed hollow now, especially seeing the dead man close-up.

Indeed, Jez was staggered by the man's appearance. He was old and frail with wild, white hair and a leather patch over one eye. The one good eye almost seemed to be twinkling, mocking him, and even though the old man was quite dead, there was a definite smile on his face.

This was the man who had shot him, who had put up such a terrible fight? It was utterly remarkable.

Jez was suddenly angry, all his frustration, all his bitter disappointment, boiling and bubbling up like a cauldron, fuelling his wrath and bringing the sheer scale of his failure sharply into focus which he aimed with unrestrained vehemence at the dead man at his feet.

He lashed out violently with his foot, kicking the corpse hard in the ribs. Then again and again, kicking with unrestrained ferocity.

But the dead man's smile still taunted him.

So Jez carried on kicking; smashing his boot repeatedly into the corpse's smiling face until all that remained was a bloody pulp. Yet still the image of it haunted him and no matter how he tried he could not purge it from his brain.

At last, exhausted, Jez turned and walked away in disgust. He was breathing hard, his heart pounding in his chest and still his frustration remained.

How could they have gotten away?

Christ how badly he wanted them dead. But he had blown it. His one good chance to kill them and he had let it slip through his fingers.

They had just vanished into thin air. All his men were dead yet Cassidy and Noakes were gone. *But where?*

"Fuck!" He screamed angrily, his voice carried out to sea by the wind.

Then Jez heard a noise behind him and turned, ready to shoot.

"Hey, it's me!" Said Bass Stone appearing out of the shadows. "Don't shoot."

"Where the fuck have you—" Jez began, but stopped as he saw Stone's face. He had a hand clamped over one eye, blood streaming from the socket beneath.

"That old bastard!" Spat Stone, jerking his head over his shoulder to indicate Ray, whose bloody corpse he had just passed. "Took me by surprise in the house. He blinded me, took me out of action."

Jez looked unimpressed.

"Glad to see you got him for me." Said Bass.

"A lot of good it did me."

"Why? How many we get?"

"None. Or at least none that I wanted."

"Shit."

"Yeah."

"And ours?"

"What do you mean?"

"Ours. How many we lose?"

"All."

"What?" Said Stone incredulously.

"All." Replied Jez, his voice flat, almost detached. "Thought they'd got you, too, until a second ago."

"Jesus! What about Pistoli? They get him, too."

"Dunno. I reckon. He's not here anyway."

"Shit."

"I let those fuckers slip through my goddamn fingers."

"Yeah, well—"

"Well what?" Demanded Jez.

Even though Bass was in a great deal of pain he knew that Jez now needed him more than ever before. In fact, if the whole top tier of the Vincenzi/Carboni clan had been wiped out, he was all Jez had left, apart from money. A great deal of money.

"Well you should have listened to me," said Stone honestly.

"What?" Said Jez angrily.

"It's true," replied Bass, his hand still clamped over his injured eye. "If you'd listened to me then your men would still be alive and Cassidy and Noakes would be dead."

Jez was so stunned at the other man's audacity that he did not know quite how to react. Yet before he could say anything he heard the sound of a vehicle and saw lights approaching.

He and Stone raised their guns and turned to face the oncoming truck, watching as it drove up passed the burning houses and on towards them.

Eventually, the red *Far Point* pick-up pulled up beside them and seeing Rocco and Falco inside, they lowered their weapons. But Jez showed no signs of relief that two of his men had survived, he merely showed impatience.

"You get 'em?" He asked eagerly as Pistoli climbed out.

Rocco was dripping wet, so was Falco and both looked a little shame faced as Jez glared at them, desperate for answers. He made no mention of how they came to be soaked through as it was of little importance to him.

"No, they got away," said Pistoli reluctant to enlarge too much on the details. "They had a boat waiting."

"Fuck!" Jez shouted angrily again. "Fuck, fuck, fuck!"

"Yeah, I know," added Pistoli. "But I tell you this, I want those fuckers *real bad* now."

"Well fat lotta good that does me now!" Growled Jez, staring daggers at Rocco.

"Like I said," interjected Bass, "Should have listened to me."

Jez span round to face him, pulling his gun up as he did so, ready to kill Stone for being so insolent.

"What did you say?" He demanded.

Quick as a flash, Bass snatched the gun away from him and cast it aside then, in the same swift movement, back-handed Jez hard around the face, knocking him to the ground.

"Never pull a fuckin' gun on me boy," growled Bass with meaning, "Not if you expect to live afterwards."

Pistoli and Falco stood agog, unable to quite believe what they were witnessing. Both eager to see what would happen next.

Jez sat on his butt looking up, stunned. He wanted to fight, to show strength of leadership, but seeing the tall, imposing figure of Stone standing over him he hesitated. Then it was too late, the moment had gone and he knew he already looked weak.

He did not want to lose face - he was the boss for Christ's sake, but Stone was just too powerful - too formidable.

For the first time in his life Jez had been struck, hit by another individual, someone who clearly was not frightened by who he was or what his last name happened to be.

Somehow, although scary, it was also quite liberating.

Slowly he held up his hands in defeat and climbed to his feet. "Sorry," he said. "My mistake."

"You bet," replied Stone with a smirk.

Jez's anger was gone now. Suddenly he felt like a little boy whose father had just admonished him. He reached into his pocket and pulled out the small glass vile of cocaine.

"Okay," he said. "So what should I have done - how do we get 'em?"

Bass smiled inwardly. Then he grabbed the vile off him and flung it over the cliff. "First you quit that shit, okay?" He said.

"Hey!" Yelled Jez, before noticing the glare of intent on Bass' face. "Yeah, okay," he said meekly. "Then what?"

Bass regarded him for a long moment. To him, Jez Vincenzi was the golden goose; his key to power, money, everything. But more than those things, he wanted Joe Cassidy and Sean Noakes.

Somebody needed to pay for his ruined eye. If not Ray Reece then either Cassidy or Noakes would do. Preferably both.

Finally, he lifted his gaze from Jez and looked to Pistoli and Falco who had been enjoying the show. The boy had long deserved a whupping and it was good to finally see it.

"What about you two?" Bass asked. "You in?"

Falco nodded, a little awe struck, water still dripping off his forehead, his clothes sodden.

Pistoli was not eager to follow Stone's orders but he would play along for the time being, see where things led. He still had a score to settle with Matt Mason, his brother's killer, as well as with Brett Cassidy and the girl. If Stone could lead him to them then so be it.

However, if Bass fucked up then Rocco would take matters into his own hands. But for now he nodded his agreement, too.

"Good," said Stone as he turned and looked out to sea.

In the distance he could see a small spec of light - a lamp or a torch maybe, but he could not make out to what it belonged. Although he was willing to bet that it was a boat of some kind and on it, he strongly suspected, would be Joe Cassidy and Sean Noakes, who were both now out of his reach, at least for the time being.

They had won this round, he conceded, but next time things would be different.

"So come on then," Vincenzi pressed, "what now?"

"What now?" Bass replied as he turned and looked back at the others. "Now we do things my way."

PART TWO

Chapter Fifteen

Las Vegas, five days later

Ethan Ridgeway's small hospital ward at the rear of his Las Vegas home was presently full to capacity. Matt Mason occupied the first bed; his condition still serious but he was out of the woods according to the Doc. Indeed, he had regained consciousness a couple of days earlier and was now chaffing at the bit to get back on his feet but Ethan had forbidden it.

To make matters worse, Matt was now under the watchful eye of Rose, too. Since her arrival, she had assumed the role of protective lioness and was determined that her son should follow the Doctor's advice to the letter.

Matt knew from experience that it would be pointless to argue with her so had reluctantly resigned himself to a long, boring convalescence consisting of hours of butt numbing bed rest. But it did not mean he had to like it.

In bed number two, Joe Cassidy was propped up on his pillows reading the newspaper; a cup of coffee in his hand. His wounds had been tended to and were now expertly dressed in clean bandages. Fortunately, the gunshot in his arm was what the Doc called a 'through and through' - which meant that the bullet had passed cleanly through leaving clearly visible entry and exit wounds. Because of this, Ethan was confident it would not cause any lasting damage, although advised Joe that he may feel a little stiffness in his upper arm in cold weather.

The bullet wound in Joe's thigh, however, was a different proposition and had needed all of Ethan's considerable skill as a surgeon to remove the many tiny fragments of bullet which had broken away as it burrowed into his flesh. What is more, a lesser surgeon might not have been able to save the leg at all.

As it was, Joe had been lucky and the only lasting reminder he was likely to have of the injury was perhaps a slight limp.

The same could not be said for Sean Noakes who was laying in the last remaining bed, his condition critical.

Miraculously, Sean had survived the rough, jostling sea voyage to Montego Bay in the tiny dinghy. Somehow, he had also made it through the subsequent flight to Las Vegas which took off just minutes after he and the others arrived at the Jamaican airfield in the early hours of the morning.

However, by the time the plane touched down at McCarran and they had been whisked away to Doc Ridgeway's in Bernie Dufresne's personal limousine - usually reserved for millionaire high rollers en-route to *The Villa Continental* - Sean's condition had deteriorated severely and he was very close to death.

Ethan had operated immediately, enlisting Louretta, Victoria, Violet and Rose as nurses to assist him with the complex and lengthy surgery.

Sarah, meanwhile, had not left Sean's side - neither during or after the operation. She had slept and taken all her meals in the chair beside his bed, awaiting the moment he would finally wake and come back to her. She had already lost her son and had no intention of losing her husband as well.

Presently, however, his eyes remained resolutely shut, his body unmoving, and only the *beep, beep, beep* of the monitor and the shallow rise and fall of his breathing assured Sarah that Sean was still alive.

Virgil Nash and Josh Noakes had been on kitchen and laundry duty - the Hollywood movie star, complete with broken arm and gashed forehead, together with his privileged step-son, knuckling down to their chores without so much as a word of complaint. They had kept everyone fed, watered and freshly laundered.

The women, for the most part, spent their time tending to the three patients in the hospital ward, doing their utmost to ensure each of the men returned to full health as soon as possible. They changed bed linen, scrubbed the floor - even emptied soiled bedpans when necessary and none flinched in the task.

Vicky had worked hardest of all, trying desperately to keep her mind occupied, doing everything she could to prevent herself from worrying about Liv and Brett but it was not working and their safety was all she could think about.

Rose, meanwhile, fussed around both Matt and Joe, the two great loves of her life. Matt, her son, had a free, independent spirit but he had been away from her too long and although the circumstances were far from desirable, it was so good to have him close once more.

As for Joe, she knew him too well and could almost interpret his every thought. He was supposedly reading the newspaper and enjoying his coffee but as she tended to Matt's bedclothes, Rose noticed that her husband had not turned the page in several minutes; his gaze elsewhere. The coffee, too, had not been touched and was, by now, quite cold.

He was lost in thought. Joe was a proud and capable man; both resourceful and reliable, yet he kept his emotions tightly bottled and never let anyone know how worried - or, indeed, how scared he was.

But Rose knew that he was desperately worried about Sean, frightened that his best friend might die and leave Sarah, his twin sister, widowed. He was concerned for Matt, too, who, himself, had almost died. If not for a tremendous effort by Doc Ridgeway then Joe could easily be mourning the loss of his friend and his son.

However, Joe had two sons and one was still unaccounted for.

They had not heard a word from Brett or Liv since leaving *Far Point* and Joe was deeply concerned for their welfare. As were all of them.

However, Joe put on a brave face and kept his emotions in check, staying determinedly strong for others who might need him but still his mind kept drifting back to *Far Point* and Brett - and Rose could tell.

As Violet entered the ward and walked past her, Rose could also tell that Matt seemed to visibly brighten and she smiled inwardly to herself. Her son truly was on the road to recovery.

Considering all that had happened, Violet had been overwhelmed by everyone's warmth towards her. They all sympathised with her for the loss of Alfie and Richie and each, in their own way, could empathise. Bass Stone had destroyed her life and now, with Jez Vincenzi, he had also destroyed the lives of everyone else.

Indeed, Violet, along with all those who had sought sanctuary at Ethan Ridgeway's home, now shared a common enemy and she drew solace from that.

Even though each and every one of them had suffered, she knew that they were stronger together and was confident that Stone and Vincenzi had made a strategic error by inadvertently uniting them all.

An error which she was determined to exploit.

Violet was still sore and stiff but her injuries were healing well enough now thanks to Doc Ridgeway who had been a key factor in her recovery. She and everyone else had much to thank the good doctor for but Ethan modestly shrugged off their praise and made light of his efforts.

Yet it was not just his medical expertise they were grateful for. He had also given up his home and now, instead of living alone he was sharing his house with ten other people. His kindness was remarkable, yet he had taken it all in his stride - although it was fortunate his house was large enough to accommodate all of his new guests.

Indeed, the house had become something akin to a field hospital in wartime and it seemed to Violet there was an essence of the Dunkirk Spirit about their little band of refugees. No matter how wounded or hurt they might be, there was still a definite grit and determination about them. This was coupled with a general sense that they were all in it together and it somehow made her feel much better.

Furthermore, being at Doc Ridgeway's made her feel as if she was part of a family again and she liked it.

Since her arrival, Violet had taken it upon herself to help care for Matt, even though he had been unconscious for much of the time. Nevertheless, she would dress his wounds, change his bedding and, on occasion, even give him a bed bath.

Caring for him, she could not help but notice him, too.

His face was so handsome and rugged yet also very sad. It was as if happiness had somehow eluded him and Violet felt deeply sorry for him although she knew not quite why.

His body was something she rather ashamedly noticed, too, and even though he was injured, there was no avoiding the fact that his torso was firm, his stomach flat and his shoulders broad and powerful. What is more, Violet could not help but wonder what it would be like to have his thick, muscular arms wrapped around her.

And then, one day, as she watched him sleep, he quite unexpectedly awoke. Indeed, the first person he saw when he opened his eyes was her, bending over him, staring back.

Briefly, he looked into her face and smiled - a fabulous movie star kind of smile - before immediately falling back into unconsciousness again. But in that instant, even though she was loathed to admit it,

Violet was hooked.

Now the highlight of her day was the morning shift in the hospital when she would attempt to feed Matt his breakfast, although it was never an easy task.

Matt was too proud to admit he needed assistance - even though he was still in a great deal of pain and could not properly sit up. Consequently, since fully regaining consciousness, his and Violet's relationship had been something of a battle of wills.

Ultimately, however, he knew that if he wanted to eat then he had no choice but to rely on Violet's help - but he hated being so useless and was unaccustomed to depending on anyone.

Nonetheless, as the days passed, they slowly got to know each other and now they had formed an uneasy truce - albeit one that predominantly consisted of Violet trying to force feed Matt who was still not inclined to admit his frailties.

However, they both enjoyed these minor skirmishes each morning even though they fervently denied it to themselves.

To the others, however, their mutual attraction was clear to see and it was a source of minor amusement in what was otherwise a fairly sombre existence.

***

As darkness fell on his fifth day at Doc Ridgeway's, Virgil Nash wandered out onto the front porch and sat down on the stoop.

It felt good to be outside after having spent so long cooped up indoors. Indeed, even though his life as a movie star prevented it for much of the time, Virgil was an outdoorsman at heart. He loved the fresh air, the sun on his face and the feeling of being at one with nature.

Before he was famous Virgil had been an avid surfer and could even have turned pro if stardom had not come his way - although he was still unsure as to whether that was a blessing or a curse.

Undoubtedly fame had taken away his freedom; the ability to

walk down the street unrecognised or to buy a pack of cigarettes without having to sign umpteen autographs were simple pleasures that were now impossible and his days of blissful anonymity had long since passed. In fact, if he tried to walk down almost any street in the world nowadays he would undoubtedly be mobbed by adoring fans. In some ways, this was wonderful and he was truly grateful for the opportunities he had been given but he did miss those days of obscurity terribly.

This feeling of ruefulness had been exacerbated by his recent confinement to the house - an unavoidable consequence when pretending to be dead as it meant having to stay out of view, hidden behind closed doors for the majority of the time.

Indeed, because Virgil was so famous, he could be instantly recognised by almost anyone.

What is more, should any passer-by happen to spy him then the whole deception, which was presently so crucial to everyone's safety, would be over.

Within minutes, news of his miraculous return from the dead would be all over the news and before long media vans would be parked out on the lawn; dozens of reporters, cameras at the ready, all clambering to get a glimpse of the missing movie star and his equally famous wife.

A horrific scenario which he did not relish.

As with most great movie stars, Virgil had grown more handsome with age. His once sun bleached hair had now silvered somewhat which only served to highlight his golden California tan which, in turn, seemed to make his legendary blue eyes just that tad more appealing.

However, these good looks, which had unquestionably aided his career and significantly added to his enormous success, had now become something of a hindrance and he was beginning to feel a little like a caged animal.

He reached into the sling of his wounded arm and pulled out a pack of *Luckies,* then dragged one out with his teeth and lit it up; the flame from his solid gold *Zippo* glowing brightly in the dusk.

He knew he should not really be out on the stoop but Doc Ridgeway's place stood alone on Canyon Hill Drive, high up, so he could see anyone coming - but it was still a risk and he knew it.

But he had to get out, just for a minute, just to clear his head and get his thoughts together.

Virgil had known Liv since she was a little girl and even though she was not his by birth, he was as much a father to her as Sean was. He was desperately worried for her well-being, afraid that she might be lying dead somewhere with Brett alongside her and the thought of this troubled him greatly.

Virgil was also worried about Sean. Even though Vicky's previous marriage to him complicated things a little, the two had managed to remain good friends. Indeed, aside from Joe, Virgil was Sean's best friend.

He, Sarah, Virgil and Victoria had worked things out extremely amicably and the four of them had raised Liv and Josh together - the kids each spending equal time at either home.

But now Sean lay unconscious, close to death and events of the past, long thought buried, had suddenly come hurtling back to haunt them all.

It was very troubling indeed.

Of course, Virgil knew the sensible thing to do would be to stay hidden. Start a new life somewhere - anywhere - where they could live in relative safety - as Sean and Joe had a decade earlier.

Yet that had just been proven to be catastrophically ineffectual.

Furthermore, whilst it was not their fault that Sean and Joe had been forced into hiding - effectively playing dead for ten years - it was a lifestyle they had become used to. Indeed, Sean had been on the run for the best part of his life and it had almost become second nature to him.

But for Virgil and Victoria it was just not practical.

As much as Virgil craved anonymity, as much as he wanted a life away from the public glare, it was not a realistic option, not at present.

Like it or not he was famous. Vicky, too. There was nowhere they could go where people would not recognise them.

He also had commitments he must honour; movies he was tied to - which he had signed contracts to appear in; big budget pictures that he had a great deal of his own money invested in as producer as well as star. To pull out of them now would be an extremely costly exercise most probably involving legal action against his remaining estate - meaning he would lose millions even if he stayed 'dead'.

In contrast, Joe and Sean had diversified their assets. They had taken steps years earlier to ensure that any monies from their business interests could not be traced directly back to them. Furthermore, their former notoriety had all but evaporated nowadays with the media in general much more interested in the new generation of villains who made their exploits seem tame by comparison, so they could live out the rest of their days in wealthy anonymity if they so desired.

But Virgil could not hide. His business was making movies, his face was his fortune and even though he had more than enough money to last him several lifetimes he could not just simply walk away now. Neither could Victoria. Much as it appealed. They could get away with 'being missing' for a couple of weeks, perhaps even a month but any longer than that would be utterly impossible.

What is more, Josh was at college and his future prospects, at least until very recently, appeared to be rosy. Liv, too, if by some miracle she was safe, also had her whole life ahead of her. To ask them to give it all up, to go into hiding for the rest of their lives - for reasons of things that took place before they were even born was just not fair.

He could not do it to them. Nor could Vicky - and Virgil was pretty sure that if Sean was conscious he could not either.

Which presented something of a dilemma.

Virgil drew on his cigarette whilst he pondered these things, hearing the front door open behind him as he blew out a long plume of blue smoke.

A second later Victoria laid her hand gently on his shoulder. "It's not safe to be out here, honey," she said softly.

"I know. It's okay. Just having a smoke - I'll be back inside in a minute."

Vicky sensed his anxieties as they reflected her own. She sat down next to him. "Everything okay?" She asked.

"My arm's fine. Doesn't hurt at all," he replied.

"I didn't mean your arm - I meant—"

"I know, Vic," he interrupted, then felt immediately guilty for snapping. "Sorry," he said, turning to her, his voice full of remorse, "I know what you meant."

"And?" She asked, her eyes showing deep concern for him.

"And the answer is I don't know, Vic. I just don't know what the hell we're gonna do."

"No, I know, honey. Me either. But let's get Liv home safely first - her and Brett - then once they're back we can make some decisions."

"Yeah, I guess you're right. I just hope we hear from them soon."

"You think we will?" Vicky asked, suddenly emotional. She was a strong, smart woman but the last few days had been extremely tough on her. Tears were never far away and her thoughts were constantly with her daughter; the worry for Liv's safety ever present even though she did her utmost to carry on as best she could.

Virgil understood this completely. He placed a comforting hand on her knee, "I'm sure we will. Just a matter of time, that's all."

Vicky took the cigarette from him and put it to her own lips, closing her eyes as she sucked on it, the stress etched on her face.

A tear rolled down her cheek as she thought about her daughter again, very aware of what had happened to Michael. Jez Vincenzi had already claimed the life of one of Sean's children, had he now taken another one too?"

"Hey, c'mon," Virgil encouraged. "It'll be fine, I know it will. Brett will look after her - that boy won't let anything happen to Liv, you know he won't."

Victoria sniffed and wiped the tear away with her fingers before taking another long drag and handing the cigarette back to her husband. "I know Virge - I do - somehow I just know she's still alive. I think I'd feel it if she wasn't - it's just the worry, that's—." Then the flood came, she could hold back no longer, her shoulders began to shake and the tears flowed like a river.

Virgil cast away the cigarette and wrapped his good arm around her. "I feel it, too, Vic. I *know* she's okay - she'll come back to us, I promise. We've just gotta be strong. You just gotta hold it together until we get word. But we *will* get word - I know we will."

Vicky snivelled a nod as she tried to compose herself. "Yes," she said with forced confidence, "then we can work out what to do afterwards as a family - make the decision together."

"Yeah, course. Sounds good," replied Virgil breezily, trying to reassure his wife. But he knew whatever decision they finally arrived at would undoubtedly have massive ramifications on the rest of their lives.

***

Ethan and Louretta were sitting at the kitchen table. Josh was in the background stacking dishes on the drainer. The room was quiet; Ethan was tired and Louretta was letting him have a moment's peace whilst also keeping him company and Josh was occupied with his chores.

At nineteen, Josh Noakes was a fine young man; intelligent, quick-witted and focussed. Aside from his love of fast cars - a passion which both he and his sister shared, Josh was more than just the average teenager. Indeed, he had two distinctly different sides to his personality. On the one hand he liked sports and girls and having a good time, but on the other he was studious and bookish with an eye firmly set on the future.

At school he had been the star quarter-back and naturally, being the son of a movie star, he was also blessed with good looks. His hair was long and blonde and facially he was unmistakably his mother's son. Yet because of his square jaw and strong, straight nose, people assumed him to be Virgil's son, too. For his father's safety he never corrected them. Indeed, when Virgil and Sean were younger they could easily have been mistaken for brothers so it was not a surprising assumption for people to make.

Josh was currently on vacation from *CalTech* - the California Institute of Technology - although his present circumstance could hardly be classed as a holiday, in fact it had been anything but. However, he had not complained, had not once thought about himself or what might become of his plans for the future which he knew, instinctively, depended heavily on what happened in the next few days or weeks.

Yet he did not care about that at the moment. All he cared about was getting Liv and Brett home safely.

Josh's parents had always been honest with him and Liv, never disguising the fact that their father and Uncle Joe were in hiding and supposedly dead to anyone beyond their immediate circle. As he and Liv got older it became perfectly normal to never discuss their father in public and if anyone should ask, the answer that he was dead rolled effortlessly off their tongues. It was almost like a game which only they knew how to play. Which kind of made it unreal, too.

But after recent events Josh had gained a whole new perspective on things and it was certainly not a game any longer.

Nevertheless, Josh was determined not to be a hindrance and was eager to help in any way that he could. His mother had enough to worry about with Liv, she did not need to be concerned about him, too.

So Josh kept his head down, did his chores and did not ask questions that he knew nobody had answers to just yet. But it did not stop him from worrying about his sister - or his father, who was currently unresponsive and hooked up to a monitor in a hospital bed just along the corridor. As he stacked the last of the dishes on the drainer, Virgil and Victoria walked into the kitchen. It was clear his mother had been crying but there was no need to question why.

Whilst she sat down at the table, immediately wrapped in a hug from her own mother, Louretta, Virgil walked over and joined Josh at the sink.

"You okay, kid?" He asked.

"Uh-huh."

"You should've let me help with that."

"It's okay. I got it. You sit down, I'll pour you some coffee."

Virgil smiled and patted Josh on the arm. He could not have been more proud. "You're a good boy, you know that?"

"Yeah, I know," replied Josh with a grin, brushing the complement aside and picking up the coffee pot.

Virgil went and joined the others at the table as Josh placed four mugs down in front of them.

However, just as he was about to pour the coffee, Rose rushed into the room.

"Hey, Doc, Come quick!" She cried.

"Why - what's the matter?" Asked Ethan, already on his feet.

"It's Sean," replied Rose. "He's woken up."

Chapter Sixteen

A small island off the coast of Haiti

L iv looked over at the pitiful sight of the stranded boat laying listlessly in the shallow water. She was standing ankle deep in the surf, the waves breaking gently over her calves, the crystal blue of the Caribbean Ocean stretched out endlessly before her.

Immediately behind her was the white sandy beach of the tiny island she had inadvertently marooned herself and Brett upon.

Five days after she had so disastrously beached *The Rachel* there, she was still cursing her stupidity. How she had missed an island the size of Jamaica was still beyond her, although at the time she had rather more pressing matters to attend to.

When Brett collapsed, shortly after their escape from *Far Point*, Liv did everything she could to staunch the bleeding from the bullet wound in his side.

Furthermore, with very few supplies on board and no medical equipment whatsoever, she'd had to use every ounce of her ingenuity to prevent him from dying.

After using her own vest top to soak up the blood, she then folded it and used it as a makeshift pad. Next she removed Brett's jeans and tied the legs of them tightly around his waist to keep the vest firmly in place, applying as much pressure on the wound as possible to stem the bleeding.

In retrospect, it was an almost laughable situation; her dressed only in a lacy bra and skimpy cut-offs and Brett in nothing more than a T-shirt and boxers. Indeed, had it not been so serious then she could not have dreamt up a better scenario than to have the pair of them alone together wearing very little clothing.

But it was serious. Dreadfully so. And over the course of the days that followed Brett could have very easily died.

Yet thanks to Liv's efforts he had not.

That first night, as Brett lay unconscious, his head in her lap, she had never felt more afraid. With the small craft bobbing silently in the blackness, she cried herself to sleep, praying that Brett would still be alive when she awoke - and much to her relief he was.

However, his condition had deteriorated. He was pale and shivering and groaning with delirium. Being careful not to disturb his wound, she took him in her arms and tried to warm him. But he would still not stop shivering, so she ripped down the canvas awning at the rear of the boat and covered Brett with it. This seemed to work a little better, although his body still trembled with cold.

As the sun came up, Liv knew she had to find land soon - somewhere with a doctor, preferably a hospital, otherwise Brett would surely die.

Her stomach rumbled with hunger as she started the engine, but all she had been able to find below deck was a half packet of stale biscuits and a litre bottle of water. Both of which she decided to save until later. Hopefully Brett would be up to eating something then, although she was not entirely convinced.

However, the lack of supplies had not been their only problem. As *The Rachel* had still been in the restoration process at the time of their hasty departure, there was no navigation system or radio installed. So without Brett to assist her, Liv had no way to accurately set a course and without a radio she could not call for help.

Fortunately, there was a compass and chart on board and she

knew roughly where Jamaica was in relation to *Far Point*, although she presently had no point of reference to guide her, just the compass and a vague idea of their position.

By noon, Liv could feel the sun burning her bare skin yet she had no choice but to endure it as there was nothing she could cover herself with.

Brett still needed the canvas awning as he had not yet stopped shivering and was looking more ill with every hour that passed.

However, Liv had managed to get him to take some water, allowing herself just two small mouthfuls, only too aware that she needed to make it last as long as possible. Yet Brett would not eat. She tried feeding him a biscuit but he would not keep it in his mouth as he was too addled to even bite.

This worried her greatly as she knew he had to eat in order to maintain his strength - which, in turn, would hopefully keep him alive. Nevertheless, she returned to the helm and set off once more, hoping the afternoon would bring the sight of land.

Yet it did not and as dusk fell on that first full day at sea, Liv could not understand why they had not yet reached Jamaica. *Surely it was not that far away?*

She kept going until the last of the daylight had been completely extinguished, making any kind of navigation impossible, and with her no longer able to even see the bow, she shut the engine down and weighed anchor for the night.

Only now, when it was cooler, did she feel the true soreness in her limbs where the unrelenting heat of the punishing Caribbean sun had severely burnt her. But she had no care for herself and instead set about tending to Brett.

Yet there had been no improvement in his condition and he was still feverish and babbling incoherently. However, he seemed to be no worse either, which was something of a relief.

As the night went on, she managed to get Brett to take a few more sips of water but still he would not eat and kept spitting out the small pieces of biscuit she placed in his mouth.

Liv tried crumbling one up but he still would not keep it in. In the end, the only way she could make him swallow was by chewing the biscuit into a pulp herself, then pressing her mouth against his and pushing the biscuit in with her tongue.

When he responded with his own tongue, entwining it with hers as he took the biscuit mush from her, it was so intimate, so tender, that Liv almost wept. Nevertheless, she was elated that he had finally accepted the food. Indeed, after the first taste he seemed keen for more, opening his mouth in readiness like a baby bird, eager for the next morsel.

After each small portion, she would close his mouth and massage his throat to encourage him to swallow. Thankfully this worked and she managed to get him to take two whole biscuits - although the process took well over an hour.

Liv, herself, ate nothing. She decided that if they still had not reached Jamaica by noon the next day then she would allow herself a biscuit, but until that time she would go without. Brett required sustenance more than she did presently and she was painfully conscious of needing to conserve their meagre rations.

She slept that night cuddling Brett with the awning wrapped around them both.

Before sun up the following morning, however, Brett's condition had worsened considerably. His face was almost grey and his breathing slight. He was still muttering gibberish - although Liv could have sworn he uttered her name more than once.

Very carefully she untied the jeans from around his waist and gently pulled away her folded vest top which was now heavy with dried blood. The wound looked livid and swollen and she was worried that it might be infected. Without any medical knowledge, she thought perhaps she should try to clean it, hoping that would help. But as soon as she poured a little drop of water on the nasty looking injury Brett's eyes flew wide open with shock and he screamed loudly in agony, as if scolded by a kettle. He then promptly passed out.

Suddenly panicked, scared that she might have inadvertently made Brett's condition more serious, Liv ran to the helm and opened the throttle. She aimed the boat in the direction she hoped Jamaica to be and powered it onward, a renewed sense of urgency in her desperate search for land.

She kept *The Rachel* going for as long as possible, monitoring Brett as best she could from the wheel, still worried that she may have done more harm than good.

Yet after his initially adverse reaction to her attempt at cleaning his wound, he seemed to have settled and was thankfully still breathing. Although Liv was deeply concerned for him as he looked utterly dreadful.

However, her efforts to find land came to nought and before the sun reached its zenith, the engine sputtered and died, the fuel tank empty.

Suddenly it felt useless, all hope gone, as they drifted aimlessly on the calm sea, the sun beating down on them uninterrupted in the cloudless blue sky and nothing but sea all around.

Filled with despair, her limbs aching terribly from sunburn and her lips chapped and peeling, Liv finally broke down and cried. *Was this how it was to end for her and Brett?*

At last, when she could cry no more, she went back and crawled under the awning next to him, sheltering herself from the harmful rays of the sun as she cradled his fevered head in her lap. If they were to die then at least they would be together.

They seemed to drift endlessly; all the remainder of that day and through the night that followed. Liv, using the same method as before, fed Brett twice more, rather guiltily enjoying the touch of his lips on hers and the warm taste of his tongue in her mouth.

Each time she fed Brett, she also took a single biscuit for herself, although the water was now all but gone with just an inch remaining in the bottle. Her head throbbed with sunstroke and bright lights played across her eyes whenever she closed them but at last she fell into a deep, exhausted sleep.

She was still asleep under the awning in the early afternoon of the following day when they ran aground.

As *The Rachel* shuddered to a halt in the shallow waters just meters offshore, Liv was thrown forward and Brett's head slipped from her lap with a bump; the remaining water from the bottle spilling out onto the deck and running away in tiny rivers.

For a moment Liv was dazed, a little disorientated. Her body was stiff with pain and her thoughts befuddled but she forced herself up onto her feet and looked out over the rail. Then, upon seeing the white sandy beach before her and the lush green palms beyond, her heart soared.

Quickly, Liv made certain that Brett was shaded and comfortable, then set about going ashore to explore, hoping desperately to find food, water and medical supplies.

However, just minutes after jumping waist deep into the sea and wading up to the beach, a small group of people emerged from the trees.

Liv breathed a huge sigh of overwhelming relief and fell to her knees with gratitude. *Thank God, they were saved.*

***

"Hey, you okay, girlie?" A tall man with ebony coloured skin and a Franco-Caribbean accent called out to her.

"Yes, I'm fine - but the person I'm with needs urgent medical attention!" She yelled back. "Please help me!"

As it turned out, the man was called Felipe, and he informed her she had landed on a tiny island off the Western tip of Haiti, over three-hundred miles due East of Jamaica.

Liv was stunned that they were so far from their original destination, realising they must have passed Jamaica en-route, somehow missing it completely. *No wonder the journey had taken so long.*

Nevertheless, Felipe and his friends were from a small fishing village just a short distance away and they seemed keen to help.

Unfortunately, the village had no phone or medical facilities but the small group carried Brett back there anyway, taking him directly to the thatched mud shack in the centre of the village which was Felipe's home.

They laid him on an ancient brass bed that nearly filled the entire floorspace of the tiny shack, then sent for a doctor.

Ten minutes later, a short, round, extremely wizened old woman arrived who, Felipe assured her, was the only doctor on the island. Although to Liv she looked nothing like any doctor she had ever seen before.

Nevertheless, the woman entered the hut and headed straight over to where Brett lay. With her she had an old wicker basket covered with an equally old gingham cloth that Liv assumed to contain a variety of potions and cure-alls. Yet, at this stage, she was willing to give anything a try, so merely looked on without raising objection.

Tenderly the woman examined Brett's wound, gently prodding the area around it with her fingers.

"Careful!" Cried Liv.

The woman turned and gave her a withering look before resuming the examination. Brett, however, lay unmoving and silent, seemingly oblivious to her touch.

After a thorough inspection, the old lady then rummaged around in her basket for a moment, clearly hoping to find the correct remedy. A second or two later, she pulled out a plastic tub containing what could only be described as an assortment of dried leaves and flaky powder which she tipped into a grubby wooden bowl. Next she sifted through the contents of the basket again and brought out a dirty looking bottle with a cork stopper from which she poured several drops of thick brown liquid into the bowl. She then set about mixing everything into a muddy paste.

She inspected the wound once more before scooping out a large dollop of the paste with her long, crooked fingers.

"Please be careful!" Liv piped up. "He's in a lot of pain—"

Suddenly the old woman glared at her. "Sssh!" She hissed vehemently.

Liv decided it was best to do as ordered and let the old hag get on with her work. After all, what harm could she do, Brett could hardly be any worse off.

As it was, Brett did not even flinch as the women carefully lathered the revolting mixture onto his wound; caking a large lump of the muddy goo all around the bullet wound and surrounding area.

When finished, she stood up and sprinkled some highly pungent liquid around the bed - again taken from the wicker basket. After that, she brought out a rattle made from what appeared to be a tiny skull of some kind and chanted some incomprehensible words.

Finally, she marched over to Liv and stared hard into her face, scaring her half to death in the process. One last time, the old women rummaged in the basket and withdrew yet another bottle of potion which she thrust into Liv's hands.

Then she left, obviously quite satisfied with her work.

Liv glanced quizzically at Felipe who was standing beside her. "What did she give me this for - have I got to make Brett swallow it?"

Felipe laughed, a deep baritone rumble, "No, girlie," he said. "Tis balm for your sunburn - rub it in well, all over. Tomorrow it be much better I promise."

Oh, okay, sure," replied Liv feeling a little silly. "Thanks."

"Same with your man," continued Felipe, "He be better in morning, too, you see."

Liv looked at him with surprise. "Oh, wow - that's great," she said, elated Brett's prognosis was so good, although not entirely sure how the muddy goo would help, yet she was willing to trust in its healing powers for his sake.

However, Felipe had referred to Brett as 'her man' and she frowned regretfully, "But you're wrong on the other thing. We're just friends, he's not my—." Her words trailed off as she found herself suddenly unwilling to admit that he was not *hers*.

What had happened on *The Rachel* was extremely intimate and, for her at least, something had definitely changed in the dynamic between them.

Involuntarily, she reached up and touched her mouth with her fingertips, recalling the feel of his lips on hers and the taste of his warm, probing tongue as it searched for her own. It was a memory that would stay with her forever and maybe, in some way, that did make him hers, just a little.

Felipe smiled knowingly at her. "Like I say, your man be fine."

Liv simply blushed and argued no more.

***

When Brett opened his eyes it was only just getting light. His fever had gone, his delirium had passed and his head felt properly clear for the first time in days.

However, he was more than a little confused by his surroundings having awoken on an old brass bed, in what appeared to be a hut of some kind.

What is more, a black man who he did not recognise was asleep on a mattress against the far wall.

However, what interested him more was Liv, who was asleep next to him. She was sitting in a chair beside the bed although bent over so that her head was cradled in her arms on the bed itself.

Her face was turned towards him. It was deeply tanned, although her cheeks were rosy with sunburn and her nose was peeling a little - her lips were also somewhat chapped, yet to him she looked astonishingly beautiful.

The sight of her lips triggered something in his brain, a memory perhaps, a faint recollection of the two of them kissing - their mouths pressed together in the darkness as they drifted silently on a blackened sea. *Was it real or just a dream?*

Brett was unaware of any pain until he tried to sit up and then he felt it acutely; wincing loudly as he inadvertently angered his wound, reminding him sharply that he had recently been shot.

The sound disturbed Liv and her eyes flickered open.

"Brett?" She queried groggily, unable to quite believe that he was conscious and apparently feeling better. "My God, you're awake - how do you feel?"

"I feel okay," he replied, "although kind of sore I suppose. How long have I been out?"

Liv sat upright, "Nearly four days," she said. "Thought I was gonna lose you there for a while."

"Four days - Christ!" Exclaimed Brett, utterly amazed.

Still half asleep, Liv yawned deeply; stretching out her arms above her head and arching backwards in the chair, trying to relieve the ache in her spine from being curled over all night.

However, in doing so, she noticed that her sunburnt limbs no longer hurt at all; the balm given to her by the old woman had worked wonders on her delicate skin, turning it from a livid red to a rich, dark brown overnight. *'Well I'll be damned,'* she thought.

"Where the hell are we?" Brett asked. "What is this place?"

Liv looked a little shame faced as she replied, "Ah, well, I was aiming for Jamaica but I kinda overshot it a little."

"A little? How much is a little?"

She grimaced, "Erm, I'd say about three hundred miles or so."

"Three hundred miles - Jesus, Liv!"

"Hey, don't knock it, bub," Liv snapped, taking exception to his accusatory tone. "If it wasn't for me you might not have been anywhere at all - and besides, I kinda like this place."

Brett smiled, he could not help it. Nor could he deny that she had saved his life. "Yeah, well I guess you're right. Where are we anyway?"

"Somewhere off the coast of Haiti—"

"Haiti? Bloody hell!"

"Yeah, I know, wild right?"

Brett was utterly gobsmacked, "Yeah, I'd say *wild* is about right."

Liv smiled and shrugged. "Could be worse I guess."

He looked at her. "I suppose," he replied, lacking the strength to stay cross with her.

His face was pale and his eyes sunken. He was still very weak and suspected any attempt to get out of bed would be foolish at present.

"You've phoned your dad, though, I take it? They all know we're safe?" He asked.

Again Liv stared back at him guiltily. "Erm, not exactly."

"I don't understand. What do you mean? You have spoken to them haven't you?"

"Well, you see, that's just it. When I said it couldn't be worse, well that's not entirely true."

"Why, what do you mean? They *do* know we're alive, don't they?"

"No, they don't - and I'm not sure that they are either." Thinking of her family now, Liv suddenly felt emotional and tears sprung up unexpectedly, taking her a little by surprise. "I've been out of my mind with worry - what with you nearly dying and everyone else back at *Far Point* in so much danger. I just didn't know what to—" the words choked in her throat as she fought to compose herself, feeling foolish and embarrassed for becoming upset, knowing it would serve no purpose. She had to remain strong but the joy she felt at Brett's sudden recovery had weakened her defences.

"I think what the young miss is trying to tell you, brother," said the deep baritone of Felipe who had stirred from his slumber and was now standing behind Liv's chair, "Is that there are no phones on the island, no way to make contact with the outside world - so nobody knows you're here except those of us who live here."

Brett stared wide-eyed at the tall, mahogany skinned man who had spoken.

"Bloody hell," he said with astonishment.

***

Brett remained bed-ridden for three more days on the strict orders of the old woman who visited daily; each time applying more of her medicinal gunk to his rapidly healing wound.

Liv, in the meantime, helped out around the village. Also, in return for Felipe's kindness, she tidied and cleaned his hut from top to bottom and did all of his chores whilst he, himself, was out all day fishing.

In addition, Liv spent much of her time with Brett; fussing around him, helping him wash and eat - she even assisted him whenever he needed to use the dunny, although left him to perform his business alone. Nevertheless, she was always there, waiting outside, to help him back to the bed.

On the fourth day, Brett ventured out of bed properly for the first time and with Liv's help took a slow stroll around the village.

By the fifth day he was walking unaided and by the sixth he seemed almost back to his old self, although his wound was still tender and would need several more days of gentle recuperation. However, in general, the old woman's concoction had worked wonders and neither Brett nor Liv could quite believe how quickly he had healed.

On the seventh day since her and Brett's unceremonious arrival on the island, Liv stood ankle deep in the crystal clear ocean just offshore, looking over to where *The Rachel* was beached just a short distance away.

Felipe and his gang of fishermen, supervised by a seriously concerned Brett, who was fretting about any possible damage to his pride and joy, were trying to push the small cruiser off the sand bank she had grounded herself upon.

The old woman had warned Brett that any over exertion might lead to his wound opening up again and advised that he rest for at least a few more days. But he and Liv were both anxious for the safety of their loved ones and desperate to make contact - both to tell them they were okay and to be certain the others had escaped from *Far Point* alive.

In order to do that they had to get to Jamaica. There they would find not only a phone but also, hopefully, a plane which would take them to join the others.

***

Twenty minutes later and *The Rachel* was once again floating freely, re-fuelled and laden with enough fresh fruit and clean drinking water to see Brett and Liv safely to Jamaica.

Standing waist deep in the water beside the small boat, Liv hugged Felipe warmly and kissed him lightly on the cheek. "Thank you for being so lovely," she said.

"Twas nothing, girlie," he replied, embarrassed and delighted in equal measure by her show of affection.

Brett then shook Felipe's hand. "I can't thank you enough. You saved my life. You're a good man, Felipe and a good friend too now."

Again, the older man looked embarrassed by the kind words but could not prevent himself from grinning broadly with pride; his teeth brilliant white against his dark brown skin.

Then Brett and Liv finally clambered aboard the newly launched cruiser; Brett taking particular care so as not to disturb his wound.

"You got your chart, brother?" Felipe asked, shielding his eyes from the glare of the sun as he looked up from the sea at Brett who was now standing on the deck of *The Rachel*.

"Yep, got it," replied Brett. "And I've charted the course so all being well we should be okay."

"Good. Then you should reach Jamaica by midday tomorrow at the latest," said Felipe. "God speed, brother. You, too, girle."

"Thanks Felipe. Goodbye," said Brett as he turned and headed for the wheel house.

"Bye," said Liv tearfully to the kindly Haitian as the engine sparked into life.

She remained at the stern as *The Rachel* headed out to sea, waiving to Felipe and his friends who stayed standing in the sea waiving back.

Liv waived until the small group of people were little more than tiny specks in the distance then turned and joined Brett at the helm, hoping that before too long they would finally be reunited with all those they loved.

***

By sunset that evening they had been going for sometime, however Brett's wound was now feeling tight and painful from the long hours spent at the wheel. So, as the light faded, they dropped anchor on a calm sea and settled down on the cushions donated by Felipe at the rear of the craft. He had given them blankets too as the sea air after dark was prone to be chilly.

Brett, currently in less than peak physical condition and tired from the hours on his feet, slumped wearily down beside Liv and rested his head on her shoulder.

"Sure you're comfy?" She asked, feigning indignance.

"Uh-huh, very - thanks", he replied with a grin, then added cheekily, "although you could do with a bit more padding."

"Hey!" She cried, slapping him playfully, "You saying you'd

rather me be fat?"

"No - not all of you - just your shoulder maybe. It's way too bony to be properly comfortable."

Liv laughed, happily playing along. "Well that'd look just great wouldn't it? A nice, slim body and one freakishly fat shoulder!"

"I'm just saying," continued Brett mischievously as he snuggled into her, "It'd be a lot more cosy, that's all."

"Ah, quit the whining," replied Liv. "Sides, I don't get any complaints."

Brett smiled, his eyes shut. "Nope, I bet you don't."

Liv turned her head sharply to look at him, "What's that supposed to mean?"

Brett opened his eyes to see her glaring at him. "Nothing," he laughed, holding his hands up in defence, worried that she might decide to slap him again only next time a little harder. "I mean it - it was a compliment, honest!"

She eyed him cautiously. "Hmm, yeah well it'd better be, buster" she warned with mock anger. "I saved your life - and don't you forget it."

Brett closed his eyes again and snuggled into her shoulder once more. "I won't," he said sleepily. "Ever."

Liv regarded him for a moment more, "Hmm, yeah, well we'll see about that."

As she watched, he appeared to nod off, but as she studied his tanned, peaceful face, she could not help but remember the last time they were on the boat together.

A warm feeling filled her belly and she suddenly felt extremely content. Indeed, in that moment she could have happily spent the rest of her life there, with Brett, just bobbing in their boat on the ocean with the stars up above and him laying beside her.

After a time, she turned her attention to the large bag of fresh fruit that Felipe had given them. She rummaged through the contents and finally selected a large, round orange for herself. Piercing the skin with her long thumbnail, she swiftly pealed it then broke it up into segments, placing each one in her lap. Next, she picked up the fattest segment and bit into it, the juice spurting out and spilling down her chin.

The mouth-watering scent of the orange was enough to rouse Brett from his slumber and Liv felt him stir beside her as her mouth filled with the tangy taste of the juicy fruit.

As Brett's eyes flickered open, everything suddenly seemed extremely familiar - like déjà vu. He could not quite think why but somehow he had the sense that he had lived this moment before. The starry night sky, the rhythmic lapping of the gentle waves against the side of the boat and the motion of *The Rachel* as she rocked soothingly on the quiet sea.

Yet it was more than just those things - it was Liv, too. The closeness of her; her very proximity to him - the familiarity of it was so vivid in his mind that it just had to be real, not just an imagined moment.

And then he spoke, before the thought had properly formed in his mind, before he had a chance to stop himself.

"We kissed, didn't we?" He said.

Liv stopped chewing instantly. "Sorry?"

"We kissed didn't we?" Brett repeated, squirming round to look at her directly in the face. "Last time we were out here, we kissed - I remember. *Didn't we?*"

Liv stared back at him, her eyes big and round and blue, orange juice dribbling enticingly from her plump lips and onto her chin. "Yes," she replied softly, stricken with guilt as she remembered the intimacy of feeding him as he lay wounded; their lips pressed together, their tongues entwined. Technically not actually kissing but in reality so much more. She could not deny it.

"Yes," she said again. "I'm sorry, I was just—" but then her voice deserted her.

Brett hotched up, his eyes never leaving her face which was now merely inches from his. She looked utterly adorable with her plump lips all sticky and juicy. Indeed, as they slowly parted he could not resist the taste of them any longer and unable to control himself, he leant in and kissed them lightly.

He relished the sweet succulence of their orangey tang as he gently pulled away again, yet he could still feel her breath on his face and smell the delicious citrusy aroma of her beautiful mouth.

Liv was momentarily startled, but she rallied quickly and responded in kind, pressing her lips against his, her tongue offering him another glorious taste of her.

Suddenly they were kissing frantically, as if their very lives depended on it; hot, passionate and deep; the years of lust erupting like a volcano.

Within seconds they were clawing at each other's clothes, tearing them off with urgent abandon and unrestrained desire.

Yet still they kissed, feasting off the others lips, their passion unquenchable, their tongues entwined as they hungrily craved for more.

Soon they were both naked, their firm, tanned bodies writhing together on a hastily strewn blanket at the rear of the boat, the culmination of a shared longing that each had held secret from the other.

But the secrecy was now gone as they made love long into the night.

Chapter Seventeen

Las Vegas

Sean's timing could not have been better. He had roused from his coma just a few days earlier yet for most of the time since, as a side-effect from the strong pain killers Doc Ridgeway had given him, he had been in a permanent state of drowsiness.

However, they had now flushed through his system and he was clear-headed at last; the pain in his chest now easing and much more bearable without the assistance of the powerful meds.

Indeed, Sean had not known a thing about Liv or Brett's disappearance until just hours before Liv telephoned so had been spared almost all of the worry that every other person in the house had been grievously afflicted with for the past week.

Now though, the mood in the house had been transformed. Liv and Brett were alive and in just a few short hours they would all be reunited on Canyon Hill Drive.

Victoria was almost giddy with delight, a wide smile etched permanently on her face. Rose, too, was humming a little tune as she flung the drapes wide and pushed open the window at the far end of the hospital ward, letting the bright Las Vegas sunshine stream into the room.

Sean was the only full-time patient in the ward now as both Joe and Matt had been deemed fit enough to be discharged - although

Matt was presently confined to a wheelchair and was still required to sleep in the ward at night.

Once the thrill of the news had subsided and the furore had died down a little, Sarah came into the ward and took her place in the chair beside Sean. She looked beautiful, as always to him, but he could tell she was tired. There was something else too; a wistfulness perhaps, that her son, Michael, would not be coming home with Liv and Brett.

Whilst she was delighted and relieved that they were safe she could not help but wish that Michael had been spared too. *Why had he had to die?*

"You okay?" Sean asked softly, understanding his wife's emotions completely as he placed his hand on hers.

She smiled. "I'm fine. Just a little teary I suppose and feeling a bit sorry for myself. But it's nothing, it'll pass. Just silliness."

Sean knew it was not as he felt it too. His daughter had lived but his son had not and he could not quite decide what he should be feeling - elation and relief at Liv's survival or sorrow and despair at Michael's death.

However, he knew how fortunate it was that anyone had survived the assault on *Far Point* at all. Not least himself.

But what had happened could not be changed and he and Sarah *had* to move on, *had* to get passed it.

"I love you, you know that?" He said as he studied his wife, still seeing in her the girl he had loved since he was ten years old.

She smiled again, this time there was a genuine happiness in it as she picked up his hand and kissed it fondly. "And I love you."

"Everything will turn out fine, Sarah, you'll see," he said.

She nodded, "I know."

Although the truth of it was, as they sat there in silence thinking about what might have been, neither of them could be certain everything would actually be okay.

Unlike Virgil and Victoria, who were reluctantly confined indoors, Matt was free to enjoy the well cared for garden that surrounded the house on Canyon Hill Drive. Ethan kept it in immaculate condition with not a blade of grass out of place and not a flower bed disturbed - except for the devastated section of hedge, border and turf where Matt's truck had ploughed onto the property. Ethan had hurriedly done his best to patch-up the hedge so as not to attract any unwarranted attention from passers-by, but it was far from perfect and still needed extensive repair.

"You sure made one heck of a mess," Violet remarked as she surveyed the scene, her South London accent strangely out of place in the all-American suburb in which Canyon Hill Drive was located.

"Yeah, well I don't like to do things by halves," Matt grinned before taking a deep pull on his half-smoked cigarette.

By comparison, his English accent was now all but gone, replaced by a definite Californian drawl; America being his home of many years.

Much to his chagrin, he was having to use a wheelchair and chomping at the bit to be fit once more. The frustration of not yet being able to walk unaided was truly infuriating as he hated being dependent on anyone. But he knew he had to be patient and that eventually he would heal fully, thanks to the Doc - however patience was not his strong suit.

Violet was behind him, leaning on the handles of the wheelchair as the pair of them took a break from their tour of the garden.

The sun was beating down on her back, the strappy top she was wearing allowing her to tan nicely in the Las Vegas afternoon. Indeed, over the preceding afternoons, her skin had turned a golden brown which, when complimented by her striking green eyes and long, dark hair made her look thoroughly irresistible.

Matt had tried his damnedest not to notice but that plan was failing miserably.

For years Matt had done his utmost to stay clear of relationships and commitment. Not since he was a very young man had he stayed with anyone for longer than a couple of weeks and actively avoided situations where he might find himself entangled.

Of course there had been women, many of them - in fact they practically fell at his feet and he was only human after all. But not since Suzie, the girl he had loved with all his heart; the girl he had intended to marry and spend the rest of his life with, had he felt the desire for something more permanent.

Suzie had been gunned down in the street; shot to pieces right in front of him in a botched gangland assassination and the horror of witnessing it, of seeing her lying there, lifeless and torn, her dress soaked through with her own blood, had never left him.

It had not been Matt's fault but he still felt guilt, even now. If she had not been with him she would not have died and that was the inescapable truth.

The assassins were trying to kill his father, Joe, but Suzie had selflessly thrown herself in front of him and their bullets had torn into her instead.

She had sacrificed herself so that Matt might know his father and he would be eternally grateful to her for that.

But her death haunted him and he could not forget.

For a long time Matt blamed his father for the atrocity of her death but then came to realise that it was not Joe's fault at all and simply forgave him. Over the years that followed they rebuilt their relationship, forging it ever stronger so that their bond was now totally unbreakable.

Yet all these years on Matt could still not forgive himself.

It was one of the reasons why he had never settled down. There was no doubt he had a wanderlust; a nomadic, free-spirit, but he was now approaching forty and knew it was time he set down some roots.

However, that was easier said than done. Firstly he had to meet the right person and so far he had not - or not anyone who could erase the memory of Suzie.

At least not until recently.

Indeed, since Violet's arrival at Ethan Ridgeway's home, Matt had found himself thinking about Suzie less and less. In fact the image of her face in his memory had been replaced by that of a woman with striking green eyes and long dark hair.

But still he fought against the obvious attraction, bridling against his natural instincts, steadfastly trying to remain aloof and immovable.

But it was proving more difficult as each day passed.

Particularly now, with Violet so close, leaning in next to him, her womanly perfume filling his nostrils and fuelling the intensity of his feelings towards her.

Her very presence was intoxicating and he found himself fighting the urge to kiss her.

But instead he sat in his wheelchair impassively smoking a cigarette, pretending he was barely aware of her.

Matt was usually supremely confident around women and naturally self assured. Yet with Violet he was trying not to give too much of himself away, subconsciously afraid perhaps that if he did, something dreadful might happen to her too.

But Violet was no delicate flower. She was slender and beautiful but had a core of steel and the tough resolve of a gangland dynasty running through her veins.

When she set her mind on something she would not be easily put-off - and that now applied to Matt Mason too.

For the better part of her life she had dedicated herself to her father and *The Golden Gloves* pub. Indeed, she had been pretty much running the place since she was seventeen years old. For all intents and purposes, even though her father's name was above the door, it was her place.

It had kept her busy and she had devoted almost every minute of her time to it. The clientele was primarily made up of old-time villains like her father but she loved them all dearly and they loved her. She was *their girl*.

But, regardless of her heritage, she remained a good girl. Alfie had made sure of it. He had kept her, the youngest of his offspring, honest and on the right track. Most of his other children had followed his path - yet all aside from Violet and Richie had eventually left him and gone their own way - no longer even keeping in touch.

However, Richie had stayed forever loyal and had risen through the ranks to eventually take his place at the head of the table alongside Manno O'Keefe.

But not Violet. Alfie had determinedly kept her on the straight and narrow and she was grateful for it.

She had thrown herself wholeheartedly into the pub, keeping it profitable even through the tough times. She was a grafter, no doubt about it, which had left little time for romance.

Many men had tried their luck but she was just not interested as all seemed to pale in comparison to her father.

Alfie was a villain but he had honour and his heart was true. He was a fierce ally and supremely dependable; a man with quiet dignity who was deeply respected by all who knew him.

To Violet he was everything and she put him on a pedestal which very few other men could ever hope to assail.

Yet there was something about Matt which intrigued her; something she found incredibly attractive. Not just his looks or his physique - although both were magnificent - but something much deeper than that.

Like Alfie, Matt, too, had a quiet dignity. She sensed that like her father he would also be extremely dependable and a strong, unflinching ally.

Yet, within him she saw pain, too. An inner sadness of some kind which had clearly left its mark and made him seem strangely lost and alone even though his family clearly loved him.

A few days earlier, Victoria had hinted that there was a tragedy in Matt's past; something about a former girlfriend who had died suddenly in horrific circumstances. Violet did not like to push for information as at the time Vicky was still wracked with worry over Liv, but what she had told her did explain Matt's obvious pain.

Violet's heart went out to him; the attraction she initially felt when first she set eyes on him suddenly becoming much more significant.

Maybe it was that she, too, had recently lost her father and brother in horrific circumstances; maybe it was that she found in Matt a kindred spirit. Violet could not be sure what it was but there was a definite connection between the two of them and she was almost certain Matt felt it too.

"I reckon I owe the Doc a new hedge, don't you?" Matt said as he surveyed the damage.

"Yeah, I'd say it's the least you could do after he patched you up - you could patch his hedge up in return," replied Violet.

"That's what I'll do then, when I'm fit enough to get out of this goddamn chair and back on my feet, I'll repair that hedge and make it as good as new."

Violet smiled. Even though he tried well to disguise it, he was a real boy scout at heart. Without thinking she bent and kissed him on the top of the head. "I think that'd be very nice of you," she said.

Then she froze, suddenly aware of what she had done. It was an innocent gesture which came so naturally to her that she could hardly believe she had done it. *What the hell was she thinking?*.

In the few seconds of silence that followed something changed and the dynamic noticeably shifted between them, as if a barrier had been broken.

The air became more charged, the atmosphere more intense.

"Hmm," said Matt, slightly taken aback by the show of affection and trying to make light of it even though a fire had been lit within him. "Well, I do my best."

"My God," Violet said, clearly mortified and ready to rush back into the house to hide her embarrassment. "Sorry - I don't know what—"

But Matt grabbed her arm as she tried to pull away. "Don't." He said firmly. "Don't apologise. There's no need."

Violet paused for a moment, her arm straining in his grip. But then, after a beat, she finally relaxed and Matt let go of her.

Again something shifted, as if there was now an acceptance of the growing bond between them and there was silence for a while as they absently studied the hedge and digested this unexpected change in their relationship.

"Do you mind if I help you?" Violet suddenly said. "Fix the hedge, I mean? The Doc's helped me too - fixed me up, taken me in and put a roof over my head - I'd like to repay him if I can."

Matt looked up and smiled at her. "Sure, I'd like that," he said.

***

After a while, they resumed their tour of the garden but before going back indoors Violet, who had obviously been in deep thought, said, "What about after we've fixed the hedge. What are you going to do then?"

Matt shrugged. "Dunno. I haven't really got that far - it all depends on my dad I suppose - what him and Sean have got in mind. This damn vendetta has gotta stop soon. It was all supposed to have been done and forgotten. We'd all left it behind but now Michael's dead and so are Ray and Ruby. Somebody's gotta put an end to it before somebody else dies. What about you - what are you gonna do?"

266

"Not sure. I think that rests on whatever your dad and Sean want to do, too. It's why I came out here to Vegas - Bass Stone killed my father and brother and I want that bastard to pay!"

Matt considered her for a moment and his mind flashed back to that awful moment when Suzie was killed. The same vendetta that killed her was still raging, still claiming victims. He could not bear the thought of Violet being another.

"Be careful what you wish for Violet," he said with meaning. "You never know where it might lead."

"Yeah?" She replied, suddenly angry, "Well I wish Bass Stone was dead and I for one won't be happy until he is—"

"Hey, hold on, just wait a minute—" Matt interjected, but Violet's hatred of Bass Stone had got the better of her.

"No, I won't bloody wait - and if no one else is gonna kill him then I'll damn well do it myself!"

With that she marched off.

"Violet! Please, listen—" Matt called after her.

But it was too late, she was already halfway back to the house and he was left sitting in his wheelchair all alone.

***

Violet flung open the back door and stomped through the kitchen, nearly knocking both Victoria and Rose over as she ran past them, obviously very upset. "I'm sorry!" She yelled behind her, emotion in her voice, as she rushed down the hallway and bounded up the stairs.

Vicky and Rose looked at each other with concern then both hurried after her.

They arrived outside Violet's bedroom door a few moments later to find it closed.

Again, Rose looked at Vicky who nodded her encouragement, indicating that she should knock.

Very lightly, Rose tapped on the door. "Hello? Vee, it's Rose and Vicky - are you okay sweetie?"

"I'm fine, thanks," replied a choked voice from inside, clearly not 'fine' at all.

"Can we come in?" Rose asked tentatively.

"Er, well..." Violet began, feeling slightly silly now for her irrational outburst and the tears which were presently streaming down her face.

"It's alright, honey," said Vicky, "We understand - we know it's tough. Please, let us help."

There was no reply which Vicky interpreted as a positive sign and signalled Rose to open the door.

Silently she turned the handle and the pair of them crept into the room.

"You okay?" Rose said, seeing Violet sitting on a stool by the dressing table, her head bowed.

"I don't know," Violet sniffed. "I'm just emotional, that's all."

"Is it Matt?" Asked Vicky.

"Matt? Why, what do you mean?" Replied Violet, surprised by the question.

"Please, honey. It's as plain as day," said Vicky in her typical no nonsense way, "The pair of you can't keep your eyes off each other."

Violet looked up, her expression one of alarm. "Really? Is it so obvious?"

"Mmm hmm, 'fraid so," said Vicky.

"Really?" Violet now looked at Rose.

"I'm afraid Vicky's right Vee," said Rose. "But it doesn't matter, we all think it's lovely - Matt's a great guy and he's been on his own too long."

"Ain't that the truth," agreed Vicky. "About time that boy settled down."

"But there's nothing going on with him - not really," said Violet. "I think there could be but—"

"But what, sweetie?" Encouraged Rose.

"I don't know. It's like there's something holding him inside that won't let go. Does that make sense?"

Rose and Vicky looked at each other once more, both thinking the same thing.

"There is, isn't there?" Violet asked. "It's about that girl years ago isn't it? The one you spoke about Vicky. Is that why?"

Victoria turned to Rose. "I think we need to tell her about Suzie."

Rose nodded her agreement.

"Please tell me," begged Violet, "help me understand."

Slowly, Rose sat down on the bed. "Well," she began as Vicky squatted on the edge of the stool next to Violet, "It all happened a long time ago…"

Over the minutes that followed, Rose told Violet all about Suzie; how she and Matt were in love; how they intended to leave London and spend the rest of their lives together in America - how Suzie was going to work for Victoria as her assistant in Hollywood whilst Matt worked for Sean on his ranch. But then Rose explained how it had all gone tragically wrong and before their planned departure for America Suzie had been brutally gunned down in the street; the circumstances truly horrific.

She went on to say how badly this had affected Matt, that he had never fully gotten over it and how it undoubtedly explained his reluctance to settle down.

"But give him time," she said finally, "He's got a good heart and I can tell he's really fond of you - he just needs to get used to the idea and accept that whatever happened in the past can't be changed - it's what he does next and for the rest of his life that matters."

"Wow, I had no idea," said Violet. "That explains a lot."

"He's a great guy," Vicky reiterated, "Believe me - he saved my life. If not for him I wouldn't be here now I guarantee it. Just give him time."

"Why, what happened to you?" Asked Violet.

"It's a long story, honey, but suffice to say Matt is one of the best. Him, Virge, Joe and Sean, all of them really good guys and we're lucky to have 'em."

Violet smiled, she admired Vicky's loyalty and obvious love for them all.

"So what did you argue about anyway?" Said Rose to Violet.

"Oh, nothing. It was not really an argument just me being all mixed up that's all. This thing with Bass Stone, him killing my dad and Ritchie - it's got me all—" suddenly she teared up again.

"Hey, c'mon. We know, we've all been there and it's tough. Sean and Sarah have lost poor Michael and everyone's feeling the loss of Ray and Ruby - your dad and Ritchie, too. It's terrible. Joe and Sean have lived with this for most of their lives and still it goes on—"

"But don't you feel angry?" Violet blurted.

"Of course we do," said Vicky. "Two days ago I didn't know if my daughter was dead or alive - her and Brett both missing without a trace. I feel so goddamn angry I could rip Jez Vincenzi's heart out with my bare hands - but there's more to consider than just that."

"What do you mean?"

"She means all the dead, Vee," said Rose. "All the bodies piling up. God knows how many were killed on *Far Point* along with Ray and Ruby - and too many have died in the past. Your dad and Ritchie are just two of the many. But what would you have us do?"

"Fight!" Snapped Violet. "Fight with everything you've got until those bastards are dead!"

"Don't you geddit?" Vicky asked.

"Get what?" Replied Vicky hotly, her eyes burning with rage.

"We have all been fighting. Joe and Sean have been fighting for over thirty years. Matt and Virge, too. All of us. Ten years ago we all thought we had seen an end to this goddamn stupid vendetta

- started by a madman in London before you were even born. Him and his associates killed or hurt almost everyone Joe and Sean came into contact with - caused countless pain to those that they loved - me, Rose and Sarah included. He tried to destroy everything they ever had - wreaked havoc on their lives time and time again. So they fought back. Fought with everything they had until finally Sean killed Benny Vincenzi and put an end to his worthless life."

Violet was quiet now, her anger subsiding; the realisation of what the others had been through slowly sinking in and the comprehension that it was not her alone who had suffered finally dawning.

"But it didn't end," said Rose, picking up where Vicky left off. "We went into hiding, thinking, praying that all that death, all that violence was behind us. For ten years we rebuilt our lives, raised our children, allowed ourselves to believe everything was all okay. But it wasn't."

Violet looked at her guiltily, sorry now for losing her temper.

"Well, you know the rest of it," Rose added. "Somehow this Bass Stone found out where we were - killed your father, Ritchie and Manno, too, as well as Michael and God knows how many more. Now we're on the run yet again, our lives in tatters."

"So what would you have us do, Vee?" Vicky asked. "Fight again? Lose more people that we love - maybe Matt or Virge, Sean or Joe - perhaps even one of us three in this room?"

"No, course not - I just—" Violet began.

"I know, honey," said Vicky. "It's a goddamn sonofabitch and it hurts like hell but it ain't just a simple fix. There's a hell of a lot to consider."

"I'm sorry," said Violet. "I'm just so angry, that's all."

"Of course you are," said Rose. "You're grieving too. We understand - all of us do. But you're not alone, not anymore. We're all here to help and we all know what you're going through."

271

"Thanks," Violet said sheepishly, her voice little more than a whisper. "I've been so selfish. So stupid. I never really gave much thought to anyone else - I've been just so blinded by hatred. All I could think of was my dad and Ritchie and getting even with Bass Stone."

"Hey, don't sweat it, honey," said Vicky, "It does you good to be selfish once in a while."

"But I was so mean to Matt, too," said Violet.

Vicky put an arm around her and gave her a hug, "Don't you worry about it, Vee - besides, that boy's a tough one, he can handle it, believe me."

Rose smiled. "I know I shouldn't say it but sometimes I think Matt could do with a bit of 'mean'. Every woman he meets practically swoons in front of him so it won't hurt to give him a bit more of a challenge. It'll do him good and probably make him realise exactly what he might be missing."

"Exactly," agreed Vicky.

"And you two don't hate me for being such a selfish little bitch?"

Now Rose came over and hugged her too; all three of them there in front of the dressing table with their arms around each other. "Of course not," Rose said, giving her a kiss on the cheek, "You're one of the family now whether you like it or not."

Violet smiled with relief, overwhelmed by their kindness. It felt good to be part of a family again.

***

Two days later Virgil called everyone into the kitchen for a family meeting.

Over the past couple of days he had held several long consultations with both Joe and Sean and Brett and Liv. Whilst he was absolutely delighted and extremely relieved to have the two younger ones back, as was Victoria, it was now time to make plans for the future.

Virgil had listened to the opinions of the others and taken their views on board and now, with his wife by his side, he had finally reached a decision.

"I guess most of you know what this is about," he began. "And firstly let me say that it's absolutely great to have Liv and Brett back safely."

"I'll drink to that!" Agreed Sean, gingerly raising a steaming mug of coffee, the effort of movement showing on his face. He was now occupying the wheelchair recently vacated by Matt and was positioned at the far end of the table next to Sarah. Still in pain but healing satisfactorily.

"Hear, hear!" Said Joe, voicing his approval.

"Sssh!" Hissed Rose with mock sternness.

"Good to have you back, too, Sean," Virgil added.

"And I'll drink to that!" Injected Sarah.

Everyone smiled and echoed their agreement.

"We thought we'd lost you for a while," continued Virgil, "And you two as well," he said, looking now at Brett and Liv. "But somehow you made it off that island alive and we're all thankful for that."

"So what is it you wanna say, honey?" Asked Louretta who was sitting next to him with Ethan tucked neatly in beside her. Already they looked like an old married couple.

"Well, after a lot of discussion and a whole lot of soul searching," Virgil replied, "Vicky and I have decided that it's time to go back to our lives - so we'll be heading back to LA in the morning."

"What?" Exclaimed Louretta. "Are you goddamn kidding?"

"It's okay, Mom," chimed in Victoria. "We've got it worked out - we'll be fine—"

"What do you mean 'you'll be fine' - how do you know?"

"They will Rett," said Sean calmly. "Listen to Virge - let him explain. It's a good plan."

Louretta looked from Sean to Joe, seeing him nod his

agreement. "Fine," she said at last, "What's this foolproof plan then?"

"Not foolproof," Virgil said, "but hopefully it'll work."

"So tell me, then," Louretta said sharply.

"He's trying to, Rett," said Ethan coming to Virgil's defence, "If you'll just let the boy speak."

Virgil had not been called a 'boy' for many years but he was grateful of Ethan's support and Louretta suddenly seemed suitably admonished - which in itself was an extremely rare occurrence. Clearly the Doctor had a calming influence on her.

"Thanks, Doc," Virgil said.

"So what's the plan, Virge?" Rose asked, smoothing the way.

"Simply this," he replied. "It's just not practical for Vic and me to stay 'dead'. The fact of the matter is, like it or not, we are famous; our faces are everywhere - magazines, billboards - movie theatres - all over. Short of extensive plastic surgery neither of us could ever walk down the street unrecognised again. So, like I said, it's just not practical.

"We've also got major commitments which, if not honoured, could bring about our ruin - alive or dead cos our estates would be effected, too.

"So we go back to Malibu. Back to Hollywood. Go to the police, tell them we - Vicky, me, Josh and you Rett, were all victims of a kidnap and murder plot orchestrated by Jez Vincenzi and Bass Stone. We tell 'em the truth, that they tried to kill us - to run us off the road and that we were forced to go into hiding, to pretend to be dead, for the sake of our own survival."

"But what if the cops don't believe you?" Asked Louretta.

"They will, Rett," continued Virgil. "I'm sure of it. If there's one thing I get being a famous movie star it's influence. There'll be no need to mention Joe and Sean at all - we can keep their names and everyone else's completely out of it. With both Vicky and me telling the same story the cops won't have a choice but to believe us. We can

274

get the TV and media on our side - I'm sure Beau Brewster can help with that - and the cops will be under pressure to bring in Vincenzi and Stone as soon as possible. The pair of them won't dare make a move - not with that kind of attention on them."

"Do you mean the media mogul Beau Brewster?" Ethan asked. "Weren't you married to him, Rett?"

"Yeah, honey, I was," said Louretta.

"He was just one of my many step-fathers, Ethan," said Victoria with a mischievous grin.

"Yes, thank you, Vicky, that's correct," Louretta said succinctly.

"Oh," said Ethan, sounding a little forlorn.

"Don't worry, sugar," said Louretta placing a hand over his. "That flame burned out long ago but he's still a good and reliable friend - I reckon Virge might be onto something."

"Anyway," continued Virgil, "As I was saying. I think the cops should keep Vincenzi and Stone busy but Vicky and me will step up our personal security at all times and we'll get a detail sorted for Josh, too, so he can head back to *CalTech*—"

"What? You're going back to school?" Louretta exclaimed, turning to Josh with amazement. "Surely not?"

"It's what I want Grandma," said her grandson. "I wanna go back to school, finish my studies. I'll be okay."

"Sean - have you agreed to this?" Louretta asked.

"I have, yes." He said. "It's what he wants, Rett. Virge, Joe and me we'll get him the best goddamn security detail available and they'll protect him at all times. I don't like it but I can't expect him to live in hiding - not like Joe and me have had to do. It's just not fair."

"But aren't you scared?"

"Course I'm scared," Sean said hotly, "I'm bloody terrified. I've already lost one son and nearly my daughter, too. But Josh has got to do what's best for him - Liv, as well. I can't stand in their way. All I can do is protect them the best I can."

"He's right, Mom," said Victoria.

"He is, Grandma," Liv agreed.

"What? You've both signed up for this madness, too?" Louretta was clearly shocked.

Vicky nodded. "Uh-huh. Reluctantly, yes. But I can't put a leash on him. Josh is his own man and if that's what he wants to do then I won't stop him, much as I wish I could."

"And what about you, sugar?" Said Louretta now talking to Liv. "Are you going too?"

"No Grandma," said Liv, linking her arm through Brett's in a show of togetherness, their new found love no secret from anyone gathered there at the table, "We thought we'd stick around here for a while if that's okay with you Doc."

Everyone knew there had always been a spark between Liv and Brett. Indeed, it was widely suspected that it was only a matter of time before that spark turned into a burning flame. So it came as no surprise to anyone that they had finally taken things to the next level. In fact the news was greeted with a great deal of delight, particularly from Rose, Sarah and Victoria who were already imagining the sound of wedding bells.

"Of course," Ethan smiled kindly at Liv. "You're very welcome, both of you." He had already informed his realtor that the house was no longer for sale.

"Well I ain't staying here," Louretta said. "If Josh is going back to *CalTech* then I'm going to my bungalow where I'll only be thirty minutes away if he needs me."

Louretta's main residence was the *Wildwood Ranch* in Palm Springs, but she also owned property in New York, Hawaii and a luxurious beach fronted bungalow in Santa Monica where she was currently proposing to go.

"But Virge and me will only be up the coast in Malibu—" Vicky protested.

"Don't care," Louretta was adamant. "My place is still closer."

"It's okay Grandma, I'll be fine—" Josh began before being cut off.

"Fine or not. I want you close," Louretta said firmly.

"But Rett, I thought you might stay here for a while?" Ethan said.

"Yeah well, I was gonna but—" suddenly she broke off as an idea occurred to her. "Hey! Why don't you come to the bungalow with me?"

"It's hardly a bungalow Grandma," Liv pointed out, "More of a grand villa."

"Yeah, well," Louretta winked at her, "I like a little luxury when I'm away from the ranch."

Ethan was somewhat surprised by the offer but it immediately had appeal. He could think of nothing more pleasurable than spending some time with Louretta alone - away from Canyon Hill Drive and the house that was filled with memories of his dead wife. "Sure - I'd love to go with you," he said, "but I can't just up and leave this place - what about everyone else? Where would they go?"

"Well, I was gonna speak to you about that, Doc," Joe interjected. "I was wondering if Rose and I and Sarah and Sean could stay here for a while - lay low until we can plan what to do next.

It was not in Joe's DNA to run from a fight but in order to take down Vincenzi and Stone he would need to be at his best, as would his allies. Yet he, Sean, Matt, Brett and Virgil, too, were still licking their wounds from the last encounter and few of them would be in a fit state to rise to the challenge any time soon. They would all need to recuperate properly before entering the fray once more. However, Joe and Sean were no longer convinced that was the way to go. Too many had already died and they, themselves, were not getting any younger. So why not do as Virgil suggested and leave matters to the police - it would cost nothing and their names would never have to be mentioned so their anonymity would be assured; their families safe. Virgil had worked out a good strategy so it was certainly worth a try.

"If you want to go with Rett to Santa Monica," Joe continued, "why don't you let us rent this place from you, we'll take good care of it—"

"Yeah," Matt broke in, "I've been meaning to fix that hedge for you, Doc - make it as good as new. I'd be happy to tend your garden, too, if you'll let me?"

"Me, too," added Violet. "This place has been like a home to me and you've all been like family - I'd love to stay for a while and pay back your kindness - I'd be happy to pay—"

"Nonsense!" Said Ethan. "I won't hear of it. You're all welcome to stay here for as long as you like. Take your time, get well - plan out what you're going to do next. Matt, I appreciate your offer and thank you - it'd be very kind and Joe, please treat my home as your own."

"So does that mean you'll come to Santa Monica with me?" Asked Louretta.

"It does - if that's okay with you?" Ethan smiled.

"Well sure it is, honey - I wouldn't have asked if it wasn't!"

"Careful Doc," giggled Victoria, "You might end up being husband number four!"

Louretta narrowed her eyes at her outspoken daughter and Ethan merely bowed his head bashfully. But neither argued with her.

"So," Virgil said at last, "are we all in agreement?"

Louretta looked around the table, everyone nodding. "Looks that way," she said. "Let's just hope this plan of yours works."

"Yeah," agreed Virgil. "Let's hope that it does."

Chapter Eighteen

Miami

Jez Vincenzi awoke to the sound of feminine laughter echoing around the empty corridors of his grandfather Tito's vast mansion in Key Biscayne, which now belonged to him.

Slowly he roused from beneath the black silk sheets, which had not been changed in many days, and climbed reluctantly out of bed, intent on finding the source of the apparent hilarity.

In staggering from his palatial, yet disorderly room, he briefly caught a glimpse of his reflection in the mirror. The left side of his face now bore a permanent peppering of tiny scars caused by the scatter of pellets from Ray Reece's shotgun. This ugly cluster of blemishes, which was repeated on his neck and left arm, shone pink against his olive skin and served not only as a constant reminder of his disastrous assault on *Far Point* but also of his abject failure as a leader.

In one ill-judged, hastily planned and poorly executed offensive he had wiped out almost all of his men and brought about the total ruination of the Vincenzi/Carboni organisation. Worse still, he had lost any modicum of respect he may have inherited as his grandfathers' sole heir and left himself vulnerable to a takeover - which he was now completely powerless to prevent.

Yet, as he stared at his reflection, the scarring on his face barely registered. Nor did the deaths of all those men he had taken to The Caymans and neither did the loss of his grandfathers' empire.

None of it meant anything now.

It had at first, straight after the battle at *Far Point*, when he felt his failure acutely but now he just felt dead inside.

The past few weeks he had spent mostly alone, either in his room or wandering aimlessly around the near empty Vincenzi mansion. He was in a daze, like a lost little boy with no one to guide him - except for Bass Stone who Jez now relied upon for everything.

Indeed, Bass now made all decisions and Jez simply obeyed without question.

In short, Jez was a broken man. There was nothing left of the arrogant, obnoxious youth he had been prior to the botched attack on *Far Point*.

He had lost interest in women, partying and even cocaine. His flash cars stayed undriven in the garage and his fancy clothes hung unworn in his vast closet.

As it was, the only thing he wore lately was a pair of grubby silk pyjamas and the only thing that interested him was vengeance.

Nowadays, he only really felt two emotions; the first being anger, which was aimed squarely at those who, in his deluded opinion, had brought about his terrible downfall; and the second, was fear.

Jez had become completely paranoid and lived in constant fear of being assassinated by a rival family - or worse, of being murdered in his sleep by either Rocco or Falco who were clearly disgruntled and becoming more so as each day passed.

But it was Stone who Jez feared more than anyone as he was the biggest, meanest predator of them all. However, Bass had used this to his advantage and, using every ounce of his fearsome persona, had managed to manipulate the younger man to his will.

As a result, Jez had rather misguidedly assumed Bass to be an ally; a formidable guardian whom the others were mindful of and clearly intimidated by.

Capitalising on this, Bass had also taken on the role of chief advisor and it was a position he exploited to the full. Yet even though his motives were transparently obvious Jez seemed content to let Stone ride roughshod over him.

However, deep down he knew that Stone's allegiance would cost him dearly and for his help in killing Joe Cassidy, Sean Noakes and the others the price tag would undoubtedly be extortionate but it was a bargain he was prepared to make.

Vengeance was more important to Jez than all the money in the world - indeed his desire for it had consumed him since he was ten years old and, just like his father before him, it had now driven him to the very brink of insanity.

Stone sensed this and knew he had to tread carefully. It would be easy to tip the boy over the edge so he had to proceed with caution, play the long game and, for the time being, be the strong right hand that Jez so desperately needed which, Bass confidently felt, would bring about its own reward.

Vincenzi was Stone's ticket to the big payoff he had long been seeking so he was determined not to let the opportunity slip through his fingers for a second time.

Bass had waited over ten years for the same chance with Big Jack Anderson back in London, which in the end had never materialised, so a few more weeks in Miami for a prize far greater than Anderson could ever have delivered was well worth the wait.

And this time success was almost guaranteed.

***

The sound of laughter and general frivolity grew louder as Jez padded down the white marble corridors of his inherited home; the feminine voices now joined by Bass Stone's deep baritone.

It was clear to Jez now that all this noise, which was echoing off the clean, cool walls, was emanating from the enormous bathroom that formed part of his grandfather Tito's grandiose bedroom suite.

The main room was opulent in style; rich fabrics, expensive rugs and heavy, ornate drapes that reflected Tito's more traditional tastes. The furniture was dark, classical and Italian which was at odds with the mansion's uniquely 'Miami' appearance. The bed, which took centre stage, was a big four-poster with an embroidered throw and blood red sheets which were all mussed up and had clearly seen recent action.

A naked girl with a shapely derrière and a tattoo of a half-eaten popsicle on the cheek of her left buttock lay face down in the pillows. She was fast asleep, all partied out, with a line of coke sitting beside her on the night stand.

Jez was somewhat taken aback as he entered through the wide open door. This room was Tito's inner sanctum and as such it was off limits. Not even Jez, himself, had thought to claim it. Yet Stone had clearly decided to use it as his own personal playground.

As Jez wandered across the large room, he could see items of clothing strewn all over the floor, including several bras and at least three pairs of lacy panties.

Finally he ambled into the bathroom and found the source of all the laughter.

Sitting at one end of the enormous square bath, being lathered, fondled and generally amused by three more naked girls, was Bass Stone. Hot water was pouring out of the gold taps at the opposite end and warm steam was filling the air like a sauna.

The girls, who each had spectacular figures, were of varying colours. One was black with a tight round afro and a tight round ass; another was Puerto Rican - dark haired, light brown skin with enhanced breasts and nipples that stuck out like thumbs. The third was white, bottle blonde with small titties and a colourful tapestry of intricate tattoos covering the whole of one arm.

All were having a wonderfully debauched time and Bass was enjoying himself immensely as ringmaster.

Around the edge of the gold-plated tub were assorted glasses; some empty, some half-full, as well as three drained magnums of champagne. A fourth bottle was being swigged decadently by Stone as the black girl straddled him amidst the copious amounts of soapy bubbles filling the bath. As some of the expensive liquid escaped from his mouth and dribbled down his chin, the Puerto Rican girl licked it hungrily off before then sticking her tongue into the mouth of the white girl who sucked on it with relish.

"Hey, what's going on?" Jez asked, disturbing them all from their pleasures.

Stone pulled the bottle from his mouth and turned to see the boy standing there in the doorway.

Jez was no more the chisel-jawed young buck with carefully tousled hair and clearly defined six-pack that Bass had first encountered when he arrived, not so long ago, in Miami with Michael Walsh as his captive.

All Jez's former swagger and cockiness had evaporated; replaced by this dishevelled and bloated creature who stood before him now.

A small pot-belly was visible beneath Jez's open pyjama jacket and the satin bottoms were dirty and stained with spatters of spaghetti sauce and piss which made him look like some sad, pathetic vagrant.

How the mighty have fallen, Bass mused as he replied. "What do you mean - what's it look like?"

As he spoke, the black girl kissed him and wriggled on his lap to ensure his continued arousal, whilst the Puerto Rican turned to face Jez and made a provocative show of lathering her fake breasts teasingly.

But Jez was immune to her charms and instead focussed his attention on Stone.

Against the three slender girls, Bass looked enormous; his huge, muscular bulk dwarfing them. His caramel skin glistened wetly to emphasise the sculpted contours of his physique whilst his tightly cropped curly hair gave him a sleek, streamlined appearance.

However, his glare was quite daunting. Jez had always known him with the jagged white scar above his right eye; apparently the result of a fight back in London, which made him look decidedly menacing. But now, after having his cornea pierced during his encounter with Ray Reece at *Far Point*, the right eye, beneath the wide scar, was now completely white and resembled a shiny glass cue ball.

Even though the eye was useless, it still managed to give him an air of pure evil which unsettled Jez more than he cared to admit.

"This is my grandfather's room," he blurted.

"Yeah, so?" Bass replied, "Are you expectin' him back any time soon?"

The girls giggled at his joke.

"No," said Jez, a little befuddled, "It's just that—"

"Just that what, kid?" Asked Bass, feigning ignorance. "I'm sure your grandpa wouldn't mind me an' the girls here havin' a bit of fun for a while - after all, he ain't using the place is he?"

Again the girls giggled as Stone's deep, South London accent echoed around the Italian marble walls of the bathroom.

A huge TV was inset into the far wall which Bass had been playing a porno video on to get the girls in the party mood. However, the movie had now finished and the TV was playing a rolling news feed with the volume muted and nobody paying it any mind.

"No, course not," Jez continued, "it's just that I wasn't expecting you to be here that's all."

"Well why don't you join us honey?" Said the white girl with the colourful tattoo, "You look like you could use a bit of fun."

"Leave the kid alone, Crystal," Stone said. "He ain't up to

284

partying right now - an' I ain't ready to share."

"Is that so sugar?" Cooed the Puerto Rican girl, turning back to Stone and rubbing her hands across his torso.

"Yeah, that's right," he replied, enjoying her attentions, "I want you ladies all to myself - an' I got a whole lot to give."

"You got that right, lover," said the black girl, writhing steadily on his lap, "You sure is one whole lot of man and I want filling up real good."

Bass responded by grabbing her buttocks and pushing himself into her. The pair of them kissing deeply as she rode him, signalling that they were done with Jez and his inconsequential irritations. Taking their cue from this, the other two girls also began kissing and fondling each other, clearly no longer interested as to whether Jez was there or not.

Dismissed from his own grandfather's bathroom, Jez was about to turn and slink away when Crystal, the white girl, suddenly broke off from kissing her friend and yelled, "Christ, he's alive!"

"Jesus!" Exclaimed the Puerto Rican, joining in with her amazement. "I don't believe it - thank God. That guy's too damn pretty to be dead!"

"What the fuck are you two on about?" Bass snapped, "What guy?". However, as he spoke, he saw what they were staring at.

On the TV, set in the far wall, the news was showing footage of a handsome man in sunglasses surrounded by a mass of reporters. A scrolling banner ran along the bottom of the screen which read, *Hollywood legend found alive and well - star tells of family's ordeal at hands of Mafia killers - police to make significant arrests.*

"What? What is it?" Jez asked.

"Look at the fucking TV, kid," Stone said flatly. "This party's over and we better get out of here fast."

Jez turned to look at the TV as instructed and slowly what he was seeing began to register. *But surely it was impossible.*

Virgil Nash was still alive.

***

Rocco Pistoli felt like a traitor as he drove away from Johnny Magisano's magnificent Fort Lauderdale residence, but his patience had finally run out and something had to be done.

He had given Jez Vincenzi the benefit of the doubt, stuck by him in the aftermath of *Far Point* even though his handling of the raid had left Rocco fuming. Indeed, many of his friends had died there due to Jez's inept planning and ineffectual leadership but still Rocco had remained loyal.

His reason for this loyalty, aside from the fact that the pair of them were supposed to be friends, was that Jez had promised to deliver Matt Mason to him; the man who had killed Rocco's brother, Enzo, but so far nothing had happened.

Indeed, Rocco had been forced to rely on Bass Stone, whom he neither liked nor trusted, to help him find Mason as Vincenzi had delegated the task to him.

Infuriatingly, Jez had chosen Stone as his consigliere over Rocco himself who, in his opinion, should have been the natural choice.

As it was, neither he nor Jez knew anything of this half-caste interloper from London and had never even set eyes on him prior to his arrival in Key Biscayne with Michael Walsh. Yet, Rocco had to admit, the information Stone had extracted from Walsh had been integral to the initial tracing of Cassidy, Noakes, Nash and Mason - even though things had subsequently gone array.

So Rocco had been inclined to give Stone a chance. After all, if he had delivered Mason to them once, he could possibly do it again.

But now, several weeks on, Jez had sunken into himself and Stone seemed to be running riot doing just as he pleased.

Rocco remembered Stone's words on *Far Point* well, 'Now, we do things my way,' he had boldly stated. Well it seemed *his way* was to sit on his dark-skinned ass milking Jez for every penny he could get.

Rocco did not doubt that Bass would like to get his hands on Cassidy and Noakes to make them pay for the eye he had lost on *Far Point,* but at present he seemed much more content to live it up in the lap of luxury on Jez Vincenzi's dime.

Over the past weeks, Rocco had witnessed Stone enjoying countless alcohol fuelled romps with an endless stream of whores. What he had not observed, however, was any effort on Bass' part to find Matt Mason or the others and Rocco had finally decided that enough was enough.

All the loyalty he had originally felt for the Vincenzi and Carboni families, not least to Jez himself, had all but evaporated. Indeed, he viewed Jez now with nothing more than disdain; his contempt for him undisguised.

To Rocco, Jez was now nothing more than a useless brat who had squandered his inheritance and pissed away the respect his grandfathers had earned. What is more, he had proven himself to be totally incompetent and, quite possibly, mentally unstable.

This was a view shared by Falco, too.

As for Bass Stone, Rocco could read him like a book. Stone, even though undoubtedly very capable and extremely formidable, was clearly more interested in getting his hands on the Vincenzi/ Carboni fortune than in helping Rocco find Matt Mason.

Indeed, by the time he had finished whoring and partying and rinsing Jez of all his money, Mason and the others would be long gone - if they were not already.

And Rocco was sick of waiting.

A change of leadership was badly required and Falco was in complete agreement.

Even though he was merely a foot soldier, Falco needed to follow someone he deemed worthy of his respect. He had been loyal to Tito Vincenzi for many years and had become one of his most trusted men. Indeed, Tito and Carmine had both been men who commanded respect and no one would have dared rise against them. But Jez was an entirely different proposition and the other families were already beginning to sense his weakness.

With this in mind, Falco, in all good consciousness, could not, *would not,* be subordinate to Tito's snivelling pup and his half-caste monkey any longer.

He knew the vultures were already circling and was desperate to avoid being on the wrong side in a turf war; a war which could not only end in a rival family seizing control of all Vincenzi/Carboni interests but also, quite possibly, in Falco's death.

However Rocco had shown him a way to avoid this most probable and rather unappealing eventuality.

Johnny Magisano's organisation spanned the whole of Miami and most of Florida but he was eager to expand his operation across the whole country. Yet the Vincenzis had been holding him back, keeping him in his place and preventing his empire from growing.

For years he had been paying them a hefty tariff - a huge percentage of his profits - and in return, they graciously granted him permission to operate in their territory.

Naturally Johnny resented this. In fact, having to pay them anything at all burned him deeply but to refuse them would have been tantamount to suicide.

They were too powerful to go up against, particularly after forging their game-changing alliance with the Carboni family.

Indeed, to them, as a united organisation, Magisano was little more than a gnat, just a small cog in the wheels of their enormous money making machine. Nevertheless, Johnny had ambitions to be much more and always had his sights on greater things. It was all just a case of waiting for the right opportunity.

Rocco knew Johnny a little from way back as their fathers had come over from Sicily together - not enough to trust him but enough to be confident that any conversations they might have would not be repeated back to Jez Vincenzi.

With this in mind, Rocco had tentatively reached out.

His initial approach had led to a series of clandestine phone calls and finally to the meeting that had taken place just a few moments before at Johnny's home.

In that meeting Rocco had made Johnny a deal; he would get rid of Jez Vincenzi, the last remaining obstacle of the now largely defunct Vincenzi/Carboni organisation, thereby clearing the way for Magisano to take over. Whilst in return, Johnny would appoint Rocco as consigliere and provide him with any means necessary to track down and kill Matt Mason.

The two men had parted company both satisfied with their part of the bargain.

Rocco's objective now was to get rid of Jez as soon as possible; and two shots to the chest and one to the head would seem appropriate; clean, efficient and, if he chose his moment correctly, completely unexpected.

However, before killing Jez, he would first have to take out Stone. But whereas murdering Jez would cause him a modicum of pain, the two of them once being close, killing Bass would be of no consequence to him at all. Indeed, he would positively enjoy it and intended to make the most of it.

As he turned onto the highway for the short drive back to Key Biscayne from Fort Lauderdale, Rocco amused himself by conjuring up imaginative ways of killing Bass Stone.

**

Falco was drinking an espresso in the kitchen when he heard all the activity.

From his stool at the central island he had a clear view of the hallway and stairs. He placed his coffee down on the counter top and watched with interest as Bass Stone, wearing only his boxer shorts, lumbered down the stairs. Over his shoulder, Bass carried one half-naked girl who was kicking and screaming angrily, another of the hookers was being forcibly dragged by the hand and two more scantily clad girls were following along behind, clearly not amused.

"C'mon!" Stone growled, "We ain't got all fuckin' day, you gotta get out of here - so move it!"

Intrigued by all this commotion, Falco stood up and craned his neck to see Stone very nearly throw each of the girls out of the front door.

"And keep your mouths shut!" He yelled after them, "Otherwise you'll be seeing me again - and next time it won't be no party!"

As he slammed the door he saw Falco staring at him bemused.

"What is it? What's going on?" Falco asked innocently.

"Switch on the fuckin' TV and take a look for yourself - then pack a bag cos we gotta move, quick!" With that Bass bounded back up the stairs, presumably Falco assumed, to get his own stuff together.

Quickly, Falco found the remote on the counter and clicked on the TV, instinctively punching in the number for the news channel.

Immediately he saw the footage of Virgil Nash and the scrolling news feed that accompanied it.

He watched, transfixed, for a minute, a sense of panic rising within him. Then, an instant later he realised that Rocco's deal with Magisano would count for nothing if Jez was arrested. Johnny could simply take over without any help from Pistoli as the boy would already be out of the picture. Furthermore, as the only remnants left of the Vincenzi/Carboni organisation, Rocco and Falco, himself, would undoubtedly be surplus to requirement.

With no bargaining chip, there would be no deal and he and Rocco would find themselves out in the cold, maybe with a bullet in each of their heads for good measure.

"Shit!" Falco exclaimed. He had to think but everything was

moving too fast, there was no time. Stone and Vincenzi were moving out and at any moment the place was sure to be crawling with cops. What to do? *What to do?*

Falco was not blessed with an over abundance of intelligence and was incapable of formulating a contingency plan by himself. He needed Rocco to tell him what to do - but he was presently with Johnny Magisano putting together a deal that was already worthless.

Falco had to let him know, had to speak with him, to find out what he should do. *Should he go with Vincenzi, or go to Magisano - or should he just take off on his own?*

Falco saw the phone hanging on the wall and immediately his mind was made up. He would ring Magisano's place, ask to speak to Rocco and tell him what had happened. Rocco would then tell him what to do.

It was a risk but both Bass and Jez were upstairs and would not hear if he used the phone in the kitchen. *It was the only way.*

***

Jez could not believe it. It was all like some bad dream. The last person he ever expected to see alive again was Virgil Nash but there he was, on the TV screen, surrounded by a gaggle of reporters and photographers.

Yet, Rocco had killed him - run him off the road in California. Pistoli had apparently even seen his lifeless body in the wreck of the car. *So how then could Nash still be alive?*

Jez suddenly felt angry. Bass had ordered him to go to his room and pack a bag and he had meekly obeyed. But now he did not feel meek at all - or compliant or intimidated - he felt madder than hell; his temper bubbling like a volcano about to blow.

He burst into his room, tore off one of his monogrammed slippers and flung it violently at the mirror over the dresser, shattering it into jagged shards.

"Piece of shit mutherfucker!" He raged through gritted teeth as frothy saliva sprayed from his mouth. "Why couldn't you just stay fuckin' dead and leave me in peace!"

Then he roared with wild, unrestrained frustration and swept the dresser free of ornaments with one violent swoop of an arm so that they crashed noisily onto the polished marble floor and smashed to pieces.

"Aaaah!" He yelled again, balling his hands into fists and punching himself several times in the head. "Stupid, stupid, stupid!" He berated himself.

Again he had failed. Cassidy and Noakes had escaped him, Matt Mason was in the wind and now, it turned out, Virgil Nash had somehow eluded him, too.

After years of waiting, he had finally been given a chance to kill the four men he held responsible for the death of his brother, Vito.

Indeed, for the briefest time he had held their very lives in the palm of his hand; his to extinguish at will. But that chance had been squandered and they had all now slipped through his fingers.

It was a bitter disappointment and Jez felt as if he might explode with the agonising humiliation of it all.

Was the whole fucking world conspiring against him!

Breathing heavily but making an effort to reign in his emotions, he truculently stripped off his pyjamas and blindly threw on some clothes, still simmering with rage. As he shoved his feet into a pair of canvas espadrilles he slid open the drawer of his night stand and pulled out a gold-plated Smith and Wesson .38; his eighteenth birthday present from Carmine, which he tucked into his belt at the small of his back. *Christ, what he would give for an excuse to use it.*

Nevertheless, regardless of how he felt, he knew he must presently act with some urgency as it would do him no good at all to stay around until the police arrived.

With that in mind, he grabbed a large suitcase from the closet, threw it onto the bed and set about bundling some essentials into it.

However, as he did this, he noticed the red light flashing next to the word 'kitchen' on the phone beside his bed.

Already highly paranoid, Jez was immediately suspicious. *Who the hell was making a phone call now?*

Curious to know, he snatched up the receiver and placed it to his ear, then pressed the button adjacent to the blinking light which would allow him to secretly eavesdrop on whoever it was.

Indeed, as soon as he hit the button, he heard someone speaking on the other end of the line and immediately recognised it to be Falco.

"*…but please,*" Falco was saying, "*If you could just interrupt Mr. Magisano for a moment…*"

Upon hearing that name, Jez froze and listened more intently, hooked on every word being said as murderous thoughts flooded his mind. Yet there was a feeling of relief too, with his weeks of paranoia now clearly vindicated. He was not crazy after all and had been right to be suspicious; his underlings *were* conspiring against him - a discovery which raised his sense of persecution to a whole new level.

"*…he's meeting with my buddy, Rocco Pistoli*" Falco continued, "*they're working out a deal - but things have changed an' I gotta speak to Rocco for a second - it'll be real quick…*"

Jez had heard enough to know what he must now do. Very gently he set down the receiver on the night stand and crept out of his bedroom, pulling the *.38* from his belt as he stealthily descended the stairs.

***

Falco had not been able to speak to Rocco. After a lengthy and frustrating conversation with Johnny Magisano's housekeeper, who had done nothing but give him the runaround, it transpired that Pistoli had left several minutes earlier.

Falco had missed him. For a second he had toyed with speaking to Magisano himself but knew that to be a bad idea. Johnny would find out the news soon enough, at which time all deals would be off. So there was no point in hastening the inevitable.

With the weight of the world seemingly on his shoulders, Falco put the receiver back on its hook and turned to leave, intending to pack a bag as Bass had advised. *Better the devil you know,* he thought, resigning himself to fleeing with Vincenzi and Stone.

However, as he turned around he saw Jez standing in the kitchen doorway; the gold-plated *.38* in his hand and pointed directly at him.

"Had a good chat with Johnny, did you?" Vincenzi asked casually. "Everything cool with him?"

"No!" Falco begged, suddenly desperate, knowing his conversation had been overheard, knowing that he had been caught as a traitor. "Please, Jez - it ain't like that. I just—"

But his pleas fell on stony ground as Jez cared nothing for explanations and with his finger poised so temptingly on the trigger, he could restrain himself no longer. Indeed, before Falco could utter anything more, his words were violently snatched away by the destructive force of the Smith and Wesson.

The shot rang out in an ear-splitting crash and echoed loudly around every wall of the mansion. It struck Falco hard in the stomach and he staggered backwards against the refrigerator from the brutal impact, a look of complete shock registering on his face.

Then Jez fired again.

This time Falco was hit in the groin. Squealing in terrible agony, his legs buckled under him, blood pissing from his wounds as he lay helpless on the kitchen floor. As he writhed in excruciating pain, he was terrified to see Jez Vincenzi's grinning face staring down at him; his evil eyes filled with blood lust and glistening maniacally with the thrill of it all.

"Please!" Falco begged as blood erupted from his throat and spilt over his lips, "Please—".

"Please what?" Said Jez, enjoying himself immensely, "Please can you die? Hey, why sure, Falco. Why didn't you just ask?"

Then he fired again. And again. And again, until the clip was spent along with the last remnants of Jez's sanity.

***

Bass could not fail to hear the gunshots from Tito's bedroom and still only half dressed he rushed from the room and flew down the stairs four at a time.

As he burst into the kitchen, Jez span round and aimed the .38 in his direction.

"Whoa!" Hold it kid," Bass yelled seeing the madness in his eyes, "it's only me, I ain't gonna hurt ya!"

"Yeah?" Jez replied, "Well how do I know that, huh? How do I know you're not in league with Magisano too?"

"Who or what is Magisano?" Queried Bass, genuinely in the dark. As he spoke he saw Falco's bullet riddled body on the floor behind Vincenzi laying in an enormous pool of blood. It was a macabre sight which shocked even Bass.

"Who's Magisano?" Jez sneered incredulously, "Don't get cute with me, Stone, I ain't in the mood. You know who the fuck I mean - *Johnny Magisano,* head of the Magisano family - so don't play the fuckin' innocent!" He was clearly irritated by the question and no longer displaying any sign of his former timidity towards Bass. In fact, quite the reverse as his whole demeanour seemed to have changed since witnessing Virgil Nash on the TV a few minutes earlier.

"Jez, please," said Stone, his hands up in surrender, "I don't know who he is, honest. I ain't from round here - I never heard of the guy!"

"So you're saying you ain't working with him?" Jez said, still pointing the .38 and his voice full of disbelief. "You ain't conspiring against me like Rocco and Falco?"

"What?" Stone was clearly surprised to learn of Rocco and Falco's betrayal and Jez could see it written all over his face. "No, course not," Bass continued, "I wouldn't trust those guys for a moment and whoever this fuckin' Magisano is, let me kill him - let me prove my loyalty to you."

"So you're on my side?" Asked Jez cautiously, although his inclination was to believe him now that the red mist of rage had subsided.

"Course I am," replied Bass, relieved to see Vincenzi lower the gun. "I'm here for you. I promised I'd get those guys for you and I will."

"But only if I pay you a fortune right?"

Bass was slightly wrong-footed by the remark. "What? No, that's not why—"

"It's okay, Bass," Jez interrupted, "You can quit the bullshit. I know why you're here and what you want."

"Jez, please, no—" Bass tried, but again he was cut off.

"It's alright, I don't care," said Vincenzi honestly. "Just get me what I want and you can write your own ticket."

"What?" Bass was a little taken aback. "Just so I know for sure, what is it *exactly* that you're saying?"

Jez was calm now, placated, satisfied that Stone was not a threat to him - at least for the moment, so tucked the .38 back into his belt. "What I'm saying, to be clear, is if you deliver Cassidy, Noakes, Nash and Mason to me, I will pay you whatever the fuck you want."

Stone's face was a picture. There it was, straight from the horse's mouth. No need for anymore cajoling, no need for anymore pussy-footing around as everything had suddenly, rather unexpectedly, been put on the table.

However Bass still required complete clarification. "So what sort of figure are we talking about?" He asked.

Jez shrugged. "Name it."

Suddenly the cogs in Stone's brain started pinging like a cash register as he quickly considered Vincenzi's net worth, working out what he would be willing to hand over. A number kept lighting up, flashing like a neon sign in his mind's eye, a figure so huge he could barely comprehend it but greed was getting the better of reason. *Fuck it, what the hell. Give it a try.*

"Two million," he said, unabashed, staring the boy straight in the eye without the slightest trace of reserve.

He saw Jez waiver slightly upon hearing the huge sum and thought for a moment he was going to counter with a considerably lower offer, as would have been expected.

But no.

"Fine. Do we have a deal then?" Jez said, offering his hand.

Bass could not believe his ears and forcibly had to restrain himself from whooping with joy. However, instead he just smiled widely as he grabbed the boy's hand which was half the size of his own. "You bet your fuckin' arse we have a deal," he said.

Then, after shaking hands firmly but briefly, Stone added, "But now I think we'd better get the hell out of here before the bloody law arrives."

***

By nightfall, Rocco had checked into a *Best Western* just outside of Orlando.

Seven hours earlier, driving back to Key Biscayne from Fort Lauderdale, he had been overtaken by several squad cars, lights flashing, sirens wailing, and all heading very fast in the same general direction as him.

Curious as to what was going on, he proceeded with caution, his suspicions aroused and his instincts bristling. Then his misgivings were confirmed as he turned onto the tree-lined boulevard upon which the Vincenzi mansion was situated; the whole area swarming with cops.

At least eight squad cars were parked on the street with uniformed officers enforcing a taped perimeter. A further six patrol cars were strewn at various intervals along the sweeping driveway and a squadron of media helicopters were circling overhead.

The place was a bustling hive of activity with looky-loos and news crews all crowding the scene.

Nevertheless, even though Rocco had pulled up a safe distance away, the wrought iron gates which normally concealed the property from view were presently open allowing him a glimpse of the activity within.

To better assist him spy on what was going on, Rocco swiftly retrieved the telescopic sight from his rifle case in the trunk of the car.

The rifle was his most prized possession; a *Valmet* made in Finland with a polished wooden stock and a powerful *Zeiss Diavari* sight. A couple of years earlier, he had been sent to Europe at Tito's request to kill a businessman who was making a move on the family's interests there. After fulfilling his contract, Rocco had found the rifle in the guy's apartment. It came in a hard leather case with snap locks. The rifle and sight both mounted neatly in perfectly shaped sponge mountings. He had loved it instantly and claimed it as a prize. After all, the businessman had no more use for it.

Since then, Rocco had kept it in his car; using it on occasion for things other than simply target practice; things which his talents were far more suited to.

What is more, the sight doubled as makeshift telescope and using it now he could see an ambulance parked immediately in front of the steps that led up to the front door. Then a few minutes later, he watched as a couple of medics wheeled out a gurney with a body on it covered with a blanket.

However, the telescopic sight gave Rocco a remarkably clear view and even though the blanket covered most of the body, from the knees down the pants and shoes were visible, as was the left hand which was hanging exposed

Rocco's heart sank as he recognised the tan chinos and penny loafers that Falco always wore. The hand was also missing a pinkie, which was further proof in any were needed. Indeed, Rocco had been with Falco several years earlier when he had lost his little finger, which had been severed after catching it accidentally in the breach of a shotgun.

There could be no mistake, his friend and ally was dead.

Tragic as this was to Rocco, personally, it also raised several pressing questions. Firstly, who had killed Falco and why? Secondly, where were Jez and Bass now? And finally, and possibly most importantly, what the hell had happened in the short time since Rocco had been gone?

It was all most troubling and Pistoli continued to watch for a long time in search of answers. Yet none were forthcoming and after a lengthy period of waiting there was still no sign of Vincenzi or Stone anywhere.

Eventually Rocco gave up his surveillance and drove to a nearby bar to think about his next move. However, he had no sooner bought a drink when most of his questions were answered. The TV on the wall was showing all the footage; first of Virgil Nash, then the subsequent raid on the Vincenzi mansion.

Rocco's first thought was of his deal with Magisano and how this would change things.

Quickly he rushed to the pay phone in the far corner of the bar room and called Johnny, hoping he could still salvage something in the light of recent events; painfully aware that his grand plan had just spectacularly backfired. The Vincenzi/Carboni empire was now ripe for Magisano's taking and with Jez suddenly out of the picture, he could easily do it without Rocco's help.

Clearly Johnny was aware of this too, having seen the news

footage for himself. "Deal's off, kid," was his opening statement as he came on the line.

"No, Johnny, wait, please - I can still help, believe me—" Rocco pleaded.

"Maybe so, kid, but I reckon I'll take my chances." Magisano interrupted.

"No, please, give me a—"

"Hey, I needn't have taken the call," Johnny said honestly, sounding a little irritated, "I coulda just left you hanging, but I told you, myself - I owed you that. I showed you respect. But now it's done, kid, leave it at that. Okay?"

Rocco thought about begging some more, thought about trying to convince him to see it from his angle but ultimately he knew it would be futile. The truth was he was now surplus to requirement so there would be no changing Magisano's mind.

"Sure, Johnny," he said flatly, "I understand. Thanks for telling me yourself. I appreciate it."

"No problem, kid," replied Johnny, signalling the end of the conversation. "So guess I'll be seeing you around then, huh?"

"Yeah. Guess so," said Rocco quietly as he hung up the phone knowing there was nothing more to be said.

After replacing the receiver, he leant on the wall by the phone for a long moment feeling numb and trying to rally his thoughts.

According to the news, Falco had been found murdered at the scene - this surely meant either Bass or Jez had killed him and *not* the police. But why? *Had his treachery been discovered? And, if so, had Rocco's too?* It was the only reason he could think of for Falco being killed.

Nevertheless, no matter what the reason, there was now a manhunt on for Jez Vincenzi and his known associates - and that meant Rocco, himself, was a wanted man.

With this in mind, he went directly from the bar straight to his apartment - taking a gamble that it would still be safe to go there. All he needed was enough time to pack a bag and grab his emergency stash from the box in the closet - enough cash to last maybe six months if he was careful.

Once he had got everything, he jumped back in his car and hit the road. Rocco did not stop until he arrived in Orlando, figuring he would hide out amongst all the tourists for a while until he could formulate a contingency plan.

That night, he sat on the bed, watching the news on the TV in his modest hotel room, avidly listening for any fresh information.

Much to his relief, there had so far been no mention of his name. However images of Jez were flashing up every five minutes along with a photograph of Stone which had obviously been taken a long time ago when he was just a teenager back in England. Both were wanted in connection with the attempted murder of Virgil Nash and his family as well as the murder of Falco.

Rocco's intuition told him that Falco had been killed because of the deal with Magisano, that somehow their treachery had been discovered. Using this logic, Rocco determined that it would be best to stay well clear of Jez and Bass until he could find out more - not that he had any idea where either of them might currently be.

He was also under no illusions now that he must find Matt Mason himself if he was ever to avenge his brother. Yet this would not be easy as he had no clue as to his whereabouts either.

It was obvious to Rocco that he had several problems to ponder and until he could resolve them he deemed it wise to lay low for a while.

Once in possession of all the answers he needed, he could plan out a strategy.

And then he would strike.

Chapter Nineteen

The Cayman Islands, three months later

Even though he was corrupt and avaricious, Police Commissioner Manfred Rani was generally a decent man who had been a good friend to Joe and Sean, particularly in recent months.

In fact, in covering up the truth of what happened at *Far Point*, Rani had proved invaluable.

Joe despised having to pay bribes as it harked back to his days in London when it had been an essential form of survival - so deeply ingrained in the system that it had become just the accepted way of things.

Back then, it went hand in glove with his role as gangland supremo - a position he had reluctantly inherited from Vinnie Reece yet found himself eminently suited to. But it had never sat comfortably with him and nowadays that time was nothing more than a distant memory.

He lived a different life now and was a different man. Indeed, over the past ten years he had actually become the man he always aspired to be; an honest, law-abiding, completely legitimate businessman.

So the very act of bribing a high-ranking official and his numerous subordinates rankled considerably, but in order for him and his family to lead a normal, peaceful life, it had been a necessary evil.

Over the years Joe and Sean had become well acquainted with Manfred Rani and had learned to accept him for the man he was which, for the most part, was a friendly and gracious individual who they could not help but like. As such, the sizeable monthly stipend they paid him was something never spoken about and was considered merely to be the cost of living in such a beautiful place.

However, in return for this unmentioned remuneration, Rani guaranteed Joe and Sean their privacy and made certain that if any interested parties should come looking then no documented evidence of their existence on the island would be found.

For ten years this had been a relatively easy task as no one had come looking and Rani had very little to do to earn his monthly sweetener.

However, due to recent events, this had dramatically changed and Manfred had now more than justified his expense, undoubtedly earning every penny that Joe and Sean had ever paid him.

Indeed, one of the first things Joe had done after arriving safely at Doc Ridgeway's in Vegas, was to call Commissioner Rani and tell him what had happened, demanding that he scour the islands for Brett and Liv, telling him that if he should find them, to keep them safe. Fortunately Brett and Liv had managed this for themselves, yet Rani had still done as requested.

Joe had also instructed Manfred to deal with the mess at *Far Point* and to his credit he had.

At Joe and Sean's request, Rani's first priority had been to speak with the families of the *Far Point* security detail who had been killed in the attack and pass on their deepest condolences. He was then asked to arrange the funerals and assure their loved ones that they would be well taken care of financially for the rest of their lives. Joe and Sean knew this was scant compensation when compared to the loss of a life but they hoped that in some small way it might ease the families' pain.

Next, Manfred had organised the retrieval of Ray's body from the cliff top and had it stored securely in the mortuary in town. Sadly, there had been very little left of Ruby to salvage from the charred rubble of the house, but what remains could be saved were also put into storage at the morgue alongside Ray.

The bodies of the other men who had died in the raid - Vincenzi's murderous thugs - had also been dealt with. Their corpses had been disposed of and any evidence of them ever setting foot on the island had been magically erased.

Joe knew better than to ask questions but would be eternally grateful for Rani's assistance - which he would be properly compensated for.

Presently, however, Manfred was accompanying him, Sean, Rose and Sarah as they returned to *Far Point* for the first time since their hasty departure three months earlier.

Joe was anxious to see Ray and Ruby properly laid to rest, as were the others.

Sarah was also eager to visit her horses which, under Rani's supervision, had been rounded up, corralled and well taken care of. For this kindness alone, she was immensely grateful.

Together with Rani now, Sarah and the others walked up the driveway from the gates where, at their request, Manfred's driver had parked the Commissioner's official limousine, to see fully the scale of utter devastation that had befallen both properties.

Joe and Rose's house was completely gone with nothing but a pile of rubble remaining. Across the bluff, three blackened walls still stood at the site of Sean and Sarah's place, but that was all. The roof and all other evidence of the beautiful house that once stood there, proudly over-looking the ocean, had vanished.

The stable block was gone too, with just a charred pile of debris left to mark the place where Sean and Brett had so valiantly fought to rescue the horses.

It was a heartbreaking sight and both Sarah and Rose were in tears as they gazed upon the wreckage of their homes. Instinctively, they held hands as they made their way up the sweep of the drive, clinging to each other for support.

Slightly in front of them, Joe and Rani were in conversation together whilst Sean was a few paces behind. He had now fully recovered from the dreadful wound sustained in that very place several months earlier. Yet when he glanced at the white painted stones that lined the driveway he had a flashback to that awful night, realising, possibly for the first time, just how lucky he had been.

He then glanced at Joe who was now walking unaided, having dispensed with the stick which had, until recently, been a permanent feature. Sean knew Joe's leg still pained him but it was getting better all the time and his limp was now almost imperceptible.

In the intervening months, during their joint recovery in Las Vegas, the pair of them had spent many hours in the gym at *The Villa Continental,* which had helped immensely with their recuperation. It had been a slow process and each of them still had much to do before they reached the peak of physical fitness they had enjoyed before being shot, but they were making excellent progress and Doc Ridgeway, on his monthly visits with Louretta, was always impressed by how well they were doing.

Bernie Dufresne had also been instrumental in their recovery by closing the gym to hotel guests whilst Joe and Sean used it. This enabled them to use the facilities in private without the risk of being seen by anyone who might be interested in their whereabouts. Quite often, Brett and Matt would join them, too, both now also fully recovered and each determined to get back to their former states of fitness.

However, it was Violet who used the gym more than anyone. She was there first thing every morning for a minimum of two hours and again every evening for at least another one, which was usually followed by twenty lengths of the pool.

There was no need for Bernie to close the gym for Violet as no one knew her. Indeed, she was more than happy to mix in with the hotel guests - although the majority of the *Villa's* clientele preferred the casino to the gym so most times she had the place to herself anyway.

Nevertheless, Bernie, who felt rather protective of her now, always kept a close eye on her and would always make time in his day to speak to her personally. Violet liked Bernie a lot and the two of them had become good friends. To her now, he was something of a kindly uncle with whom she could confide - particularly with regard to her feelings toward Matt.

Yet it was the gym which Violet was most interested in. She was determined to become stronger and fitter than ever - she even had Matt training her in karate and had become almost Amazonian in her commitment to exercise and athleticism - adamant that she was *never* going to be a victim again.

And if she ever ran into Bass Stone she was damn well going to prove it.

Liv had accompanied her to the gym for a while, equally determined to improve her fitness levels, but just recently, for reasons known only to herself, she had opted to stay back at the house with Sarah and Rose.

For the moment, however, the two older women were in The Caymans on a brief trip to inspect what remained of their homes, and what they found was devastating.

However, regardless of what had happened, there was no denying that *Far Point* was a truly beautiful place; an island paradise in a spectacular location which, until recently, had been the perfect sanctuary.

Manfred Rani was now talking to Sean, leaving Joe alone

to inspect the scene. He scanned the grounds from the destroyed houses down to the gates and from the furthest reaches of the estate way off in the distance back to the cliff top upon which he presently stood. After a moment, he then turned and stared out at the ocean, witnessing again the breathtaking view which he never tired of.

And in that instant, he made a decision.

Once everything had been dealt with, when the police finally caught up with Vincenzi and Stone - and Joe was confident that they would - then he was going to rebuild.

In spite of everything, *Far Point* was still his home, the place where he felt most at peace, and at some point in the future, he was determined he would live there again.

Not, however, until he deemed it completely safe for his family to return as he had no wish to put them in harm's way ever again. Yet until Vincenzi and Stone had been brought to justice, Joe was very much aware that all of them were still at risk.

Nonetheless, Virgil's plan had been mostly a success. He and Victoria had returned to Los Angeles as arranged and told the police what had happened to them - naturally leaving out any information relating to Joe and Sean. In response, the police had initiated a nationwide manhunt for Vincenzi and Stone which was still ongoing.

Unfortunately, due to one rather zealous reporter, news had leaked of the police operation sooner than they would have liked, thus alerting Vincenzi and Stone to their imminent arrest and allowing them the vital time needed to flee.

Suddenly finding himself swamped by reporters and news crews, an infuriated Virgil had no alternative but to go public before he had intended, knowing, even as he spoke, that Vincenzi and Stone were possibly slipping away. It was galling and the only thing that marred an otherwise excellent plan.

However, trading on his fame and influence, Virgil had kept up the pressure on the police so that the manhunt stayed fresh in the public eye.

Beau Brewster had also proved invaluable once again and through his sway over the media the search for the fugitives was rarely out of the news.

Joe was convinced it was only a matter of time before the two men were brought to justice.

Due to his own experiences as a fugitive, Sean was also confident that Vincenzi and Stone's movements would be seriously restricted. With all the heat they were getting across the media, they would have no choice but to lay low and wait things out. Their faces were now splashed across every newspaper and on every TV station so they would be easily recognised by the public at large which, Sean knew first hand, would seriously restrict their options.

With this in mind, he and Joe deemed it safe enough to make the short trip to *Far Point*. Brett and Matt were more than capable of taking care of things back in Vegas should any problems arise and Josh was safely ensconced back at *CalTech* with a twenty-four hour, plain-clothed, security detail protecting him.

Josh had bridled a little at this, fearing it might cramp his style somewhat, but the head of security had assured him that his protection would be unobtrusive. Indeed, his bodyguards just looked like regular students, not highly trained specialists in combat and personal protection, so Josh was suitably appeased.

However, Louretta was also keeping a close watch on him. She had moved into her house in Santa Monica with Ethan and the pair were having a wonderful time together rekindling the flame that had sparked so long ago.

Yet, she was still as strong-willed as ever and had eschewed all attempts by Joe, Sean and the others to give her a protection detail of her own. "I'm just an old broad," she had said, "it ain't gonna do 'em no good to come after me. Heck, I'm nearly goddamn dead anyway - so if they want me, let 'em take me but I ain't gonna surround myself with a bunch of security oddbods on the off chance that they might." She then added with a mischievous smile, "Sides, they might get in the way of Ethan and me getting friendly again - if you know what I mean."

Ethan had chuckled at this, clearly signalling his opinion on the matter was much the same as Louretta's, so there was no point in trying to persuade him either.

Nevertheless, every few days he and Louretta would make the thirty minute drive to *CalTech* to check up on Josh.

Normally a boy of his age would be seriously embarrassed by the appearance of his grandmother on campus, bringing sandwiches and cookies, but this was Louretta Wild, famous ex-movie star, successful businesswoman and a sassy old broad to boot, and soon she had all Josh's friends eating out the palm of her hand, regaling them with tales of her adventures in Hollywood whilst Ethan could do nothing but stand back and admire the woman he had once again fallen in love with.

Louretta and Ethan's stubbornness notwithstanding, Joe felt relatively confident that both his and Sean's families were safe for the time being - enough, at least, to feel able to make the trip back to *Far Point*.

Now, gazing at the beautiful vista before him, he felt pleased that he had as the purpose of the visit was to find an appropriate resting place for Ray and Ruby.

Joe intended to find a suitable spot then, after a short service, have them buried together in a joint plot. At some point in the future, when everything settled down and all dangers had been eliminated, he and Sean would return to the island with the whole family and hold a memorial service in honour of the two people they all loved and missed in equal measure.

Yet, standing there, with the ocean before him, the white sandy beach below and the lush, green landscape behind, Joe was suddenly aware that there could be no better final resting place for Ruby and Ray than right there on the cliff top.

It was the perfect location and immediately he shared his idea with the others who were all in complete agreement.

From then on things moved swiftly and just two days later, Joe, Sean, Sarah and Rose, found themselves gathered around a beautiful burial plot on the highest point of the bluff, just a short walk from where each of the houses had been located.

Manfred Rani was also in attendance along with the vicar, who spoke some kind words over the polished oak coffins before they were each lowered into the ground.

Everyone then bowed their heads in prayer as Ray and Ruby were finally laid to rest.

They had found peace, together, at last.

***

Las Vegas

Liv had been so caught up in her love for Brett and everything that had happened since they escaped together from *Far Point*, that she had not noticed the small matter of her period being late.

Besides, even if she had, her cycle had always been somewhat erratic, so a few days either way would not have concerned her. It always happened sooner or later.

But not this time.

Indeed, she had not had a period in over twelve weeks and now knew for certain that she was pregnant.

It had been confirmed for her a fortnight earlier at a private clinic, eliminating all doubt. Like it or not, in just a few months, she and Brett were going to have a baby.

At first Liv had been stunned. Now, however, her shock had turned to delight. Although she had not yet shared the news with Brett as she had not been able to find the right opportunity - or at least that's what she kept telling herself.

Even though the house on Canyon Hill Drive was large and spacious, it seemed surprisingly small with eight adults living in it. Indeed, it was rare to have a moment alone together and even though they now shared the same bedroom, Liv was almost reluctant to break the spell of absolute bliss that she and Brett were under.

Since returning from their unplanned excursion in the Caribbean, they had been living in an idyllic bubble of contentment. Finally, after years of pent up feelings and longing glances, they had consummated their love.

It was wonderful and even though the events that brought them together had been both tragic and devastating, neither could presently be happier.

Their time together on Canyon Hill Drive had been the best of their lives, both swept up in a wild, passionate, all-consuming love affair which had completely dispelled any initial doubts.

Brett, in particular, had always been concerned that his feelings for Liv were unnatural. Because of their close family ties and because they had known each other since they were children, he worried that it might be perceived as wrong.

Their families were intricately entwined and when he was much younger he regarded Liv much like a sister. Yet as she grew and blossomed, those feelings changed completely but a shadow of guilt remained and his relationship to her became confused.

But the simple fact was they were not related and nothing they felt, nothing they were doing, was wrong.

Quite the opposite in fact. It was perfect.

Liv had helped to convince him of this and, when the family found out about their romance, they had too.

Brett had spoken at length with Victoria, Sarah and Rose, expressing the confusion he had always felt about his and Liv's relationship to each other. They, in turn, had been unequivocal in their response.

Liv was definitely not related to him in any way. Not by blood, not by birth, and there was no reason whatsoever why they should not be together.

From that moment on, it was as if a weight had been lifted from Brett's shoulders and he at last gave himself to Liv mind, body and soul, and she willingly accepted with open arms.

Since then their love had blossomed but Liv was concerned that if she told Brett of her pregnancy now it might spoil things. She hoped and prayed it would not, but she could not be sure.

Nevertheless, she had decided to wait until the house was empty before telling him the news.

And now it was.

With the older four occupants away in The Caymans and Violet and Matt karate training in the gym at the *Villa Continental*, Brett and Liv finally had the house to themselves.

Liv had already pre-warned Violet that she was planning something special for Brett so had asked if her and Matt could give them a couple of hours alone that morning.

Violet had grinned in response, her emerald eyes sparkling wickedly, "Take as long as you like, darlin," she said, "I intend to keep Matt busy for a while - I got a few anger issues to work out on him!"

"Thanks, Vee," Liv replied, aware of Violet's feelings towards Matt. The two had become close over the last few months, with the older woman now something of a big sister with whom Liv could confide - although she had chosen to keep the news of her pregnancy to herself.

Nevertheless, Violet had her suspicions. Until recently, the pair of them had been enjoying daily trips to the gym together. But then, for no apparent reason and with no proper explanation, Liv suddenly stopped going.

Violet considered this a little strange at first but then, after careful observation of the subtle, barely perceptible change in her friend's physique, she finally put two and two together.

However, she said nothing and vacated the house with Matt at the appointed time as requested, leaving the moment set for Liv's big announcement.

It was now or never.

***

It was Sunday morning and Brett was having a lie-in. Normally he would be up and about, either helping around the house or down at the gym with his father, Sean and Matt. However, this morning, with most of them away in The Caymans and Matt and Violet already gone, Liv had persuaded him to stay in bed as they had the house all to themselves.

Brett liked that idea and certainly did not need any more encouragement. A whole morning alone with Liv, *what could be better?*

The drapes were open and the warm morning sun was streaming in through the window, bathing the room in golden light. Brett rolled onto his back and linked his fingers behind his head as he reclined on the soft pillows, the bedsheets draped loosely around his waist.

Life was good and it was set to be yet another beautiful day. Presently the space beside him was empty as he was awaiting the return of Liv who had insisted on going down to the kitchen to make him breakfast. However, he had just heard her on the stairs so had sat up, ready to receive his tray - and hopefully anything else she might wish to offer him. He smiled at the thought. *God how he loved her.*

Brett could still not really believe how things had worked out. Indeed, just a short time ago he and Liv had been at loggerheads, barely speaking and actively avoiding each other. Then, due to an act of complete and utter madness, they had suddenly been thrown together.

It could not be denied, the circumstances that brought about their union were tragic in the extreme, yet those very same events had fuelled a desire within them that had reached boiling point on that small boat floating in The Caribbean.

Now they were almost inseparable. Brett loved Liv with all his heart and knew for certain, even after such a short time, that he wanted to spend the rest of his life with her.

It was perfect and he felt like the luckiest man alive.

However, it was almost too perfect. Brett hated to be pessimistic, but he was used to life being a little more difficult than it presently was.

Nothing *this* good ever lasted forever, *did it?* There was usually something that came along to spoil it.

It was just a case of waiting for the other shoe to drop.

***

Liv had butterflies in her stomach and felt a little queasy, which could have been explained as morning sickness. Yet she knew it to be merely nervousness.

She and Brett had only been together for a matter of weeks and even though it felt incredibly right, a baby was very big news - *life changing news* - and she just hoped their fledgling love affair could survive it.

Liv had risen purposely early after hearing Matt and Violet leave the house; peeking out of the bedroom window to see Matt's truck driving away, just to be certain. Violet had been as good as her word.

Brett had stirred briefly but she just kissed him and told him to go back to sleep. "I'm going to make you some breakfast," she had said, "you have a snooze and I'll be back in a bit."

He stroked her leg affectionately in response, still half asleep as she stood over him. "Really? Thanks, baby," he croaked, "Don't know what I've done to deserve it but I'm glad I did it."

Liv smiled and kissed him again, then left him in bed and went down to the kitchen to make a start on breakfast.

Now, a mere thirty minutes later, she was on her way back upstairs. She was wearing one of Brett's old T-shirts as a nightdress which fell just below her pert posterior and hung off one shoulder to expose her smooth, tanned skin. Her hair was loose and mussed up from sleep yet she looked typically beautiful and aglow with pregnancy. With her, she carried a tray full of goodies - a pot of English tea for Brett, hot coffee for her, plus a plateful of bacon, sausage, eggs, hash browns and baked beans - indeed, Rose would have been proud of her. For herself there was just a blueberry muffin. Normally she could eat like a horse but this morning her nerves had got the better of her appetite.

Nonetheless, she took a beat to steel herself before opening the door.

Yet her resolve almost failed the moment she set eyes on Brett, as even now, after all these weeks together, he still took her breath away; his dark, alluring eyes sparkling with pleasure as she entered.

He smiled warmly, "Wow! That smells good - I'm starving."

Sitting in bed with a mop of black hair messy from sleep and chiselled features that were dark with morning stubble, he looked incredibly handsome. The sheet was draped only loosely over his lower half so that his bronzed torso was clearly visible; his defined pectoral and abdominal muscles finely carved. His physique was marred only by the small pink scar on his right side, below the rib cage, which denoted the place where Rocco Pistoli's bullet had struck him.

However, to Liv, he looked like a God and she felt almost weak in his presence. *Christ he was beautiful.*

Yet she could not be sure how he might react to the news he was going to be a father.

"Hi, honey!" She said brightly. "I'm glad you're hungry cos I've gone a bit overboard."

315

"I am," Brett replied. "This is great, but you didn't have to - you could have just stayed in bed with me."

Liv scotched onto the bed next to him and placed the tray on his lap, then kissed him lightly on the cheek.

"Yeah, I know, but I wanted to—" she hesitated for a moment, her mouth suddenly dry. "I wanted to make today special."

Brett turned to look at her and kissed her lovingly on the lips, wondering if he might have missed something. *Her birthday? Their three month anniversary?* It certainly was not *his* birthday.

"Why?" He asked. "What do you mean?" Then he saw the emotion in her eyes, the tears brimming, about to flow. "Christ, Liv!" He exclaimed, suddenly very concerned. "What is it - have I missed something - have I been an idiot?"

"No," she replied, placing her hand on his arm reassuringly. "You haven't missed anything." Then she held her breath and said, "But I have."

Brett looked completely confused. "What? I don't understand, babe. What do you mean - what have you missed?"

"My period, honey," she replied softly, staring hard into his eyes to try and gauge his reaction.

"Your period?"

"Uh-huh. Three months ago. I'm pregnant Brett. We're gonna have a baby."

Brett's face was completely blank as he slowly processed the information. He frowned quizzically, "You're pregnant? What? I don't understand, what do you mean?"

Liv smiled sweetly, he looked almost like a little boy trying to fathom algebra, the details not making sense.

"I'm pregnant, honey." She repeated. "You're gonna be a father."

"I am?"

"You are," Liv smiled, yet his face was still blank, his eyes unreadable, his brain almost audibly whirring.

"I am?" He suddenly blurted, his face now animated and his eyes alive with delight. "Liv, that's great - we're gonna have a baby - I'm gonna be a dad!"

Hastily he plonked the tray down on the night stand and threw off the bedclothes, then jumped up on the bed fully naked, pulling Liv up with him, so that they were now both standing on the mattress. He held her hands tightly and started bouncing up and down with joy. Liv began to laugh, the relief she felt making her feel quite giddy, elated that Brett was as obviously pleased as she was. He was now laughing too as the pair of them jumped up and down on the bed like a pair of mad fools.

But then, without warning, Brett stopped and held Liv gently by the shoulders. "Wait," he said breathlessly, "should you be doing this? Should you be exerting yourself? You might—"

"I'm fine, honey," she grinned. "Everything's fine."

"How long?" He asked. "When are you due?"

"In just about six months from now - we're gonna have a little Christmas baby."

"Wow, Liv. That's great. I can't believe it - I really can't believe it. I'm so happy." He then took her in his arms and hugged her tightly. They held each other for a long time and then they began to kiss.

However, Liv was suddenly eager to feel his nakedness against her own bare skin and hastily pulled off her makeshift nightdress, throwing it aside as the passion erupted between them.

With urgent need, Brett pulled Liv back down onto the bed and with enthusiastic expediency she wriggled on top of him; their kissing becoming more intense, each relishing the feel of the other.

Without need for words, Liv instinctively adjusted her position and a second later groaned loudly with utter delight as Brett responded to her bidding.

For several glorious minutes their hips writhed together before Brett stopped abruptly and pulled his face away from hers, suddenly concerned for the baby's welfare. "Hold on," he said. "Is this okay? Is this alright?"

"Honey," she replied wantonly, "It's more than alright, it's goddamn wonderful. The baby's fine - don't worry. You just keep on doing what you're doing and we'll all be just dandy."

Brett smiled wickedly. "Well okay then," he said, before placing his lips over hers once more and resuming the slow, steady grind of his hips which caused Liv to cry out with pleasure once more.

***

Brett was certainly ready for his breakfast by the time they had finished, as was Liv, whose appetite had now miraculously returned. Indeed, she was ravenous after all their exertions.

The food was now almost cold and the coffee tepid, but they did not mind as they sat in bed with the tray on Brett's lap, both nibbling on lukewarm bacon, as Liv excitedly related everything the pregnancy clinic had told her.

Brett listened intently, hanging on every word, the joy of it written all over his face.

However, after a short time, his face became more thoughtful and his expression contemplative.

"Of course, you know what all this means don't you?" He said.

"No, what?" Replied Liv, her mouth now full of blueberry muffin as she tried to satiate her hunger.

"It means we'll have to get married." He said.

"What?" She spluttered, uncertain if she had heard correctly and almost choking on the muffin.

Suddenly Brett placed the tray aside once more and deftly slid out of bed. Then, with dramatic effect, turned to face her and knelt down on one knee.

"Olivia Noakes," he said most earnestly. "I love you with all my heart. Will you do me the enormous honour of becoming my wife?"

Now it was Liv's turn to be dumbstruck. She swallowed down

the remains of the muffin and stared at Brett's face in shock.

Again her eyes began to brim with tears. "Yes!" She suddenly wailed, launching herself at him, knocking the plates and cups flying as she threw her arms around his neck. "Yes, yes - I love you with all my heart, too. Of course I will marry you - of course I will!"

They began to kiss once more. Happy, delighted kisses.

Then, to seal the deal. They made love again.

Chapter Twenty

Violet really did not know where she stood with Matt as nothing more had happened with him since that awkward moment in the garden when she had rather rashly kissed him - indeed, the incident had not been mentioned again.

What is more, there was now a fractiousness to their relationship, which Violet could not quite fathom; as if her very presence annoyed him - yet at other times he would actively seek her out, which she found extremely puzzling.

Had it been anyone else Violet would have given up long ago. But something about Matt kept her permanently enthralled. Indeed every time she was close to him her heart very nearly skipped a beat.

Nonetheless, she found it impossible to disguise her irritation with him.

As it was, their relationship - either good or bad - was constantly charged with a frisson of electricity which was forever buzzing and sparking between them.

Yet they could not stay away from one another and seemed to crave more time together as the weeks went by.

At first they had busied themselves restoring Ethan Ridgeway's home. Matt had reset the hedge and Violet had re-planted the flower bed. She had then helped him replace the damaged turf on the front lawn.

They could easily have left it there but instead took it upon themselves to re-paint the whole exterior of the house, repairing boards and sanding window frames as necessary. In fact it seemed they would do anything just to be together.

To the rest of the household this was transparently obvious yet Matt and Violet still made a show of grudgingly putting up with each other.

Once the house was done, the pair of them then found exercise as an excuse to be together - in particular, karate, in which Matt was an expert.

As such, he had 'reluctantly' agreed to teach Violet, thereby ensuring that they spent at least a couple of hours together every day.

To the others, this was so obvious that it was almost laughable, yet it was also rather sweet.

Nevertheless, Violet was a quick study and a dedicated pupil and soon became quite proficient in the fighting skills Matt was teaching her.

However, what Violet did not know, was that Matt was also fighting a battle with himself.

He was extremely attracted to Violet, more so than he had been to any woman since Suzie and positively ached with desire for her. Indeed, he thought about her at almost every waking moment and found her presence around him utterly intoxicating.

Even though he had loved Suzie with all his heart, he was little more than a boy when they were together with feelings not yet fully matured. Now, however, he was a man, with a wealth of experience and recognised the difference between his youthful love for Suzie and the sheer depth of his feeling for Violet and, to his eternal shame, the two bore no comparison.

He wanted nothing more than to take Violet in his arms and declare his love for her but he could not as it felt like an unforgivable betrayal of the girl who had died so that his father might live.

So, instead, he rebuffed Violet, fought against his feelings for her, which often took the form of irritability. But the irritation was not that she was close to him, but in his inability to react in the way he so desperately wanted to whenever she was around.

He knew that she found this confusing and he hated himself for it and it was certainly not how he acted with other women, but Violet was different. She meant something.

In fact, she meant *everything*.

Nonetheless, much as her very presence exacerbated the annoyance he felt with himself, he could not bring himself to be without her, much as he was loathed to admit it.

The fractiousness between them was caused merely by his conscience constantly bridling against these feelings, knowing that the memory of Suzie, indeed his very love for her, was fading and the guilt of it was almost too much to bear.

***

They drove in silence to the *Villa Continental* in Matt's recently repaired truck. Violet had the window down, the warm Las Vegas air rushing in, so that her long, dark hair billowed in the wind and her subtle perfume wafted alluringly into Matt's nostrils which he found deeply distracting. Indeed, he had to focus his attention fully on the road ahead, forcibly concentrating on mundane things such as traffic and road signs, to prevent the arousal he felt from the scent of her becoming too pronounced.

Upon arrival, they pulled into a space in the private parking lot reserved for hotel employees. Still without speaking, they then each grabbed their gym bags and strode in, as normal, through the staff entrance.

When they reached the bank of service elevators stationed a short distance within, Matt punched the button and they waited together, again in silence.

As they stood in anticipation of the elevator's arrival, the air was charged with sexual tension and barely restrained anger - hers for his continued refusal to acknowledge his feelings - and Matt's for his own inability to shake off the sense of betrayal he felt whenever he was with her.

They rode the elevator to the tenth floor without so much as a word; Matt was once again very aware of Violet's intoxicating scent in the confined space and was therefore incredibly relieved when the doors finally pinged open.

They stepped out of the elevator onto a polished marble floor, facing an ornamental Greek fountain with a statue of an ancient Olympian at its centre. Beyond the fountain was the impressive glass frontispiece, framed by two Grecian columns, which formed the grand entrance to the state-of-the-art gymnasium.

However, it was immediately apparent to Matt and Violet that they had the place all to themselves with the numerous and varied exercise apparatus all standing vacant in the deserted space - the hotel guests clearly preferring the gaming tables to treadmills or so it appeared.

Nonetheless, without acknowledging this emptiness, they went straight to their respective locker rooms to get changed. A few minutes later they met up in the spacious open area at the rear of the gym where the floor was covered with large padded crash mats.

Matt and Violet were now wearing sports shorts and stretchy gym vests. In addition, they were also wearing head guards and sparring pads on both their hands and feet for maximum protection against a stray fist or foot catching them accidentally.

Dressed for battle, with the gleaming Las Vegas skyline sparkling in the early morning sunshine through the floor to ceiling windows at their back, they eyed one another like a pair of ravenous tigers. Two fine specimens of prime physical excellence; Matt with his golden tan and hard muscular frame; Violet with her dark hair, generous breasts and long, athletic legs.

Yet her green eyes sparkled with annoyance as Matt adopted a defensive position in front of her, inviting her to attack.

And she was more than ready.

The drive in had angered her - all that brooding masculinity, all those pent up feelings, yet much to her chagrin, he still refused to open up and insisted on giving her the silent treatment instead.

Well she'd show him.

"C'mon then, show me what you've got, Matt said, finally speaking to her for the first time since leaving the house.

Violet did not need asking twice, because *boy, was she ready,* and the moment he finished speaking she launched herself at him.

Matt was quite taken aback by the ferocity of her attack and had to take urgent action to defend himself. Indeed, it was immediately apparent to him that this was no mere sparring session - at least not to Violet. To her, this was real. She was obviously angry and clearly had some serious aggression to work out.

Since her training began, Violet had made great progress in learning the combination of styles Matt had taught her and was becoming quite skilful in her own right. Although she still had a long way to go before she could even come close to Matt's level of expertise.

He had become a black belt in karate in his teens and since then had been adapting his technique; borrowing heavily from Tae-kwon-do, Kung fu and kick-boxing to develop his own unique fighting style - at which he was extremely proficient.

He had been teaching Violet this same method and she had taken to it instantly, undoubtedly helped by her already high standard of fitness.

Today, however, Violet was out for blood and she came at him time and again with a barrage of well co-ordinated combinations. Matt had them adequately covered but still had to use all his skill to counter them.

Nevertheless, the zealousness in which she was going about this unrelenting onslaught was proving to be her downfall as several times she overextended on a kick or mis-timed a punch, leaving herself wide open to a counter.

Matt had purposely overlooked this at first, hoping that she would eventually settle into a more considered fighting strategy - which would have been much the wiser choice.

Yet this was not the case and he was now getting a little bored of being her punching bag.

If she was to learn properly, then she must also learn to protect herself - and leaving her guard open was a very serious error indeed.

In previous lessons, Matt had repeatedly warned Violet of this but she appeared to have forgotten so it now seemed an appropriate moment for a timely reminder.

As Violet laid into him with yet another high stretch kick, she overextended once again to leave herself dangerously off balance. Immediately seizing the opportunity, Matt countered with a move of his own design which he knew would harmlessly but effectively end her attack.

With her leading foot raised high and aimed directly at the padded cheek of his head guard, Matt expertly shifted his stance and countered with breathtaking speed. Whipping a leg around her waist, he easily held her with it in a vice-like grip. He then twisted his body to force her down onto the crash mat so that she landed on her back with him on top of her.

Before she had time to react, he swiftly pinned her down with both his legs locked over hers and his hands clamped on her wrists to prevent her from struggling.

Violet's green eyes blazed with indignant fury as she glared up at him; the gentle glow of perspiration gleaming on her forehead and glistening in the deep channel between her full breasts as they heaved with exertion and rage.

Matt stared back; her lustrous black hair spread out on the crash mat, her beautiful, yet angry face fixed on his as her lithe body wriggling frustratedly beneath him.

Suddenly he was lost in the deep emerald pools of her eyes, helplessly bewitched by their hypnotic allure. At the same time he became very aware of her hips and thighs as they rubbed tantalisingly against his through the flimsy material of their gym attire and the feel of her firm breasts as they pounded repeatedly against his chest with the rise and fall of her breath.

Without warning his loins stirred and as he looked into Violet's face, he saw her eyes widen with delighted surprise; the fury suddenly gone as her pupils dilated with desire. He felt her body surrender with compliance and saw her plump lips part - willing him, imploring him, to kiss her.

Anxious to be free of restrictions, he tore off his head guard and gloves and cast them aside.

With Matt making no attempt to stop her, Violet pulled her arms out from under his knees then tore off her own head guard and gloves before lifting her chin provocatively.

Unable to resist a second longer, he then bent his head and pressed his soft lips against hers.

In that moment it was as if an ocean of lust washed over them. Suddenly they were locked together at the mouth, their tongues entwined in a glorious dance of passion too long restrained.

Violet shifted her position a little so that he could be more comfortable, then slid her legs free and placed the backs of her ankles on Matt's tight buttocks, pulling him down onto her as she thrust her hips upwards to meet his.

She wanted him more in that moment than she had wanted anything in her whole life; desperate to feel his naked flesh on hers as they kissed and pawed at each others bodies in a crazed frenzy of lust on the floor of the deserted gymnasium.

Violet pulled at the hem of Matt's vest, freeing it from the waistband of his shorts before tugging it upwards to expose his hard, tanned body. He briefly broke away to allow her to pull the vest off over his head but then, as he bent back down to kiss her again, he suddenly froze.

Violet watched helplessly as the passion faded from his eyes, seeing it replaced immediately by the tortured guilt that she had so often seen before.

"I'm sorry, Vee," Matt said, tearing his eyes away from hers in shame and hurriedly jumping to his feet. "I can't - I just can't."

"What?" Replied Violet suddenly bereft, her body still aching with desire for him. "No, please—"

But Matt was adamant. "I'm sorry."

Violet sat up and tried to calm him. "Why? Please tell me - help me understand, let me help you."

"It's no good," said Matt turning away and walking off towards the changing rooms. "I wanna be with you, Vee - more than anything. I just can't that's all. I just can't!"

Violet sprung to her feet and made to go after him. "Please Matt! Don't leave - please—"

But it was too late, he had already passed through the polished glass doors that led to the mens locker room and she was left standing in the gym all alone.

***

Matt burst into the changing room and smashed his fist hard into one of the metal lockers with rage, leaving a large, angular dent.

"Shit!" He growled angrily, tearing off his padded foot guards and throwing them violently across the empty room one by one.

"Bollocks!" He cursed again, desperately infuriated with himself for the guilt he still felt over Suzie's death, knowing it to be utter madness.

Irrational as it was, it still prevented him from making love to

Violet like he so desperately wanted to.

Indeed, he was still sexually charged and deeply frustrated with unspent lust; every fibre of his being heightened with an unshakeable urgency that longed to be satiated.

But it was not to be and without further delay, Matt stripped off his shorts and strode to the showers to urgently cool his ardor.

A moment later he was standing in one of the spacious, open-fronted shower enclosures that were provided by *The Villa* for guests. As with the rest of the gym, they were Grecian in style with luxurious gold fittings and marble tiled walls.

Presently however, Matt did not care a jot for the fancy architecture or plush decor, he just needed to cool down - *fast*.

Standing under a steady stream of ice cold water with his eyes closed and his passion slowly fading, he rested his head against the imported marble tiles and thought about Suzie. In his heart, he knew that she would not have wished him to be unhappy; that she would have wanted him to live his life to the full with a woman he could love as much as he had loved her.

She would not begrudge him or think any ill of him, it was not her way.

What is more, Matt knew that her death was not his fault. Thinking about it now, he had probably known it for many years but had held onto the guilt as a way, perhaps, of staying uninvolved.

Suzie's death had hurt him deeply, cut him to the very soul and he had used that as an excuse not to get hurt again.

He had loved her with all his heart but now he loved another and it was time to finally let Suzie go.

But surely he had now blown whatever chance he might have had with Violet.

Indeed, he would not blame her if she never wanted to see him again.

That being the case, he would have no more reason to stay at

Canyon Hill Drive.

Upon his arrival back at the house, he would pack a bag and be on his way before his parents got back from The Caymans, before there could be any fuss.

There was a race meet in Kentucky in a week's time, maybe he could pick up a drive there and once he got back into the way of things he would hopefully forget all about Violet Noakes and her beautiful green eyes.

***

Matt stood there for a while longer with the water running cold. Soon, however, it began to make him feel chilly, so he adjusted the dial to a warmer setting.

The difference was immediate and hot, steamy water was soon cascading over Matt's body, soothing the pain he felt inside.

However, with his face still resting against the tiles and water rushing over his ears, he did not hear the footsteps behind him.

"Matt, I'm sorry," said a familiar voice, startling him slightly. "I know you want to be alone but I have to tell you that I love you. I can't keep it from you any longer - no matter how you may feel about me. I know you're in pain and I want to help you - I want you to let me in. But more than anything I want—"

The voice paused, seemingly struggling to continue and Matt turned to see Violet standing there naked before him.

She looked magnificent; generous breasts, a flat, firm stomach and a curly black mound of dark hair that formed a nest at the convergence of her long, shapely legs.

Immediately the ferocity of Matt's ardor was ignited once more, the sight of her utterly breathtaking.

"What?" Matt croaked, his voice hoarse with desire. "What do you want more than anything?"

Violet's lips trembled slightly with awe as she stared at the glory of his nakedness. "I want you to make love to me," she replied softly.

Matt needed no further invitation and immediately reached out his hand to her. As she took it, he pulled her to him, engulfing her in his arms as the water poured over them, her wondrous body feeling so good, so *right* against his.

With her in his arms, their passion exploded as they kissed with a deep carnal desire; their tongues entwined, feasting greedily from each other.

Yet before she became irretrievably lost, Violet reluctantly pulled her mouth away from his.

"I know you don't love me," she gasped breathlessly, her lips tantalisingly close to his, "But please, just for now, pretend that you do."

"No, Vee, you're wrong," Matt whispered. "I do love you - I know I've been a fool but I realise now that I love you more than I've ever loved anyone."

"But what about the other girl" she sputtered, happy but confused. "What about Suzie?"

"She was in my past, Vee," he said. "But you are my present - my future - *my life.*"

With that, he kissed her again then turned her, so that her back was pressed flat against the warm tiles of the shower wall.

"You love me?" Violet queried, a big smile on her face as she wrapped her endless legs tightly around his waist.

"I love you," he said, grinning back.

"Good," she replied wantonly, "now prove it."

"Oh, believe me, I intend to," he said.

Then, with a shuddering wave of pleasure washing over her, Violet gasped with sheer, unbridled ecstasy as Matt set about doing exactly as he had promised.

Chapter Twenty-One

The next few days at Canyon Hill Drive were a blissful mix of love, laughter and sheer contentment; Brett and Liv together with Matt and Violet, all caught up in a wonderful whirl of romance and fun.

Their was, of course, the small matter of breaking the news of both the wedding and the impending arrival of a new baby to its future grandparents - all of whom were due back shortly from The Caymans.

Liv and Brett were both incredibly excited to tell them, knowing that their families were certain to be as happy as they were about everything. Indeed, after all that had happened, it was sure to be just the boost they needed.

It was now also abundantly clear that Matt and Violet saw their future together, too.

Furthermore, since consummating her relationship with Matt, Violet had decided to take the advice the other women had given her and put what had happened to her father and brother behind her. The police would surely catch up with Bass Stone sooner or later and when they did he would undoubtedly get everything he deserved - and Violet had at last made peace with that.

As a result, it felt as if a weight had been lifted from her shoulders and with her newly blossoming romance with Matt going from strength to strength she was like a woman reborn.

Matt, too, had never been more contented. After finally laying Suzie's ghost to rest, he had embraced life once more; suddenly it was worth living again and he was feeling invigorated and passionate about the future for the first time in years.

With so much good news to share, the homecoming of Joe, Rose, Sean and Sarah was promising to be something of a huge celebration on several fronts.

In anticipation of her parents' arrival back from The Caymans, Liv had invited Louretta and Ethan to Vegas to share in the festivities - so that she and Brett could announce the news of her pregnancy to everyone all at once.

Furthermore, she had arranged for Josh's security detail to be given a few days off so that Louretta and Ethan could pick him up from *CalTech* on the way. Liv had been purposely coy on the phone about her reasons for the family get-together but Louretta, being a wily old bird, had pretty much guessed. However, she did not let on as she had no intention of spoiling her granddaughter's plans.

Nevertheless, with a view to letting her grandson drive to Las Vegas after picking him up, Louretta and Ethan had chosen the Shelby Mustang GT500 for the trip, knowing how much Josh loved it.

Ethan was behind the wheel as they left Louretta's bungalow in Santa Monica and headed off on the short, half-hour drive to Pasadena to collect Josh. From there it would be another four hours or so to Vegas but there was no particular rush and they would probably stop on the way for some lunch.

As it was, they set off early, just after nine, with a view to arriving at Canyon Hill Drive sometime around mid afternoon.

Yet as the Mustang roared away from the Santa Monica bungalow, neither Louretta or Ethan noticed the dusty green sedan that pulled out into the line of traffic a few cars behind them.

Life in hiding had proved much harder than Rocco Pistoli had previously imagined. Indeed, even though he assumed himself to be something of a loner, he was used to the companionship and camaraderie of the Vincenzi crew and was quite surprised by just how much he missed both.

In fact, life on his own had been a miserable existence. From Orlando, he had lurched from one city to another, living in squalid roadside motels in run-down out-of-the-way neighbourhoods in a bid to stay under the radar and avoid places where he might be known or recognised as a Vincenzi associate.

What is more, he had burned through almost all of his cash in just three short months even though he had been trying to conserve it. Yet boredom and loneliness had got the better of him and a relatively serious coke habit which he had kicked back in his twenties had once again taken hold of him.

Presently, he was managing it well enough but he could feel his need for it growing daily and was becoming ever more reliant on the brief buzz that it gave him.

As a side-effect of the cocaine, Rocco's sex drive had also increased significantly and he had blown another bundle of cash on hookers. This was partly to relieve his loneliness - after all, an hour spent with a whore was one less spent alone - but his rapidly depleting funds had prevented him from being choosy and he had taken to picking up women in the seedier parts of town; women whose priority was not necessarily cleanliness or hygiene but to fund their own drug habit.

Consequently, things had recently taken a downward turn and what had begun as an annoying itch in his genitals had swiftly turned into a nasty little rash coupled with a severe burning sensation whenever he peed.

Worse still, he was down to his last few hundred bucks and

needed funds rapidly to keep him afloat.

Briefly he entertained calling Jez Vincenzi and begging his forgiveness. Rocco had heard through the grapevine that Jez and Bass Stone were holed up in an old Carboni safe house in Vermont; a mansion previously owned by Carmine for the specific purpose of laying low until whatever heat he might be getting at some hypothetical point in the future had died down.

The place had never been used but a caretaker and a housekeeper were kept on the payroll to keep it in a habitable order in case it should ever be needed.

After Carmine's untimely end, Jez had inherited it and as such, was taking advantage of its isolated location to stay under the radar for a while - or at least that's what Rocco had heard from a very reliable source, but it was not common knowledge.

Pistoli had the phone number written down on a crumpled piece of paper in the back of his wallet somewhere, given to him personally by Carmine himself, and briefly he had been tempted to use it, thinking that maybe he could wrangle his way back into Jez's good graces.

But then he thought of Bass Stone and the hold he now had over Jez and realised it would be futile. There was no such thing as a free pass and with nothing to bargain with Rocco would be as good as signing his own death warrant.

The hard reality was that he was unable to rely on anyone's help and it was up to Rocco alone to get himself out of the mess he was currently in.

Which led him there, to the small, Asian run *7-Eleven* in East Brooklyn at midnight.

Rocco had not robbed a store since he was a kid but desperate times called for desperate measures and it was the only remaining option which would guarantee a quick injection of cash.

He stood outside in the darkness, leaning against a broken

street light, waiting his moment. A *Knicks* cap was pulled down over his forehead and the hood of his zip-thru fleece pulled up over that. A fully loaded 'Saturday Night Special' was tucked into his belt, hidden by the ex-army jacket he was wearing over the hoody.

Around his neck he wore a loose bandanna and tucked in his pocket was a pair of cheap wraparound sunglasses.

Rocco felt antsy but excited, his adrenaline pumping as the last remaining customer left the store leaving the owner all alone.

Rocco gave it a count of twenty, just to make certain the coast was clear then swiftly marched across the dark, deserted street towards the *7-Eleven*. A moment before pushing the door open, he pulled the bandanna up over his nose and slid on the sunglasses to disguise himself and mask the very distinctive hairline scar that ran from the top right of his forehead to the bottom of his left earlobe - a facial feature which any witness would be sure to remember.

As he burst into the store, startling the little old Asian man behind the counter, he pulled the gun from his belt and yelled, "Hands where I can see 'em grandpa!"

The shop owner immediately did as instructed and threw his hands up in the air. "Don't shoot, don't shoot!" He wailed in a heavy Chinese accent.

"Just do as I tell ya, okay?" Replied Rocco sternly, pointing the gun directly at the old man's head. "Now give me all your money - and no fuckin' funny stuff."

The little Asian did not even hesitate as he popped open the cash register. "Here, take it - no funny stuff, I promise," he said.

Rocco looked into the cash drawer and saw a meagre pile of bills; a few hundreds, a couple of fifties but mostly twenties and tens along with a handful of coins.

"Where's the fuckin' rest of it?" He demanded, his adrenaline pumping even faster and his anger rising along with the need to score. "Don't you lie to me now!"

"I not lie, I swear. This is it - wife went to bank earlier - this all I have left."

"I said don't fuckin' lie!" Rocco roared, pushing the barrel of the pistol hard against the man's forehead.

The little Asian whimpered slightly as he replied, "Please, I tell truth. This all I have. Don't shoot - I beg you, I have wife and fam—"

"Ah, shut the fuck up!" Rocco growled irritably as he pulled the trigger, the report of the gun deafening in the deserted store.

The little Asian's eyes flew wide as he dropped to the floor dead.

Rocco's patience had run out. He needed money not excuses and the old man was just getting in his way. Indeed, the *.22* calibre revolver was still smoking as Rocco leapt over the counter and pushed the store owner's body aside with the heel of his boot before proceeding to empty the cash drawer of its contents.

He hurriedly stuffed the notes into his coat pockets then, with his gloved hands, scooped out the change, down to the very last dime. Yet he was certain there must be more, *surely this could not be it?*

He pulled out the cash drawer and tossed it aside, swiftly checking underneath to make sure no bills were stashed underneath, but there was none. Then, working quickly, he rummaged through several drawers and cupboards at the back of the counter, hoping with growing desperation to find something more. But again he came up empty.

"Sonofabitch!" He yelled angrily, aware that he had run out of time. He had to get the hell out of the store before the cops arrived as someone was bound to have heard the gunshot.

As he turned to leave, he caught sight of a wizened Asian woman sitting on a deck chair in a doorway to the side which led to the living area in the back. She was just staring at him, tears of confusion filling her eyes.

The image of her stirred something within him and Rocco

froze for a moment, transfixed by her gaze.

However, his attention was ripped away from her as the door burst open and two black teenagers entered the store.

One of them opened his mouth to speak, "Hey man, what's goin—" he began, but his voice was snatched away by yet another blast from Rocco's gun. The boy fell like a stone, his face smashing against the tiled floor, blood pissing from the hole in his forehead.

Rocco was startled and panicked now; shocked by what he had done. Yet his need to score made him dangerously erratic and heightened his anxiety.

The other teenager just stood there numbly for a moment, his eyes locked on Rocco, unable to quite comprehend what had just happened. But then, as the realisation hit him with a rush, he was suddenly terrified for his own life.

He turned to run but he was too late as Pistoli gunned him down, too, with a shot to the back of the head.

As the boy hit the ground, Rocco bolted for the door. Yet the bodies of the two teenagers were barring his exit. Quickly he dragged them aside; the door banging against the second boy's head as Pistoli finally managed to swing it open.

Before leaving he instinctively turned and looked back at the grey-haired old woman.

Still her gaze bored into him and Rocco felt the hairs prickle ominously on the back of his neck. Suddenly he felt disgusted with himself, yet she would not stop staring.

"Stop it!" He yelled, but still she persisted. Rocco could feel his anger rising. "Stop it, you old crone!" He yelled again, but her response was unchanged.

Finally, Rocco raised the revolver and took aim at her but just as he was about to pull the trigger, he heard the sound of a police siren growing ever louder as it sped towards the store.

"Looks like it's your lucky night," he said, the sound of the siren distracting him from his murderous intent.

He lowered the gun. "Goodnight grandma," he said softly as he then turned and ran from the store leaving three dead in his wake.

He arrived back at his seedy little motel room just after 1am with a freshly purchased sachet of coke. Hurriedly, he chopped and sifted it, then eagerly snorted a couple of lines. The effect was immediate and suddenly his anxieties and frustrations faded away.

With the coke now relaxing him, he went to the bathroom and stripped off his clothes to ease the constant irritation of his inflamed and itchy genitals. Indeed, free from material and with the air circulating freely around them, the relief was enormous. Yet he could not help but be concerned by the sight of the red, angry rash and cluster of round, pustulant spots he saw speckled on his crotch in the cracked bathroom mirror.

Nonetheless, he forcibly put his worries aside and sat down naked on the bed; his legs spread wide to allow maximum airflow around his sore testicles. He then picked up his jacket and pulled out his pathetic proceeds from the *7-Eleven*.

The small pile of notes and assorted coins did not take him long to add up and when he had finished it amounted to a grand total of four-hundred and seventy-three dollars and forty-nine cents.

Not nearly enough to keep him in hookers and coke for long and he knew he would need to hit another store before the week was out.

Firstly, however, he needed to see a doctor to get some pills for the persistent itch in his groin before it drove him absolutely insane.

***

The next morning, Rocco was sitting in the busy waiting room of a free clinic in Brownsville, not far from the store where he had killed three people the night before. Indeed, news of the incident was the main topic of conversation in the noisy bustle of the room but Rocco pulled his cap down and spoke to no one.

338

He held a ticket in his hand, taken from the machine on the counter, which denoted his place in the doctor's queue. His number read *56*, whereas the corresponding machine on the wall was displaying only number *18*, meaning thirty-eight people were ahead of him.

Rocco was not a patient man and would have gladly walked out but his genitals now felt as if they were on fire and the itching had become almost unbearable. He needed some antibiotics or some penicillin - anything to relieve his considerable discomfort. So he settled in for a long wait.

He thought maybe a magazine might help to keep his mind off the itching and ease his need for yet another hit of cocaine, even though it had only been a few hours since the last.

In front of him, on a low table, was a huge stack of ancient, extremely well thumbed magazines - some of them years old which had probably been there since the clinic opened.

Rocco leant over and sorted through them, trying to find something to take his mind off things.

Vogue, Cosmo, several *Time* and umpteen *People* magazines were laid out before him along with numerous others but it was a copy of one particular *Life* magazine which finally caught his eye.

It was tatty and obviously quite old; the pages all ripped inside, but it was the large black and white photograph on the front cover which encouraged him to select it.

The full width photograph was a classic archive shot of a legendary Hollywood beauty taken, Rocco guessed, in the 1940s. It featured a platinum blonde in typical western attire sitting astride a glossy, dark horse. The small caption beside it simply read; *Louretta Wild: Then and Now.*

His interest piqued, Rocco picked it up and flicked through the pages until he found the article he was looking for.

Again, there was a photograph of Louretta as she was in her

heyday, this time laying beside a pool in a swimsuit and sunglasses. But on the facing page there was a photo of her as she was now - or at least how she was at the time of the magazine's publication which, upon checking the date, Rocco found was 1979.

Knowing of Louretta Wild's association with Matt Mason, Pistoli read the accompanying article with a great deal of interest.

It covered her formative years as a movie star, before moving onto her success as a horse-breeder, explaining how that had far surpassed her acting career. The article then went onto highlight her latest triumph as joint owner of *The Villa Continental*, the most exclusive hotel and casino in Las Vegas, and her recent part in overseeing its lavish refurbishment.

Across the ten page feature were many more photographs; some of the *Villa*, some of *Wildwood*; her ranch in Palm Springs, and several more of her bungalow in Santa Monica. It was this which Rocco found particularly interesting.

Both *Wildwood* and *The Villa Continental* were risky propositions as he would have little hope of getting to Louretta easily at either of those. Indeed, even Carmine Carboni and Tito Vincenzi had considered them too much of a gamble, as proven by Jez's father Benny, who had come to grief at *The Villa* himself.

However, Rocco had not previously been aware of the bungalow in Santa Monica and it struck him now that security might not be as tight, making the prospect of grabbing the old woman much less hazardous.

Furthermore, if he could get close to Louretta Wild, he could force her to tell him where to find Matt Mason and that was a tantalising concept indeed.

Suddenly, all thoughts of doctors and penicillin were swept away and even his groin stopped itching as the idea of catching up with Matt Mason played over and over again in his mind.

Feeling greatly invigorated, Rocco rolled the magazine and

stuffed it quickly into his jacket, then stood and strode purposefully out of the clinic to where his dusty green sedan was parked.

He tapped his pocket and smiled as he started the engine. Four-hundred and seventy-three dollars and forty-nine cents - just enough for gas and cocaine to get him to Santa Monica.

***

It was a long, arduous drive coast to coast, but Rocco eventually checked into a cheap *Ramada* on Santa Monica Boulevard just after nightfall, six days after starting out from New York.

Nevertheless, he was still staked out bright and early next morning in front of Louretta Wild's palatial, ocean view bungalow, hopped up on coke and digging hungrily into a piping hot *McMuffin*.

His tired green sedan, an old Crown Vic, was strewn with the debris of fast food wrappers and empty drink cartons which were only in part from the journey. A sleeping bag was spread out messily on the back seat which had been used more than once on his drive across country.

Yet sitting there, swallowing down a mouthful of tasty *McMuffin* and sucking on a refreshing strawberry shake, looking across the street at the old woman's home, it all seemed worthwhile and he suddenly felt optimistic that his luck was finally about to change.

Indeed, he had only been watching the house for an hour or so when its high gates opened and a shiny blue Shelby Mustang with Louretta Wild in the passenger seat and some old guy driving edged out onto the street.

Pistoli, his heart now beating a little faster, started the engine of his Ford sedan as the beautiful blue Mustang roared off down the road.

Rocco gave it a second or two, then pulled out into the line of traffic a few cars behind, hoping that the old woman was about to lead him directly to his brother's killer.

He followed at a distance but never lost sight of the Mustang as they headed out through Culver City and on passed Dodger Stadium towards Pasadena.

A half-hour after leaving the bungalow, they turned off the highway following the signs to *CalTech*. Rocco was a little confused but continued to stay with them. However, when they drove onto campus and pulled up, he hung back and parked a suitable distance away where he could keep an eye on them without being noticed.

He looked on curiously as Louretta Wild and her elderly companion got out of the Mustang and waited on the sidewalk beside it.

After a minute or so, a tall, blonde kid carrying an overnight bag came bounding out of the main block. He hugged the old woman and kissed her on the cheek then shook hands with the man, happy smiles on all of their faces.

Rocco guessed that this boy was Louretta Wild's grandson whom, from Vincenzi's many rants, he remembered was called 'Josh'.

He watched as the boy stowed his bag in the trunk before jumping into the driving seat of the Mustang, the old man moving into the back. Louretta Wild took her place once again in the passenger seat.

The presence of the bag suggested to Rocco that the three of them were going on some sort of trip and as the Mustang started off, he once again slipped in three or four cars behind. Instinctively, he checked the fuel gauge again to see what was left in the tank and to his relief, saw the needle had barely moved. His mind at ease, he settled comfortably in for what could possibly be another long drive in the space of just two short days.

Nevertheless, it soon became abundantly clear that they were all heading to Las Vegas, a mere four hours away and the more Rocco thought about it, the more convinced he became that at the end of this journey he would, indeed, find Matt Mason.

Chapter Twenty-Two

Brett picked up Joe, Rose, Sean and Sarah from McCarran Airport just before midday.

It was great to see them all and he was bursting to tell them the news but he knew he must wait until everyone else arrived and for when Liv was standing beside him.

On the short drive back to Canyon Hill Drive, Joe told his son all about the trip; relating the details of the small but intimate service held on the cliff top for Ray and Ruby as well as a first-hand account of the complete devastation they had all found at *Far Point*.

The news of this saddened Brett yet he was heartened by Joe's decision to rebuild and make his life there once more.

Although Brett said nothing to give things away, he could think of no better place himself than *Far Point* to raise his child and knew Liv would wholeheartedly agree.

They arrived back at the Ridgeway home a short time later where Liv, Matt and Violet were waiting to greet them - not letting on that Louretta, Ethan and Josh, together with Virgil and Victoria would be joining them later for a small celebration.

Even though Joe and Sean remained blissfully ignorant to the nuanced shift of dynamics in the house, as was fairly typical of the male species in general, both Sarah and Rose picked up on something subtly different about the mood between the four young people that greeted them.

Indeed, Liv was positively glowing and Violet could barely stop smiling.

As the two older women went upstairs to freshen up, Rose said to Sarah, "Is it just me or is there something different about those four?"

"Nope, not just you," Sarah replied. "Did you see that smile on Vee's face - and how Matt was looking at her?"

"I sure did," Said Rose with delight, "You reckon—?"

"Yep. I reckon alright," Sarah grinned, "Those two have been at it."

Rose giggled. "Really? You think?"

"I'd put money on it - it's written all over their faces and they can't keep their eyes off each other!"

"I know," agreed Rose. "Ooh, I'm so pleased - although it's about damn time!"

"I'll say," chuckled Sarah, "Before we left there was so much pent up emotion between those two that I thought one or both of them might explode!"

Rose, laughed and nodded. "You can say that again. But what about Liv and Brett? Something's going on with them too, don't you think."

"Yeah," replied Sarah, the two women now standing on the landing outside the doors to their respective bedrooms, "But I'm not quite sure what. Still, I expect we'll find out soon enough. First though, I need to take a shower and freshen up."

"Agreed," said Rose, opening her bedroom door. "See you in a bit."

"Yeah, see you."

Then both disappeared into their bedrooms.

***

Virgil and Victoria jetted into McCarran later that afternoon from London where Virgil had been filming on location - and where both were due back in just four days time.

Whenever possible, Victoria liked to accompany her husband on location, but in this instance she was actually producing the movie, too, so her presence on set was more vital, hence the reason for Louretta and Ethan picking up Josh.

However, because Virgil and Vicky were big name movie stars, their presence in Las Vegas, as with anywhere they went, was documented by the press which made it impossible to go straight from the airport to Canyon Hill Drive.

Instead, they were picked up by a limo from *The Villa Continental,* arranged, of course, by Bernie Dufresne - promoting the charade that the married couple were staying there whilst taking a short break from shooting. *The Villa,* famously owned by Victoria's mother, naturally being the obvious choice.

Upon arrival at the hotel, where much press attention was focussed on them entering the lobby, they were escorted by Bernie, alone, in a private elevator, down to the staff parking garage below.

There, away from the glare of reporters and photographers, they were picked up by Matt in his truck and driven incognito to Ethan Ridgeway's home, the media and public at large completely unaware that they had ever left the hotel.

However, both Virgil and Victoria were uncertain as to why Liv had summoned them home. All she had said was that it was important that they be there so, of course, they had agreed.

***

With Louretta, Ethan and Josh's arrival mid-afternoon, it completed the full family gathering much to everyone's delight and surprise - yet they were all as much in the dark as each other as to the reason for it, although speculation was abound.

Nevertheless, Brett and Liv remained tight lipped and arranged for everyone to meet up on the patio under the pretty pergola at the rear of the house at eight o'clock that evening.

At the appointed hour, everyone was there as requested, all seated around the large wooden table used for dining alfresco on warm Las Vegas evenings such as the one they were presently enjoying.

Liv and Brett, sitting together at the head of the table, made for an extremely handsome couple and it was clear for all to see that they were very much in love.

After a little chatter, Brett finally called for silence and stood to address the small group of friendly onlookers.

"Thanks everyone for coming," Brett began. "Pop, Rosie - Uncle Sean and Aunt Sarah, it's good to have you back. Vicky, Virge - thanks for making the trip, we appreciate it."

"Hey, no sweat, kid," replied Virgil. "So what gives?"

"Yeah, what you called us all here for, sonny?" Asked Louretta.

Brett turned to her. "Grandma, Ethan - glad you could make it - and you Josh."

"C'mon, boy - enough with the 'thank yous'," Joe protested, "stop teasing us and spit it out!"

"Ssh!" Said Rose, slapping her husband lightly on the arm. "Let him finish."

Brett smiled at his father's well-intended impatience. "Okay, Pop," he said before clearing his throat and taking Liv's hand. She, in turn, gazed lovingly into his eyes and nodded her encouragement.

"Well, as you all already know," he said, turning again to face his captive audience, "Liv and I love each other very much."

As Rose looked proudly on, she raised a hand to her mouth to stifle her emotion, suddenly realising what her stepson was about to say.

Meanwhile, Victoria's eyes began to fill with tears of joy and Sarah grabbed hold of Sean's hand and squeezed it tightly with anticipation.

346

"So, with that in mind," Brett continued, "whilst you were away - and we had a little peace and quiet for a change," he grinned, "I asked Liv to marry me and—"

"And I said 'yes", Liv blurted, jumping to her feet. "We're getting married!"

Suddenly everyone erupted with cheers of congratulation and whoops of joy.

Matt and Violet, who were standing at the back, ready with the champagne, popped the corks and quickly handed everybody a glass.

"I knew it! I goddamn knew it!" Yelled Louretta delightedly as she stood up and rushed to give Liv a hug. "Well done, honey - you got a good one there, trust me."

"I know, Grandma, thanks."

"Congratulations sweetie," Sarah said, now also on her feet and joining in, giving Liv a kiss on the cheek. "I thought something was going on - I just couldn't put my finger on it."

"Are you pleased?" Liv asked.

"What? Are you kidding? I couldn't be happier." Sarah replied.

"I know - I just wish Michael was here too, that's all," Liv said, taking her by the hand.

"Me too, sweetie," Sarah said softly, placing her hand over Liv's, "He would have been so happy for you - for both of you."

"Thanks," Liv nodded, her eyes brimming, "I know he would."

Their conversation was abruptly broken off by the clinking sound of Brett tapping a paper knife on the base of his champagne flute.

"Wait! Wait - there's more," he said above the din. "We're not done with our news yet!"

"What?" Said Victoria, "there's more?"

"Uh-huh," said Liv, rejoining Brett and taking his hand once more."

"Are you gonna tell 'em or am I?" He said.

The room fell silent as everyone stared at Liv with baited breath.

She turned to look at them, her face beaming with joy.

"We're going to have a baby," she said. "I'm three months pregnant."

***

After a prolonged period of back-slapping and congratulatory hugs, the garden settled down again into a rather noisy but happy throng of excited conversation, the women forming a circle around Liv on one side of the patio, the men in a masculine huddle on the other.

"So when are you going to get married?" Asked Vicky. "Soon, I imagine, if you want to do it before the baby arrives - and before you start showing too much."

"Yeah," replied Liv, "That's the plan. We want to get married straight away - or at least as soon as we can find a place to do it."

"You haven't decided on a venue yet?" Rose broke in.

"No, not yet," said Liv. "Brett and I both would've liked the ceremony to be at *Far Point* but that's out of the question at the moment."

"How about *The Villa?* Sarah asked.

"We did consider that," replied Liv, "but we thought there would be too many cameras, too much press."

"You can say that again," said Vicky. "Hell, all we did was walk through the lobby earlier and we nearly got mobbed."

"What about here?" Louretta said, "We could decorate it, maybe put a marquee up in the garden - I'm sure Ethan wouldn't mind."

"I know he wouldn't" answered Liv, "and we did think of this place, too. We both love it here and we've been so happy - but security would be a major issue and, again, the press would be crawling all over the front lawn - I can see it now. Same thing with the beach

348

house in Malibu - the media would turn it into a circus and none of us want that."

"Well then, why not do it at *Wildwood*," Louretta stated. "We can pretty much guarantee your privacy there - and there won't be any press, not on the ranch anyway. We can step up security and pitch a marquee on the back pasture behind the house so that none of those goddamn media helicopters can get a look at you - what do you think, honey?"

"My God, Grandma, *Wildwood*, of course! It didn't even occur to me," exclaimed Liv, suddenly excited. "But it would be perfect - especially as both Brett and me have got such fond memories of it - we spent some great times together there as kids. Thank you Grandma - it would be wonderful! But you're sure you don't mind?"

"Hell, kid, you're my granddaughter ain't ya," replied Louretta, "An' Brett may as well be my grandson - so of course I don't mind. It'd be my pleasure."

"Oh, thanks Grandma!" Liv gushed, wrapping her arms around her grandmother and kissing her fondly on the cheek. "But can we do it soon - I'm not sure how long it's gonna be before I start to show?"

"Sure - how 'bout next week? A June wedding at the ranch will be real pretty."

"Yeah, it would, it'd be lovely - how about Saturday week, then - ten days from now, would that be okay?" Liv asked.

"Sure, honey," Louretta smiled. "That'd be just swell."

"Would that work with you, too, Mom?" Said Liv to Victoria. "I know you're busy with the movie shoot and everything but I really think we'd better—"

"Of course, sweetheart," interrupted Vicky. "Virge and me can make a few calls, rearrange the schedule a little - that comes with the perks of being the star and producer."

"But it means you'll have to fly back here again in a just week or so," said Liv guiltily.

"Nonsense. I ain't going anywhere. You're my only daughter and you're getting married - we've got lots to do before Saturday week - like getting you a dress to start with!"

"Mom, that's great, thanks!" Exclaimed Liv with delight, "But what about the movie - won't that be a problem?"

"Like I said, sweetie, perks of being the boss - 'sides we've pretty much wrapped in London now, just a few additional exteriors to do and we can fly back after the wedding to shoot those."

"You sure?" Asked Liv, stifling a happy grin.

"Sure."

Liv hugged her mother tightly. "Thanks, Mom, you're the best!"

"Yeah, well I'll remind you of that in just over a week," chuckled Vicky.

"Let me go tell Brett," said Liv, "he'll be so pleased - I just know he will." And with that her daughter was gone.

As Victoria watched her go, she saw her pleasure mirrored on the faces of the women around her.

However, whilst it was clear that Violet was extremely happy for Liv, Vicky sensed a wistfulness about her, too, which she assumed might have something to do with her feelings for Matt.

So as not to draw attention away from Liv and Brett's moment, Victoria whispered conspiratorially in Violet's ear, "Come on," she said, taking her hand affectionately, "Let's go get another drink."

"Er, okay, sure," replied Violet, allowing herself to be led back to the table.

"You can tell me all that's been going on with you since I've been away," said Vicky.

***

Whilst the women discussed wedding venues, the men had been having an entirely different conversation.

"So, boy," Joe said to Matt, "everything been alright here while we've been gone?"

"Yeah, Pop, fine," he replied. "Everything's been good."

"*Really* good, I'd say, wouldn't you, Matt?" Brett chipped in.

Matt smiled at his step-brother's heavy-handed attempt at subtlety, "Yeah," he grinned, "I guess so."

"What?" Joe asked, suddenly curious, "What's going on between you two?"

"Not between *us two*," chuckled Brett, "But between Matt and Vee."

Sean could not help but overhear, "What's going on between Matt and Vee?" He asked.

"What's that?" Said Virgil, joining the conversation, "Something's going on between Matt and Vee? Vicky thought there might be - she told me earlier."

"Jesus!" Exclaimed Matt with a wide, guilty grin spreading across his face, "You guys are worse than a bunch of gossipy old women!"

"So tell us then," said Joe, leading the interrogation, "Have you and Violet got a thing going?"

"A thing?" Matt said, raising an eyebrow at his father's choice of words, uncertain as to whether he had ever heard Joe say such a thing in his life, "Who are you, Oprah?"

Everyone laughed, including Joe, suddenly realising that he must be getting old. "Yeah, maybe," he said. "So come on, spill the beans."

Matt regarded Brett with a look of good-humoured contempt, "Thanks, bro," he said sarcastically.

"Hey, my pleasure," replied Brett, "but you might as well tell 'em - it's written all over your lovestruck face!"

Matt chuckled. "Okay, okay - alright, I give in," he said. "Yes, Pop, Vee and me have got *a thing* going on."

"Really?" Said Sean and Virgil in unison whilst Joe just beamed with pride. Between the men, in private, Violet was considered to be what Joe called 'a bit special' and whom they all regarded as *all woman*. Indeed, had any of them been twenty years younger they may all have given Matt a run for his money - had they not all been so happy in their own relationships of course.

"So what? Are you two together now then?" Joe asked.

"Uh-huh," Matt replied.

"And you're happy?"

"Yep. Never been happier," Matt said with an absolute certainty that could not be mistaken.

Again Joe looked at him; pride bursting from every pore. "That's great, son," he said, placing a fatherly hand on Matt's shoulder. "Really great and I'm very pleased for you."

"Well go on," prompted Brett, "You might as well tell 'im the rest while you're about it."

"What do you mean," queried Joe, "what rest?"

Again, an exasperated Matt gave Brett a sideways glance, although secretly he was grateful for the excuse to tell his father everything. "I've done with wandering, Pop, that's what it means," he said, turning back to Joe. "It's time I settled down, put down some roots - I wanna make a home close to you and Mum - build a future with Violet. It's what we both want."

Sean and Virgil were looking on, completely rapt in the conversation, both knowing how long Joe and Rose had wanted Matt nearer to them.

"What? Are you getting married, too, then?" Joe asked, slightly taken aback.

"Not yet - but sure, sometime in the future, I reckon. We've not really talked about that yet but we do want to be together so I guess that would be the next logical step - although I don't wanna rain on Brett and Liv's parade. Today's about them, not about us - even though Brett clearly thought the state of our relationship needed bringing up."

"What can I say," Brett smiled, "That's what younger brothers are for isn't it? Besides, I can't have my best man keeping secrets now can I?"

"Best man, eh?" Joe said, sliding an ironic glance to the eldest of his offspring.

"Uh-huh," Matt nodded, "That kinda got lost in the whole 'relationship' conversation."

"Yeah, well, he'll be lucky to have you" said Joe, taking a playful swipe at Brett.

"Hey!" Brett replied with mock indignance.

"I'll tell you another thing," Joe added as he regarded Matt, "What you've just told me will make your mum really happy, too."

"I know," said Matt earnestly.

Joe then wrapped a powerful arm around each of his sons' shoulders. "Today is a good day," he said, "a real *good* day and I could not be more proud of either of you."

Sean gave Matt a friendly slap on the upper arm, "I guess congratulations are in order for you, too, then, eh?"

"Er, yeah - well, I guess," said Matt, suddenly a little embarrassed.

Virgil was just about to offer his congratulations also when Liv bounded over, all excited. "Hey, Brett! Guess what," she exclaimed, "Grandma says we can get married at *Wildwood* - next week!"

***

After topping up their glasses at the table, Violet and Victoria stepped away to the outer perimeter of the garden. It was a clear, bright evening with a million stars lighting the sky; a gentle breeze played over the women's bare arms to give a pleasant coolness in the otherwise stifling Las Vegas air.

"I thought you and Matt might've gotten things sorted out whilst we were at *Far Point*," Victoria said, "but I guess I was wrong—"

"No, Vicky," Violet contradicted, "You were right - we did. We sorted everything out - in fact we did more than that. Much more, actually," she grinned unashamedly.

"You did?" Victoria said, sounding a little surprised.

"Uh-huh."

"You mean you—?"

"Mmm hmm," Violet giggled, "Lots of times."

"Wow! That's well, I mean it's great," Victoria blathered, quite taken aback but also delighted. "So are you a couple now then?"

"Uh-huh, I think so," said Violet. "Matt's even talking about us setting up home together."

"And you're pleased - that's what you want?"

"Yes," Violet said with certainty, "I love him and I want to be with him more than anything - it's wonderful."

"Christ, Vee, that's great to hear," Victoria exclaimed, immediately throwing her arms around Violet and hugging her tightly - I'm so happy for you, truly I am."

"Thanks - I was so excited to tell you, I thought I might burst!"

"Well now you've told me," Victoria said releasing her from the embrace before adding, "But I don't understand, you looked so lost in your thoughts a moment ago, so wistful. I thought there must be something wrong, that maybe you and Matt had fallen out again—"

"No, it was nothing like that," Violet interrupted. "It was just me being silly, that's all."

"What do you mean?"

"Oh nothing, I was just thinking how lucky Liv and Brett were to be surrounded by such a loving family and I suppose, for a moment, I was reminded of how much I miss my own - my dad and Richie in particular."

"Hey, it's alright, honey, I understand," said Vicky, "we all do - but like I told you before, you're part of *our* family now - you're one of us and we'll always be here or at the other end of a phone if you ever need to talk."

"Thanks Vicky, I appreciate it - I just hope I wasn't being too much of a misery during Liv and Brett's big announcement - I'd hate them to think I wasn't pleased for them cos I am, really."

"I know, honey. Of course you are and nobody thought anything of the kind," Victoria reassured her. "Hell, it was only me who noticed anything at all."

"You sure?"

"Positive."

"Good, that's a relief, I'd hate to be a downer," said Violet.

However, as she spoke, she could suddenly see Victoria deep in thought as if something had just occurred to her.

"Vicky?" She said, "Is everything alright?"

"Yeah, honey, everything's fine," replied Victoria, "But I've just had an idea which I reckon might do you the world of good."

"You have? What?"

"Well," Vicky began, "over the next few days this house is going to jammed to the rafters with people jabbering on about weddings and babies. Everyone's gonna be so busy fussing over Liv and Brett that nobody else is even gonna get a look in - I guarantee it - especially as we've only got a few days to get everything organised."

"Yeah, I know, I realise that," said Violet a little confused, "but I don't understand what you're getting at?"

"Just this, honey," continued Vicky, "You and Matt are gonna be so swallowed up in it all - there's not gonna be hardly any time for you two to spend alone."

"So?" Said Violet, even more perplexed.

"So, after the wedding, Virge and me will have to fly back to London to finish the movie which means our beach house in Malibu is gonna be sitting empty," Vicky replied. "You and Matt could go there for a few days, spend some time together alone - there's a pool, a beautiful view of the ocean and plenty of space for you to just relax and enjoy yourselves. Hell, the freezer's stocked and there's beer in the refrigerator, so all you'll need to buy is a couple of cartons of milk! What do you think?"

Violet was quiet for a moment as she mulled the proposition over in her head. The idea certainly had appeal; a few days alone with Matt in a luxurious beach house overlooking the ocean, it sounded absolutely perfect.

"You could leave *Wildwood* on the Sunday after the wedding and head straight there - you'd be on the beach in less than three hours," Vicky encouraged.

"Are you sure you wouldn't mind?" Liv said at last. "I mean it's your house after all."

"Honey," replied Vicky in typically practical style, "it's like I said, you're family now and that means you're more than welcome to whatever I've got. Besides, I got a soft spot for that fella of yours and it's about time someone made an honest man of him."

Violet chuckled. "Well, in that case then," she said, "I'd love to."

"Good," agreed Vicky, then that's settled."

***

Rocco Pistoli had been very careful, following at a discreet distance until the Mustang finally pulled up at the house on Canyon Hill Drive.

Rocco, himself, had parked his car off the road behind a small stand of trees; close enough to observe what was going on but far enough away so as not to be noticed.

As he watched, he soon realised that the house was packed with people. In addition to the three he had followed there, he had counted at least seven others walking around outside at various intervals, amongst them Joe Cassidy and Sean Noakes.

However, it was one person in particular that caught Rocco's eye. Standing less than fifty yards from where he sat in his car was the man who had killed his brother and whom he had vowed to kill in return; Matt Mason in all his glory.

Bingo! But he had not just struck gold, he had hit the whole goddamn mother load - Mason, Noakes, the Cassidys - both father and son - and Virgil Nash, too, all wrapped up neatly together in one place.

Yet as fortuitous as this was, Rocco knew there was far too many of them to take on alone. Indeed, they had already proved their resilience and resourcefulness at *Far Point* - to the cost of nearly all of Jez Vincenzi's most dependable soldiers.

Even though it was incredibly galling, Pistoli knew he must simply bide his time and hopefully catch Mason on his own when he would have a much better chance of success.

So he settled back in his seat and watched the house until long after sunset when it was completely dark and the only lights in the street were emanating from the one solitary house.

When he was certain that he could not be spotted, Rocco slipped out of the sedan and sprinted stealthily across the road, flattening himself against the hedge on the other side which surrounded Doc Ridgeway's home.

From this place of concealment, he could clearly hear people talking in the garden, their voices carrying loudly in the still of the night.

Brett Cassidy, the boy who had eluded him and Falco in The Caymans, had just announced his wedding and everyone was celebrating. As Rocco listened, he heard every detail of their plans for a ceremony at *Wildwood*, the ranch owned by Louretta Wild in Palm Springs.

Upon overhearing this vital snippet of intel, an idea started to formulate in Rocco's head; one which might not only lead to him killing Matt Mason but which also might prove to be his own salvation.

Indeed, he was just about to slink back to his car to set his plans in motion when he heard voices immediately beside him on the other side of the hedge.

The two women were standing maybe less than three feet away from him, completely oblivious to his presence. Rocco froze, so as not to be discovered, keeping his breathing low and steady as he silently eavesdropped on their conversation.

It soon became clear that one of the women was Victoria Wild and the other, apparently, Matt Mason's girlfriend.

At first they were expounding a load of emotional crap which Rocco thought extremely dull but then there was mention of a beach house in Malibu and their girlie chat suddenly got very interesting.

Rocco mentally logged all he had discovered then, when the women finally moved away, he furtively sneaked back to his car, knowing that if Mason should somehow elude him this time then he would be afforded a second bite of the cherry.

Perfect.

***

By 11pm Rocco was certain that everyone was staying for the night as the lights had been turned off in the garden and the party, it seemed, had moved inside. By now he was desperate to score and also needed to lay his hands on some more cash - which he felt confident he could liberate from another *7-Eleven* without too much trouble.

So, he took his leave in the darkness, not switching on his headlights until he reached the junction at the end of the road.

From there he headed to seedier parts of town to find what he was looking for.

An hour later he was considerably richer, having stolen over a thousand bucks from a drug store and assuring its owner a long stay in hospital.

Afterwards he headed for The Strip to score some coke - and even did a couple of lines in the men's room at *The Villa Continental* just for the hell of it.

Whilst he was in there, he went into a cubicle and lathered

some antiviral cream onto his testicles. The ointment, also stolen from the drug store, was supposed to ease the symptoms of genital herpes which Rocco was now convinced he had - and, much to his relief, it had alleviated the itchiness considerably.

With the coke in his system and the ointment doing its job, Rocco now felt much more relaxed. Enough, in fact, to give his plans greater consideration.

With his discovery earlier he knew he now had the valuable bargaining chip he needed to turn his life around.

What is more, it was finally time to play his hand.

Indeed, as he pulled the crumpled piece of paper from his wallet and lifted the receiver in one of the phone booths that skirted the lobby, it seemed entirely apt for Rocco to be placing a call to Jez Vincenzi from *The Villa Continental.*

Chapter Twenty-Three

Vermont, New England

The ornate stone-built mansion was situated next to a beautiful clear lake with a backdrop of rolling hills and lush, green woodland. The sky seemed vast in its cloudless blue splendour with only the calming chatter of bird song to disturb the peaceful tranquillity of it all.

Yet as Jez Vincenzi sat hunched in a lawn chair by the empty swimming pool, wrapped up in a thick overcoat, the sheer wonder of nature's bounty was completely lost on him.

He was clutching his gold-plated .38, the present given to him by Carmine on his eighteenth birthday, and taking pot shots at a mock Roman statue that sat on the far side of the pool; half its head now missing as well as an arm and part of a leg.

Indeed, the gun was constantly with him nowadays and had served to change the dynamic between him and Bass Stone considerably.

In the months since fleeing from Miami, Jez had gained over forty pounds in weight, his hair had grown long and lank and his face, now bloated beyond all recognition, was hidden behind a bushy fuzz of patchy bumfluff.

His mood had become morose and solemn as he constantly plotted ways in which he could find and kill the men who had blighted his existence.

He hated Vermont. Hated the air, the scenery, the loathsome silence of it all that constantly seemed to remind him of just how much his life had changed since the raid on *Far Point*.

Jez was born in Miami, a child of the sun; he had enjoyed riches, wealth and power - money, cars, women at his fingertips and a lifestyle most would envy.

Now he found himself marooned in the middle of nowhere, in a soulless mansion with only Stone for company and a future that was far from certain.

Everything had gone but he cared not.

The only thing of importance to Jez now, the thing that got him out of bed each morning and what he fixated on until the day was done, was vengeance.

Yet still it eluded him and he had no more idea today than he had three months earlier where the men were that he so despised.

Virgil Nash was the only one whose whereabouts were known but an attempt on his life was impossible as he was surrounded by either security or reporters at nearly all times.

Furthermore, it was Nash who had been instrumental in ensuring Jez and Bass were never out of the news and largely responsible for them having to stay holed up in Vermont - an enforced and prolonged vacation that was seriously starting to grate. But with their images constantly flashing up on TV or plastered over the newspapers, they had no choice but to stay in hiding for fear of being recognised.

Since killing Falco, Jez's relationship with Stone had evolved. No longer was the younger man frightened of the older one and no more did he rely on his advice. Indeed, since Jez set out the terms of their relationship, things between them had become more even handed. If anything, the balance of power had shifted slightly and it was Jez who was now in control.

Bass had become wholly reliant on Jez keeping his word, trusting that whenever they finally caught up with Cassidy and Noakes and put them in the ground, Vincenzi would pay him the two million dollars he had promised.

However, trust was a two-way street and Bass had been most clear on what would happen to Jez if he failed to honour the agreement.

Nevertheless, whilst they were holed up in Vermont, Carmine and Tito's fortune was of very little use to either of them.

What is more, Bass hated Vermont and their predicament as much as Jez did - although being cooped up with the sullen and sulky boy made it doubly insufferable as he was far from being Stone's ideal companion for a long stint in solitary - no matter how picturesque the location.

In fact, Bass was starting to wonder if it was all going to come to nought and was seriously considering putting a bullet in the back of Jez's skull and heading back to England.

However, the pull of the money was too strong and he knew it would be complete madness to give up on the chance of so much cash.

He also still had a score to settle.

Bass had been entrusted to deliver Cassidy and Noakes but on his first opportunity to do this, at *Far Point*, they had slipped through his fingers and even though he had not been in charge of the operation, he had been an integral part of it and the failure still galled.

Furthermore, he had lost an eye in pursuit of them and had been taken out of the fray long before he had a chance to prove himself, which seriously damaged his pride.

Stone was not accustomed to failure and certainly not used to defeat. So now it was not just a matter of money but a matter of honour and Bass was chaffing at the bit to finally show his worth -

especially as doing so would win him such an enormous prize.

Being removed from the many distractions of Miami; such as the palatial luxuries of the waterfront property and the constant stream of nubile hookers, had helped to re-focus his mind. His goals were clear once more, absent of any previous diversions.

All he needed now was news of where to find his prey.

Whilst in hiding, he had dreamt many times of ripping Joe Cassidy and Sean Noakes limb from limb; relishing the image of his big, powerful hands crushing their skulls until they burst. The vision of it amused him and helped while away the long hours of boredom in the hope that it might soon become a reality.

During their confinement, Bass' once tightly cropped curls had sprouted into a bushy Afro which was lightly sprinkled with the first specks of grey. Like Jez, he too had grown a beard, although his was thick and dark, which prevented him from being recognised whenever he went to the store to get supplies.

Again like Jez, Bass had also gained weight, but whereas Vincenzi's was fat his was all muscle.

To keep himself busy, Stone had spent his time chopping down trees from the nearby wood and hauling logs from there to the yard where he cut them into firewood. An enormous stack now stood at the back of the house; enough to last several long, New England winters.

But it was better that than mope around like Vincenzi, waiting for a time when they could finally be free of this never ending monotony.

As a result, Stone's bulk was now huge; his shoulders wide and his muscles hard - a man-mountain possessed of enormous power with the skill to know how to use it.

And he could not wait for the opportunity.

As the sun reached its zenith in the cloudless blue sky, Bass laid down his axe on the old wooden chopping block in the yard and headed for the kitchen for a cold drink, the sweat of his labours glistening on his bulging biceps and dripping from his brow.

He reached into the refrigerator a moment later and pulled out an ice cold *Bud* then flicked off the cap with his thick, gnarled thumbnail. As he gulped down the instantly refreshing beer, he glanced out of the window and saw Jez sitting out by the pool.

The boy had his overcoat on like it was eight below, yet it was summer, the sun was beating down and the day was warm and free from breeze. Stone, himself, wore only a white vest, smeared with the dirt of the wood pile, and a pair of jeans which hugged his chunky thighs. He shook his head at Jez's attire, "Bloody kid's gotta be out of his mind wearing that in this heat," he said to himself as he drained the last of the cold *Budweiser.*

He continued to watch with bemused amusement as Vincenzi fired off another couple of shots at the statue, both missing their mark by quite a margin and hitting the wall in the distance beyond with a loud crack.

Bass shook his head again and laughed derisively, "Christ almighty!" He chuckled.

However, as he turned to head back to the yard, the phone began to ring. This was an extremely rare occurrence as very few people had the number and Stone, concerned by the irregularity of it, automatically looked to where the cordless handset normally sat on its base unit on the counter top.

But the base unit was sitting empty. Bass turned back to the window, realising that Jez must have the handset out by the pool and immediately saw the boy pick up the ringing receiver.

As he looked on, Bass became increasingly intrigued. *Who the hell could be calling?*

Suddenly Vincenzi was on his feet and talking animatedly into the cordless handset. Then, through the window, Stone saw Jez grin as the call ended. Next thing he was marching purposely back towards the house.

Something had happened. Something big. Bass could tell.

A moment later Jez flung open the kitchen door and burst into the room to see Stone standing before him. The grin was still on his face.

"What is it?" Bass asked, "What's happened - who was that on the phone?"

"It was Rocco," replied Jez.

"Rocco? What the fuck does—" Bass began.

"He's found 'em," Interrupted Jez. "All of 'em."

Stone instinctively knew to whom Vincenzi was referring. It was the news they had both been waiting to hear for many months although the messenger was the last person either had expected.

"Where?" Bass asked, his manner becoming more intense, "Where are they?"

Jez smiled. "At the moment they're in Las Vegas and next week they'll be in Palm Springs."

"Palm Springs - you sure?"

"Uh-huh," replied Jez gleefully. "Pack your bags, Stone, we're going to a wedding!"

***

Four days later they were sitting in the diner of a truck stop outside of La Quinta; both bearded with caps pulled down over their faces and running the risk of being recognised. But the opportunity they had driven all the way across the country for was more than worth it.

It was a slow night and Jez and Bass were amongst only four other customers in the diner but no one was paying them any mind as they sat and waited for the green Crown Vic to pull into the parking lot.

Jez had been contemplating the meeting during their long journey; considering what to do with Rocco when he eventually met up with him and he had still not decided.

He pondered this again as he stirred his coffee, not noticing the lights of the green sedan as it turned off the highway and pulled up on the far edge of the parking lot.

"He's here," said Stone, draining the last dregs from his mug and sliding from the booth onto his feet. "Come on, let's go."

Jez glanced out of the window and saw the dusty Crown Vic sitting in the space next to the second-hand Chevy Suburban he and Stone had driven from Vermont to California - a vehicle far removed from the beautiful, bright yellow Lamborghini Tito had given him for his twenty-first birthday and yet another reminder of how far he had fallen.

But things were about to change.

Jez threw down a couple of bucks on the table then slid from the booth and followed Stone from the diner.

By the time they had crossed the parking lot, Rocco was out of the car and standing nervously beside the trunk. His genitals felt as if they were on fire, the itchiness driving him out of his mind and for a second he considered asking Jez to wait for a moment whilst he used the rest rooms to smear some more of the soothing antiviral ointment on his testicles but he dismissed it as a bad idea. *His balls would just have to wait.*

He shifted apprehensively as Jez and Stone approached. Stone looked enormous - far bigger and even more of a brute than he remembered - but recognisable nonetheless. Jez, on the other hand, looked completely different - fat and bloated with long greasy hair and a fluffy beard that made him look like a bum. Indeed, Rocco had to look twice to be sure it was him and the difference, even from the last time he saw him, was quite shocking.

However, Jez noticed a significant change in Rocco, too. His sharp features were now gaunt and sallow and his hair greasy and unkempt. Furthermore, his demeanour was twitchy and he had the glassy stare of a tripped out junkie and as Pistoli stepped forward to greet him, Jez felt disgusted; a buzz of annoyance triggering in his brain.

"Jez!" Said Rocco, a little louder than intended, "Good to see you."

"Hey, speak up, why don't you," snarled Stone."

"Sorry, man," replied Pistoli contritely, "Just pleased to see you both that's all."

"Yeah?" Said Jez, the buzz in his brain growing stronger, "Not sorry that I ain't Johnny Magisano maybe?"

"What? No - that's all a big mistake, Jez, honest. It was all Falco, not me," Pistoli lied.

"No? Well it sure didn't sound like that when I heard Falco talking on the phone," Jez sneered. "Sounded like you and Magisano was playing house - like you and him was all cosied up together making plans behind my back."

"That's not right, I'd never—" spluttered Rocco.

"Don't lie!" Jez interrupted. "It ain't gonna play well for you if you keep on spinning me stories."

"He caught you red-handed, son," smiled Stone, "your hand was right inside the cookie jar - so don't try to bluff your way out of it."

Rocco looked from Bass to Vincenzi and back again. At last he turned to Jez once more, his shoulders slumping in defeat. "Okay, you're right, maybe I did. But I was wrong Jez, I realise that now and I'm sorry - really I am and I'm offering you a gift to prove it - that's gotta be worth something right?"

Jez was quiet for a moment but inside his head the buzz was still a loud and constant monotone driving him insane.

"You wanted Cassidy and Noakes," Pistoli pressed on, hoping he was getting through, "well I've delivered them to you along with Nash too - surely that proves my loyalty."

367

"And what about Mason?" Asked Jez.

"Yeah, he's with 'em but I was kinda hoping I could save him for myself - he killed my brother and I've got a score to—"

"What? So you think I still owe you - is that it?" Jez said incredulously.

"No, no - I was just hoping—"

"Hoping what? That I'd just sweep everything under the rug, forget about your betrayal?" Jez could feel his anger rising, the weight of the .38 in his coat pocket temptingly heavy.

Stone could sense Jez's frustration; knew that at any moment he could blow but they could not afford a scene. If Vincenzi murdered Rocco now, in that parking lot, so close to *Wildwood,* it would be the end of everything. Their plan would be over and they would have to retreat back into hiding, their one opportunity gone.

Yet Stone also knew Jez had struggled with Pistoli's betrayal since leaving Vermont and suspected that when the time came, when they finally stood face to face, Vincenzi's temper would get the better of him and he would want to shoot Rocco dead.

Stone had no loyalties to Pistoli whatsoever, could not have cared less whether he lived or died - so long as it was not in that parking lot. Not when so much was at stake.

But Jez was dangerously unstable and Rocco was still talking.

"No, I was hoping I could somehow make it up to you," he implored, "I thought if I gave you Cassidy and Noakes it would prove my loyalty, prove how much I want things to go back to the way they were - that you might let me back in."

"You think I'm a fuckin' fool?" Vincenzi growled, his voice rising by several octaves. If someone came out of the diner now they could not help but hear their conversation and that could create even more problems.

"No - I don't, I swear!" Pleaded Rocco, his voice also getting louder.

"Then why treat me like one?" Spat Jez. "You meet me here, lie to my goddamn face, then think you can strike another deal?"

"Deal? I don't know what you—"

"A deal you fuckin' moron - a deal about Mason when you know he's mine!"

"But he killed my brother—"

"So fuckin' what?" Jez yelled. "Your brother was nothing - just a fuckin' foot soldier, a worthless nobody. But my brother was part of me - my twin - we were young princes born to be fuckin' gods and Mason and the others took that away from us - so they belong to me. Every single one of 'em belongs to me - *not you!*"

By now several people inside the diner had heard the ruckus and were peering out the windows into the darkness.

"Jez, please—" Pistoli begged.

"No!" Vincenzi roared, instinctively reaching for the .38 in his pocket. "You fuckin' betrayed me and now you're gonna pay!"

Matters had quickly spiralled out of control and Bass knew he had to act fast before Jez did something incredibly stupid.

He laid a hand firmly on Vincenzi's shoulder. "Stand down," he hissed. "People are looking. If you want Cassidy and Noakes then think about what you're doing. Think about the bigger picture."

Jez shrugged Stone's hand off angrily. "I want them all."

"Fine," said Bass, "Take 'em and I'll help you. But you need to quieten down otherwise somebody's gonna call the cops."

Rocco's heart was in his mouth. He had always hated Stone but at the moment he was extremely grateful for his presence.

Jez was seething, consumed by anger, but Stone was right, he had to keep an eye on the bigger picture and it was not worth losing sight of it for the sake of killing Rocco.

"Okay," he said at last, his voice once again quiet and his anger evaporating. "We'll do it your way."

"Good," said Stone. "Now leave the gun in your pocket and let everyone in the diner go back to their coffee. Nothing to see here."

Rocco breathed a huge sigh of relief. "Thank you, Jez. Thanks Stone, I mean it. Really."

"Hey, don't thank me yet," said Stone with a wicked smile, "If you can't tell us what we need to know then I'll kill you myself and then I'll kill every one of them rubberneckers in the diner just for fun - so get fuckin' talkin' and pray that I like what I hear."

Vincenzi grinned, extremely glad that Stone was on his side.

***

For the past two days, Rocco had been recceing the *Wildwood* ranch; trying to isolate any possible weaknesses in the perimeter fence unaware that years earlier, an intruder had brutally murdered someone on the property. Security had been significantly beefed up as a result, which was why Carmine and Tito always regarded *Wildwood* as something of a stronghold.

However, in the intervening years, due to a lack of further breaches, the security team had become lax and procedures subsequently overlooked. In fact Rocco found several places along the boundary where an incursion would be entirely possible - and perhaps even go unnoticed for days.

There was one point in particular, close to a small wooded area, where it would be easy to enter. Furthermore, because of the tree cover, it would be safe to hide out there for a day or so completely unseen. Then, at an appropriate time, using the cover of darkness, hike the few miles to the ranch house and hole up in one of the surrounding barns to await an opportune moment to strike.

Rocco laid out his findings to Vincenzi and Stone who listened intently, both impressed by what Pistoli had discovered.

"Well, what do you think?" He said when he had finished.

"I think it might just work," said Stone.

"Yeah, me too," agreed Jez. "We'll have to sleep rough though - we're gonna need sleeping bags, definitely some wire cutters."

"Already thought of that," grinned Rocco flipping open the trunk of the Crown Vic to reveal what was inside, next to his cherished rifle case. "I got wire cutters, some torches, supplies for a few days and three sleeping bags - everything we should need."

"Three sleeping bags?" Jez queried, his curious tone obviously exaggerated.

"Yeah," Rocco replied, his grin slipping, "One for each of us."

"Then you bought one too many," Jez said, clearly enjoying himself.

"Eh?" Said Rocco. "What do you mean?"

"I mean you ain't going nowhere," smiled Vincenzi triumphantly.

"No, Jez, please," implored Pistoli, "It's my plan - I've worked it all out for the three of us."

"Not anymore," said Jez. "You're done Rocco. You're outta here - and be grateful you're still alive."

"Please, no!" Pistoli sounded pathetic as he looked to Bass for support. "Stone, please, tell him - it's my idea, my plan. We can get 'em all together if we—"

"Hey," Stone broke in as he set about removing the bags from the trunk. "Don't look at me. I reckon you're getting away lightly so I'd cut my losses if I were you and be on my way."

"But—" Rocco tried again.

"Beat it!" Jez growled. "Before I change my mind and kill you!"

Pistoli knew there was no more arguing with him and his heart sank. Matt Mason would die but it would not be by his hand and he felt completely robbed. However, there was nothing more he could do.

As Stone lifted the last of the bags from the trunk, Jez regarded the rifle case sitting beside them, knowing how much Rocco cherished it, and a malicious thought occurred. He smiled evilly, "Bass, take the rifle, too. Its telescopic sight could be useful."

"No, Jez, please," Rocco wailed, desperate not to lose his beloved rifle. "It's the only thing of any value I've got left - I got nothing else."

"Quiet!" Snapped Stone as he grabbed up the case, "And get on your way."

"Oh, and Rocco," added Jez. "Don't ever let me see you again. Not if you know what's good for you. Understand?".

Pistoli nodded in defeat, his testicles burning like a fire and the need to score suddenly all consuming. "Yeah, I understand," he said, sounding completely broken as he slunk to the front of the car and slipped into the driver's seat.

A moment later the engine roared into life and the Crown Vic screeched away in a cloud of dust.

As Stone loaded up the Suburban, Jez watched his former friend drive off into the night.

He would never see him again.

Chapter Twenty-Four

For the sake of the press, Brett's surname had been announced as 'Davenport', which was, in fact, his mother's maiden name. It was deemed safer by all concerned to keep any reference to the name 'Cassidy' out of the media as the wedding would be covered by news agencies all over the globe.

Beau Brewster, the media tycoon and Louretta's former husband, had conjured up an elaborate back story for Brett which painted him as the son of a wealthy foreign businessman from an unspecified country.

Beau had also seen to it that coverage was focussed on Liv - the daughter of Hollywood movie stars Victoria Wild and Virgil Nash - and not on the man she was marrying. Although, in truth, this was not difficult as it was mostly Liv, not Brett, whom the media were interested in.

Nevertheless, it would have been much easier to have a small, private wedding with just family and close friends but it was Liv's rite to have the wedding she wanted and Victoria's rite, as mother of the bride, to help with all the preparations for her daughter's big day. This meant decorating the venue, organising the catering, sending out invitations and, of course, helping Liv find the perfect dress.

However, this was no simple task as it was almost impossible for Victoria to go anywhere without being recognised - her every movement photo-documented in a whole host of celebrity gossip magazines.

So, from the moment she and Liv stepped into the bridal boutique on *Rodeo Drive,* the media buzz began and by the day of the wedding it had been whipped up into a frenzy.

News teams and press wagons were jamming the roadway immediately in front of the *Wildwood* gates and media helicopters were circling overhead - although only on the periphery as the airspace immediately above the ranch was restricted - therefore ensuring Brett and Liv a completely private ceremony.

In addition to the massed media, fans from all over the world were also lining the fence.

To cope with this, ranch security had been stepped up significantly for the big day and the team who had been manning the guard posts with little to do for so many years suddenly found themselves stretched to the limit keeping out eager fans and over zealous reporters.

Louretta had also asked them to undertake hourly border patrols, even though she knew it would stretch the team even further, but she considered it a vital precaution to ensure no uninvited guests gained entrance to the property.

Indeed, these patrols should have been initiated several days before the ceremony, as she had instructed, but her head of security had disregarded these orders thinking them wholly unnecessary.

In fact, rather than ask for additional support he had, instead, chosen to restrict these patrols to the morning of the event in order to save on manpower.

Only after all the crowds arrived did he realise just how spectacularly he had underestimated the situation but by then it was far too late.

However, fearing for his job, he had chosen not to inform Louretta of this.

Nonetheless, his failure to initiate the patrols when requested did not surmount the extent of his failure as he had also decided that the abandoned Chevy Suburban which was found close to the boundary line did not present a threat either.

The vehicle, registered in Vermont, was noted by his team, who after checking with the police, found it to be reported stolen.

Yet this discovery did not concern the new security head unduly as he assumed it to belong to a devoted fan who was just desperate to be at the wedding - even though the car itself had arrived significantly earlier than all the other vehicles that were now strewn up and down the roadside.

In his view, the car was innocuous enough, other than the fact that it was stolen, and he was far too busy to concern himself with such trivial matters.

Things were equally hectic up at the ranch house, some distance inside the gates and beyond the view of the crowd outside.

Indeed, it was a bustling hive of activity. A huge marquee had been erected on the back pasture and decorators, catering crews and wedding organisers formed a constant stream in and out. The house itself was also alive with decorators; the wedding planners working flat out to make the day as special as possible.

To their credit, they had worked wonders in such a short space of time and with so little notice - which was due in no small part to the star power of Victoria and Virgil.

Nonetheless, by 1pm, a full hour before the guests were due to arrive, everything was miraculously ready. The various teams of organisers and decorators packed up their vans and went on their way leaving just a few key people to orchestrate things in the marquee. Likewise, once everything was in place, the caterers confined themselves to the kitchen to prepare for what was bound to be a very busy afternoon and evening.

With the preparations completed, the house suddenly became

unexpectedly quiet. The women were upstairs fussing around Liv, attending to her, helping with her dress and make-up whilst enjoying a glass or two of champagne to celebrate the occasion.

Similarly, the men, all smartly dressed in their tuxedos, were downstairs in the kitchen, chatting, joking and purposely keeping things light to help ease any nerves Brett might be feeling.

However, he was coping well enough even though he and the others were all nursing sizeable hangovers from the impromptu bachelor party thrown for Brett by the ranch hands in the bunkhouse the night before.

Only Ethan Ridgeway, who knew better, and Josh, who had been under strict orders from Victoria not to get too drunk, remained reasonably clear-headed - even though the others were doing their best to pretend otherwise.

Indeed, Matt was feeling particularly fragile. Whilst he enjoyed the occasional *Bud* after a race to unwind, he had never been a big drinker due to his strict fitness regime. So the effects of his over-indulgence last night, coupled with the nerves he was feeling in his role as best man, were proving to be a heady mixture and his stomach was complaining loudly as a result. Nonetheless, he was determined not to let this spoil the occasion and was putting on a brave face for the sake of his step-brother, but he did feel decidedly rough.

Coincidentally, he and Josh happened to be standing together in the kitchen when Matt realised he had left the folded piece of paper upon which his best man's speech was written on the table in the bunkhouse. Through the fog of his hangover he seemed to remember scrawling some notes on it last evening whilst the others were telling beer soaked stories of Brett's childhood visits to the ranch - stories which Matt thought might enliven his speech. Unfortunately, he too, had become caught up in the telling of these tales and had subsequently forgotten all about his speech which, he assumed, still remained on the small table in the communal area that the ranch hands used to make coffee.

"Shit!" He exclaimed.

"What's up?" Asked Josh.

"Ah, nothing. Just left my goddamn speech in the bunk house that's all."

"It's okay, I can go fetch it," said Josh, taking pity on Matt, aware of how rough he was feeling.

"Hey, no - that's okay. I can—" Matt began.

"It's no trouble," interrupted Josh. "You stay here and take care of Brett and I'll go get it."

"You sure?" Asked Matt, his head pounding as he gratefully surrendered."

"Uh-huh. Where is it?"

"On the table - at least I think so. If not I'm in a whole heap of trouble."

"No problem," said Josh. "I'll be back in a sec." And with that he was gone.

However, a few moments after his departure, Matt suddenly felt incredibly queasy and had an overwhelming desire to puke. With no time to waste, he rushed from the room, almost knocking Joe and Sean over as he bolted out of the back door heading for the *Guest Washroom.*

"Hey! You okay?" Joe called after him but Matt had no time to hang around.

"Yeah, I'm fine!" He yelled behind him, "Just gotta go throw up that's all!"

Some years earlier, Louretta had commissioned the washroom to be built at the rear of the house, close to the corral. She regularly hosted rodeos and other equine events which involved hands from various ranches and groups of other invited guests. However, she did not particularly want them using her facilities in the house, so it made sense to have a washroom built for specific use of guests during larger gatherings.

Nevertheless, the *'Guest Washroom'* was far more grand than its name suggested. Panelled in dark mahogany with a black and white marble floor, it featured both ladies and gents rest rooms. Each rest room had eight spacious cubicles, all with spotlessly clean porcelain fittings and gold-plated fixtures.

Running parallel to the cubicles was a polished onyx unit containing eight pristine basins with an ornate gold mirror fixed above and spanning its entire length. Beside every basin was a vase of flowers, a selection of luxury soaps and a neat stack of fluffy towels. To top it all off, a spectacular row of small crystal chandeliers hung overhead.

On several occasions, the washroom had been used by sheiks, movie stars and various foreign dignitaries all visiting the ranch in search of the thoroughbred stock Louretta was renowned for.

Today, however, it was to be used by the wedding guests but presently, as Matt flung open the door and threw himself into the nearest cubicle, it was going to be used for his more urgent needs.

Normally at large gatherings, a rest room attendant would be present but he would not be on duty until the guests arrived, which Matt was glad of. It was embarrassing enough having to puke but even worse if someone was there to witness it.

As it was, he had the place to himself. *'Thank heaven for small mercies,'* he said to himself as he slammed the cubicle door shut and bent over the toilet bowl.

***

The ranch seemed unnaturally quiet to Josh as he made his way from the ranch house to the bunk house.

Usually it was a busy working environment and he would have expected to meet any number of the hands, whom he had known since childhood, en-route. But today they were all too busy getting gussied up into their Sunday best - all invited to his sister and Brett's wedding. Indeed, all three of them; Josh, Liv and Brett, had spent many happy times on the ranch when they were growing up so they had a great deal of affection for the ranch hands, and the feeling was mutual. Nevertheless, tuxedos and bow ties were far from the hands' natural attire as they were much more at home in T-shirts and Levis, so the day was going to be one of considerable discomfort but to see Liv and Brett married they would happily endure it.

Yet without them wandering around the place it did seem eerily strange and Josh half expected to see tumble weed rolling across the deserted corral as he passed it.

It was not until he was almost to the huge barn which stood close to the bunk house that he heard the sound of voices.

At first he thought it was maybe a couple of the hands still finishing up their chores, but as he listened he did not recognise either of the men's voices, which seemed to be deep in the midst of some heated argument.

He glanced upwards to the hayloft where the voices were emanating from and was immediately struck by the sight of what appeared to be a rifle barrel protruding from loft opening. Instantly concerned, he was about to turn and run to warn the others when the argument abruptly stopped. Josh then heard someone climbing down the ladder that led to the ground level.

Quickly he realised that at any moment that individual, whoever it may be, would be confronted by the sight of him standing there. Furthermore, instinct told him it would not be wise to stick around and wait for that to happen.

With no time to escape back to the house, Josh threw himself into the bushes beside the barn and cowered low to conceal himself.

A couple of seconds later, an enormous mixed race man with bushy Afro hair loped menacingly out of the barn and stood for a second right in front of where Josh was hiding. The man appeared as if he was trying to decide where best to go. But then, after a couple of beats, he hurried off, keeping his head low as he ran back past the corral in the direction from which Josh had just come.

Josh was suddenly torn; *did he run back to warn the others or did he tackle whoever was still left in the hayloft?* In the second he took to consider this, he glanced up again at the rifle barrel and realised with horror that it was aimed directly at Liv's bedroom window.

In that instant his decision was made and without considering the consequences of what he was about to do, he leapt clear of his hiding place and ran headlong and unthinking into the barn.

***

Jez Vincenzi and Bass Stone had both massively underestimated the public's interest in the wedding. Neither had the slightest idea that coverage would be so intense or that crowds of fans would arrive at the ranch en-masse. In fact they had not even considered it.

As a result it had proved to be a huge surprise and now their actions seemed incredibly rash.

They had cut through the perimeter fence three days earlier, when the road that ran adjacent to the ranch had been deserted and no evidence of any fan activity was present.

Once inside, they had embedded themselves in the small wooded area that Rocco had pointed out; sleeping under the stars in the sleeping bags he had so generously provided and eating the food he had also supplied. Although without cooking equipment they had been forced to eat the food cold, straight from the can - and only then because Bass managed to slice the cans open with his razor sharp hunting knife, otherwise they would have starved.

For three days they had lived like this; eating, sleeping and shitting in the woods with only each other for company which soon became very tiresome indeed.

Nevertheless, they had somehow made it through without killing each other and at midnight on the third day, using the cover of darkness, they emerged from the copse and made a run for the small cluster of buildings a couple of miles distant.

By the time they reached the barn, just a stone's throw from the ranch house, it was almost two in the morning and the whole place was quiet.

Quickly and as stealthily as possible, they snuck into the barn and clambered up to the hayloft where they concealed themselves behind a stack of bales to await their moment.

It was only at first light, when Bass very carefully emerged from his hiding place to risk a look out of the loft window that their huge error became known to him.

From his vantage point, Stone could survey the surrounding area clearly. It was even possible for him to see the main gates and the perimeter fence in the distance - and to his extreme shock, the crowds of people lined up, three rows deep along it. Behind them were perhaps a dozen media trucks and buzzing over the heads of the hordes of expectant onlookers were at least three news helicopters. Even though it was not yet six in the morning, the activity beyond the fence was staggering and for a moment Bass was completely dumbstruck by the unexpected sight of it.

"Jesus!" He exclaimed finally.

"What?" Said Jez, still groggy from just three hours of fitful sleep.

"You'd better come over here and take a look," replied Stone. "Be careful though."

"Hey, I ain't a complete moron," snapped Jez irritably as he crawled from the soft hay that had made for a comfortable bed.

"No?" Sneered Bass, "You might wanna revise that when you see what I'm looking at."

"What the fuck do you—" Jez began as he peered over Stone's shoulder. "Jesus Christ!" He yelled more loudly than intended when he saw what Bass was looking at. "Holy shit. What the hell is going on?"

"My guess would be that we aren't the only ones who planned on turning up to this shindig unannounced."

"Yeah, I think you're right - hey, are those media trucks?"

"Yep. And those things in the sky are news helicopters. Smile Jez, I reckon you're just about to be the main story on *Good Morning America*."

Jez immediately darted away from the window, back to the safety of the hay bales. Bass followed but with less haste. He suspected that the helicopters were not allowed to fly directly over the ranch, possibly because of some sort of enforced 'no fly zone'. So, for the moment at least, they were safe enough. But time was running short.

"So what do you wanna do?" He said.

"What do you mean?" Replied Jez.

"Well, I reckon if we make a break for it now we could probably make it back to the woods without getting noticed. Then we'll just have to wait it out there until things die down."

Vincenzi looked appalled. "You mean you wanna go? You wanna just leave without killing those bastards?"

"What other choice do we have?" Asked Bass reasonably. "If we stay and finish what we came here for it'd be suicide. There's no way we can make it outta here ali—"

"So you're chicken, is that it?" Snapped Jez contemptuously.

"What? No—" Began Bass before getting interrupted by a snarling Vincenzi.

"You lead me here, tell me you're my man, tell me that I can rely on you no matter what - then, at the first sign of trouble, you just wanna up and leave."

"Hey," Said Bass, not appreciating the other man's tone. "First, I ain't scared of nothing. Second, you talk to me like that again and I'll rip your fuckin' head off with my bare hands. And third, this wasn't my idea. This was all you and Rocco. I'm just the hired hand and I intend to be alive to spend my reward - and staying here ain't the way to do it."

Jez was about to respond when they heard movement outside.

"Ssh!" Bass said, the look on his face completely murderous. He could cheerfully kill Jez now and walk away happy but that was no longer an option.

Silently he slithered away from his hiding place and peeked out over the ledge of the window.

Immediately he saw a couple of ranch hands in the corral. Then two more wandering down from the bunk house. The ranch was waking up and the hands were readying to start their chores before the wedding. Bass and Jez had missed their chance to escape unseen and now they were trapped.

"What is it?" Hissed Jez.

"Ranch workers. People moving about," whispered Bass. "We're stuck here now like it or not."

Vincenzi looked smug. "Good. Then we might as well finish what we came here for."

Reluctantly Stone slipped back beside Jez behind the bales where the two of them sat and stewed in silence.

For over six hours they waited, dozing sporadically but never allowing themselves to completely drop their guard just in case they should be disturbed by some poor unsuspecting soul. Bass had his silenced *Glock 17* in his lap the whole time, ready for such an occurrence, but fortunately it was not needed.

Whilst they waited the ranch came alive and bustled with frantic activity as the working day began and preparations for the wedding started in earnest.

The ranch hands exercised the horses and went about their daily chores as the wedding organisers arrived and set about the business of making everything perfect for Liv and Brett and all the while Bass and Jez sat and waited.

It was not until after midday that things quietened down again.

The ranch hands all disappeared to go freshen up for the main event and the wedding organisers, with their work completed, all packed up and went on their way to leave Bass and Jez alone.

With the coast clear, Vincenzi snapped open the long, slim case that he had taken from the trunk of Rocco's car and lifted out his prized rifle.

"So you're still going ahead with it then?" Asked Stone, tucking the *Glock* back into his belt at the small of his back, its fat silencer resting just above the crack of his buttocks.

"Yep. Either with or without you." Replied Jez as he removed the telescopic sight from its sponge housing and began screwing it in place.

"You're fuckin' crazy, you know that?" Bass said, watching incredulously as Vincenzi crawled over to the window and rested the polished wooden stock of the *Valmet* on the ledge so that the long black barrel stuck out.

"Yeah, well no one's asking you, Stone," Jez replied, putting his eye to the scope and sweeping the area through the powerful lens.

Bass' first instinct was to pull out the *Glock* again and shoot Jez in the head. But his preferred weapon was the knife; he liked the sound of it as the blade sliced through muscle and sinew, enjoyed the delicious thrill of it as with every tiny push life was slowly extinguished.

As he considered this, he wrapped his thick fingers around the hilt of the hunting knife hanging in the sheath on his belt. It would be so easy to kill Jez now, with his back to him. *So wonderfully easy.*

He felt sick to his stomach that everything had all boiled down to this. Sick that all those months spent with this whining, spoilt kid for the chance of one massive payout had all been for nothing.

With all the security and media coverage he knew, too, that there was little chance of Jez's plan succeeding. However, if by some miracle it did, then he would undoubtedly spend the rest of his life in prison and Bass would never be able to collect his money.

And he was damned if he was going to let that happen.

Yet all was not lost. His only hope now was to somehow get off the ranch before Vincenzi started killing people. But first he needed the number of Jez's Swiss bank account where all his funds were safely stashed away from the American authorities and he was not going to leave without it.

Silently he withdrew the hunting knife from its sheath, the wide, serrated blade gleaming in the midday sun as Bass stepped closer to Jez, knowing the information he sought was written on a piece of paper in Vincenzi's wallet.

Jez was still scanning the area through the telescopic sight, his eye travelling from the corral to the lower windows of the house and then on up to the upper level. So far he could see no signs of life but then he suddenly spotted exactly what he was looking for. A cluster of clucking women in one of the bedrooms. He knew them instantly. Louretta and Victoria Wild, Rose Cassidy, Sarah Noakes and the blonde haired beauty who had escaped his clutches at *Far Point*, the one whose firm breasts he could still feel on the palms of his hands when he closed his eyes; the same girl who was now wearing her wedding dress; Liv Noakes.

Jez smiled as he lined her beautiful face up in the centre of the cross-hairs. Just the slightest squeeze of the trigger and her pretty little head would explode into a thousand bloody pieces. Then, as everyone rushed about in blind panic, running out into the yard desperately searching for help, Jez would pick them off, too, one by one until he had killed them all.

However, with his finger resting gently on the trigger, the hairs on the back of his neck suddenly began to prickle and he had a premonition of imminent danger. Immediately he removed his finger and reached down for the .38 in his belt.

Quickly, he rolled over, raising the gold-plated gun in the same swift movement, to see Bass standing over him, the knife held firmly in his grip, poised to strike.

Bass froze as he suddenly found himself staring down the barrel of the gun. He was certain he was about to die as Jez pointed the loaded pistol directly at his chest, but as he awaited death, no shot came. Bass then realised that if Jez fired the alarm would be raised, thus immediately ending any hope Vincenzi had of a surprise attack.

Unlike the *Glock* in Bass' belt, Jez's automatic did not have a silencer and the sound of the gunshot would be heard far and wide, warning everyone within earshot of their presence.

He could not fire for risk of failure.

It was a stand-off as the pair of them faced each other; Jez with the *.38* outstretched and Bass clutching the murderous looking knife.

Stone smiled. "You can't do it can you boy? You shoot me you lose any chance you might have of killing Cassidy and Noakes."

"I can do what I fuckin' like. No one can stop me!" Jez growled, making no attempt to keep his voice low. "Not even you, Stone."

"Maybe. Maybe not." Replied Bass calmly. "But you know I'm right don't you?" As he spoke he could see the frustration in Vincenzi's eyes; the boy obviously knew as well as he did.

"So go then. Walk free," said Jez, lowering the *.38* in defeat. "Leave me to it - I don't need you anyway."

"Sure, no problem," said Stone. "First though, I'll need that piece of paper in your wallet with the number of your Swiss bank account written on it - if you don't mind."

Jez's eyes widened, clearly surprised that Stone knew he possessed such a piece of paper. "You can kiss my ass!" He spat vehemently. "I ain't giving you a goddamn thing."

"Fine, okay." Said Bass. "Maybe I'll just go and knock on that ranch house door then - tell everyone what's about to happen. Hell, I might even get a reward."

"You wouldn't fuckin' dare!" Yelled Jez.

"Just you bloody watch me!" Stone yelled back, neither of them being mindful of their present whereabouts.

"You do and I'll fuckin' kill you!" hollered Jez.

"You could," Bass flew back. "But you won't. Not if you want Cassidy and Noakes dead, not if you want your precious vengeance." With those words he knew suddenly that he had struck a chord and decided to press his advantage. "Look, lets face facts. We both know that if you continue with this action you ain't gonna be getting out of here. There'll be no escape - not with all the news crews and security guards - they'll be on you before you've even made it halfway back to the trees. So you're either in or you're out - and if you're in then you won't be needing your Swiss bank account anytime soon cos they're either gonna put you in the ground or lock you away for life. So what's it gonna matter?"

Jez stared hard at Bass, his teeth gritted together his eyes burning with anger but there was no getting around it. Stone was right.

This was what the last ten years had come down to. This was the moment he had been waiting for since he had cradled his twin brother's lifeless body in his arms in that hotel suite at *The Villa Continental.*

This was when those responsible would pay for what they had done.

But there would be no escape for him. He knew it. For what he was about to do he would pay a heavy price - either death or life imprisonment.

The only question was, would it be worth it?

As for the answer, he did not even need to consider it. "Fine," he said, reaching into his jacket pocket and pulling out his wallet. "Take it and fuck off!" He slung the wallet at Stone who snatched it greedily out of the air.

Quickly Bass rummaged through the contents and was relieved to see the number written on the back of a business card with the address and embossed logo of the Swiss Bank printed on it.

"Nice doing business with you," Stone said with a wry grin.

Jez made no response but his face was a picture of disgust.

"Happy hunting," Bass added as he stuffed the wallet into the back pocket of his jeans, "But now I'll be on my way and leave you to finish your little crusade alone."

He then nodded a goodbye before turning and heading for the ladder that led to the ground level.

"That's it - you fuckin' go!" Jez yelled after him but Stone could not have cared less. He was finally done with Jez Vincenzi.

All he required now was his money.

Chapter Twenty-Five

Violet looked absolutely beautiful in her bridesmaid's dress. The jade satin gown fitted her curvaceous form superbly and perfectly complimented the emerald green of her eyes. Both were contrasted by her dark, lustrous locks which had been pinned up purposely for the occasion and held in place by a pretty comb decorated with delicate jade rosebuds.

She felt like a princess and so far removed from her South London roots that she could hardly believe it possible.

In just a short space of time, her life had changed dramatically. Indeed, after the utter despair she felt at losing her father and brother she feared she would never know happiness again.

Yet here she was; happy, content and in love with a remarkable, warm, kind, strong man who, quite wonderfully, was in love with her, too.

She felt extremely fortunate that things had turned out the way they had and knew in her heart that her father would be so pleased for her.

Presently, however, she was a little concerned for Matt who, it transpired, could not handle his liquor. Violet, who had been practically raised in a pub, had seen way too many drunkards in her life and was pleased that Matt was not like them. However, she had also seen many severe hangovers and was conscious of how much he must be suffering.

With the women all fussing around Liv, Violet saw a moment to quickly slip away to go check on him. Also, if she was honest with herself, she was keen to show off to him in her dress, knowing he would find her irresistible in it.

She scampered down the stairs excitedly and wafted gracefully into the kitchen only to see Matt's back as he hastily ran out of the back door.

She looked quizzically at Joe and Sean who seemed to be rather amused by his swift departure.

"Wow!" Said Joe as Violet approached them, "You look sensational."

"Yeah," agreed Sean. "Stunning."

"Thanks," said Violet. "You wait 'til you see Liv, she looks amazing."

"I'll bet," said Sean proudly. "Hey, you just missed Matt."

"Yeah, I know. I just saw him leaving. Where's he gone?"

"He's not feeling too good, darlin'" answered Joe. "Bit too much booze last night I think. He's gone to be sick."

"What, outside?" Violet queried.

"No, darlin'" chuckled Joe. "He'll have gone to the washroom just round the corner - it's the nearest loo."

"More of a palace if you ask me," added Sean.

"Had I better go?" Asked Violet concerned.

"Can't hurt, Vee," said Joe. "He's sure to brighten up when he gets a load of you in that dress."

"Without a doubt," agreed Sean.

"Okay then," nodded Violet. "Where's this washroom - round the corner you say?"

"Yeah, just out back. You can't miss it," said Sean helpfully. "It's got chandeliers and everything!"

Violet was not sure if he was joking but she smiled anyway.

390

"Right, I'll be back in a minute - better not be gone too long otherwise Liv might start to wonder where I am."

"Don't worry, luv. We'll cover for you," grinned Joe as Violet headed out the back door in search of Matt.

***

Bass Stone kept low as he sprinted past the corral, heading for the gate that led to open ground and the trees which lay some two miles beyond.

He knew he was taking a tremendous risk, as the route led passed part of the main house and it was entirely possible that at any moment he could be seen, but he had no other choice.

It was either run or get caught and he would rather not spend the rest of his life rotting in some American prison.

However, he had just reached the far side of the yard when he heard the sound of a door opening. Instantly wary, he quickly dived for cover behind a nearby water trough.

Laying in the dirt on his stomach, he peeked out from his hiding place in time to see a stunning young woman crossing the yard, heading towards an outbuilding just a short distance away.

As Bass watched the woman's movement in the form-fitting jade dress, he ogled her generous breasts as they jiggled enticingly under the satin material. Yet as he watched, there was something strangely familiar about her which evoked a memory from the past.

No, it couldn't be.

He squinted his eyes in order to see her face more clearly. *Were his eyes deceiving him?*

At the risk of being spotted, he leaned out further to get a better look and upon closer inspection was certain it was no mistake.

It was her, the woman he had assumed he had killed months ago back in London at the *Golden Gloves* pub.

The same woman he had desired for much of his youth but who had considered herself too good for the likes of him.

391

All thoughts of escape deserted him as he considered the immensity of what he was witnessing.

Yet even though it seemed utterly impossible for her to be in this alien place, *alive,* he was in absolutely no doubt.

The woman he was staring at was Violet Noakes.

***

With Stone gone, Jez was left alone to get the job done. Shaking off the deep annoyance he felt by the other man's departure, he bent to the task in hand.

Everything Stone had said was correct. This was now a suicide mission, or as good as. Either way it would not end well. But Jez had waited too long, had invested so much time and emotion into his unrelenting quest for vengeance that he simply could not give up now.

He and come too far. Indeed, it was all he had left.

Jez wondered often about Vito, his brother, about what sort of man he might have become. Would he have been better than him? Would he have made the decisions Jez had? Would he have been driven to the very brink of insanity too?

Because Jez knew that was where he was. He was teetering on the edge, his mind a mishmash of thoughts; totally consumed by hatred. Everything he had was gone and there was nothing more to look forward to.

All he had was death. The death of Joe Cassidy, of Sean Noakes, of Matt Mason and of Virgil Nash - along with any of their loved ones who happened to get in his way. In fact, the more the better because that is what they had done to him; taken his life away along with his brother's in that hotel room in Las Vegas ten years earlier.

The strange thing was, Jez had been so wrapped up in his unrelenting search for vengeance that he could barely even remember Vito, except that he had been sweet and kind and the complete opposite of him.

392

Jez could not remember his father either, not really. His only memory of Benny was of a cold, aloof man who angered quickly and whose rage was formidable. *Had he been insane too?*

By doggedly pursuing this course of action, Jez had to consider for the first time whether he was following rather too closely in his father's footsteps.

Benny had been obsessed by Cassidy and Noakes and so, too, was he.

After careful consideration, he decided that he and his father were the same. Perhaps that was what his grandfathers were trying to protect him against. They hardly ever mentioned Benny when Jez was growing up and whenever they did it was rarely complimentary, thinking him to be a loose cannon, both unpredictable and erratic. A dangerous combination.

Would Benny have single handedly destroyed their empire in one fateful night as Jez had at *Far Point* in his pursuit of vengeance?

It was impossible to know but if his father was anything like him then Jez thought it entirely likely.

Their shared obsession had cost them both much over the years; power, position, wealth - as well as their sanity.

But it ended here. No matter the consequences, no matter the cost. For Vito and for Benny, this was where he would finish it.

***

Jez nuzzled his eye into the viewfinder of the telescopic sight once more and targeted the bedroom window where a moment earlier he had spied Liv Noakes in her wedding dress.

After a second or two he found her again; she was standing on some sort of raised platform, a stool perhaps, with the other women fussing around her skirts. *An easy target.*

Again he captured her pretty face in the cross hairs. *If only she knew.*

But then, as Jez made just the slightest adjustment to the focus,

Liv looked up and stared directly at him.

Jez smiled. "Hello baby," he said, "give me a smile."

She was like a rabbit caught in the headlights and in just the briefest moment he was going to shoot her dead.

***

Liv was feeling particularly girly, which was most unlike her as she had always been something of a tomboy and never happier than when dressed in greasy overalls with her head stuck under the hood of a car.

Indeed, she often thought of her cherished Chevy Monte Carlo which she had last seen on the roadside shortly before all the madness exploded at *Far Point*. But her father and Joe had assured her that Manfred Rani had taken care of it and that it was being well looked after in her absence, but she still missed it.

Yet today, that part of her life seemed to belong to someone else. In fact *she* seemed to be someone else because she was having a lovely time being pampered and taken care of by those she loved. What is more, she was practically revelling in the feeling of looking pretty and extremely feminine as she excitedly looked forward to marrying Brett in just over an hour.

She looked every inch the movie star's daughter exuding old Hollywood glamour in a vintage silk dress with sculpted satin bodice and long white veil.

So wonderfully slim and elegant did she look that no one would ever have guessed she was in her second trimester. Indeed, the pregnancy gave her an added glow which made her appear even more radiant.

What is more, it did not concern her in the slightest to abstain from the champagne the other women were drinking and was happily standing on a stool as they all fussed around her dress, making certain that it would flow perfectly when she eventually walked down the aisle.

Standing on the raised podium, she had an excellent view through the wide french windows that led onto a balcony prettily fringed with purple bougainvillea. From this vantage point she could survey not only the grounds immediately around the ranch house but also the fence line in the far distance beyond. Squinting, she could just make out the hordes of fans who had turned out to catch a glimpse not of her and Brett but of her mother and Virgil. Indeed, her wedding was just a sideshow in comparison to their immense fame but it did not concern her. She was, however, very grateful that the ranch was so private which, in turn, prevented any outsiders from intruding on her and Brett's big day.

Or so she thought.

Yet as she turned her attention back to the area around the corral and surrounding outbuildings, her eyes fell on an unusual object protruding from the hayloft of the barn to the right of her view.

Squinting again, she could also see what appeared to be a hunched figure behind it. Only after a couple of seconds did she realise with horror that it was a man with a rifle pointed directly at her.

Furthermore, standing there on her podium, up above the other women, it suddenly dawned that she was a sitting duck.

***

Violet opened the door to the mens washroom and stepped inside. As Sean had suggested, it was very grand in design and slightly out of character for a working horse ranch but it was certainly in style with the ranch house which was equally opulent inside. Louretta may have been a no-nonsense business woman but she was also an ex-movie star and, as such, still enjoyed the luxurious trappings that came with that status. Indeed, she was a successful woman with style and taste - traits which Violet could not help but admire.

The washroom was deserted, as the wedding guests had not yet arrived, and the only sound she could hear was that of Matt retching in one of the cubicles.

"Matt! It's me," She said loudly. "You okay, baby?"

There was a groan from the nearest stall. "Yeah, I'm fine, Vee," he replied, "just feeling a bit rough, that's all."

"You sure? You want a glass of water or something?"

"Yeah, please, honey, that'd be great, thanks."

Violet looked about her and saw a paper cup dispenser on the wall next to the hand-drier. "Hold on," she said. "I'll be right there."

She stepped quickly over to the dispenser and pulled out a cup, then crossed to the nearest hand basin and ran it under the cold tap.

As the water filled the cup, Violet heard a door swing open behind her and assumed it to be Matt exiting the cubicle. But as she looked up into the mirror, expecting to see her lover standing behind her, she instead saw the enormous form of Bass Stone looming over her, grinning evilly with his gold tooth glinting in the light of the chandelier hanging overhead.

A jolt of terror shot through her body as she stared into the malevolent face of the man who had killed both her father and brother. Yet Stone looked different now; even more sinister, even more menacing. His hair was a wild, unkempt afro and he had the appearance of a tramp; his clothes dirty and dishevelled but it was in his face that she saw the most significant difference. The jagged scar above his right eye now seemed startlingly pink against his caramel skin, giving him an air of extreme menace, but it was the pure white eye below that she found most disturbing. The blank eye, like a shiny glass cue ball, gave him the look of the devil incarnate and a shiver of dread ran down Violet's spine.

"Hello, darlin'" he said, the South London accent clearly discernible in his deep voice, "It's been a while."

Violet, still reeling with shock, spun to face him and was just about to speak when she heard the sound of the toilet flushing and the latch on the nearest stall unlock.

"Is somebody else in here?" Matt asked groggily as he inched open the door.

"Matt, watch out—!" Violet yelled but her warning came too late.

"No one you need worry about mate," answered Stone who, quick as a flash, whipped round and smashed the hard oak door into Matt's unsuspecting face, catching him high on the temple with a hefty thud.

"Matt!" Screeched Violet as the toilet door juddered on its hinges and slowly swung open to reveal her boyfriend standing unsteadily in the cubicle, stunned by the impact and staring blankly at her.

"Matt—!" She squealed again as he dropped to his knees and slumped awkwardly against the cubicle's partition wall, clearly out cold.

Briefly Violet's heart sank as she filled with despair. But then, as she stared at Matt's unconscious form, she heard Stone's gravelly laugh and suddenly she was fuelled by an entirely different emotion.

A violent rage began bubbling within her, a wild anger that she had only ever felt once before; on the night that her father and brother had been murdered. Without conscious thought, she bunched her hand into a fist and flew like a wildcat at Bass Stone; punching him with devastating force on the dead centre of his nose, exactly as Matt's training had taught her.

"Fuckin' bitch!" He yelled as pain shot through him.

But Violet was not done.

Before Bass had a chance to react, she span round and whipped her trailing foot up behind her like a slingshot; the heel of her stiletto sandal smashing against the curve of Stone's jaw and the sole slamming into his lower lip, opening up a wide bloody gash.

Clearly shocked, he staggered unsteadily as Violet maintained the momentum. She leapt forward into the air, flinging her leading leg high with another lightening fast kick; the sole of her sandal striking his bearded chin with brutal effect and snapping his head backwards.

She landed light as a cat as Stone shook his head in disbelief, blood pissing down his chin, unable to quite believe the way in which this girl was attacking him nor how skilful she obviously was.

He spat out a gob of magenta saliva and wiped his bloody lip with the back of his hand, smearing a streak of red across his cheek as he nodded his respect.

He was impressed. Clearly she had learnt much since last they met.

However, Bass was an old dog and had hardened himself to pain, shaking it off as if it was nothing more than a gnat bite. Yet also like a dog, he was very dangerous when injured, so when Violet attacked again he was ready for her.

"You bastard!" She cried as she leapt into the air, hurtling towards his face with her leading leg again outstretched in a carbon copy of her previous move, hoping it would have a similar effect. *Christ, how she wanted to take him down.*

But this time she had over-extended, leaving herself open, which Matt had repeatedly warned against in the training room.

Seizing this briefest of opportunities, Bass swiftly dodged aside and snatched Violet bodily out of the air mid-flight and smashed her down hard onto the onyx unit so that her back crashed painfully against one of the porcelain hand basins, just narrowly missing its gold taps as the back of her head whacked down on the solid unit.

Violet cried out in agony, her body reeling from the impact, the breath sucked from her lungs.

Just to be sure, Bass punched her in the stomach then banged her head down again hard. Briefly she saw a blinding white light as her skull connected violently with the solid surface of the onyx counter top.

The fight left her immediately as she lay there winded, stunned and defenceless, desperately trying to stay conscious as darkness closed in all around her.

The room was spinning, Stone's face just a dizzying blur as she saw him standing over her.

She was exposed and vulnerable, her limbs completely unresponsive, splayed out on the vanity unit like some sacrificial lamb with its scent in the wolf's nostrils.

Dazed and unable to move, she was helpless as Stone's huge hands slithered all over her body; groping her with deliberate, unrestrained roughness.

Then he suddenly thrust her legs wide apart and slid his enormous bulk between them; Violet completely powerless to prevent him.

Stone bent low over her, so that his face was mere inches from hers; his vile smelling breath hot on her cheek. He was gurning with desire, his lips thick with lustful saliva as he whispered to her in a gruff, animalistic tone. "Think you're too good for the likes of me do ya princess?" He said, as his grubby fingernails dragged up the hem of her dress. "Well now you're gonna get what you deserve."

A long, slimy spindle of drool dribbled down from his hungry wet lips as his other hand grabbed at her breasts, pawing them greedily in a bid to satiate his basest desires.

Violet, still concussed, bravely tried to fight back, willing her limbs into action as she thumped her fists feebly against his shoulders, kicking as best she could in a pitiful attempt to remove him from between her thighs. But it was futile.

"Get off me!" She breathed, her voice little more than a hoarse gasp, the air not yet having returned to her lungs. "Get off!"

"Not a chance darlin'" Stone growled as he ripped at the neckline of her dress, tearing it open so that both her plump breasts spilled out. "You're mine now and there ain't nothin' you can do about it," he added, licking his bloodied lips at the sight of the feast before him.

Years earlier, he had fantasised about the exquisite taste of Violet's flesh and had longed to sample it. Moreover, he had been tantalisingly close to doing so just a few months before at *The Golden Gloves* but his pleasure had been cruelly interrupted by Alfie Noakes.

On that fateful night, he thought he had killed Violet along with her father, but it was not the case and here she was now, his to do with as he desired, just as he imagined. A second opportunity - and this time there would be no such interruptions.

Violet did her best to fight but her body was still too weak to properly respond.

Stone was going to rape her and there was not a damn thing she could do about it.

As he groped her maniacally, Violet's head lolled to the side and through her starred and blurry vision she saw Matt still crumpled in the stall.

"Matt!" She cried weakly. "Matt, please help me!" But she knew he was out cold and could not save her.

Devoid of all hope, she turned back to Stone once more and, using every ounce of force she could muster, beat her fists repeatedly against the sides of his head.

Yet even though her strength was slowly returning, he seemed completely impervious.

He pulled his face away from her breasts and smiled at her. "That's it," he spat lustfully, "You fight back darlin'. Fight me hard - but it ain't gonna do you no good, cos that sweet little arse of yours belongs to me!"

Chapter Twenty-Six

Instantly aware of the danger they were all in, Liv flung herself off the stool and onto the floor behind her dressing table. "Get down! Quick -behind here!" She yelled to the other women, "There's a goddamn sniper out there and he's aiming his gun right at us!"

For a moment, Louretta, Victoria, Sarah and Rose all looked slightly nonplussed. "A sniper? I don't understand. What do you mean?" Louretta queried.

"A sniper Grandma - a guy with a gun trying to shoot us!"

"What? Are you sure?" Louretta still did not seem convinced and neither did the others.

"Yeah, Grandma, I'm sure," snapped Liv, grabbing at her grandmother's hand and pulling her down onto the carpet. "Now get down, all of you - he's trying to kill us!"

The other three women immediately did as instructed and threw themselves down onto the ground, all of them wearing their finest and Liv, herself, in her wedding dress.

"Where is this guy, honey?" Asked Victoria.

"In the main barn - hayloft window," her daughter replied. "From there he's got a clear view of the whole of this room."

At those words, the rest of the women all looked unconsciously towards the door which sat some distance away at the opposite end of the room.

They were trapped.

"But who—?" Rose began, "—it couldn't be Vincenzi, surely. I mean he'd be mad to—" her voice trailed off as she considered the implications.

"I think he might just be desperate enough to try anything," said Sarah, "The guy's out of his mind. Got to be him. I mean who else?"

"Never mind that," interrupted Louretta, "Where's Violet?"

"Downstairs with Matt I think," answered Liv, "I saw her nip out a few minutes ago - I guess she's worried about him."

"Hell," said Louretta, "I'm worried about him too now - along with the rest of them."

"Someone's got to warn them," stated Rose with alarm, "If one of them goes outside with that mad man watching, then who knows what might happen!"

"I'll go," declared Liv. "I'm damned if I'm gonna let that sonofabitch ruin my wedding day!"

"No sweetie," said Sarah, fully aware that Jez Vincenzi - or, indeed, whoever the shooter might be, would have an uninterrupted view of the killing ground between the dresser and the bedroom door. "You stay here - take care of yourself and that baby of yours. I'll go."

"But Sarah, it's too dangerous," said Rose, her voice full of concern, knowing all too well the trauma her sister-in-law had been through in the past. "You stay here with Liv. Let me go."

"Don't worry," replied Sarah reassuringly, "I'll be fine. Besides, you're the groom's stepmother - Brett would never forgive me if anything happened to you."

"And Joe would never forgive me if anything happened to you either," countered Rose.

Sarah smiled reassuringly, "I'll be fine," she said again, "I've got every intention of being at that wedding today and Jez bloody

Vincenzi is not going to stop me."

Rose took her hand and squeezed it. "Please, be careful," she said. "I want you there too."

"So do I," said Liv.

Sarah nodded as she slipped off her shoes, "I will."

As she crouched on her haunches, preparing for the dash across the room, Louretta said, "Keep your head down honey."

"And don't stop until you get out that door," added Vicky. "We're all rooting for you."

"Don't worry," Sarah grinned, "I'm famously hard to kill - just like my brother." Then she launched herself out from behind the dresser like a sprinter off the blocks.

***

Jez had Liv squared up nicely in his sights, her head now in full focus and the cross hairs targeted at the dead centre of her forehead.

However, at the very moment he was about to pull the trigger, she suddenly dived out of view.

"Fuck!" He growled, as his target disappeared, knowing her to be on the ground, out of his line of sight. Obviously she had seen him and sensed the impending danger.

Jez quickly scanned for the other women but before he had a chance to shoot they, too, dropped to the ground behind a dressing table where he could not see them.

"Fuck!" He spat again.

Nevertheless, as he surveyed the room for other signs of life, he realised that the women were trapped. There was no way they could make it out of the room without him seeing them. If any of them should emerge from their hiding place to make a break for the door he would easily cut them down before they could make it halfway across the room.

He just had to be patient and hope there was not some other way they could raise the alarm. Yet he could see no telephone and in a house that large, with the bedroom door closed, someone would have to shout extremely loudly to be heard - especially over the excitement of the wedding preparations.

At least that's what Jez was banking on, so he stayed put and waited, certain that an opportunity would soon present itself.

Sure enough, just a few moments later, a dark-haired woman - a beauty even though she was old enough to be Jez's mother - leapt up and made a bolt for the door.

Jez grinned with evil delight. He knew this woman to be Sarah Noakes - wife of Sean Noakes and sister of Joe Cassidy. It was almost too poetic. How utterly perfect.

Vincenzi zeroed in on her as she made her pathetic dash for freedom, then held his breath to ensure his shot was true.

"Bye bye Sarah," he said.

***

As stealthily as he could, Josh slowly climbed the ladder that led to the hayloft.

His adrenaline was pumping as he reached the top, uncertain who he would find up there but instinct told him to beware.

A long, wooden-handled pitch fork was stuck in a bale beside him, left there no doubt by one of the ranch hands the day before.

Silently Josh pulled it free and clutched it in his grip, the four sharp prongs aimed out in front, guarding against the possibility of attack.

He chose each step carefully so as not to alert whoever he might find, hoping it would be a friendly face, praying he was just being overly cautious.

But the voice in his head knew it to be a forlorn hope.

Then, as he rounded the stack of bales, his worst fears were realised. He suddenly saw the man lying prostrate by the loft opening, his eye pushed against a telescopic sight and the rifle on the ledge aimed at Liv's bedroom window. A gold-plated pistol was sitting in the soft hay by the man's side and at the sight of it Josh stumbled slightly, disturbing the straw beneath his feet which made just the slightest rustling sound.

He held his breath and prayed that the intruder had not heard him.

But by then it was too late.

***

After watching Violet leave through the kitchen door, as she headed out to the washroom in search of Matt, Joe and Sean continued to chat and enjoy the general banter of the men in the room for a while.

However, Joe suspected that he should perhaps go and check on Matt himself. If his son was suffering then he should help particularly as Violet was all dressed up in her bridesmaid's dress and he did not want her getting all ruffled - mainly because Rose would never forgive him.

"Reckon I might go give Violet a hand," he said.

"Want some help?" Asked Sean.

"Sure, can't hurt. We can't do much here but wait any how."

With that, the two old friends exited the back door and wandered over to the *Guest Washroom* to see if they could make themselves useful.

***

Jez was just about to pull the trigger when he heard the sound behind him. The noise distracted him from his target at the worst possible moment, allowing Sarah Noakes to scamper away to safety, out of his sight.

Incensed by the untimely interruption, Jez, vitriolic, turned assuming it to be Bass Stone slinking back, having thought better of leaving his paymaster alone.

However, as Jez spun to reprimand him, he saw that it was not Stone at all but a kid just a year or so younger than him.

405

He knew it instantly to be Josh Noakes - not a primary target but definitely a secondary one and as consolation for missing the opportunity to kill Sarah, he would certainly be suitable.

Quickly, Jez swung the rifle around but Josh was faster. Using the pitch fork to excellent effect with a well-aimed jab, he somehow managed to scoop the rifle out of Vincenzi's grip.

It was nothing more than a pure fluke but it worked superbly and the rifle flew out of Jez's hands and landed well out of harm's way in the far corner of the hayloft.

Unable to believe his good fortune, Josh thrust the pitch fork again, hoping to pin Jez down and hold him captive whilst he called for back-up.

But it was Vincenzi now who was too quick and as Josh stabbed down, Jez grabbed the pitch fork by the handle and snatched it out of his hands.

However, Jez's grip on the tool was only tenuous and from his awkward position, could not keep hold of it. As a result, the pitch fork slipped from his fingers and cartwheeled over his head, helicoptering out of the hayloft window to spear in the ground below.

Josh was unsure of what to do as he and Vincenzi stared at each other for a second in silence, both now unarmed. But then, at the exact same moment, they each remembered the gold-plated *.38* lying in the straw beside Jez.

As Vincenzi's hand flew to it, Josh leapt onto him, desperately grabbing at Jez's wrists to prevent him from using the gun, knowing that his life and the lives of those he loved depended on it.

The two young men scrambled desperately in the hay, wrestling for control of the weapon. Jez may have been paunchy and out of shape but he was still strong and even though Josh was naturally fit, his opponent, fuelled by anger, was putting up one hell of a fight.

Evenly matched, the two of them struggled madly to gain advantage, each as determined as the other.

Whilst his hands were occupied, trying frantically to prise the gun from Jez's fingers, Josh was using every other method he could think of to disarm him. He kneed him in the groin but Jez then countered with an elbow to the chin.

Josh butted him on the bridge of the nose but his angle was poor and the blow ineffectual as Vincenzi retaliated by biting down hard on Josh's earlobe.

The pain was excruciating as Jez's teeth sunk into his opponent's soft flesh. Josh jerked backwards involuntarily; violent spasms of unbearable agony shooting through the whole side of his head as the lower portion of his lobe was savagely ripped away from his ear.

With his adversary temporarily incapacitated, Jez seized his opportunity. Using all of his strength he forced Josh off of him with his forearms, then slammed his feet into his chest and propelled him backwards into the hay.

As Josh reeled in agony; blood from the jagged wound pissing over his dress shirt and new tuxedo, Jez scrambled to his feet and spat out the meaty piece of ear lobe triumphantly.

Josh glared at him, his eyes burning with anger, his heart beating like a war drum in his heaving chest.

Jez was puffing breathlessly, too; his lips blowing and his fleshy cheeks ruddy with exertion from the fight. But he had emerged victorious and as he stood on the ledge, his back to the hayloft window, looming over Josh's helpless form, he raised the gold-plated .38 and smiled maliciously.

***

Sarah bolted across the room, expecting each step to perhaps be her last. Yet miraculously she made it to the bedroom door, amid whoops and cheers of encouragement from the other women, as she threw herself onto the safety of the landing unable to believe her luck.

However, there was no time to waste, she had to warn the men.

She hoisted up her long bridesmaid's dress and hurried along the landing, kicking off her high sandals as she went and leaping down the steps of the sweeping staircase three at a time.

Without a second to spare, she burst into the kitchen a few moments later, her heart racing but her nerves steady.

She could not see either Joe, Sean or Matt - or even Violet - and a tremor of dread fluttered in her belly but she could not give in to it as there was too much at stake.

"There's someone out there!" She cried, as Brett, Virgil and Ethan turned to face her. "Someone with a rifle - a sniper in the barn - aiming at Liv's bedroom!"

For a moment, the men looked stunned as they took in this alarming information, but then, in unison, they rallied.

"Wait here!" Ordered Brett, "Ethan, please look after her - we'll go check."

"Of course, yes," replied Ethan. "But please be careful."

Brett nodded his assurance.

"Where's everyone else?" Sarah then asked, her voice trembling with concern.

"They went out there, honey," replied Virgil gravely, pointing through the window to the corral. "They're all outside."

***

Violet was terrified as she stared up at Bass Stone's enormous bulk towering over her.

She was pinned down and helpless, her most intimate parts exposed to him but as her strength returned so did her anger.

Suddenly she was like a wildcat once more, kicking and clawing, fighting to be free.

But Stone was a powerhouse of muscle and bone; broad shoulders, thick arms and a body that was hard and immovable as he stood over her, easily fending off her harmless assault.

"I'm gonna kill you!" Violet wailed with rage, her voice now stronger, too.

"You are?" Stone smirked as he bent and licked his wet tongue all the way up the side of her face, savouring the delicious taste of her. "Well you said that once before, remember? And see where that got you."

"Yeah?" Said a man's voice from behind, "Well that time she didn't have us to help her."

Bass Stone shot upright in surprise and span round to see the two men who had just entered the washroom.

"Well, well, well," he grinned at them, quickly regaining his composure, "If it ain't Butch and Sundance themselves - hi, fellas, I was hoping we might meet up one day."

"Who the hell are you?" Growled the taller of the two men.

"Me? I'm Bass Stone - maybe the princess here has told you about me - I knew her old man."

He then glanced at Violet, making no attempt to stop her as she rolled off the unit and onto the floor, desperate to escape him.

"Looks like our love session might have to be put on hold for a minute or two, darlin'," he said, "but don't fret, I shouldn't keep you waiting long."

He then turned again to the two men as he unclipped the leather sheath on his belt. From it, he swiftly withdrew his keenly sharpened hunting knife, its lethal serrated blade polished to a mirror-like sheen.

Holding the knife comfortably in his expert grip, Stone casually switched position, adopting a more natural fighting stance.

"Come on then boys," he invited, "show me what you got."

Then, as Stone eagerly eyed his prey, Joe Cassidy and Sean Noakes readied themselves for attack.

***

It was the first time Joe and Sean had ever set eyes on Bass Stone but Violet's description of the man did not quite do him

409

justice. Indeed, nothing could have prepared them for the beast that was now standing before them.

Stone was huge and clearly very strong with arms like tree trunks, hands like dinner plates and the supreme confidence of a silver back gorilla.

He was also in his prime; just thirty-two years old yet a veteran brawler and a ruthless killer. He had almost twenty-five years on Joe and Sean who, in comparison, were practically in their dotage.

Both of them were now in their mid fifties and even though extremely fit for their age, their greying hair and lined faces told their own tale.

Once they were kings; the toughest around - Joe in particular had been feared far and wide, although Sean came a close second. Together they had been unbeatable. It had made them infamous and earned Joe the title *Godfather of Gangland*, bestowed on him by the London media.

However, their natural toughness had also served Sean well in surviving the many trials life had thrown at him.

But that was all in the past. Today, up against an adversary such as Bass Stone, they were nothing more than a pair of old men - formidable and redoubtable without question - but still old men.

Stone was in an entirely different class and also armed with a very sharp knife. Joe also thought it safe to assume that he would undoubtedly have a gun secreted about his person somewhere too.

"You okay, Vee?" Asked Sean, glancing quickly to Violet who had now managed to cover her nakedness.

Cowering beside the vanity unit, with her back to them, she nodded her response; hurt, concussed and dreadfully embarrassed that Joe and Sean had found her so defenceless and exposed. But above all she was angry that she had allowed Stone to get the better of her once more. Angry for her father, her brother and herself. She had failed and because of it Sean and Joe were now in terrible danger, too.

Joe saw Matt crumpled in the toilet stall. "Matt? You alright, boy?" He asked, praying that his son was still alive.

"Don't worry, he ain't dead," said Stone with a bloody grin. "Not yet anyway." He made a show of glancing at his watch, clearly enjoying himself. "But I reckon he will be in a couple of minutes - but hey, you will be, too, so it ain't gonna matter none."

Joe said nothing as he ripped off his bow tie and popped the top button of his dress shirt.

"That's it. Make yourself comfy," said Stone. Go ahead, take off your jacket too - I'm happy to wait. After all, I want you at your best."

Joe remained silent as he stripped off his jacket, throwing it aside before rolling up his shirt cuffs, his eyes never leaving Stone's.

Sean followed suit, taking his lead from Joe - just like when they were kids. *Joe the enforcer, Sean the voice of reason.* Only this time there would be no reasoning.

Sean was watching Stone carefully too, still awed by the sheer size of him; his eyes conveying fear.

Bass saw it instantly. "You're right to be scared," he said to Sean, posturing confidently, "I'm gonna crush you when I've finished with your boyfriend here."

Sean made no reply, his face saying it all, as the three of them continued to face off.

A moment passed. "We got this, right?" Sean whispered nervously to Joe out the corner of his mouth.

"We'll know in a couple of minutes, I reckon," Joe replied.

"Great. Thanks for the pep talk," said Sean sarcastically, "I feel much better now."

Joe gave a little smile and allowed himself a sideways glance at his friend. "Hey, no problem, glad I could be of help."

However, in that briefest of glances passed an innate understanding between the two of them.

411

They had always had it. It was what had made them so effectual. In just one look Joe had conveyed his thoughts to Sean and he had picked them up clearer than any radar.

As the pair of them turned back to face Stone, Joe suddenly shouted, "Go!" and, as if hearing a starting pistol, Sean reacted instantly.

For a moment, Stone was caught wrong footed, falling into the same trap that so many had before. He had been focussing all his attention on Joe, discounting Sean as a serious threat.

But, like the others, Bass had failed to realise that Joe and Sean were a team and, although eminently capable individually, they were far more effective when working together.

Stone had been played and by underestimating Sean he had made a serious error.

Sean, although sensibly wary, had purposely shown 'fear' to give the impression that he was of little consequence, thus convincing Stone to be more wary of Joe.

The ruse had worked exactly as intended. However, as Sean threw himself at Bass Stone, he knew that whatever happened next was way beyond anyone's control.

***

Keeping their heads down, Brett and Virgil bolted from the house and sprinted to the cover of the *Guest Washroom*, completely unaware of the battle unfolding within as they threw themselves flat against its outer wall, relieved to still be alive.

They had expected the sniper to try and pick them off during their mad dash from the back door, but it had not happened. Indeed, there had been no gunshots at all.

After a brief pause, Brett risked a peek around the corner of the wall, his gaze travelling immediately to the hayloft window of the large barn that stood a short distance beyond the corral.

"Well?" Asked Virgil. "What can you see?"

"There's definitely someone up there," whispered Brett, pulling his head back in, "they're standing with their back to the window. Can't see a gun though."

"Who is it, any idea?"

"No. I can't see their face but I'm pretty sure it's no one we know."

"So definitely an intruder then?"

"Yeah, I'm sure of it. And if Liv said they've got a rifle then I sure ain't gonna argue."

"So what do you wanna do?" Virgil asked.

Brett thought for a moment. "We've gotta get over there, check it out, I reckon."

"I was afraid you were going to say that," said Virgil.

"You got a better idea?" Asked Brett hopefully.

"Nope," Virgil shrugged, "Just not too keen on our chances, that's all."

"No, me neither," Brett agreed. "But I guess it's gotta be done."

"Yep."

"You ready then?"

"As I'll ever be."

"Okay then. After three," Brett said, gearing up for the hundred yard sprint across open ground. "One… two… three!"

Upon 'three,' the two men shot away from the washroom wall and ran hell for leather towards the barn.

Chapter Twenty-Seven

For a few seconds, Matt had no idea where he was or how he got there, still foggy from the blow as he slowly roused from unconsciousness. His head was spinning, there was a severe throbbing at the centre of his forehead and his limbs were heavy and lethargic.

He looked about him, surprised to find himself crumpled on the floor beside a lavatory in a toilet cubicle.

Then he remembered what had happened. The last thing he had seen before everything went black was the image of a very large man with a pure white eye and skin the colour of caramel - followed by a brief vision of Violet standing behind him.

Immediately concerned, he looked up, his sight still blurry, to see a foggy image of that same man facing off against his father and Sean. Furthermore, as he blinked his eyes, desperately trying to clear his vision, he saw Violet cowering on the floor beneath the row of hand basins. She looked hurt and scared and Matt felt a sudden surge of anger burn through him.

Yet as he made a move to rush to her aid, his legs refused to respond properly and he fell back onto the toilet, weak as a kitten and still struggling to throw off the effects of the heavy blow that had knocked him out.

Sitting there, trying in vain to get up, he could do nothing but watch as his father and Sean charged into battle. Worse still, as his vision finally cleared, he saw a flash of deadly steel as the huge brute they were facing lashed out with his knife.

***

Sean was like lightening as he sprung forward, grabbing the hand in which Stone was holding the knife and twisting it counter-clockwise with all of his might. In the same swift movement, he thrust his knee up into Bass' groin, slamming it into his balls.

Bass roared with pain, unable to hold onto the knife as Sean twisted it from his grip. It clattered to the ground and was kicked away as the two men struggled.

However, Stone was quick to recover and powered a blistering body blow into Sean's ribs before Joe leapt in to join the fray.

Both Joe and Sean knew that if they were to stand any chance against this monster then they had to end it quickly. If not, Stone's younger, more superior stamina and his significant age difference would undoubtedly come into play.

With this strategy in mind, Joe landed three jack-hammer punches on Bass's jaw in quick succession then head-butted him hard on the bridge of the nose for good measure; the force of it utterly devastating.

There was an audible crack as Bass' nose split open, blood erupting from it as he staggered backwards. Yet he ignored the pain and using his huge strength, flung Sean off him as if he was nothing more than a rag doll.

Momentarily airborne, Sean smashed violently against the row of cubicles before dropping to the ground with a hard slap as Stone charged to meet Joe.

He swung his mighty fist with bone shattering force but Joe expertly dodged aside and hammered Bass in the ribs with two more brutal jabs, swiftly followed by a third to the centre of his stomach.

Stone rocked backwards again but there was to be no respite

as Sean leapt up and smashed his fist into Bass' ribs from behind, feeling a rewarding crunch as one of them snapped. Stone reeled with pain once more but before he had a chance to react, Sean kicked at the joint behind his right knee to send him crashing to the ground.

With Stone on his knees, Joe went to work on him with a blistering right hook to the jaw, followed by a left - then repeating the combination twice more before finishing with a well-placed uppercut, landing it squarely under Bass' chin, which would render almost any other man unconscious, but miraculously Stone's eyes stayed open.

By now Sean was standing beside Joe, the pair of them looking on as Bass spat out a gob of red saliva, his face bruised and bloody, his chest heaving and blood pouring from his shattered nose. Yet even on his knees and apparently beaten he still looked strangely formidable; the top of his head reaching the level of Sean's chest, such was his bulk.

"Had enough?" Asked Joe, panting heavily from adrenaline and exertion. "Are we finished now?"

It was at that moment when Joe knew his past was truly behind him. In days gone by he would have made certain that Stone would never trouble him again. But standing over Bass now, he lacked the killer instinct he once had; the instinct that had kept him on top of his game for so many years and had earned him respect and renown in equal measure.

But now the fight had left him as it had with Sean, too. They were different men now. Better men. Content and happy, their previous lives forgotten and their past long buried.

Making peace with this realisation, he asked Bass again, "So, we done here?"

Stone took his time, letting his breathing settle. Then, with his head bent and staring at the floor, he finally spoke. "I'll tell you this," he said, his voice calm and even, "you two are good. Very good - and believe me, I've seen a few and fought the best. I can even see why people still talk about you in such reverential terms. Hey, I might even concede that in your heyday you could've maybe taken me down."

Then suddenly Bass looked up. "But have I had enough?" He sneered. "Have we finished?" He smiled. "Boys, we've only just begun."

Joe immediately saw the danger and launched another powerful punch. However, with unbelievable speed, Stone caught him by the wrist, stopping the blow dead, killing its momentum and sending a violet spasm back up Joe's arm that ricocheted painfully throughout his whole upper body.

At the same time, Stone's other hand shot up and seized Sean vice-like by the throat.

As he squeezed, he sprung to his feet, suddenly towering over the two men caught in his snare. Then, before either could react, he smashed Sean's head hard against the side of Joe's.

Joe saw a blinding white light as he fell aside, crashing down onto the tiles like a punch-drunk boxer hitting the canvas.

Meanwhile, Stone picked Sean up by the throat, physically lifting him clear of the ground with one powerful arm. Already dazed from the clash of heads, Sean could do nothing to respond as Bass then clamped his other hand on his knees and hoisted him high above his head, holding him easily like a champion weight-lifter.

Sean's eyes were bulging, his face slowly turning purple as Stone's thumb crushed his windpipe. But then, with an enormous animalistic roar, Bass threw him bodily across the room.

Sean found himself hurtling through the air once more. This time, however, he smacked violently into the back wall, his head colliding hard against the dark wood panelling with devastating force, as his neck snapped backwards with impact.

He dropped to the ground and hit the tiles heavily for a second time but by then, his world had gone black and whatever pain he might have felt was immaterial.

With Joe sprawled on the ground, concussed from the brutal clash of heads, Stone reached down and picked him up by the scruff of the neck. "So you're the famous Joe Cassidy," he said, staring at him curiously as if he were some kind of specimen in a Petri dish. "London legend and famous tough guy. Well, maybe you were once - but you ain't no more."

Joe forced a smile, his head pounding, feeling as if it was about to explode. "Can't argue with you there," he said, "but I can still pack one hell of a punch."

As the last word left his lips, Joe powered a crippling blow into Stone's gut using every ounce of force he could muster.

Stone threw him back to the ground as he curled over in pain. "I'll kill you for that you bastard!" He growled, "You and your whole fucking family."

"You'll have to get passed me first," said Matt, finally managing to find the strength to stagger out of the cubicle, still dazed and fuzzy, but on his feet nonetheless.

Trying to shake off the effects of Joe's crippling punch, Stone regarded Matt for a moment, his face a picture of contempt as he assessed the man who was now standing before him.

He looked weak and unsteady and there was a huge purple bruise on his forehead where the cubicle door had smashed into it. He was swaying like a sapling in the wind, barely able to stay upright.

Bass grinned derisively. "You?" He said. "What the hell can you do against me?"

"This," snarled Matt, suddenly producing the hunting knife from behind his back and plunging it forcefully into the centre of Stone's chest.

Bass looked down, amazed to see the hilt of his own knife sticking out; its blade buried deeply within.

A moment earlier, he had inadvertently kicked it during his struggle with Sean and it had skittered across the floor, coming to rest at Matt's feet.

Shock briefly registered on Stone's face as he slowly lifted his head again to stare glassily at Matt who, himself, was struggling to stay upright.

But then, astonishingly, the gritty determination returned to Stone's eyes as he reached up and grabbed the hilt of the knife.

Matt could do nothing but watch in horror as Bass proceeded to pull the murderous blade from his chest; blood pouring down the front of his shirt and spurting forth from the hideous wound amid the grotesque sound of flesh sucking at polished steel.

At last Stone tugged it free and he stood staring at Matt, the knife held in his bloody grip, his hand stained completely red. "You haven't earned the rite to kill me," he gurgled, glaring at Matt with murderous intent.

"No. But I have," said a voice from behind.

Stone felt a sudden tug at the small of his back as his *Glock 17* was pulled sharply from his belt.

He turned at the sound of the female voice, knowing already to whom it belonged.

Violet was standing there, Stone's silenced *9mm* held steadily in her outstretched hand and aimed squarely at the centre of his forehead.

"I said I'd kill you, remember?" She said. "Well I always keep my word. This is for my dad and my brother you murdering son of a bitch!"

Then Violet pulled the trigger.

***

Sean roused just in time to see Stone's body drop; the deadly thud of the silenced *Glock* completely inaudible beyond the confines of the washroom.

Quickly, Matt pulled off his jacket and wrapped it around Violet, protecting her modesty as she lowered the pistol. "You okay, Vee?" He asked, his voice full of concern.

Violet was staring down at Bass Stone's corpse; a perfect round hole in the centre of his forehead and a steadily growing lake of deep red blood leaking from the exit wound at the back, spreading thickly across the black and white tiles. "Yeah," she replied, her voice steady and calm. "I am."

Joe climbed to his feet, his head still aching as he walked over to help Sean up. "What about you - you okay?" He asked.

"I reckon," answered Sean, taking his friend's hand and allowing himself to be pulled to his feet, "you?"

"Uh-huh. Just feeling old, that's all," Joe said with a smile.

"Hey, better that than dead," replied Sean, raising an eyebrow, knowing how close they had come.

"You can say that again," agreed Joe.

"Sorry about the mess," said Violet apologetically, still staring at Stone's lifeless body. "I didn't mean to—"

"Don't you worry about that darlin'," interrupted Joe. "You ain't got nothin' to be sorry ab—"

Suddenly, his words were cut short by the sound of a blood-curdling scream coming from outside and even though they were all still bruised and shaky from battle, all four of them immediately rushed from the washroom to find out what the hell was going on.

***

Jez wiped his wet mouth; his fluffy, unkempt beard stained red and matted with the blood from Josh's ear lobe.

"You're Reilly's kid aren't you?" He said.

"What?" Replied Josh, his anger still raw and the pain from his detached lobe stinging unbearably.

Jez then realised his mistake and smiled. "That's right, he's Sean *Noakes* to you, isn't he?"

"Yeah, he's my dad," Josh spat. "So what - what's it matter to you?"

"Oh, it means everything to me," said Jez. "Everything in the world."

Suddenly it all fell into place for Josh and he realised this intruder was not some random madman but someone with a very serious grudge. The same man who had orchestrated the raid on *Far Point* and who was responsible for the deaths of Ray and Ruby.

"Jesus!" Josh exclaimed as the realisation dawned. "You're Benny Mottola's son aren't you?"

Jez smiled again as he waved his gun menacingly. "Ah, I see you've heard of me," he said. "Yes, my name is Giuseppe Vincenzi and your father and his friends killed my brother, Vito."

"No - that's not right!" Countered Josh. "You've got it all wrong - that's not what happened at all. It's all a huge mistake - they didn't kill your brother it was—"

"Yes they did!" Jez wailed, squeezing the gun tighter, his eyes crazed and glaring. "Don't you lie! They murdered him - shot him down in cold blood—"

"No!" Josh tried again, knowing the truth of it from both his father and Uncle Joe. "They didn't—"

"Quiet!" Jez screamed, jabbing the gold-plated .38 angrily at Josh, his total insanity now clear to see. "Shut up! Just shut up - don't you say another fuckin' word. They did kill Vito - they did - and now I'm gonna kill you!"

Suddenly Jez stuck the gun out straight, his aim now still and unwavering. "You're fuckin' dead, kid," he said. "Dead like my brother."

Staring down the barrel of the gun, Josh was absolutely terrified but he knew it was too late, he was going to die and there was nothing he could do about it.

Determinedly holding back tears of anger and fear, he closed his eyes and waited for the shot that he knew would end his life.

***

Brett, being younger and quicker, was several paces ahead of Virgil as they raced down to the barn. As he neared the building he could hear the angry exchange between Jez and Josh quite clearly, yet he was still several yards away when he saw Jez raise his gun.

From Brett's viewpoint, Josh was unseen somewhere beyond the hayloft window, but there was no mistaking his voice or the terrible thing that was about to happen.

Without breaking stride, Brett ducked down and scooped up a baseball-sized rock from the ground. Then, whilst still running at full pelt, he tossed it as hard as he could, hoping to distract Vincenzi from his murderous intentions.

The rock span through the air with Brett willing it onwards, praying his aim was true. Its silent trajectory carrying it high and fast before arcing downwards to strike Jez on the temple with a solid thunk, very nearly knocking him cold.

His head was slammed sideways with the brutal shock of impact and his eyes rolled upwards as the world began to spin. Like a wilting branch, his outstretched arm dropped; the gold-plated .38 falling from his grip and landing harmlessly in the soft hay at his feet.

As his legs buckled, Jez turned slightly, briefly seeing Brett and Virgil skidding to a halt, before he tumbled backwards out of the hayloft window.

"No!" Brett shouted with horror as he saw what was about to happen.

But there was nothing he could do.

The pitch fork was stuck firmly in the dusty earth directly below the window; its long wooden handle pointing skyward, like a tall, thin spike and Brett and Virgil looked on helplessly aghast as Jez's bloated body plummeted onto it.

The handle speared into his back and stabbed through his

meaty torso before bursting out of his belly in a hideous squelch of skewered flesh; blood spurting like a fountain from the terrible wound as he let out a dreadful, almost inhuman cry of unbearable anguish.

Brett and Virgil rushed to his aid but it was clearly useless; his injuries were way beyond anything anyone could possibly do. Yet miraculously Jez still lived.

Flat on his back, in a spreading lake of his own blood, he stared at Brett and Virgil. His eyes were bulging, his breath quick and harsh.

Brett heard the sound of footsteps approaching and turned to see his father and the others hurrying towards them. They all looked battle weary and somewhat dishevelled but Brett could not concern himself with that at present. They were alive and for now that was all that mattered.

He stepped aside to let his father and the others through, his expression grave as his eyes met Joe's, silently conveying that the man on the ground was done for.

As Joe, Sean, Virgil and Matt crowded round, they each recognised Jez Vincenzi, remembering him from that fateful day ten years earlier at *The Villa Continental.*

Yet he was no longer the small boy from memory; the elder of Benny's 'young bulls', the surviving twin who had been so proud and resolute as he courageously carried his brother's body from the penthouse bedroom without shedding a solitary tear - an image that had forever stayed with all those who witnessed it.

Now, however, that same boy, ten years on, was barely recognisable; ruined by hate and driven by obsession. He was bloated and dishevelled with a wispy bumfluff beard but underneath it all his resemblance to Benny was unmistakeable. With age he had grown into the image of his father and for those standing over him there was a definite sense of déjà vu.

Yet what struck Joe the most was just how young Jez was.

Indeed, he looked barely older than Josh.

It was such a terrible waste of a life, and no matter what Jez had done in the past - the deaths of Michael, Ray and Ruby and the torching of *Far Point* amongst them - Joe's heart still went out to him.

He crouched down and took Jez by the hand. "It's alright, son," he said, "don't fight it, soon all the pain will be gone."

Jez sputtered and choked, the blood bubbling in his throat, his body convulsing as the length of the red-stained pitch fork handle protruded from the grotesque wound in his belly; his life steadily slipping away.

He turned his head slowly so that his deathly white face was staring directly at Joe as he valiantly tried to speak; the words coming in short, staggered bursts. "You… killed… my… brother," he gurgled. "All… four… of you. I swore… I would—"

The words trailed away as blood erupted from his lips. Joe squeezed his hand tighter. "No, son. You're wrong - it didn't happen that way - you need to know." He said. "We were there, yes, but we had nothing to do with the death of your brother." Joe could feel Jez fading, he only had seconds left. "It was a terrible accident - your father - he didn't mean to - but it was him, not—"

"Liar!" Jez spat, forcing the words out in a last violent gush of blood as his body briefly spasmed before finally falling still; his hatred travelling with him to the afterlife as his glazed eyes stared lifelessly back at Joe.

The threat from the past was finally over but as Sean placed a comforting hand on Joe's shoulder, the pair of them felt nothing but sadness for the dreadful loss of someone so young, no matter how misguided he might have been.

Even at the last Jez had been unable to accept the truth, his obsessive vendetta still burning strong; the madness inherited from his father blinding his senses and dismissing all reason.

Yet maybe in death he would eventually find peace.

***

The wedding took place a little later than scheduled, as was the bride's prerogative - although in Liv's case it was to give everyone the necessary time to clean up.

Cancelling the ceremony at such short notice would have required an explanation, from which many questions would have inevitably arisen. Questions which no one wanted to answer.

Furthermore, police involvement was not an option either.

Nonetheless, the area surrounding the corral was declared out of bounds, as was the *Guest Washroom* which was where the bodies of Jez and Bass had been stored until after the festivities. Then, under the cover of darkness, Joe and Sean would drive out to the Mojave desert and bury them.

Vincenzi and Stone were already listed as missing - they would simply never be found.

During the delay before the ceremony, Ethan stitched and dressed Josh's ear, assuring him that a good plastic surgeon could easily repair his damaged lobe. Meanwhile, Rose carefully applied make-up to everyone's bruises so that none of the other guests would suspect a thing.

Fortunately, Louretta had enough foresight to have an additional bridesmaid's dress made, just in case of unforeseen eventualities, and with a few swiftly executed alterations it fitted Violet perfectly.

Josh's dress shirt and tuxedo were covered in blood but again Louretta had the answer. In her wardrobe hung one of Beau Brewster's old tuxes, tailored for him when he was a much slimmer man. With a few pins and a stitch here and there, it made for an excellent replacement and in it Josh looked as good as new.

So, after many trials and tribulations - and a wedding day no one would ever forget - Brett and Liv were finally married.

Regardless of the events prior to the ceremony, the joining of Sean and Joe's two families was a union worth celebrating, as was

425

the end to all the bad blood which had blighted their existence for so many years.

   After more than four decades, it was finally over.

Chapter Twenty-Eight

During the wedding reception, Violet suddenly remembered her conversation with Victoria at Doc Ridgeway's place in Las Vegas and her generous offer of the beach house in Malibu for a little getaway. Thinking it would do both her and Matt the power of good after the events of that day, Violet broached the subject with Vicky once more and she happily agreed to let them use it for as long as they liked.

So, the next day, after Brett and Liv had set off on their honeymoon, Matt and Violet headed to Malibu for a few days of much needed rest and relaxation.

However, the 'beach house' that Violet had envisaged turned out to be far grander in reality than she could ever have imagined.

Made predominantly from glass, it was set high up on a cliff with spectacular views of the ocean and surrounding coastline. Resembling something straight out of a Hollywood movie, it was elegant, light and oozing with an understated air of refined opulence.

Indeed, it reminded Matt of a 'Bond' villain's lair, particularly the magnificent master bedroom which sat directly above the cliff face and featured a balcony that stretched out over a sheer drop to the ocean washed rocks below.

On the opposing side of the property, was a large sun terrace with a huge free form pool, a sunken hot tub and a host of luxurious loungers.

Inside the house it was equally spectacular; both hi-tec and chic, decorated in contemporary fashion with minimalist furnishings set upon a palatial open plan.

All in all it would make a very welcome retreat for Matt and Violet to spend a few precious days alone.

***

They arrived at the beach house a little after midday, having taken a fairly leisurely drive from *Wildwood*.

After a quick tour or the place - in which Violet marvelled at the splendour of Vicky and Virgil's home, they both slipped into their bathing suits and made their way down the cliff to the house's private beach using the wooden staircase that led from the sun deck.

Matt found a spot midway between the cliff and the sea and spread out a blanket on the ground before setting the large chest-style cooler down on it which Rose had prepared for them that morning. In it she had packed a bowl of fresh salad and another full of fruit. There was also a huge parcel of turkey sandwiches, several muffins and an apple pie along with two bottles of wine.

"Wow!" Said Vee, inspecting the contents as she sat down on the blanket in her tiny bikini, "Rosie knows it's only the two of us, right?"

"Yeah," smiled Matt, admiring the bikini and her tanned skin as it glistened in the sunlight, "You keep eating my Mum's food and you ain't gonna be fitting into outfits like that for much longer!"

"Good," Violet giggled, "I need fattening up a bit."

"Oh, no you don't - I like you just as you are," Matt protested as he cosied up next to her on the blanket.

"You do, huh?"

"Yep."

"Well then," said Violet with a salacious glint in her eye as she turned to face him, "I think you'd better show me."

428

With that she lifted her chin and Matt kissed her; the pair of them falling back onto the warm blanket as their semi-naked bodies basked in the golden Malibu sun, the picnic quickly forgotten.

***

From the sun deck above, Rocco Pistoli watched them, jealous of Matt Mason as he cavorted with the dark-haired beauty on the beach. She was obviously the girl Rocco had overheard talking with Victoria Wild in Las Vegas and now, seeing her for the first time in the flesh, she did not disappoint.

When he was finished with Mason then maybe he would take his turn with with the girl before killing her, too.

He felt a stir of annoyance; the mere thought of sex making him aware of the irritating rash on his genitals. Indeed, the rash had now spread to his face; the area around his mouth red and blotchy with spots making him look like a pubescent teenager.

The ointment, which had proved so effective, had all been used up, as had his very meagre supply of cash - the last of it spent two nights ago on a few grams of coke, which was also gone.

He was antsy now from withdrawal and fidgety with desperation; he needed money to score, to eat, to live. But first he had to do what he had gone there for - then the rest would take care of itself.

Focussing on that helped to calm him, although he wished now that he still had his prized rifle.

Briefly he reminisced about his beautiful *Valmet*, with its polished wooden stock and powerful *Zeiss Diavari* sight, sitting prettily in the sponge housing of its slim leather case.

Such a marvellous weapon.

With it he could have taken Mason out right there and then. Rocco could visualise targeting his head in the cross hairs and watching it explode just an instant after squeezing the hair trigger.

He smiled at the prospect but knew it was not to be as Jez

Vincenzi had robbed him of that pleasure.

Nevertheless, rifle or not, Mason was now within his grasp and very shortly he was going to be dead.

Rocco pondered this for a moment more then turned and went back inside the house.

The two love birds on the beach would not be back for a while so there was plenty of time for him to search the house for valuables. Rocco was confident that in a home owned by such wealthy stars as Victoria Wild and Virgil Nash he would surely find riches galore; money, jewellery, valuables of every kind - all of which could be used to buy him the things he so badly needed. Hell, he might even move into the beach house for a while himself - after all, with Mason and the girl out of the picture it would only be sitting empty.

With Wild and Nash's money he could afford proper treatment for his annoying dose of pox, buy coke by the bagful and screw hookers galore, two, three at a time and all of the highest calibre. He could even throw parties for them at his very own beach front pad.

But he was getting carried away. Firstly, he had to find the valuables, secondly he had to deal with Mason and the girl then, and only then, could he consider what to do next.

One thing at a time.

After being dismissed and humiliated by Jez Vincenzi outside the diner in the parking lot in La Quinta, Rocco had joined the throngs of people flocking outside the gates of *Wildwood* on the day of Liv Noakes' wedding.

However, unlike everyone else who had been expecting a happy ending, he had been anticipating a bloodbath.

But nothing happened. For some reason Vincenzi and Stone did not make their move. It was all very strange.

Nevertheless, Rocco waited until after the wedding, when all the guests had departed - he even waited until long after the last of the devoted fans had gone - certain that at any time he would hear the sound of gunshots - perhaps even the distinctive report of his own beloved *Valmet*. Yet still nothing happened.

Intrigued, he sat in the green Crown Vic a discreet distance away from the *Wildwood* gates and watched patiently with his last few lines of coke and a stale donut to keep him company.

In the early hours of the morning, he saw Joe Cassidy and Sean Noakes leave the property in a pick-up. For a moment he was tempted to follow but, instead, decided to stay put and wait for Mason.

As it turned out, Cassidy and Noakes returned just before sunrise; the pick-up they were driving, which was previously spotlessly clean, now coated in a thick layer of dust which all seemed very mysterious - and still no sign of Jez or Stone. *Could the two things be somehow connected?*

Rocco thought it entirely possible but decided to stick around nonetheless.

Several hours later, Brett Cassidy and his new bride drove out through the gates; their vintage Porsche dragging several tin cans from its rear fender. A hand-written 'Just Married' sign stuck to the back. Clearly they were off on their honeymoon.

Again, Rocco was tempted to follow as he had a score to settle with both of them but, again, he thought better of it. His primary target *had* to be Mason, everyone else could wait.

As time dragged on, Rocco witnessed an airport limousine enter the property but soon afterwards that, too, left carrying Virgil Nash and Victoria Wild, obviously they were flying off somewhere.

At long last, Matt Mason's truck finally appeared through the *Wildwood* gates, him behind the wheel and the dark-haired girl sitting by his side.

Maintaining a sensible distance, Rocco tailed them all the way back from Palm Springs to Malibu; a two and a half hour drive in which he had plenty of time to consider what might have happened to Vincenzi and Stone. But nothing jumped out except for Cassidy and Noakes' moonlight trip. Maybe Jez and Bass had tried and failed, maybe their bodies were in the back of that pick-up and now buried in some unmarked grave in the desert.

Had it been Rocco, that is what he would have done with them.

It was pure speculation but the more he thought about it the more convinced he became. Jez and Stone had failed once again and now they were both surely dead.

The same would not happen to him.

Pistoli watched from across the road as Mason parked up in the driveway of the palatial beach house in Malibu which seemed even more impressive than the one Louretta Wild owned in Santa Monica.

From the conversation Rocco overhead in Las Vegas he thought this to be Victoria Wild's and Virgil Nash's house, but it was best to be sure.

A guy walking his dog happened to be passing as Rocco got out his car and leant on the hood. "Hey, buddy," he said to the man with the dog, "I gotta package to deliver - do you know who lives there?" Rocco pointed to the house across the street.

"Yeah, man, sure," said the guy, "Some movie star I think - you know, the one from that thing last year? Virgil Nash, is it? Him and his wife, what's she called? Victoria something. Sorry man. I hope that helps - I'm not really up on movie stars but I'm pretty sure a whole bunch of 'em live around here."

"Hey man, no problem," Rocco said, "Thanks anyways."

Pistoli's suspicions were correct. He had also watched Wild and Nash heading off in an airport limousine earlier that day so he was fairly confident that they would not be returning home anytime soon.

Mason and the girl had the place to themselves and they would not be expecting a guest.

The rest was easy.

For a movie star residence, Rocco gained entrance without too much trouble; the security system turned off thanks to Mason's arrival there.

By the time Pistoli was inside, the loved up couple were already down on the beach, affording him plenty of time to look around before killing them.

***

"Hey, I'm starving," said Matt pulling his lips away from Violet's. "We got three whole days of this so I reckon we should eat now - keep our strength up for later, what do you reckon?"

Violet beamed with contentment before giving him another peck on the lips, "Oh, believe me, handsome, you're gonna need all the staying power you can muster."

"In that case," he smiled back, "I'd better grab me a sandwich and start working on my stamina right away."

Violet giggled, lovingly watching Matt's boyish expression as he rummaged hungrily through the cooler. The bruise on his forehead was still a deep blue although yellowing around the edges. Aside from that, however, he was back to full fitness which was a relief considering the hefty blow he had taken the day before.

Violet was still revolted by her encounter with Bass Stone and the memory of his hands pawing over her, but she felt no guilt for killing him. The man had been a vile, sadistic murderer and he got what he deserved so she refused to waste her life grieving for him.

The future was what was important now and that was sitting in front of her, sorting through the cool box. "I'll take one of those," she said, as Matt opened the parcel of turkey sandwiches. "I think I'd better if I'm gonna keep up."

Matt grinned wickedly and winked, "Maybe you'd better take a few."

"Yeah, and maybe a muffin, too," she replied, happily playing along.

433

"Shall we open the wine?"

"If you think you can take it," Violet teased, remembering his severe hangover from just twenty-four hours earlier.

"Hey, I maybe a lightweight," Matt replied, "But even I can handle a glass of wine or two."

Violet smiled. "Well, if you're sure, then why not. Let's push the boat out."

"Damn it!" Matt exclaimed as he continued to hunt through the cooler. "No glasses."

"You sure?"

"Uh-huh. None here. Don't worry," he said, closing the lid, "I'll run and fetch some, won't take a minute."

"Baby it doesn't matter, we can make do without—"

"Nonsense, it's no problem. You stay right here, I'll be back in a jiffy."

"Okay," conceded Violet, "But if you're heading back up there, would you grab my sunglasses, too, please? I think I left them on the bed."

"Sure thing. Back in a sec." With that, Matt scampered away toward the wooden steps, his bare feet burning on the hot sand.

***

Rocco made a cursory sweep of the ground floor before heading upstairs. In his experience, all the good stuff was usually hidden away in a bedroom, so that was where he intended to start. There would be plenty of time to look around downstairs properly later.

He was well-used to the opulence of the Carboni mansion in Biscayne Bay but this place was in a completely different class. Indeed, he could not help but marvel as he made his way up the sweeping staircase and along the galleried landing to the master suite.

As he opened the door, he was immediately awed by the

434

staggering view from the open french windows. Unable to resist, he crossed the spacious, beautifully decorated room and walked out onto the balcony.

It was as breathtaking as it was dramatic; the balcony jutting out over the drop to the sea, with nothing beneath only waves and rocks.

Christ, this place must have cost a fortune, he mused.

Again he considered the parties he might have there after offing Mason and the girl. He could have drugs and hookers on tap, indeed women would be clambering to get a piece of him if he lived in a place like this. Hell, he might not even have to pay them at all.

He wandered back in from the balcony and studied the room, considering where best to search first, and to his right spotted a huge walk-in closet.

Thinking back now, Rocco remembered Bass Stone saying something about this place; about how plush it was and how spectacular. Yet he particularly recalled him mentioning the walk-in closet in the master bedroom.

Months earlier, shortly before that whole goddamn debacle in The Caymans, Jez had sent Stone there to kill Louretta Wild and her grandson who were supposedly staying there at the time, yet they had failed to turn up.

Nevertheless, what Stone had said about the walk-in closet had stayed in Rocco's memory. Indeed, he distinctly recalled Bass showing off a pair of diamond set cuff links and a solid gold Rolex he had stolen from it. Stone had also remarked how there was 'still rich pickings to be had there.'

Greedily, Rocco rushed over to the closet, his face like a kid at Christmas as he pulled open the doors and stepped into the cavernous space.

On one side hung row upon row of dresses, skirts and coats - all colour co-ordinated with pristine uniformity on neat chrome rails. On the opposite side, hung dozens of mens suits in a variety of masculine shades together with vast array of blazers, shirts and trousers. Beneath the rails were racks of shoes suitable for every conceivable occasion. On either side of the closet stood a tall boy, one for him, one for her, stacked full of expensive underwear.

However, it was the twin *his* and *hers* cabinets at the back of the room which interested Rocco the most.

In *her* side were drawers full of highly-valuable jewellery - all beautifully crafted in gold, silver and platinum and adorned with precious stones of every kind.

In *his* side, Rocco found cuff links, lighters, tie-pins and watches, again all made from gold or silver - many with diamonds inset.

It was like an Aladdin's cave stacked with thousands of dollars worth of highly desirable extremely valuable trinkets.

With such an abundance of riches, Pistoli did not quite know where to start. He felt light-headed with elation; all his problems having just melted away.

He had hit the jackpot and in an overwhelming rush of avarice quite forgot the original purpose of his visit.

Quickly, he returned to the bedroom and stripped off his dirty old clothes, discarding them carelessly on a plush armchair in the corner of the room.

Before pulling off his stained trousers he removed the *.22* calibre revolver from his belt and tossed it onto the bed - the same second hand 'Saturday night special' that he had used to murder the little Asian shopkeeper in New York; its serial number coarsely filed off.

Once completely naked, Rocco strode back into the closet and chose a pair of blue silk boxers, knowing they would feel cool and light against his inflamed genitals. He slipped them on before proceeding to choose a shirt, tie and suit - opting for a classic blue pinstripe, single-breasted.

Finally, when fully dressed, he selected a pair of shiny black wingtips.

Aside for the shoes being maybe a half-size too big, everything else fitted perfectly and could actually have been made for him.

In his brand new suit of clothes, Rocco then moved onto the *his* and *hers* cabinets at the back of the room and took his time selecting just the right accessories, eventually choosing a solid gold *Brietling* with matching cuff links and tie pin.

As he admired his reflection in the mirror above the cabinet, checking out his new look, he felt like a million dollars. Only the blotchy rash around his mouth and greasy, slicked back hair marred his otherwise affluent appearance. He also needed a shave but he quite liked the dark growth of fresh stubble as it gave him something of a roguish air.

Unfortunately, the cabinet mirror only reflected his top half and Rocco was keen to check out the overall effect.

He remembered seeing a full-length mirror next to the chair in the bedroom and decided to go take a look.

However, as he ambled back out into the main room he discovered with surprise that he was no longer alone.

***

Matt padded through the house, his bare feet virtually silent on the polished hardwood floor. He had entered through the patio doors from the terrace and made straight for the kitchen to get the wine glasses.

As he headed back out, he popped the glasses down on the table at the bottom of the stairs then bounded up the steps two at a time to fetch Violet's sunglasses from the bedroom.

His feet making no sound on the glass treads of the spiral staircase as he reached the first floor and hustled along the galleried landing.

He strode into the bedroom, going straight to the bedside cabinet where Violet had left her sunglasses a short time earlier.

Snatching them up, he was turning back towards the door when he spotted an unusual object on the bed.

Indeed, he did a double-take, so out of place did it seem but his eyes were definitely not deceiving him. The snub-nosed revolver was old and chipped from years of being shoved in and out of holsters and belts; The varnish on its wooden handgrip worn and scratched, yet it was still every bit as deadly as the day it was made.

Matt was confused by its sudden appearance and looked about the room to see if anything else was amiss; immediately seeing the stack of discarded clothes on the chair beside the full-length mirror and the pair of scuffed mens shoes on the floor beneath them.

However, he had no chance to consider them further because at that moment, a man appeared - a complete stranger, as if from nowhere, taking Matt quite by surprise.

The man was tall and slim with pointed features; a long hairline scar ran diagonally from the top right of his forehead to the bottom of his left earlobe. He was unshaven with greasy, lank hair and a seriously unpleasant rash around his mouth, giving him the look of a vagrant down on his luck, although in stark contrast, his clothes were sharp and expensive - and most likely Virgil's Matt guessed.

The two men stared at each other, both equally shocked to see another person in the room, neither expecting it.

They stood there motionless for a moment, temporarily dumbstruck with stunned silence.

In that brief space of time Matt mentally weighed up the intruder whom he guessed to be a couple of years younger than himself. The guy had the strung-out appearance of a junkie, although he also looked lean and fit - his face displaying the scars of a fighter. *Definitely not someone who should be dismissed lightly.*

Likewise, Rocco was also evaluating the opposition. From

a distance, Matt had looked in good physical shape, but close-up, wearing nothing but board shorts, he was considerably more impressive; his ripped abs and honed muscles superbly defined.

Pistoli knew he would have to be wary but he relished the challenge; he had faced far bigger men than Matt before now and had always come out on top. His skill and ruthlessness as a hardened killer always winning through.

The gun, however, would make it a much easier proposition and as Rocco's eyes flashed to it he signalled his intent.

"Hey, man, don't do it!" Blurted Matt. "Everything's cool - whatever it is you want we can work it out."

Pistoli smiled derisively, "Oh, you think, mutherfucker?"

Matt's brain was whirring, trying to figure out what this guy was doing in the house. *Was he robbing it? Did he want cash?*

"Listen, if it's about money—" Matt began.

"You think this is about money, asshole? Is that what you think?" Rocco could feel his temper rising.

Matt was momentarily perplexed. *But if not money then what?*

However, It was then that the penny finally dropped. "Jesus, you work for Jez Vincenzi don't you?" He said.

"That's it, lover boy, now you're getting warmer," sneered Rocco, mentally working out the distance between him and the gun, calculating his chances of reaching it before Matt.

"But Vincenzi's dead now," said Matt, "so is Bass Stone."

Pistoli shrugged. "Yeah, I figured as much. At the ranch, right?"

"Uh-huh," Matt nodded. "So you see, it's over - finished. There's no need to—"

"You think this is about Jez?" Barked Rocco. "This ain't' nothin' to do with that snot nosed brat. It's about what *I'm* owed - not him. Look closely at my face, asshole, see if you recognise anything!"

Matt was now even more confused as he stared at Rocco's face. There was something vaguely familiar but nothing more. "I'm sorry," he said, "do I know you - have I somehow caused you—"

"Arizona, mutherfucker!" Growled Rocco, "A few months back. You killed a couple of guys, *remember?*"

"What? I don't understand."

"Think mutherfucker - think!" Pistoli shouted.

So as not to antagonise the intruder any further, Matt did as instructed, casting his mind back to Arizona where, not so long ago, he had been shot - very nearly dying as a result of the wounds. Indeed, had it not been for Ethan Ridgeway's considerable skill as a surgeon then he undoubtedly would have.

"Yeah, I remember," he said, bitterly recalling the pair of cold-blooded killers who had tried to murder him.

"But those guys came after me. I was lucky to escape with my life!" He could picture the men in his mind's eye as he spoke; one severed in two after being mown down by the Dodge Matt had hot-wired; the other fatally wounded, yet still defiant, still spitting vitriol as he lay bleeding out at Matt's feet.

Matt could even remember the guy's name. '*Enzo*'.

The same thug who had not only been in Arizona, but also in the penthouse suite at *The Villa Continental* the day Benny Vincenzi had killed his own son. The very day that had sparked Jez's own misguided quest for vengeance, which had ended so tragically, so bloodily, just twenty-four hours earlier at *Wildwood*.

Or so everyone had thought. Yet now someone else had shown up, someone else with a grudge, asking about Enzo of all people - the guy who had been sent by Jez to kill Matt in that hotel room just East of Phoenix.

Thinking back, Matt could still picture Enzo's face as he lay dying on the ground in that side street in Arizona.

Then he saw it; the clear resemblance between Enzo and the man who now stood before him in the bedroom.

"Christ," he said. "You're Enzo's brother aren't you?"

"Give the guy a cigar - got it in one, asshole. You killed him you sonofabitch and now I'm gonna kill you."

As the words left his lips, Rocco made a sudden dive for the gun.

Matt reacted a second slower, caught off-guard by the stunning realisation of who Rocco was.

However, he recovered quickly as Rocco threw himself towards the bed, his arms at full stretch, making a grab for the vintage revolver. With his fingers just inches away from its worn, wooden grip, Matt bundled into him, slamming an elbow hard into his ribs.

Pistoli buckled with pain, pulling one arm down sharply to protect his exposed side whilst swinging an arcing right hook to the side of Matt's head.

Yet even though the blow hurt like hell, Matt was far more concerned with keeping the gun out of Rocco's reach and as pain exploded through his skull, he slashed the revolver away with the palm of his free hand.

The gun flew from the bed and rebounded off the bedside cabinet before bouncing across the carpet and coming to rest in the space between the open french windows.

Meanwhile, the two men were still tussling on the bed, fighting in close quarters with a desperate variety of short jabs and knee kicks. Locked together, their heads clashed on numerous occasions as they each scrambled to gain the upper hand, but in such a confined brawl neither could find an opening to unleash their full power.

Finally, Rocco somehow managed to slither away; throwing himself off the far side of the bed and hurriedly jumping to his feet as he ripped off his jacket to free himself from its constraints; his eyes never leaving his opponent as Matt leapt up onto the mattress.

"Come on then, you sonofabitch!" Pistoli spat, his anger burning as he ripped off his tie and popped the collar on his newly acquired shirt, "Show me what you've got."

"Glad to," snarled Matt, leaping into action; his movement now unhindered and blindingly quick.

Rocco believed himself to be ready. Moreover, he arrogantly considered himself to be a superior combatant to Matt in every way having proven himself time and again against serious opposition.

Yet nothing could have prepared him for the devastating speed of the attack that followed.

Indeed, the initial strike almost knocked him to the ground as the heel of Matt's leading foot slammed hard into Rocco's chest. It was so unbelievably fast that he barely saw it coming, yet before he could react another lightning kick snapped his head sideways before Matt had even landed.

Rocco desperately tried to throw up his guard but Matt's skill was way beyond anything he could contain and blow after crippling blow got through his weakened defences.

In just a few seconds, Pistoli had been systematically destroyed and was now paying the price for his over-confidence.

He knew he was beaten as there was simply no way he could keep taking this kind of punishment and no chance of launching a counter attack. For the first time in his life Rocco had come up against a far more skilful opponent and the realisation fuelled the rage that had been boiling inside him since the news of his brother's death.

As yet another punch landed on his jaw, Rocco reeled away in retreat, desperate to escape the onslaught.

"We done?" Matt growled, his fists clenched ready for another round, the adrenaline pumping through his veins. "Are we finished now? I've got no beef with you, man, but if you want to I can go at it all day!"

Rocco was bent double, one arm wrapped protectively around his aching torso and his shoulders hunched with pain. He held up his hand in surrender, "Yeah," he panted; his nose bleeding and his lower lip split open, blood dripping down his chin as he spoke, "We're done."

Matt exhaled with relief and lowered his fists.

Although with his head bowed in defeat, Rocco could see the gun on the ground just a couple of feet away from where he was now standing and he was instantly infused with a fresh glimmer of hope.

During the fight, he had been steadily backing towards the french windows in retreat, unwittingly heading for the very object that could assure him victory.

With the gun he could emerge from this fight undefeated and Enzo's death properly avenged.

Yet, more importantly, he could still kill Matt Mason.

Seizing the opportunity, Rocco suddenly leapt sideways and snatched up the gun.

However, as he raised his arm, clutching the revolver in his grip, poised to blow the man's head off who had so skilfully taken him apart, a foot struck him in the chest with devastating force.

A split-second earlier, Matt had seen the imminent danger and had reacted instinctively by launching a well aimed kick to throw Rocco off balance.

Pistoli staggered onto the balcony from the force of the blow, firing the pistol harmlessly into the sky as he stumbled outside. But he refused to give up and whilst still tottering backwards, levelled his aim and attempted to shoot again.

With no choice but to defend himself, Matt reacted, his reflexes super fast as he span round and whipped his leg round in a powerful back kick that caught Rocco directly under his chin, launching him off the ground.

As Matt turned, he saw Rocco flip backwards over the balcony rail and instantly dived to save him.

The gun fired again as Rocco pitched over, toppling into the empty space beyond as the bullet ricocheted off the vertical cliff face beneath the overhanging balcony.

Indeed, he was fully over by the time Matt snatched hold of his foot; the whole of Pistoli's body now dangling precariously over the sheer drop and held tenuously by just one ill-fitting shoe.

"Hang on, I've got you!" Yelled Matt, trying desperately to secure a tighter grip on the shiny wingtip that Rocco had stolen from Virgil's wardrobe. But Pistoli was wriggling frantically and Matt could feel himself being pulled over the rail too as he tried to find better purchase on the polished shoe.

"Stop moving about - I can't get a grip!" He shouted as the shoe, a half-size too big, suddenly seemed to loosen causing Rocco's foot to slowly slip free. "I can't hold you - you need to keep still or you'll fall!" Matt cried again.

Yet staring down, vainly trying to hold on with all his might, he saw Rocco gazing evilly back at him.

The expression on the Italian's blotchy, unshaven face was wild and deranged as he brought the gun up once more and pointed it at Matt. "Then we'll both be dead, mutherfucker!" He growled.

As he fired, Rocco's foot slipped free of the shoe and he plummeted down to the waiting rocks below.

Matt reeled backwards from the sudden release of the heavy weight; the black wingtip still clamped tightly in his grip as the speeding bullet whizzed past just a hair's breadth from his cheek.

Yet, mindless of his own safety, Matt lunged forward again hoping there might still be a chance of saving Pistoli.

But it was useless.

Rocco, unrepentant to the last, fired three more times in quick succession, each shot flying wide of the mark, their sound lost to the crashing of the waves, as he fell to his certain death.

Matt scrunched his eyes closed with horror as Pistoli's body splattered on the rocks below.

For several long seconds Matt stayed there, his head bowed

against the balcony rail; the sound of the ocean playing its mournful tune in his ears.

After a moment he sensed Violet standing beside him. She had been concerned that he was taking a long time and had come to find him; the events of the previous day still playing on her mind.

"Everything alright, baby?" She asked. "I thought I heard gunshots."

Matt opened his eyes and stared down at the rocks again. But where he had expected to see Pistoli's bloody corpse he saw nothing but a mass of sharp, jagged rocks washed completely clean by the ocean.

"Yeah, honey, I'm fine," he replied wearily. "Everything is just as it should be."

Epilogue

Eighteen months later. The Cayman Islands.

Brett snapped the lid back onto the large tub of wood varnish then rinsed off his brush with white spirit before jumping down onto the quayside to admire his handiwork.

He arched his back, stretching out the knots in his aching muscles; it had been hard work but *The Rachel* was finally ready for its first passenger excursion and as he admired her gleaming, freshly varnished, lovingly polished lines he could not be more proud.

He had been working since first light and it was now almost lunchtime, yet before he could eat he needed to take a shower and get changed into something a little more presentable than a pair of grubby cut-offs and a stained T-shirt.

"Hey! You ready?" He called to Matt who was working on their sister vessel, *The Ruby*, which was moored up alongside. The pair of them had bought it together and when ready, she would become the second cruiser in their planned fleet.

"Yeah, just finishing up!" Matt yelled back. He had also been hard at it since the crack of dawn and was equally ready for a break.

Forming a business partnership with Brett had seemed like a natural fit for him after so many years wandering alone. He still had his freedom and a life spent predominantly outdoors, yet he also had something he could build upon and the support of a loving family. In

446

particular, Violet, whom he had married in a small beach ceremony in Cabo San Lucas shortly after their stay in Malibu, neither of them wanting to wait a second longer than absolutely necessary in the wake of what had happened.

Life was too short.

Now they were settled and happy with a baby boy of their own; 'Alfie,' born almost a year ago.

Likewise, Brett was a father now too and after marrying Liv he knew he had to support his growing family. No longer could he muddle along serving beer and burgers to the locals at *Calico Jack's*.

His long term plan had always been to own a small fleet of cruisers and *The Rachel* had been the first step towards making his dream a reality. But as his circumstances changed, he realised the need to step up his time frame and when Matt expressed an interest in going into partnership it seemed like the perfect opportunity for them both.

It had proved to be an excellent decision and soon *'Cassidy & Mason's Island Tours'* would be open for business.

It was an exciting proposition and as Matt wiped the grease off his hands with a dirty rag, he could not wait.

He had spent the better part of the morning tinkering about with the engine on *The Ruby*, giving it a few final tweaks so that it now purred as smoothly as a kitten.

Next week, he and Brett would start on the paintwork and, with luck, should have it ready for paying customers within the month.

Presently, however, they had to get back to the estate as today was the big day.

***

It had taken a great deal of effort, an enormous amount of planning and a hell of a lot of money but finally the renovations to *Far Point* were completed.

The stunning location, so badly ravaged by fire just two years

447

earlier had now been fully restored to its former glory. However, where once stood two houses up on the bluff, there now stood four.

Putting their fabulous wealth to good use, Joe and Sean had offered a house to each of the two newly married couples as a wedding gift - giving them carte blanche to design whatever they desired. It was a wonderfully generous offer which Brett and Liv and Matt and Violet gratefully accepted.

If the events of the past had taught them anything it was that they were all stronger together, so with acres of space available at *Far Point* it seemed like the natural solution. It also served to put everyone's concerns to rest.

For over a year they had all been living in a little encampment of caravans within the grounds of the estate where they could oversee the building of the four new houses which stretched out across the bluff and overlooked the ocean.

In addition, a brand new stable block had been constructed and Sean and Sarah's thoroughbred stock were once again ensconced safely within.

However, whilst the equine inhabitants of *Far Point* had settled into their new residence sometime ago, the human contingent were due to move into their beatiful new homes that afternoon.

Yet it was not that which brought Matt and Brett rushing from the quayside but the small memorial service that was soon to take place up on the hill, immediately above the cliff path that led down to the beach.

An hour after returning to the estate Matt and Brett were standing around just beyond the circle of caravans at the foot of the hill. Both were dressed in their best suits and busily trying to keep their children occupied whilst they waited for everyone else.

Soon Josh came to join them, quietly amused by how quickly these two outwardly tough guys had shown their soft, gooey centres.

Matt was holding little Alfie in his arms who was sucking

hungrily on his bottle whilst Brett was playing peek-a-boo with Rae, his beautiful blue-eyed daughter. She was a toddler now with her first birthday just a week away; her mass of blonde ringlets tied in pigtails with pretty pink ribbons. She was the image of her mother and had a sunny, mischievous disposition just like the old pirate who was her namesake.

Josh, meanwhile, was in his final year of Marine Biology at *CalTech,* and soon to be taking up a position at *The Cayman Oceanic Institute of Marine Science* where he would put his education to good use.

Presently, he was spending his days on campus and his weekends at Louretta's place in Santa Monica but shortly he would be joining the others at *Far Point* on a more permanent basis.

Louretta and Ethan, who had arrived on the island the day before with Josh, were the first of the others to appear, closely followed by Virgil and Victoria who had been there for the last week.

In that time, they had been working on the plans for their own vacation home which they hoped would be completed by Christmas. Indeed, now Vicky was a grandmother she intended to make the most of it and even though she and Virgil had incredibly busy schedules, they were both determined to visit as often as time allowed.

Joe and Sean had sold them a generous parcel of land at the Southern end of the estate where they would have ample space to enjoy their privacy but still be close enough to their grandchildren. In fact, it was an ideal situation all around as it also provided Virgil with an excuse to spend plenty of time with his two best friends away from the fast-paced hullabaloo of Hollywood. Furthermore, late summer in The Caymans was excellent for surfing and Virgil was keen to set aside more time for the sport he had loved for most of his life - he might even talk Joe and Sean into taking it up too.

A few moments after Virgil and Victoria, the remaining women made their way over from the circle of caravans to the small gathering at the foot of the hill. Rose and Sarah first, followed by Violet and a heavily pregnant Liv.

Any day now, she and Brett were expecting their second child and if it was a boy, they were going to call him 'Michael.'

Manfred Rani turned up next, accompanied by the vicar, they were met by Joe and Sean who shook their hands and chatted with them briefly.

After a moment or two, Rani and the clergyman moved on up the hill to make the necessary preparations for the service.

As they walked away, Joe and Sean wandered over to the waiting group who were watching them with quiet admiration.

These two old warriors who had been friends since they were kids and had remained united in good times and bad. They had experienced much and survived it all with an unbreakable resolve; their faith in each other unwavering throughout.

They had endured attack, beaten off enemies and buried far more than their fair share of loved ones but in spite of the many tragedies they had always made it through.

In the process they had raised their families and made the world a safer place for their grandchildren to grow up in.

Now, in their fifties, it was time to hand over the reins to the next generation - to Matt, Brett, Liv and Josh.

In their remaining years they intended to make the very most of every day amongst those that they loved and who loved them.

The rebuilding of *Far Point* signalled a new beginning, finally unshackled from the threat of the past. Standing shoulder to shoulder, just as they had when they were boys, when they had declared themselves to be blood brothers forever, they would face the future together.

With the sun high up in the clear blue sky, the smartly dressed, tightly knit party of family and friends slowly began to make their way up the gentle slope of the hill towards the small cemetery plot overlooking the stunning vista that lay beyond its crest.

Upon their arrival a few minutes later, they all stood around the three gleaming headstones in the pristine family plot, waiting for the vicar to begin the service.

On each stone read the name of someone they had lost; Ray Reece, Ruby Reece and Michael Walsh. Michael's body had never been found but it was Sarah and Sean's strongest belief that he was there, with them, in spirit and his headstone marked a place where they could feel a little closer to him.

With everyone gathered around, their heads bowed in silence, the vicar began his memorial sermon, his voice carried on the wind along with the sound of the ocean waves softly breaking on the shoreline below.

With the demons of the past finally put to rest, it was now time to honour the fallen.

THE END.

About The Author

Kris Lillyman is based in Northamptonshire, England and has worked as a freelance graphic designer and illustrator for over twenty-five years. He is married with two grown up children.

In addition to adult thrillers, he also writes and illustrates children's books - to find out more about these, please visit: **www.boomboombooks.com**

Alternatively, search 'Kris Lillyman' in iTunes, Amazon, Barnes & Noble or most other online bookstores.

www.ingramcontent.com/pod-product-compliance
Lightning Source LLC
Chambersburg PA
CBHW031051260626
47172CB00001B/27